In the magical Christmas season, the journey home is filled with wondrous surprises . . . unexpected attractions . . . and the promise of a love to treasure for a lifetime.

Praise for the beloved *New York Times* bestselling authors whose Regency holiday tales sparkle in

Snowy Night with a Stranger

Jane Feather

"An accomplished storyteller . . . rare and wonderful."
—*Los Angeles Daily News*

"Jane Feather will enchant readers. . . ."
—*Romantic Times*

Sabrina Jeffries

"Entertaining, sensual historical romance."
—*Booklist*

"Warm, wickedly witty and brilliantly plotted."
—*Romantic Times*

Julia London

"Lusciously sensual and delightfully witty."
—*Booklist*

"London's characters become so real they become part of your life while you are reading her books."
—*The Oakland Press*

Also by Jane Feather

To Wed a Wicked Prince

A Wicked Gentleman

Almost a Lady

Almost a Bride

The Wedding Game

The Bride Hunt

The Bachelor List

Also by Sabrina Jeffries

Let Sleeping Rogues Lie

Beware a Scot's Revenge

Only a Duke Will Do

Never Seduce a Scoundrel

One Night with a Prince

To Pleasure a Prince

In the Prince's Bed

Also by Julia London

The Book of Scandal

The Dangers of Deceiving a Viscount

The Perils of Pursuing a Prince

The Hazards of Hunting a Duke

Highlander in Love

Highlander in Disguise

Highlander Unbound

With Alina Adams

Guiding Light: Jonathan's Story

Jane Feather
Sabrina Jeffries
Julia London

Snowy Night with a Stranger

Pocket **Star** Books
New York London Toronto Sydney

Pocket Star Books
A Division of Simon & Schuster, Inc.
1230 Avenue of the Americas
New York, NY 10020

Lettering by David Gatti. Illustration by Alan Ayers.

This Pocket Star Books paperback edition November 2010

Manufactured in the United States of America

10 9 8 7 6 5 4 3 2

ISBN: 978-1-4516-0943-1
ISBN: 978-1-4165-7883-3 (ebook)

Contents

Snowy Night with a Stranger

A Holiday Gamble

Jane Feather

Chapter One

It seemed to have been snowing forever, Ned Vasey reflected glumly. His breath in the closed carriage had misted over the glass at the window, and he leaned forward and rubbed at the pane with his gloved hand. It cleared the mist but the outside was thickly coated with snow, offering only an opaque square of whiteness that gave little light and no visibility.

He sat back against the thick leather squabs and sighed. The carriage was in the first style of elegance and comfort, as well sprung as such a vehicle could ever be, but after close to three weeks' traveling, Viscount Allenton found it as comfortable as a donkey cart. The snow had started in earnest as they'd left Newcastle, but now that they were lumbering through the lower reaches of the Cheviot Hills it was a blizzard. The horses were struggling to keep their footing on the sometimes steep road that for long stretches was barely a cart track winding its way through the foothills. God knows what it would be like higher up, Ned thought. The upper passes would certainly be blocked. But fortunately he was heading out of the hills, not into them.

Alnwick, a small, pretty Northumberland town. That was how he remembered it, but the last time he had visited his childhood home had been ten years ago, before he'd been packed off, the family's so-called black sheep, into exile over a scandal that struck him now as utterly stupid. Since then his blood had thinned under the Indian sun, and he couldn't seem to get warm anywhere in this godforsaken frozen north.

And if his brother, Robert, had managed to keep himself alive, Ned would still be warmly content in India's sultry heat. But Rob, as so often in their childhood, had ridden his horse blindly at a hedge during a hunt, and both horse and rider had gone down into the unseen ditch on the other side. The horse had broken both forelegs, and Rob his neck. Which left the previously contented younger son, Edward the black sheep, to inherit the family estates and the title. And the younger son infinitely preferred the life of plain Ned Vasey, Indian nabob, to that of Edward Vasey, Viscount Allenton.

But such is fate, Ned reflected, huddling closer into his greatcoat. Ten years ago the estate had been going to rack and ruin under his father's reckless negligence, and it seemed from the agent's letters that Rob had finished the job. Which left the younger son, who had somehow managed to turn his exile into a very good thing, to pick up the pieces. And a very expensive picking up it was going to be, Ned had no doubt.

The carriage shuddered as the horses stumbled on the deeply rutted and now slippery track. Stopping was not an option. They would all freeze to death, coachman, postillions, horses and all.

The carriage was still moving, but very slowly. Ned

opened the door with difficulty against the crust of snow and ice, and stepped out into the blizzard. He struggled toward the coachman and the near-side postillion. "How much farther before we're out of here?" he called up, snow filling his mouth and blocking his nose.

"Hard to say, m'lord," the coachman called down, flicking his whip at the striving horses. "At this speed, it could take an hour to do a mile."

Ned swore into a gust of snow, his words snatched by the wind.

"Best get back in, sir," the coachman shouted down. "Your weight don't make no difference to the 'osses, and ye've no need to freeze yet a while."

Ned nodded and climbed back into the coach, still swearing as he realized he'd allowed himself to get frozen to the bone with no way of warming himself up again in the frigid interior.

If he ever made it to Hartley House, at least he'd find a warm welcome there. And a house bursting with Christmas revelry. Lord Hartley's bluff camaraderie and generous spirit would be a welcome antidote to what was bound to be the dank neglect of his own house. Sarah would make him a good wife. . . .

"Whoa . . . whoa, there."

The coachman's yell broke into Ned's thoughts and he reached for the door handle again as the carriage juddered to a halt. He pushed open the door and jumped down. A torch flickered just ahead on the track showing four figures, barely visible in the swirling snow, milling around an overturned gig. The pony had been released from the traces and stood blowing steam through its nostrils and stamping its hooves.

"Stay with the horses," Ned instructed over his shoulder. He plowed through the snow toward the scene. "What happened here?"

A youth turned from the group. "Pony caught a hoof in a rut, sir," he said in a broad Northumberland accent that Ned hadn't heard in ten years. To his satisfaction, however, he found that he could still understand it without difficulty. For strangers to the county, it might as well have been a foreign tongue.

Ned bent to check the pony's legs, running his hand expertly over the hocks. "I can find no damage," he said, straightening. "Why would you bring a pony out with a gig on a night like this?"

"Why would ye bring them 'osses out in a bleedin' blizzard?" the youth demanded on a clearly combative note.

Despite the snow, there had been no signs of a storm when they'd left that morning, but Ned was not about to bandy words with this insolent young man. He turned away, back to his own conveyance.

The blow to the back of his neck surprised him more than it hurt him. He stumbled to his knees in the snow and something—no, someone—jumped lightly onto his back, legs curling around his waist as he knelt. Hands slipped into the deep pockets of his coat, and then fingers slid inside his coat. It was all over in the blink of an eye. The slight weight left his back, and as he struggled to his feet, his assailants and the pony disappeared into the blanket of snow behind him. The gig remained where it was. Presumably it was a permanent fixture, designed to catch any unwary traveler on these seldom-used tracks.

Ned cursed his own stupidity. He knew that the Cheviots were plagued by bands of rapscallions and highwaymen; he simply hadn't expected to fall victim on such a filthy night. He dug into his pockets. He had kept a pouch with five guineas close to hand for easy distribution at roadside inns. It was gone.

"What 'appened there, m'lord? Couldn't see a thing in this." The coachman had climbed down from his box, but neither he nor the postillions had left the horses.

"Nothing much," Ned said, climbing back into the carriage, now as wet as he was cold. "Keep going."

The carriage lurched forward again and he felt inside his coat. His fob watch was gone from his waistcoat pocket. Those light fingers had demonstrated all the sleight of hand of an experienced pickpocket. He hadn't been able to see the features of any of his cloaked and hooded assailants behind the veil of snow, but he was fairly certain he would recognize the feel of those fingers against his heart.

The financial loss was no great matter, but the blow to his pride was another thing altogether. Ten years ago he wouldn't have fallen for such a trick, but his sojourn in India had clearly softened him, he thought disgustedly. He had learned how to make money, a great deal of money, but he'd lost something in the process. Something he had to retrieve if he was to assume the life of a North Country English gentleman once again.

God, he was cold. He could only begin to imagine what those poor buggers outside were feeling.

Something hammered on the roof. The coachman. He struggled with the frozen door again and leaned out. "What is it?" His words disappeared into the snow but the coachman, just visible on the box above him, pointed with his whip. Ned stared into the whiteness, then saw it—a glimmer of light, flickering like a will-o'-the-wisp in the distance.

"We can't go no farther, m'lord," the coachman bellowed. "The 'osses won't make it, an' me blood's freezin'. Reckon we 'ave to try an' rouse someone."

"Agreed," Ned shouted. "I'll go ahead and see what's there. I can make better time on foot." He jumped down into snow that reached his knees. "Postillions, release the horses from the traces and lead them after me."

The two men dismounted and stumbled through the snow to the horses' heads. Ned plunged forward, still up to his knees, keeping the flickering light in his sights. And after fifteen agonizingly slow minutes the lights grew steady and close. He could hear the wheezing of the postillions behind him and the puffing of the beasts, but salvation lay just ahead.

A long driveway led up to a large stone mansion, lights pouring forth from many windows, piercing the veil of snow. The strains of music could be heard faintly as the travelers approached the flight of steps leading up to double front doors. Ned drew his greatcoat tight and dug his way up the steps to the door. He banged the big brass knocker in the shape of a gryphon's head. And he banged it again, ever conscious of his freezing horses, and the desperation of the coachman and postillions, all standing in the snow at the foot of the steps.

He heard footsteps, the wrenching of bolts, and the door opened slowly. Light and warmth poured forth. A liveried butler stood in the doorway, gazing in something approaching disbelief at this visitor. "Can I help you, sir?"

For a moment Ned was tempted to laugh at the absurdity of the question. But only for a moment. "Yes," he said curtly. "I am Viscount Allenton, on my way to Alnwick. My men and I are benighted in this blizzard, and we need shelter. I'd be grateful if you'd bring me to your master, but first send someone to direct my coachman and postillions to the stables, and then to the kitchen fire." He stepped past the man into the hall as he spoke.

"Yes . . . yes, of course, my lord." The butler called over his shoulder and a footman appeared. "Ensure Lord Allenton's horses are fed and watered and bedded for the night, and show his servants to the kitchen. They will be glad of supper and ale." He turned back to Ned. "May I take your greatcoat, my lord?"

Ned became aware of the growing puddle at his feet as his coating of snow melted. "Yes, please. I'm sorry to be ruining your floors."

"Think nothing of it, my lord. We are used to this weather in these parts, and our floors are prepared accordingly." The man's smile was soothing as he almost reverently eased the sodden garment from Ned's shoulders and cast it across a bench that seemed designed to receive such offerings.

"If you would care to wait by the fire, my lord, I will inform Lord Selby of your arrival." He urged Ned toward the massive fireplace at the far end of the baronial-style hall, paused for a moment to pour him a glass of sherry from a readily placed decanter, then bowed and departed.

Selby. Ned sipped his sherry. Roger Selby. One of the oldest Northumbrian landowners. A family history of roguery to boot. It was said that they had reivers in their not-too-distant past. Not that that was unusual among the families who ruled these wild borderlands. A couple of hundred years ago, the Allenton family had numbered the border raiders in their own ranks. But they had long since abandoned banditry as a means of attaining wealth. Selby's father, however, had been an acknowledged robber baron who still clung to the old ways as recently as fifty years past, and Ned's own father had always maintained that the present Lord Selby was not above a little cross-border plundering when it suited him.

Ned had met Roger Selby only once, at a horse show in Morpeth. A good fifteen years ago, he calculated as he sipped his sherry, propping one sodden boot on the andirons. Selby was about ten years older than himself, and even then in possession of the barony, his father having disappeared in mysterious circumstances on one of the high passes through the Pennines.

Ned remembered he had been fascinated by the mystery and not a little envious of the older man, who had achieved his independence and freedom from family restraints at such an early age. He spun from the fire at the sound of firm footsteps and a voice he remembered.

"Allenton . . . we heard a rumor you were returning to us . . . sorry to hear of your brother's accident." Roger Selby came swiftly across the hall, hand outstretched. "But 'tis an ill wind, eh? Welcome, dear fellow. This is no night for man or beast to be abroad." He enclosed Ned's rather slim hand in a large paw. He was a tall man, whose broad frame was beginning to run to fat in the manner of an erstwhile sportsman turned sedentary. His neck had thickened, and the starched cravat supported several double chins. His complexion was ruddy, his eyes just a trifle bloodshot, but his smile seemed genuine and his handshake was as firm as it was warm.

"Far cry from India," he said with a jovial chuckle. "By God, man, you're half frozen." He clapped Ned's shoulder heartily as he continued to shake his hand.

"I confess I had forgotten the fierceness of these northern winters," Ned said, retrieving his hand. "You must forgive me for descending upon you like this."

"Not at all . . . not at all. You know how we Northumbrians honor the claims of hospitality in our inhospitable countryside. Indeed, I doubt you'll be leaving us for a week, judging by that blizzard. The road from here to Alnwick will be blocked for several days at least."

Ned nodded. He had expected as much. "There's no way a messenger could get through, either," he said.

Roger Selby shook his head. "Someone expecting you?"

"I'm expected at Hartley House for Christmas," Ned said with a resigned shrug. "I'd hoped to arrive in Alnwick tonight."

"They'll not be expecting you now, man," Selby declared. "One look out of the window is all they'll need for an answer."

"Aye, I'm sure that's so." He turned at the sound of a discreet cough from the shadows of the staircase.

The butler who had let him in stepped forward into the lamplight. "I beg your pardon, Lord Allenton. But your coachman brought in your portmanteau. I've taken the liberty of having it carried to a bedchamber, and a servant is preparing a hot bath for you."

"Good . . . good, Jacobs. That's the ticket," Selby declared. "You'll be right as a trivet, Allenton, once you're out of those wet clothes. We'll hold dinner for you. Jacobs, tell cook to put dinner back an hour . . . that be long enough, Allenton?"

"More than long enough," Ned hastened to assure him. "You're too kind, Selby. I don't wish to inconvenience you in any way on Christmas Eve. . . ."

"Nonsense, dear fellow . . . no inconvenience at all. Not in the least. The more the merrier at this season. Take the sherry with you." He pressed the decanter into his guest's free hand and urged him toward the stairs, where the butler stood waiting to show him up.

Ned thanked his host and went willingly in the butler's wake, with his glass and decanter. Northumbrian hospitality was legendary, and with good reason. No one ever turned away a benighted winter traveler in these hills, but Roger Selby's welcome was more than ordinarily warm, and seemed to transcend mere obligation.

But of course they were neighbors, Ned reflected as he entered a large and well-appointed bedchamber. That would certainly explain the generosity of the welcome.

"This is Davis, Lord Allenton, he will be pleased to act as your valet during your stay," the butler announced, waving a hand in the direction of the manservant who was unpacking Ned's portmanteau. Jacobs bowed and departed.

He must remember to give the coachman some substantial concrete sign of his appreciation for hauling the portmanteau through the blizzard, Ned thought as he examined the contents of his bag. Most men would have abandoned it with the chaise in such circumstances, and he would have been obliged to dine in a borrowed dressing gown.

"Your bath is prepared, sir," the manservant said. "I'll take this blue coat down to the kitchen and get our Sally to press it. Sadly creased it is, an' I daresay ye'll be wanting to wear it at dinner."

"Is there not one a little less creased?" Ned inquired mildly, casting off his damp coat with a sigh of relief. "I'm sure there's no need to put anyone to the trouble of pressing something at such short notice."

"No, m'lord, there's no other less creased, and 'tis no trouble for our Sally," Davis stated a little huffily. "Lord Selby likes things to be right. He's most particular, m' lord."

"Well, I'm sure you know best. I certainly wouldn't wish to insult my host," Ned said cheerfully, unfastening his britches. "I'd be grateful if you could do something about my greatcoat while you're about it. It's sodden, quite possibly beyond repair, but I'll need it again until I can replace it. It's in the hall, I believe."

"Mr. Jacobs has seen to it, sir," Davis said. He began to take shirts and cravats from the portmanteau, smoothing the fine white linen with a reverential hand before laying them carefully in a drawer in the armoire. "Lovely cloth, sir. If I may say so."

"You may. Indian tailors do fine work with the most delicate cotton."

"These coats, sir, were never made in India," Davis exclaimed, lifting a coat of green superfine to the light. "This'll be one of them gentlemen tailors in London, it will."

"True enough." Ned stepped naked to the copper hip bath before the fire. "Schultz or Weston, I favor both." He stepped into the water and slid down with a sigh of pleasure, resting his head against the edge. "Now this was worth waiting for. Pass me my sherry glass, will you?"

Davis brought over the recharged glass. "I'll just take the coat to Sally, sir. Will you be needing me in the next fifteen minutes?"

Ned closed his eyes. "No . . . no, Davis. Take your time." He lay back in the soothing warmth, feeling the tensions of the day's travel melt from him. He was due to arrive at the Hartleys' in the morning, but they would not wonder why he failed to turn up. The blizzard would be raging from the summit of The Cheviot to Alnwick, swallowing everything in between. They might worry that he hadn't found shelter, but he could do little to alleviate that concern at present. No messenger could get through, as Roger Selby had said. It rather looked as if he would be spending Christmas Day, at least, at Selby Hall.

If truth be told, he was not sorry to postpone his arrival at Hartley House. It seemed such a long time ago that he had proposed to Sarah Hartley. He had been nineteen, Sarah seventeen. And they had known each other from earliest childhood. The border towns and villages of Northumberland provided a rarefied atmosphere, where the local county families, few and far between as they were, were entirely dependent upon each other for a social life. There were no big town centers between Newcastle and Edinburgh. It was wild, rough country that fostered both interdependence among its own and a fierce independence from outsiders.

Sarah had been a sweet young woman. He tried to conjure up her picture behind his closed eyelids. Very fair, periwinkle blue eyes, a little plump, but prettily so. Of course that could have changed as womanhood formed her. She had wept when he'd left, and she'd waited for him, these full ten years. Or so Rob had written in his infrequent letters. Sarah was still a spinster, already on the shelf. Everyone said she was pining for her first love. And when he'd been summoned home, Ned had seen no alternative but to honor his youthful pledge. This Christmas journey to Hartley House was to renew that pledge in person before he faced the unenviable task of putting right the damage that neglect had done to his own family home and estates.

Well, he had money aplenty for such a task, and it would have its satisfactions. He had his own ideas about farming, about horse breeding, about estate management, and the prospect of putting them into practice was undeniably exciting. And he would need a wife at his side, a woman who knew the land, its people and the eccentricities of both as well as he did. Sarah was a competent woman. She would make him a good wife. So why could he not summon up some genuine enthusiasm at the prospect? All he felt at present was a gloomy acceptance of a bounden duty.

The sound of the door opening jerked him back to the cooling bathwater and the unfamiliar bedchamber. "Our Sally's done a fair job on the coat, sir," Davis announced, laying it carefully on the bed. "Mr. Jacobs said as how dinner will be served in half an hour."

"Then I must not keep my host waiting." Ned stood up as he spoke, water sloshing around him. He took the warm towel off the hanger close to the fire and wrapped it around himself as he stepped out. He ran a hand over his chin with a grimace. "Do you think you could shave me?"

"Oh, aye, sir," Davis said, pouring water from the ewer on the washstand into the basin. "I'm a dab hand at it, sir. Used to shave my pa when he had the shakes on him." He took the long, straight-edged razor and stropped it vigorously.

Ned sat down on the stool before the washstand and gave himself into the hands of his borrowed valet. Davis worked quickly and efficiently, and with some pride in his handiwork. "There, sir, how's that. Good and close, I'd say."

"Indeed, Davis." Ned ran his hand over his smooth chin. "Very good. Thank you."

Fifteen minutes later he was ready to join his host. He felt a new man, the miseries of the day a thing of the past. His newly pressed coat fitted perfectly, his linen was as white as the virgin snow beyond his window, his boots had a lovely deep shine to them, and his doeskin pantaloons were as soft as butter. He did not consider himself a vain man, but Viscount Allenton liked to make a good impression, and couldn't help a satisfied nod at his image in the pier glass before he headed for the door.

He could hear the soft notes of a piano and the sound of voices coming from a salon to the right of the hall as he descended the stairs. There seemed like quite a few voices, mostly male, interspersed with an occasional female tone. He had invited himself to quite a house party, it would seem. He crossed the hall to the double doors, where a footman stood waiting to announce him.

Chapter Two

There were close to twenty people in the salon. The room was decorated with swags of greenery interspersed with the bright blood red of holly berries. Bunches of mistletoe hung from the chandeliers and Ned realized that he was standing beneath a particularly large bunch of waxy cream berries only when a woman separated from the group gathered before the fire and came over with a little squeal of glee.

"Welcome, stranger. I demand a Christmas kiss." She kissed him full on the lips before he had time to react, and the room burst into loud applause. The woman stood back and regarded him with more of a smirk than a smile. Her eyes were a little glassy, her cheeks very pink.

She was more than a little tipsy, Ned decided, but he entered into the spirit of whatever game they were playing and swept her an elaborate bow. "Your *most* obedient servant, ma'am."

"Step in, Allenton, before every lady in the room salutes you beneath that mistletoe . . . unless, of course, you've a mind to invite them." Roger Selby, beaming jovially, crossed the Aubusson carpet toward him, hand outstretched.

"It would certainly be a pleasure," Ned said, nevertheless moving quickly away from the doorway to meet his host.

"Ah, yes indeed, man, we've a bevy of beauties here and no mistake," Selby announced, linking an arm through Ned's. "Come and let me present you. Everyone's uncommon delighted at the prospect of a fresh face. . . . Here he is, ladies and gentleman. Our new neighbor, Viscount Allenton, fresh from India."

Ned bowed as each introduction was made. None of the names was familiar, which surprised him. He would have expected Selby's Christmas house party to have been made up of the local landowners, whose family names at least he would have recognized. But it dawned on him rapidly that his host's guests were not of the usual kind. There was a hint of vulgarity to the five women. It was hard to put his finger on it at first, but as a glass of claret was pressed into his hand and the group gathered around him, he began to notice the details. Voices were too loud, gowns too frilled and fussy for true elegance, and the plethora of gemstones was almost blinding. The men, for the most part, were older than the women, and there was a rough edge there too, despite the formality of their evening dress. A sharpness, a hardness, that underpinned the apparent camaraderie.

Throughout this covert assessment, Ned made himself agreeable, joining in the laughter, smiling easily at the rather frequent ribaldry, which made no concession to the women present, and answering pointed questions about his intentions now that he had returned to claim his inheritance with a careful courtesy that imparted as little information as possible. But he judged that his fellow guests were all a little too full of good spirits to be fully aware of his lack of candor.

"Anyone seen Georgiana?" a new voice demanded from the door, and the group seemed to swing as one toward a man close to Ned's age who had just entered the drawing room. He was a big man with powerful shoulders and a body that looked as if it would be at home in a boxing ring. His florid face was handsome in a bucolic way, his pale eyes were clear and focused, unlike those of the rest of the company, but there was something calculating that shifted across the light surface as he noticed the newcomer.

"Ah, you must be the benighted viscount," he declared. "Selby was telling us all about you." He extended his hand in greeting. "Godfrey Belton, at your service, Lord Allenton."

"Delighted," Ned said, shaking the hand firmly, wondering what it was about this man that instantly set his hackles rising. He did not ordinarily develop instant dislikes to strangers.

"I trust you'll enjoy our revels," Belton said, taking a snuff box from his pocket and flicking it open with his thumbnail. "May I offer you a pinch . . . uncommon fine mix, I think you'll find."

Ned shook his head. "Thank you, but I don't take it."

"I thought all you Indian folk indulged . . . supposed to combat that vile climate," Belton declared, taking a large pinch for himself.

"I didn't find the climate vile," Ned said pleasantly. "But it doesn't agree with everyone, certainly."

Godfrey Belton regarded him in questioning silence for a moment, then gave a hearty laugh that somehow lacked true amusement and repeated his original question to the room at large. "Anyone seen Georgiana? I've searched high and low."

"Wretched girl, always disappearing," Roger Selby grumbled. "She was in her room half an hour past. I sent a message to say dinner was delayed. She was there then."

"She wasn't when I knocked five minutes ago," Belton said.

"I assume you're talking about me." A soft voice spoke from a side door. "I was looking for a book in the library."

The young woman who stepped into the room was as unlike the other women in the salon as the moon was to cream cheese, Ned thought. She was slight, her slender frame straight as an arrow, and her gown of ivory silk opening over a gold slip would have caused every debutante at Almack's to sigh with envy. Her only jewelry was a three-strand collar of flawless pearls, with matching drops in her ears. Her hair was a deliciously unruly mass of copper-colored curls that she had allowed to cluster and fall as they chose. An undisciplined coiffure that unlike her gown would never find favor at Almack's. But, by God, it suited her.

She had the green eyes and flawless white skin typical of a redhead. But did she have the proverbial temperament of the redhead? Ned wondered, with a hidden smile. Now that would be interesting.

She closed the door quietly at her back and came into the salon. "I'm sorry if I've kept you waiting, cousin."

"No matter . . . no matter," Roger Selby said. "Let me

make you known to our unexpected guest. Lord Allenton . . . my ward, Lady Georgiana Carey."

Ned bowed; the lady sketched a curtsy. "I'm guessing you were caught in the storm, Lord Allenton," she said in her quiet voice. "The roads are impassable."

"They are indeed, Lady Georgiana."

"Where have you been all afternoon, Georgiana?" Godfrey Belton demanded on a slightly belligerent note. "I was looking all over for you. I told you to meet me in the Long Gallery."

"Did you, Godfrey? I must have forgotten. Do forgive me." She smiled a cajoling smile and laid a hand on his arm.

"Godfrey and m'ward are betrothed," Selby told Ned. "They're to be married in the spring."

"My congratulations," Ned said, with a half bow in the direction of the couple. He saw that Belton had placed his hand over his fiancée's as it rested on his arm. Georgiana made a move to slide her hand out from under but Belton's hand pressed down hard, his fingers closing over hers.

A slight grimace twisted her mouth. "I'd like a glass of sherry, Godfrey," she said.

"I'm not sure you deserve it, arriving so late," he said. "You'll be holding up dinner." Still holding her hand against his arm, he turned both of them to the group by the fire, but not before Ned had seen the look on the lady's face. For an instant pure fury had blazed in those green eyes and then it had vanished, to be replaced by a resigned and apologetic smile.

"Dinner is served, my lord," Jacobs intoned from the doorway.

"Good . . . we're all famished," Selby announced. "Georgiana, take Lord Allenton into dinner. As the latest arrival he's our honored guest tonight—but don't get used to it, Allenton." He laughed boisterously. "You'll be one of us tomorrow, and from tomorrow until Twelfth Night the Lord of Misrule will be running the proceedings. We elect him after dinner tonight."

Ned knew well the medieval history of the Christmas revels controlled by the Lord of Misrule. It supposedly had its origins in ancient Rome, a festival where all the usual hierarchies were turned on their heads, and the ordinary rules of civilized society were forgotten. In its present form the Lord of Misrule was elected by the celebrants and he held total sway for the twelve days of Christmas, requiring absolute obedience to his most whimsical instructions. It was a tradition still practiced among some families in the borderlands, but it had never been Ned's father's practice, and he'd never participated in the notoriously wild twelve days of revelry. He wasn't at all sure he wanted to. There were too many opportunities for unpleasant mischief when all the usual social rules no longer held sway.

"Don't look so alarmed, Lord Allenton." Lady Georgiana was by his side and he noticed she was massaging one hand almost absently as she smiled at him. "We keep within the boundaries."

"I'm relieved to hear it, ma'am," he said, offering his arm. "The ceremonies were not practiced in my father's household."

"They can be amusing," she said, walking with him across the baronial hall to the dining room opposite. "And as long as the Lord of Misrule is conscientious, matters don't get out of hand." She led him to his place at the long mahogany table.

He held her chair for her, then took his own seat on her right. "You sound very familiar with such revels, Lady Georgiana."

"Oh, I wish people would call me Georgie," she said abruptly. "Everyone does in town."

He looked at her, momentarily startled. Her voice was quite different. The low diffidence had vanished, and there was a touch of impatience beneath the sharply defined syllables.

And then she smiled at him as she shook out her napkin and said in her old voice, "I still find it difficult to get used to being called by my full name, sir. But my guardian insists upon it. And I'm sure Lord Selby knows best." Her eyes were soft, her smile sweet, and Ned thought he must have imagined that startling change earlier.

"But you don't care for it," he said.

She seemed to hesitate for a moment, looking at him with a slight wariness in her eyes, but she had no chance to say anything further on the subject.

"So, Allenton, what d'you expect to find when you finally get home?" Godfrey Belton, seated across the table from him, broke a piece of bread as he called out the question.

"I'm not really sure," Ned responded calmly. He sensed there was a point behind Belton's question, and that it wasn't a pleasant one. "It's been ten years."

"Well, you're in for a shock, dear fellow," Selby boomed from the head of the table. "God knows what your brother thought he was doing . . . letting the place go to rack and ruin like that." He shook his head. "Tragic waste, if you ask me."

"Oh, Rob Vasey was only interested in his horses, cards and dice," Belton declared, thrusting a piece of bread into his mouth and washing it down with a deep swallow of his wine.

Ned regarded him with faint hauteur. "Indeed?"

"Oh, no offense, Allenton," Godfrey said with a bluff laugh. "We're all neighbors up here, we don't have any secrets, can't afford to. You know that."

Ned's smile was tight, but he managed it. "I hope to put things right," he said, taking a sip of claret.

"You'll need deep pockets, m'boy," a man bellowed from the end of the table. "Selby has the right of it . . . rack and ruin is what I hear."

Ned struggled to remember the man's name. Giles Waring, that was it. There had been Warings around Old Berwick for generations, called themselves farmers, but they were reivers to a man. And not a gentleman among them. This offshoot of the clan looked a trifle soft for a life of raiding. But the elegancies of civilization hadn't rubbed off, either, judging by the way he was fondling the woman on his right. Definitely not his wife. That lady was seated farther down the table between two other men who seemed to find her company as alluring as her husband found his own neighbor's.

Ned turned his attention to his wineglass, contenting himself with another noncommittal "Indeed?" He glanced sideways to his neighbor. "How long have you lived here, Lady Georgiana?"

"Eighteen months, two weeks, and three days," she answered. She helped herself to a minute portion of roast pheasant from the dish the footman held at her elbow. "We were living in London when my aunt died. Lord Selby is my guardian."

Ned wondered whether to comment on the bitter precision of her answer, and then decided this was neither the time nor the place to probe. "Selby is your cousin, I believe you said." He served himself generously. He felt as if he hadn't eaten in a week.

"It's a tenuous connection." She took three green beans from the serving platter. "On my mother's side, I believe." Her slender shoulders lifted in a tiny shrug as if the issue was a matter of indifference.

"Northumberland is a long way from London, in every respect," Ned observed, helping himself to beans and moving on to the platter of roast potatoes that his neighbor had scorned.

"You never spoke a truer word, Lord Allenton," she said, and there it was again, that sharply different tone.

"Georgiana, you need to eat," Godfrey Belton called from across the table. "Look at your plate, woman. It's not enough to keep a kitten alive. Put some flesh on your bones, for God's sake. How's a man to get warm at night with a stick beside him."

Ned controlled himself with difficulty. He felt her tension beside him. It made him think of a cat bunching its muscles, preparing to spring. But instead she said softly, "I'm not hungry, Godfrey."

"You need exercise," one of the other male guests declared. "Nothing like a bit of hearty exercise to stimulate the appetite. The sooner you see to it, the better, Belton." Another round of laughter greeted this sally. Georgiana appeared to ignore it, carefully cutting her pheasant into tiny pieces.

"Jacobs, give Lady Georgiana a good spoonful of those mashed turnips and potatoes," Belton instructed the butler.

Jacobs looked uncomfortable but he brought the covered dish to Georgiana. "May I, my lady?"

"I don't think you have much choice, Jacobs," she said *sotto voce*, but it was the other voice, the one that Ned had now decided was the real voice of Georgiana Carey.

Ned watched the butler place a small spoonful onto her plate. Jacobs was ignoring the calls of "More, man, more" from across the table.

"Not enough to keep a bird alive," Godfrey declared in disgust as the butler finally backed away.

"Leave her alone now, Belton," Selby said. "She's never had much of an appetite."

Selby's word seemed to be law. Godfrey turned to his own plate and the conversation, such as it was, picked up.

"Where did you live in London?" Ned inquired.

"Brooke Street. My aunt was my guardian." She dipped the tines of her fork in the mashed turnip with a barely concealed grimace of distaste. "I never knew my parents, Lord Allenton. They died when I was a baby. My mother's sister was my guardian, and on her death I was passed along to Lord Selby."

There it was again. Acerbic as the bitterest lemon. Ned was fascinated, but he couldn't begin to explore the contradictions at this dinner table. "There are compensations to living here, ma'am," he said. "The mountains are beautiful."

"And the dales are delightful," she said, spearing a morsel of pheasant. "The fishing is spectacular, the hunting even more so. I've heard it all, Lord Allenton, and I've no need to hear it again. Instead, tell me about India." She turned to look at him, and he saw hunger in her eyes. Georgiana Carey was starved of the outside world, the world she had grown up with. And behind that hunger was a determination that intrigued him as it puzzled him.

"What would you like to know?"

Georgiana considered the question. She wanted to say *anything. Anything that has absolutely nothing to do with this place and these people.* But she could sense that she had aroused the viscount's interest enough already and she didn't dare take any more risks. She'd been foolishly self-indulgent and impulsive once today, and while she had escaped the consequences thus far, she couldn't afford to play with fate. It was time to fade into the background again.

"It's very hot there, I understand," she said in her soft voice. "Is it so all the year round? That must be tedious, I would think."

Ned tried to conceal his disappointment. He had expected a sharper more intelligent interest. She sounded now no different from the bored maidens he'd encountered in London set onto him by their mamas, anxious to snare the wealthiest and most eligible bachelor in town.

Funny how the black sheep had metamorphosed into the season's catch, he reflected, a sardonic smile twisting his mouth. Amazing what the acquisition of wealth could do for one's marital prospects.

Georgiana saw the smile and bit her tongue. In any other circumstances she would have asked him outright what unpleasant reflection had prompted it. But that would have been Georgie's question, not Georgiana's.

"I enjoy the heat," Ned said blandly. "But not everyone does." He took a sip of wine.

"Have you killed a tiger, Lord Allenton?" his left-hand neighbor asked with an elaborate shudder. "Did you hunt with one of the . . . oh, what do they call their kings? Such a silly word." She tittered behind her fan.

"Maharajahs," Georgiana said. "They call them maharajahs, Mrs. Eddington. And they ride on the top of elephants in something called a howdah, and when their trackers find a tiger, they shoot it. It's very sportsmanlike, I believe. Is that not correct, Lord Allenton?"

Ned looked at her in open amusement. Her disdain was so obvious he couldn't believe no one else around the table heard it. But it seemed that they didn't. No one evinced the slightest surprise and Belton said, "You're too book-learned, Georgiana, I've always said so. It's not good in a woman . . . gives her ideas."

"What kind of ideas, Godfrey?" she asked sweetly. "You must make it clear, so that I know what not to think."

Instantly Georgiana cursed her unruly tongue. She was sailing too close to the wind again. Not for Godfrey, who wouldn't recognize sarcasm if it hit him on the head with a cricket bat, but this Viscount Allenton was a different breed altogether.

She shrank down in her seat as if she could withdraw herself entirely from his attention.

"No, it's not in the least sportsmanlike," Ned said quietly. "But why are you trying to slide under the table?"

"I'm not," she insisted, a flush on her cheeks. She was just making things worse, she knew, but it had been two years since she'd had to worry about anyone seeing through her little performances. No one, not even

Roger Selby, suspected that her act of demure compliance lacked sincerity. But in the space of an hour, this newcomer seemed to have her measure in full. Well, not quite in full, she reminded herself. That couldn't happen.

"My error, ma'am," he said with a chuckle, and to her relief he didn't address her again until the second course had been placed on the table.

"I must congratulate your cousin on his cook," he said, taking a forkful of a pupton of creamed chicken. "This is surprisingly good."

"Why surprisingly?" she asked, toying with a teaspoon of asparagus mousse.

"I remember the food in these parts as very plain, wholesome, but lacking in delicacy," he said. "This, on the other hand, has a most subtle flavor."

"Oh, you can thank my ward for that, sir," Selby declared, reaching for the decanter, his face redder than ever. "Revolutionized the kitchens, she did, the minute she walked through the front door. And she's not above turning her own hand to a sauce now and again. Isn't that so, Georgiana?"

"I enjoy cooking on occasion, cousin," she said.

Godfrey Belton guffawed. "That's rich coming from a woman who has the appetite of a wren."

"Wrens eat twenty times their body weight in a day, Godfrey," Georgiana pointed out. "I doubt my appetite can compete."

Godfrey glowered at her amid the general laughter and she felt a twitch of apprehension. She thought she knew how far she could go before rousing his more savage side, but he could not endure being the butt of a joke in public, and this company was unlikely to put any constraints on his behavior. She gave him a placating smile, hoping that would cool his temper before it reached the boiling point, and to her relief he grunted and buried his nose in his refilled wineglass.

Ned heard her little exhalation of relief, and he felt her body relax a little beside him. Something was going on here—something decidedly unsettling. Part of him wished fate had brought him to some other port in a storm than Selby Hall, but mostly his curiosity was piqued. The stunning Georgiana Carey was a mystery he'd dearly like to solve.

Georgiana waited impatiently for the moment when, as her cousin's official hostess, she could give the signal for the ladies to withdraw. The sooner she was out of Godfrey's sight, the sooner he would forget her joke in the depths of the port decanter.

At last she pushed back her chair and immediately her neighbor was on his feet, courteously helping her with a hand under her elbow. The other women followed her out of the dining room and she allowed herself to relax properly for the first time. The women posed no threat, except for boredom, and Georgiana was used to that.

She poured tea in the salon and as soon as her companions seemed settled into noisy gossip, she went to the piano. Here at least she could find a measure of peace and quiet that would last until Godfrey arrived to demand that she play something lively, if she must play at all.

Lost as she was in the music, she became aware only gradually of the figure standing a little away from her, his back against the sofa, arms folded, brown eyes watching her steadily. Her fingers came to rest on the keys.

"Lord Allenton, I didn't realize you were there."

"No," he said. "I didn't wish to disturb you. You're an accomplished pianist, Lady Georgiana."

She shrugged. "Not really. I've known many much more accomplished than I." She looked at him with a slight frown. "You've abandoned the port rather early, sir."

"I prefer to keep a clear head," he said.

"Well, you're alone in that in this company, my lord," she declared, closing the piano with finality as she rose from the stool. "The twelve days of Christmas lie ahead of us."

"You don't sound as if the prospect pleases you overmuch," he observed, his narrowed gaze sharp as it scrutinized her expression.

"It's only twelve days," she said, brushing past him on her way back to the tea tray.

"True." He followed her. "And who should be chosen as Lord of Misrule tonight?"

"It will be between Godfrey and my cousin. And they will choose my cousin . . . if they have any sense," she said without hesitation. "He's the only one capable of keeping control if matters run out of hand, even in his cups."

"Then I shall vote accordingly." He shook his head, a frown in his eye.

"What's the matter?" she demanded. "Why are you looking at me like that?"

"I honestly don't know," he admitted. "There's just something about you . . . something familiar. I feel sure I've met you before, and yet I know I haven't. You would still have been in short skirts ten years ago when I went to India."

"I was ten," she said. "Of course we haven't met. But it's not an uncommon sensation . . . just *déjà vu*. So, how long were you in London after you came back from India . . . before coming up here?"

"Four weeks only," he said, accepting the brisk change of subject. "I thought a few weeks in the south would help to bridge the gap between India and the frozen north." He laughed. "I doubt it worked."

She gave him a distracted smile as the sound of boisterous voices swelled from the hall, heralding the arrival of the rest of the gentlemen.

"Come, come, no more of that insipid brew," Roger Selby called as he entered, bearing two bottles of champagne. Godfrey, also bearing two bottles, was on his heels. " 'Tis Christmas, ladies, and I decree that no more tea shall be drunk this night . . . or, indeed, any of the twelve nights of Christmas." He flourished his bottles. "Godfrey, open yours while I open mine."

The corks popped and the golden wine flowed. Ned tried to engage Georgiana in conversation, but she avoided him, spending her time at her fiancé's side, solicitously filling his glass, stroking his arm, smiling fondly. But Ned noticed that she barely touched the contents of her own glass, although she gave a skillful performance of becoming a little the worse for wear herself. He observed the scene with the dispassion of an outsider, even as he wondered what was really going on.

The only time Georgiana approached him was toward the end of the evening. She carried a glass bowl and a handful of paper slips. "Make your choice, Lord Allenton." She gave him a blank slip and he wrote Selby's name, folding the paper carefully before dropping it into the bowl. She gave him a brief nod and continued around the group collecting votes.

When she had everyone's vote she turned slightly away from the group, making a performance of stirring up the papers, chanting some nonsense words of make-believe magic, then she shook the bowl once again before upturning it onto the table and counting out the votes. Twelve for Selby, eight for Godfrey Belton.

Belton looked livid, but amid the general roars of approval and the genial commiserations of the company he had little choice but to put a good face on it. Selby received the vote as his due and at last the party broke up.

In the hall the guests lit their carrying candles from the branched candelabrum on the table at the foot of the stairs and dispersed, but Ned had a fairly good idea that there would be some movement between bedchambers. Not that it was any business of his, and all he wanted was the peace and quiet of his own apartment.

"Good night, Lady Georgiana," he said, lighting her candle and handing it to her, shielding the flame with his cupped palm.

"Good night, Lord Allenton. I trust you will be comfortable."

"Believe me, ma'am, I would be comfortable tonight in a barn," he said with a chuckle. "Much less a featherbed."

"Come, Georgiana, I shall see you to bed." Godfrey weaved drunkenly toward them, his candle flickering wildly.

"I can find my own way, Godfrey," she said, deftly sidestepping onto the stairs as he lurched against the newel post. "Sleep well, sir." And she was gone, light as air up the stairs, disappearing into the gloom at the head while her fiancé stumbled in her wake.

Well, Godfrey Belton wouldn't be disturbing her to-night, Ned thought. The man would be lucky to make it to his own bed in the condition he was in. He came up beside Belton and slipped a supporting hand under his elbow.

The man looked surprised, but didn't refuse the assistance. At the top he muttered a good night and weaved away around the galleried landing. Ned watched until he'd found a door and hammered upon it. It was opened, presumably by a waiting manservant, and Belton disappeared within.

Chapter Three

Ned closed his bedchamber door behind him and stood for a moment savoring the orderly peace.

"I've put out your nightshirt, m'lord." Davis straightened from the fire where he'd been adjusting a log. "Will you take a glass of cognac?"

Ned had been carefully abstemious all evening, but judged it safe now that he was alone to indulge a little. "Yes, I will, thank you, Davis. And then you may go."

"You'll not be wanting me to help you to bed, sir?" Davis brought a goblet over to him, sounding a little hurt.

"I've been managing for myself for many years, Davis," Ned said with a smile, taking the goblet. "I thank you for the offer, but you'll be glad of your own bed, I'm sure."

"Very well, m'lord." Davis bowed and went to the door. "What time should I bring your shaving water in the morning, sir?"

"Oh, not before seven," Ned said casually, taking the scent of the cognac in the wide-rimmed goblet with an appreciative nod.

"Very well, sir." Davis sounded rather hesitant as he

hovered at the door. "His lordship, sir, don't usually take breakfast before eleven."

"No matter," Ned said. "I'll break my fast with some bread and cheese. Bring it up with the hot water . . . oh, and coffee."

"Very well, sir. . . . Good night, sir."

"Good night, Davis." Ned sat down by the fire, cradling his goblet between his hands. Such a late breakfast was hardly surprising in a household that drank as late and as heavily as this one, he reflected. He set down his glass and pulled off his cravat, tossing it to the floor before easing off his shoes, flexing his toes to the fire's warmth.

Had he really seen what he'd seen? But he knew he had. Georgiana had removed a handful of paper slips from the bowl during her make-believe incantations and then, with a deft twist of her wrist, had dropped their replacements into the bowl. He would swear she'd stuffed the purloined papers into her sleeve before turning back to the room to upend the bowl on the table.

She had intended that her guardian should win the vote. It wasn't hard to guess why. Selby, even when drunk, remained in control. Godfrey Belton had a dangerous edge to him even sober. Drunk he would be savage. Not the man to keep the bawdy riotousness of Christmas revelry within bounds.

Ned sipped his cognac and let his eyes close and his mind drift. When he awoke the fire was mere ashy embers, the candles were guttering, and he was cold and stiff. Cursing, he stood up and bent to rekindle the fire. He shrugged out of his coat and was about to take off his shirt when he realized that he was wide awake. He'd dozed for over an hour and it had taken the edge off his need for sleep.

He took a sip of cognac and lit a taper in the fire's glow to light the unused candles in the branched candlestick on the washstand. He needed a book to distract him from the tumult of thoughts now crowding his mind. Sarah Hartley . . . what awaited him in the ruins of his own house . . . *Georgiana Carey.*

She, at least, would be a short-lived distraction. As soon as he could get away from Selby Hall, she would vanish from his mind.

He relit his carrying candle and took it to the door, opening it softly, listening to the sounds of the house. The usual creaks and groans of settling timbers, no sounds of life. He slipped into the corridor and padded in his stockinged feet to the galleried landing, where a dim light shone from a sconce in the wall above the staircase. He trod soundlessly down to the hall and into the salon. It was in darkness except for a residual glow from the ashes in the fireplace.

He lifted his candle, sending flickering shadows around the room. Earlier that evening Georgiana had entered the salon through a side door behind the piano. His eye found it quickly. Presumably it led into the library since that was where she said she had been. And the library was where he would find a book. A faint line of light beneath the door caught his eye.

He set down his candle on top of the piano and went to the door, pausing with his hand on the latch, wondering whether to knock. Either someone was in there or a lamp had been left lit inadvertently when the last servant had gone to bed.

Probably the latter, Ned decided. It was close to three in the morning and he had seen his host and fellow guests go up to bed soon after one. He lifted the latch and opened the door. He heard the snap and click of a drawer closing followed by a rustling as he stepped into the room. The light came from a candle on a big square desk in the window embrasure. Georgiana stood behind the desk, her copper hair glowing richly in the flickering flame. Her face was even paler than usual and something suspiciously like panic flashed for a second in her green eyes and then vanished as she saw who it was.

"What the devil are you doing here at this time of night?" she demanded in a fierce undertone.

"I might ask the same of you," he observed mildly. "As it happens I couldn't sleep and came to find a book. It seemed the logical place to look." He gestured to the floor-to-ceiling bookshelves, eyebrows raised quizzically.

"You're welcome to see what you can find," she said. "I don't think anyone's opened one of those volumes in fifty years or more. My cousin is not bookish."

"And you?"

She shrugged. "You heard my fiancé. I am altogether too much of a bookworm and bluestocking for his fancy."

It seemed she had abandoned her performance as the demure, compliant ward as soon as its intended audience had gone to bed. Ned grinned and perched on the arm of a chair. He crossed his legs, swinging one ankle idly as he regarded her. "So what are you doing at three in the morning, Georgie?"

"I was looking for something," she said, a mite defensively, he thought. "A piece of paper . . . I thought I might have dropped it behind the desk when I was in here earlier."

"Ah." He nodded gravely. "I wonder why that sounds like an untruth."

"I can't imagine why it should," she snapped. "Anyway, it's no business of yours, my lord, what I choose to do and when."

He nodded again. "That I will give you. But perhaps I can help you look for this . . . this paper?"

"No, you can't. It's not here," she said, stepping away from the desk, raising her hands palms forward as if to demonstrate the truth of her statement.

"Was it important?"

Her expression took on something of the hunted fox. "No, not in the least."

"One could be forgiven for thinking it must be. People don't usually start a treasure hunt in their nightgowns in the early hours of the morning unless they're in search of something fairly important." He rose from the arm of the chair and crossed to the desk, moving behind it so that he was standing where she had been when he'd come in.

He had heard the click of a hastily slammed drawer as he'd opened the door. The drawer in the desk was shut, but a piece of paper had not been properly replaced and a corner showed over the edge of the drawer.

He opened the drawer, aware now of her sudden swift intake of breath, the flush blooming on her cheeks, the wariness in her eyes. "Something seems to have stuck," he said, pulling the drawer out fully. "Ah, just this." He slid the errant sheet of vellum back into the drawer, smoothing it flat over its fellows, then quietly closed the drawer again. "Should it be locked?"

With a tiny sigh Georgiana slid a tiny gold key across the desk. He picked it up, locked the drawer, and then looked up questioningly.

"I'll put it away," she said on another sigh of resignation, holding out her hand. He placed the key in her palm and she turned and went over to the bookshelves on the far wall. She selected a volume, opened it, and dropped the key into a hollow in the binding. Then she replaced the volume, standing back to examine its position.

"I daresay your guardian needs to believe his secrets are his own," Ned observed in neutral tones.

"Don't we all?" she responded flatly. "Do you intend to keep mine, Lord Allenton?"

"Most certainly," he replied. "Although I'd dearly like to know what's really going on."

She turned to look at him, her hands clasped lightly against the thin muslin skirt of her nightgown. "Roger Selby is not an honest broker, Lord Allenton. I suggest you keep that in mind in your dealings with him."

"I wasn't intending to have any dealings with him," Ned said, distracted now by the slight swell of her breasts beneath the thin covering, and the hint of her shape revealed in the soft flow of muslin.

"But I think he may intend to have dealings with you," she said, seemingly oblivious of his suddenly attentive regard.

"Is that a warning?"

"A word to the wise," she said. "I don't know any details, but I do know my cousin." Bitterness laced her words, and her jaw tensed, her nostrils flaring slightly. Then she turned to the door. "Snuff the candle when you've finished, Lord Allenton. I bid you good night."

"Georgiana . . . Georgie, wait a minute." He stepped forward, one hand outstretched. She turned back to him.

"Yes?"

"Are you in some kind of trouble?"

An amazing transformation came over her then. She began to laugh with genuine amusement. "Oh, if only you knew," she said. "Good night, my lord."

And she was gone, leaving him alone, feeling rather foolish, the sounds of her laughter still echoing among the dusty volumes.

Ned waited a few moments until he could hear only the familiar nighttime sounds of the sleeping house, then he went to the bookshelves, looking for the volume that housed the key. He hadn't been able to see its title, but he had a fair sense of where on the shelf it was. He found it on the third try. *Gulliver's Travels.* He wondered absently if there was any significance in the choice.

He took the key to the desk and opened the drawer. He had no idea why he was prying into another man's personal documents—and not just another man, his host to boot. A man who had welcomed him in from the blizzard with nothing but warmth and generosity. Which he was now repaying by snooping among his private papers.

He took out the sheaf of papers and riffled through them. They seemed to refer to some kind of land deal between Selby and Godfrey Belton. A thousand hectares of lower moorland around Great Ryle. Prime land, as Ned was well aware. He had *not* been aware that it formed part of the Selby barony. But one way and another, Selby appeared to be giving this to Belton with no strings. There had to be strings—a property deal of this magnitude couldn't simply be a gift. Unless it had something to do with Georgiana's dowry. He turned the pages over, examining them closely. There was no mention of the betrothal at all.

Very strange, but really none of his business. Ned placed the papers back carefully in order, closed and locked the drawer and returned the key to *Lilliput.* He yawned, aware now of bone-deep fatigue. His second wind had clearly passed. He snuffed the candle on the desk and returned to the salon. His carrying candle on the piano had gone out so he abandoned it, picking his way back through the shadowy shapes of the furniture in the salon to the hall and up to his bedchamber.

The fire was burning merrily and he undressed by its light, climbed up into the canopied bed and sank into the deep feathers, pulling the covers over him. The bed was cold, all residue of heat from the warming pan long dissipated, but Ned barely noticed the chill. His eyes closed without volition on the day's dramas and mysteries. Tomorrow's would wait.

But his last conscious image was of the slender figure lit from behind by the candle, the shadow of her body, fluid beneath the clinging folds of muslin, the swell of her breasts and the hint of their darkened peaks.

Georgiana stood shivering in front of her own fire. She'd been in such a fever to get down to the library as soon as the house was safely asleep she'd neglected to wear her dressing gown, and she was now freezing. Not that it had done her much good. The will had not been in the desk, as she'd hoped. And any further search had been prevented by the viscount's inopportune appearance in the library.

Inopportune, but not necessarily unwelcome, she was forced to admit. It had been so long since she'd had a civilized conversation with a civilized man, one who understood the world she had come from. And Edward Vasey was *very* personable. She'd have to be blind not to notice that. Of course, it could just be the contrast between his manners and those of her cousin's other guests—not to mention those of the execrable and unmentionable Godfrey Belton. But it was more than that.

Viscount Allenton would stand out in a room full of the most elegant members of the ton. He had the air of one who gave not a second thought to his appearance, but she had spent enough time in the fashionable world to recognize the exquisite tailoring of his coat, the masterful fall of his cravat, the careful cut of his thick, dark brown hair. And he had physical attributes that owed nothing to the skills of others. A tall, slender physique that indicated a lithe athleticism, a pair of eyes more gold than brown and a delightful smile when he chose to show it.

He wasn't happy though. Something was troubling him, and Georgiana supposed she could understand that. He would be facing disaster when he eventually arrived home to take up his inheritance. It couldn't be a pleasant prospect. And if he'd loved his life in India as much as he said, then he was probably in much the same boat as she was herself. Forced into a life that she would not have chosen for herself in a million years.

But she had no intention of meekly accepting her fate.

Georgiana knelt and pulled back the rug in front of the hearth. She ran her hand lightly over the wide oak floorboards until her finger found the little depression. She pressed it and two of the boards slid soundlessly apart to reveal a small dark hole. She reached inside and drew out a soft chamois pouch. It felt satisfyingly heavy on her palm.

Georgiana stood up, kicking the rug swiftly over the opening. She wasn't expecting any visitors at this ungodly hour, but habits of caution were well ingrained; too much was at stake for even an instant's carelessness. She took the pouch to the bed, loosened the drawstrings and upended the contents into the middle of the thick quilted coverlet. Gold, silver, copper, and an occasional gem glowed in the candlelight.

Carefully she counted her horde as she did every night. There was more today than there had been yesterday. Soon she would have enough. If only she could find the damn will. She had seen it only once before, when her aunt's lawyer had explained it to her. She was her parents' only heir and the fortune was considerable, dispersed in extensive property both in London and in Northumberland and in bonds. She couldn't complete her plan without the will in her possession on the day she gained her majority. And Roger had it somewhere. He also had the most important pieces in her mother's jewel casket somewhere. The Carey diamonds. Just one of them would be enough for her present purposes. But where the devil had he hidden them?

It was six months before her twenty-first birthday, and Roger Selby intended her to be wedded and bedded with Godfrey Belton three months before that.

Georgiana scooped her treasure back into the pouch, returned it to its hiding place, secured the boards and set the rug right. She went to the window, trying to see through the thickly coated glass if the snow had stopped. A blizzard played havoc with business.

She couldn't see anything. The snow had piled up on the narrow sill, completely obscuring the outside. She contemplated trying to open the window against the barrier, but at four in the morning it seemed a pointless exercise. There was no way to keep snow from tumbling into the room, and she was cold enough as it was.

Shivering, she blew out the candles and jumped into bed, digging a nest for herself in the deep feather mattress.

Ned was still asleep when Davis came in with hot water and towels. He stirred as the manservant pulled back the curtains, then hitched himself up against the pillows, blinking in the strange white light from the snow-covered window.

"Good morning, Davis."

"Morning, m'lord. Merry Christmas. Still snowing like the blazes. No one'll be goin' abroad yet a while, I'll wager." Davis turned back to the bed. "I'll bring up coffee and breakfast now, m'lord."

"Thank you . . . and Merry Christmas to you." Ned pushed aside the covers and got to his feet. He stretched, aware of an unusual stiffness. Presumably the effects of sitting cramped in the chaise for so long, not to mention fighting his way through waist-high snow. A long walk was the answer. But not a feasible solution in the present climate.

He pulled on his dressing gown and went to the window, lifting the latch. He pushed it outward against the wall of snow and the light powder fell away, leaving only a crust of ice against the glass. And a blast of frigid air piercing the room.

Braving the blast, Ned leaned out. The snow was falling so heavily he could barely see his hand in front of him. He withdrew his hand and slammed the window closed, latching it firmly. An entire day in the close company of his fellow guests lay ahead, and short of taking to his bed with a chill he couldn't see any courteous way to avoid his social obligations.

But there was a compensation, a considerable one. Lady Georgiana Carey. She too would be immured, and he'd already noticed how adroit she was at organizing matters to her own tastes. And since Ned suspected those tastes meshed rather well with his own, he was more than willing to offer himself as a partner in crime. Two heads were always better than one.

Davis returned with coffee, hot rolls, cheese and a plate of ham. "I hope this'll do, sir, for the moment," he said, sounding rather doubtful as he set his burden on the table before the fire. "Cook's too busy with the big breakfast to prepare anything hot."

"This will do beautifully," Ned said. "I hope I haven't caused too much extra work."

"Oh, no sir, not a bit of it," Davis said cheerfully, pouring coffee. "Lady Georgiana's an early riser too. She's breaking her fast in the kitchen. Fancied shirred eggs, she did—makes 'em herself. Very good they are too."

Ned took a sip of coffee and said, "I've changed my mind, Davis. I fancy shirred eggs myself, so I shall go in search of Lady Georgiana. Direct me to the kitchen, if you please."

Davis looked startled. "It's not usual, m'lord. The guests don't usually go to the kitchen . . . Cook might not like it."

"But if Lady Georgiana is there, then there can be no objection to my joining her," Ned stated, heading for the door. "Since I'm somewhat informally clad, I'll take the back stairs, if you'll show me the way."

Davis could see no alternative. "This way, sir." He went to the door.

Chapter Four

The kitchen was bustling with activity, heat from the great range spreading into every corner. A small boy was turning a suckling pig on a spit over the fire, and a woman was pulling loaves out of the bread oven set into the bricks alongside the blazing fire. Two kitchen maids were scrubbing potatoes and chopping vegetables at one end of the long pine table that dominated the center of the room. Only one person took notice of Ned's arrival.

Georgiana, in a fur-trimmed dressing gown, was standing over the range, stirring the contents of a copper pot with a large wooden spoon. She glanced over her shoulder as Ned stepped into the kitchen and her stirring arm paused. "Good morning, Lord Allenton," she said, frowning at him. "What brings you into the kitchen of all places on Christmas morning?"

"I thought to wish you Merry Christmas," he said, then added with scrupulous honesty, "That and the prospect of shirred eggs. Davis said you were making some for your breakfast and I thought perhaps I could persuade you to double the quantity."

"Ah, well, I gave up that idea," she said, resuming her stirring. "There's not enough room in the ovens for another baking dish. They're all full of Bakewell tarts, which my cousin considers an absolute necessity for Christmas dinner, almost more important than the Christmas puddings." She gestured with her spoon to the two pots with their puddings steaming on the range. "So I'm scrambling instead."

"I like scrambled eggs just as well," he said, a mite plaintively.

She laughed. "There's plenty here. Have a seat—away from the cooking end. If you'd like to cut some bread and butter a couple of slices, that would be a help."

"Certainly." Ned found a loaf of still-warm bread sitting on a bread board at the far end of the table, a knife to hand and a crock of rich golden butter, newly churned from the look of it. He cut bread and buttered the slices liberally.

Georgiana came over with the saucepan. Without breaking her stride, she reached sideways as she passed the dresser and took two plates off a shelf. She set the plates on the table and swiftly divided the eggs between them. "There's coffee in the pot, or small beer, if you prefer."

"Coffee at this time of day," he said, watching her turn again to the dresser to fetch two shallow bowls. Her movements were swift and graceful, economical of effort, but utterly purposeful. She was very slight, her tiny waist accentuated by the tightly knotted girdle of her robe, her body moving fluidly beneath the silk folds as she stretched across the table, reaching for an earthenware jug from which aromatic steam curled. Her copper curls were roughly tied back with a green silk ribbon that matched her dressing gown. Again he had that sense of *déjà vu,* and he shook his head impatiently at the memory he couldn't catch.

She filled the two bowls with coffee. "Cream?"

"Please."

She added cream to the bowls and then sat down, cradling her bowl of coffee between her hands, savoring the aroma. "One thing I'll say for Selby, he keeps a fine dairy herd."

"Only one thing?" he queried with a raised eyebrow as he dug his fork into the mound of creamy eggs on his plate.

"Just a manner of speaking," she responded vaguely, taking up her own fork.

"I see."

They ate in silence for a while and then she said suddenly, "What took you to India? It seems a rather extreme choice of destination."

"As it happens it wasn't my choice," he replied, sipping his coffee before cutting another slice of bread. "My father had an acquaintance who owned a brokerage in London. He had contacts in India and it was decided that I should go and make my fortune . . . or die of some foreign malaise in the attempt," he added with a sardonic smile.

"Well, you didn't die," she stated. "So did you make your fortune?"

He nodded. "And enjoyed every moment of doing so. And now it seems I must put my fortune to the service of the Vasey estates."

Georgiana leaned her elbows on the table, again cradling her coffee bowl between her hands, regarding him closely across the table. "Why wasn't it your choice?"

"Ah . . . I thought you might wonder that." He buttered his fresh slice of bread. "Delicious eggs, by the way."

She nodded impatiently. "Won't you answer me?"

He shrugged. "It's no secret . . . an old story. And a common enough one."

She looked at him in questioning silence and he said bluntly, "I killed a man."

"By accident?" She didn't appear to be shocked, or even particularly surprised.

"Not exactly. In a duel. I caught him cheating at cards and called him on it. He called me a liar and the next thing I knew his seconds were waiting upon me."

He refilled his coffee cup. "We met at dawn, the usual drama . . . I intended to delope. The whole business struck me then, and even more so now, as utterly ridiculous. But one of my seconds told me that he had learned that my opponent had every intention of firing to kill. The only way he could preserve his honor, or some such rubbish. So I did what I had to do. Unfortunately for him I'm rather a good shot."

"So you had to leave the country?"

"In a certain amount of haste," Ned agreed. "Dueling is frowned upon—killing a man on the field even more so," he added dryly. "So I went to India, and until six months ago had absolutely no intention of ever returning."

"And now duty calls."

He inclined his head in acknowledgment, then said, "Your fiancé, Godfrey Belton. Is he from around here? I don't recognize the name."

Her face changed. Her mouth hardened, and her green eyes took on a glacial glint. "He's a friend of my guardian's," she said. "I don't know where they met." She rose from the table and began to gather their empty plates.

"Where will you live after your marriage?" Ned pressed. "He must come from somewhere."

"Of course he does," she snapped, moving swiftly away from him toward the kitchen sink. "I don't know where. But I believe he's acquired some land and is building a house up around Great Ryle."

The gift from Roger Selby, Ned remembered. Perhaps it was a wedding present from Selby to the newlyweds. Georgiana would get a beautiful house, and her husband some prime land. It was an explanation that would fit perfectly, but somehow Ned didn't think it fitted this particular scenario. It was too simple and pleasant for the distinctly sinister undercurrents in this household.

He watched Georgiana as she piled the dishes on a wooden draining board. Every muscle in her back seemed to have tightened, and once again he was reminded of a cat tensed and ready to strike. "So that house will be your marital home?"

She turned back to him, and brushed an errant curl from her cheek with the back of her hand. "I imagine so."

"But you have no wish for it," he declared.

She looked at him and he saw frustration and fury in her eyes, but she said only, "This is a pointless conversation. If you'll excuse me, I'm going to get dressed."

"Of course." He rose politely as she swept from the kitchen, and then made his own way upstairs again on the same errand. He seemed to have landed in a deeply mired mystery. But perhaps it wasn't so mysterious after all. Georgiana was cut off from all she knew up here in the Northumbrian wilds. She had no friends around her that he could see. And her guardian was empowered to make all and any decisions concerning her. So was she being coerced into this marriage? And if so, why?

Davis was laying out his clothes when Ned entered his bedchamber. "I thought the blue coat, sir, with buckskins," he said, smoothing the garments that he had laid with some reverence on the bed. "And I've polished your top boots, sir. How many neckcloths should I fetch for you?"

"One will be sufficient, thank you," Ned said, rather surprised at the question. "Why would I need more than one?"

"Well, I understand, sir, that gentlemen of fashion often use half a dozen before they achieve the knot to their satisfaction," the valet said. "An uncle of mine was in service to a gentleman in the city. He knows about such things."

"Ah, well, perhaps that's true for some men," Ned said cheerfully. "I for one find it perfectly simple to tie my neckcloth to my satisfaction in one attempt."

"Yes, m'lord." Davis looked disappointed and Ned felt a little guilty that he wasn't somehow living up to his valet's expectations.

"You may shave me again," he offered, shrugging out of his dressing gown. "You did a superb job yesterday."

"Thank you, m'lord." Davis picked up the dressing gown and hung it in the armoire.

"Oh, and would you find my greatcoat—I've a mind to visit the stables to see how my horses are doing," Ned said. "Do you happen to know where my coachman and postillions are housed?"

"Above the stable block, sir, with the other stablemen,"

Davis told him, pouring hot water into the basin on the washstand. "Quite snug they are up there, and they've taken their bread and meat in the servants' hall with the rest of us."

"Good." Ned nodded. Whatever mysteries there were in this house, he couldn't fault his host's hospitality in any way. It seemed rather ungrateful to dig deeper into Selby's private affairs. Nevertheless, where those affairs concerned Georgiana Carey he had every intention of doing exactly that.

Half an hour later, Davis helped Ned into his greatcoat and passed him gloves and hat. "It's coming down pretty badly out there, m'lord," he said. "Not fit for man or beast."

"I'm only going to the stables, Davis," Ned reminded him. "Hasn't anyone cleared a path?"

"All the time, sir. But it gets covered again as soon as 'tis cleared."

"I'll take my chance."

Jacobs was in the hall when Ned came down the stairs. "You're never going out there, sir?"

"Just to the stables," Ned said. "Which is the quickest way?"

"I'll show you," a soft voice chimed in, and Georgiana came out of the salon. "Could you bring my overboots and cloak, Jacobs?"

"They're barely dry from yesterday, my lady," the butler declared.

"But they *are* dry," Georgiana said with a smile. "I can't stay inside all day, Jacobs, and the stables aren't far from the house."

Jacobs shook his head, but he went off, muttering to

himself, and reappeared with a pair of sturdy overboots and a heavy hooded cloak. "Can't think why you can't stay inside in the warm like other godfearing folks," he stated, setting the boots on the floor by the bench beside the front door.

Georgiana laughed as she sat down and pulled on her boots. "You're sweet to fret, Jacobs, but believe me it's not necessary. A little snow won't kill me."

The butler went down on one knee to lace up the boots. "A gust of wind'll blow you away," he declared.

"Oh, Lord Allenton will hold on to me," she said breezily, huddling into the cloak that Jacobs held for her. "You won't let me get blown away, will you, my lord?"

Ned murmured something, acutely aware of the inappropriateness of this exchange in front of the butler, who, nevertheless, seemed not in the least shocked or surprised by it. Indeed, Jacobs was treating his master's ward as if he'd known her since she was knee high.

"Which is the quickest way?" he asked in the most neutral tone he could find.

"Through the kitchen. Follow me." She set off into the back regions of the house, through the kitchen, which was even busier than earlier, through a series of sculleries and pantries, and out into the kitchen yard.

The snow was so thick Ned felt almost as if he had to push it aside like a curtain as he plodded forward, keeping his head down. Georgiana, cloaked and hooded, was swift and sure-footed, leading the way along a narrow path through the banked snow on either side. The path was under only about four inches of snow, evidence of a recent clearing, but Ned still found it slow going. After a minute he called, "Slow down, Georgie. I can barely see my way."

"We've only about twenty yards to go," she called back, her voice muffled by the snow. She opened a gate and he followed her through, and suddenly up ahead loomed the shapes of buildings, light glowing in the upper stories. Ned heaved a sigh of relief. He was getting soft, he thought. Those years in sunny India had left him ill-prepared for his homeland in winter.

Georgiana wrestled with the bolt on the stable door, put her shoulder to it, and pushed with astonishing strength, Ned thought, for such a slight physique. But he had already come to the conclusion that Georgiana Carey was by no means the sum of the parts she showed to the world.

It was warm in the stables, braziers burning at either end. The horses were wrapped in blankets, their stalls sweet with fresh hay, and there were four stable hands in attendance. Ned found his own coachman and postillions playing cards in the tack room with a group of men, a jug of ale circulating.

"All well?" he asked.

"Aye, sir." The coachman jumped to his feet. "'Osses are doin' right good, m'lord. No ill effects from yesterday as I can see. They've 'ad a good bran mash and a rub-down. Don't know about the carriage though."

"That's of no matter," Ned said, drawing the man aside from his fellows with a hand on his elbow. "But I have to thank you for bringing my portmanteau along. It must have been hard work through the snow." Discreetly he slipped two golden guineas into the coachman's hand, which closed instantly over the coins.

"Thankee, m'lord." The man dropped his prize into the capacious pocket of his coat. "We'll be 'ere for a bit, then?"

"Until the snow's stopped and the roads are cleared," Ned agreed. "A few more days, I would think. I'm sorry you won't be spending Christmas with your family."

"Oh, that's no matter, sir," the man said easily. "We're all happy enough here. Not goin' short of anything."

Ned chuckled. "Yes, I can see that. Well, enjoy yourselves. We'll worry about the carriage when there's a point to it."

"Aye, sir." The coachman returned to his game and Ned left the tack room, wondering where Georgiana was.

He found her in a stall talking to a dappled gray mare. "What a pretty lady," he said, leaning his folded arms on the top of the half door. "Is she yours?"

"Yes. Her name's Athena." Georgiana leaned her head into the mare's neck as she looked up at Ned.

"Very warlike," he observed.

"She's a spirited lady," Georgiana replied with a smile, offering the mare a piece of apple. "All heart."

The mare nuzzled the apple from her palm and whickered softly. "Have you finished here?" Georgiana asked.

"Yes, but I'm happy to wait for you if you have something else to do."

"No," she returned. "No, nothing else. There *is* nothing else to do in this wretched weather." She stroked the mare's neck and blew softly into her nostrils in a farewell kiss before leaving the stall, bolting the door behind her.

"We should go back anyway. It's nearly time for breakfast." She moved toward the main door to the stable yard.

"Is it an obligatory meal?" Ned asked, following her.

"In a word . . . yes." She laid her hand on the latch.

Ned grimaced at her tone. He moved toward the door and then something caught his peripheral vision. The line of stalls stretched away down the block, and in one of the farthest ones he glimpsed a pony's head over the half door. The animal gazed at him with incurious long-lashed eyes. Ned gazed back, a frown in his eyes. Then he turned to follow Georgiana back into the snow.

He caught up with her as they left the stable yard. "How old are you, Georgie?"

She glanced sideways at him, a mischievous glint in her green eyes. Snow clustered thickly on her lashes and on the fringe of copper curls that had escaped the protection of her hood. "That's an impolite question to ask of a lady, my lord."

"Fustian," he scoffed. "Answer me."

"I'm twenty, if you must know. Although I don't know why you must." She plowed onward through the deepening snow on the narrow path.

"And I'm guessing that your marriage to Belton will take place before you attain your majority," he said, speaking over her shoulder because the path was not wide enough for two abreast.

Her answer was merely a shrug, but once again he felt her coiled tension. He said no more.

Ned presented himself in the breakfast room as the clock struck eleven and was mildly surprised to find all the guests from the previous evening already assembled, filling plates from the covered dishes on the sideboard and accepting glasses of champagne from Jacobs and his minions, who stood in attendance.

They had good heads and good digestions, Ned reflected, responding affably to the chorus of "Merry Christmas" from his fellow guests. He helped himself to kidneys and bacon. He declined champagne in favor of ale and sat down beside Godfrey Belton, who had a bumper of ale at his elbow and a plate piled high with kippers.

"Nothing like kippers to start the day," Godfrey observed, casting his neighbor's plate a sideways glance. "Not for you, I see, Allenton."

"No," agreed Ned. "Tell me, Belton, I've been out of the country so long I've forgotten almost everything . . . I don't recall your family. Where are you from?"

A dull flush bloomed on the man's cheek as he extracted a handful of bones from his mouth, laying them carefully against the side of his plate. "As it happens, my family is from Cumberland."

"Ah. That would explain it," Ned said amiably, spearing a kidney. "Local, and yet not." It didn't, of course. Cumberland and Northumberland were so close that if Belton's was a prominent family in the one county they would be known in the other. And he was certain he had never heard of the Beltons. Either they were not prominent county folk, or they came from somewhere else altogether.

Godfrey mumbled into his kippers.

"Lady Georgiana tells me you're building up at Great Ryle," Ned observed, lavishing mustard on his kidneys.

"Lady Georgiana should learn to keep my business to herself," Godfrey declared. "You know women, Allenton. Can't keep a still tongue." He tried for a hearty laugh of shared masculine exasperation with the opposite sex, but failed miserably.

Ned smiled. "Of course . . . of course," he agreed. "But if it's the home that's to be hers, maybe she didn't think it was a secret."

His companion was silenced and buried his head in his tankard, setting it down with a bang after a moment and calling for more. A servant hurried up with the ale jug and refilled the tankard. Across the table, Georgiana looked at her fiancé with a cool green gaze that said nothing.

Although Ned thought he could read it.

But there was a lot he could not read.

Roger Selby pushed back his chair with a screech on the polished boards. He stood up. "Ladies and gentlemen, I am Lord of Misrule, and I decree that this morning we shall play piquet for sixpence a point. After the first round of one game per pair, each winner plays another winner. At the end of the play the losers will receive forfeits decreed by the Lord of Misrule. The final winner, however, will choose the forfeit for his, the final, loser."

Applause greeted the decree and Ned resigned himself to a grim morning. The financial stakes were low at sixpence a point, but the prospect of Misrule's forfeits promised only horseplay, although perhaps less malicious in Selby's hands than in Belton's. He himself was a good card player, however. It was a required and much-valued skill in the social round among the members of the British raj in India, and he had little trouble dispatching his opponents.

He was surprised to see that only two hours had passed when he stood up, bowing to his defeated opponent. The game with the giggling Mrs. Eddington had been over quickly. He couldn't work out whether the lady was genuinely dim-witted, or just playing the part because she thought it attractive. She had handed over her fifty sixpences with much fan fluttering and exclamations of how stupid she was but how she couldn't possibly have hoped to defeat a player as skilled as the viscount.

Now he had one last game to play, and he glanced around the room to see who was still playing. There was only one couple left. Georgiana was facing her fiancé at a card table at the far side of the salon. Her expression was utterly neutral, her voice as she declared her cards without expression, her movement as she discarded and exchanged swift and purposeful. Her opponent was red-faced and clearly in a bad humor. He slammed his cards on the table, he cursed at his declarations, and he had frequent recourse to his wine glass.

Ned wandered casually over to them. He took up a position behind Georgiana, leaning casually against the wall, arms folded, watching the play. And as he watched, his astonishment grew. She was cheating. With the same sleight of hand she'd exhibited with the ballot papers the previous evening, she was sliding cards she didn't want onto her lap and replacing them with extricated cards from her sleeve. She certainly knew how to play the game; only someone really skilled at the play would actually succeed in cheating so cleverly. But why was she intent on making her betrothed so angry? Because that was certainly the consequence of her actions.

When Godfrey Belton failed to cross the Rubicon he shoved back his chair with such force it nearly fell over. He stood up. "Well, madam, you think you're very clever, I'm sure," he declared. "You had the luck of the cards, that was all."

"I'm sure I did, Godfrey," she said with a demure smile, gathering up the cards. "Will you pay me now or later?"

There was a nasty moment when Ned thought Belton

would explode with fury, but Lord Selby came over, rubbing his hands cheerfully. "All in good spirits, Belton, all in good humor," he declared. "Give the girl her due, now, there's a good fellow. She and Allenton are the only ones left standing, and judging by his play so far, she'll have her work cut out for her."

The comment didn't seem to appease Godfrey Belton, but Selby's intervention had brought him to his senses. He dug into his pocket and hurled a handful of change onto the card table, muttered something inaudible and walked off.

Georgiana appeared untroubled. She gathered up the coins and dropped them into her reticule, where they clinked satisfactorily against those already there. "Poor Godfrey," she said. "He does so hate to lose." She turned her bright eyes onto Ned. "And we shall see whether you also hate it, Lord Allenton." She gestured to the chair vacated by Belton. "Do you care to take your seat?" Her hands moved swiftly over the cards, gathering them together, shuffling, rearranging.

Ned was unsure whether he was more disturbed or amused and intrigued by what he'd seen, but he took his seat with a slight nod of acceptance. He gestured that she should make the first cut. She showed him the jack of clubs. He cut and drew the ten of diamonds.

"Will you deal?" he asked, knowing that like any experienced player she would take the option. It would give her an initial disadvantage but avoid the bigger one of having to make the final deal of the partie.

"I'll deal," she confirmed and swiftly dealt the twelve-card hands.

Ned glanced around and saw that Selby had left and

they had no audience for the moment. "I would be grateful if you would deal only the cards in this pack," he said quietly. "I don't like the ones you have in your sleeve."

He had the satisfaction of seeing her color rise. She looked up, her lower lip caught between her teeth. "Damn," she said. "You saw?"

He nodded. "Why? Did you want to make him angry?"

"No, but it couldn't be helped. I wanted his money," she said simply.

"Would you mind not taking mine in that way?" he asked with a pleasant smile.

"There's little point if you're looking out for it," she said.

"Why do you want his money?" Ned asked, examining his hand.

Georgiana said nothing immediately. She examined her cards, wondering why she had this urge to confide in this stranger. He was nothing to her. And yet there was something about him that filled her with a sense of possibility. A sense she hadn't had since she'd arrived in this palatial hell eighteen months ago. All prospect of a future she could make for herself had vanished the minute she'd understood what her guardian intended.

She was facing a life of no expectations, a life of fear under the thumb of Godfrey Belton, a life where sometimes it seemed that death would be preferable. But Georgiana Carey was not inclined to accept a future forced upon her. And she was fighting this one with everything she had. Her brain told her that she *must* not confide her secret to anyone, but something other than her brain was telling her that as far as this stranger was concerned, she should.

"Money's always useful," she said. "My guardian guards my fortune with exceptional zeal."

Ned looked at her quickly. Her face was drawn and angry although she didn't raise her eyes from her hand of cards. "I see. Or at least I think I do," he said. "It's not an unusual situation though."

She looked up at him then, her eyes bright with anger and what he would have sworn was a sheen of unshed tears. "Did I say it was?"

"No," he agreed. "You didn't. Shall we play?" He knew absolutely that if she shed as much as one tear it would be disastrous for her. He held up his cards, showing them to her quickly. "*Carte blanche.*"

She grimaced. The declaration gave him an advantage, one she couldn't match. They played intently for an hour. Ned was fairly certain she wasn't cheating but sometimes he wasn't so sure. He was half inclined to let her win, and if he hadn't had his doubts about the validity of some of her declarations, he probably would have done so, but the competitive edge that had made his fortune for him in India was too close to the surface. She was a good player, but he was a better one.

He made the final deal, which should have put him at a disadvantage, and Georgiana realized properly for the first time the viscount's skill as a gamester. He never made a mistake, making his plays with precise judgment that she couldn't help but admire despite her growing annoyance at her own shortcomings. She muttered something most unladylike under her breath as she discarded a card and realized instantly that it was a guard she should have kept. For a moment she wondered if she was facing the humiliation of failing to make a hundred points in the partie, and thus failing to cross the Rubicon, but when the game was over, and the points counted, she had at least managed to avert that fate. But there was no question who had the winner's laurels.

Georgiana gathered up the cards. "Congratulations, my lord, you are a superb player."

He regarded her with a half smile. "But you, of course, were handicapped."

"I don't always cheat," she said softly, flushing. "Only when it's necessary. I wasn't prepared to lose to Godfrey."

"It might have been politic," he responded with a frown. "He has a nasty temper." He bowed. "Thank you for the game, ma'am."

"Allenton, it's for you to choose Georgiana's forfeit," Selby announced. "What's it to be?"

Georgiana looked toward Allenton. The viscount was standing before the fire, regarding her with an air of amusement, head slightly tilted as he considered the question. The object of the forfeits was to entertain their fellow guests. Selby had been choosing the silliest activities for the previous losers, balancing full glasses on their heads, or walking blindfolded around the room. Fairly innocuous party games. Godfrey would have demanded much more vicious penalties.

"Maybe the lady would give us a card trick?" he suggested. "I'm sure she has plenty up her sleeve."

Georgiana bit her lip. He was teasing her and she was unsure whether to laugh or throw something at him. "I don't know any card tricks," she objected.

"Oh, come now, I'm certain that you do," he said. "Maybe a trick with that glass bowl over there." He gestured to the bowl she had used the previous evening to collect the votes for Lord of Misrule.

The damnable man had seen that too. Georgiana stared at him. His teasing was sailing close to the wind, and yet she was sure he would not betray her.

Ned laughed. "Never mind, I withdraw the forfeit. You are excused, Lady Georgiana." He bowed again.

There were cries of "Shame," but Jacobs's arrival to announce luncheon swiftly silenced them and the party surged toward the dining room, leaving only Ned and Georgiana in the salon.

"I suppose I should thank you," she said.

"Oh, don't thank me too soon," he said carelessly. "I'm probably going to ask for something in exchange."

Now what the devil did he mean by that? Georgiana followed him as he strode from the room, but instead of following the crowd to the dining room she turned aside and went upstairs to her own chamber. Viscount Allenton was having a strangely unsettling effect on her and she needed time to compose herself.

Chapter Five

The party dispersed after a luncheon heavy on wine, venison pasties and plum puddings, and Ned made his way to the library intent on finding a book to while away the tedium of the long afternoon ahead. Georgiana had not appeared at the table, but this seemed to draw no remark either from her guardian or her fiancé, so he guessed they were accustomed to her absences from this meal. He hadn't faced luncheon with much enthusiasm either, it coming so soon after the lavish breakfast, and he'd eaten sparingly, conscious of the vast Christmas dinner to come. He was used to the laden tables of British society in India, where overindulgence was the norm. But at least some physical activity preceded and generally followed the mountains of food and oceans of drink that were consumed under the soft wafting breezes from the punkah fans.

He sighed, wishing he were back in his office in Madras, managing the brokerage, juggling figures, organizing his empire. It would run smoothly enough without him—he had trained his subordinates well—but his brain itched for some exercise almost as desperately as his body.

He entered the library and paused. "I trust I'm not interrupting."

"Not at all, dear fellow, not at all." Roger Selby, pipe in hand, waved a welcoming arm from a deep chair beside the fire. "Come in, have a glass of port, excellent for the digestion." He raised the cut-glass decanter at his elbow and filled a second glass. "Take a pew, dear boy."

"Thank you." Ned took the glass and sat down in the chair on the other side of the fireplace. He sipped and looked for some innocuous topic of conversation but his host had his own chosen topic.

"Fortuitous your fetching up on my doorstep, actually, Allenton," Selby said, puffing meditatively on his pipe. "There's a rather awkward matter of business we need to settle . . . much easier to discuss with a glass in hand beside the fire. We can have a nice friendly discussion."

Ned felt his hackles rise but he wasn't quite sure why. But he *was* sure that Selby had something unpleasant up his sleeve. "Please continue," he said neutrally, taking another sip of his wine.

"Well, fact of the matter is, Allenton, your brother owed me money. And I was wondering when you would see your way to repaying it."

"Ah." Ned felt himself relax. When it came to money he was quite at his ease. "Perhaps you should explain the circumstances. I wasn't aware that you and my brother were on such terms."

"Oh, it was a business transaction, sir—a nice piece of land I sold him—but there was some unpleasantness. Shame your brother wasn't the man he was when you last saw him." He shook his head sorrowfully. "Very short memory he had. He disputed the transaction, although I had the bill of sale. Said the land wasn't worth the money, but we had an agreement, signed and sealed."

My cousin is not an honest broker. Ned was now convinced that Georgiana had never spoken a truer word. "Where is this piece of land?" he inquired, his expression calm and pleasant.

"Just up by Cochrane Pike." Selby puffed on his pipe, sending up a curl of smoke.

"That's not farming land, up there in the hills."

"Good grazing for sheep," Selby said. He was watching Ned closely, eyes hooded.

"We don't have sheep at Allenton—never have had," Ned said, wondering if Rob had decided to branch out for some scatterbrained reason. He had always been full of impulses and bright ideas that frittered away money and never achieved anything.

"Your brother was right keen on the idea when we talked of it, said he'd like some grazing land. I told him I had some and we sealed the bargain there and then."

Selby refilled his glass from the decanter, gestured toward his guest, then saw that Ned had barely touched his. He tapped his pipe against the hearth. "Your brother reneged on the agreement. He told me he'd changed his mind when he saw the land. But a deal's a deal in these parts, although perhaps you've forgotten our ways," he added with a sly smile.

"Do you have the bill of sale?" Ned inquired, keeping his tone pleasant.

"Aye, that I do." Selby pushed himself out of his chair

and went to the desk. "As it happens I was just looking at it a few minutes ago."

He brought the document to Ned, who took it with a nod of thanks.

Ned ran his eye over the single page. It was not a legal document, looked rather as if it had been drawn up in a tavern. Robert's signature was shaky, the lines wavering over the page. He looked up. "Was my brother drunk when he signed this?"

"What difference does that make?" Selby's tone took on just the slightest edge of belligerence. "He signed it, and promised to pay two thousand guineas. And I'm asking you, my lord, when you intend to make good on your brother's debt? You'll find yourself unpopular in these parts if you don't honor the obligation. But I daresay you've been gone so long you've forgotten how we do things." Again that sly comment, and the sudden narrowing of the eyes.

"As it happens," Ned said, "I haven't forgotten anything, Selby. Are you telling me my brother bought this land off you sight unseen? With no provision for renegotiation once he'd seen it?" Not even Rob would have been that foolish.

"Are you doubting my word, sir?" Selby sat up higher in his chair.

Indeed I am. But Ned only said calmly, "Not in the least. But before I assume the debt I claim the right to look at the land myself. I'd like to see what I'm buying . . . and also I'd like to take this document to my own lawyer for verification."

He folded the sheet and slipped it into his inside pocket. "Once those formalities are completed I shall be delighted to settle the debt." He smiled as he rose to his feet. "I thank you for the port. And for the timely reminder about how business matters are conducted in these parts." He offered a nodding bow and walked out without giving his host the opportunity for objection.

No wonder Selby had been so hospitable. He'd seen in his neighbor's unexpected arrival the opportunity to pursue a matter that he had presumably given up on when Rob died. He'd clearly thought that the obligations of a guest would put Ned at a disadvantage, and that his long absence in the Indian heat had dulled his native wit. Once a reiver always a reiver, Ned reflected. Even though the plundering was conducted in a rather less violent fashion than in the past, the end result was the same. Ill-gotten gains one way or another.

He went upstairs, deciding he had no desire for the company of his fellow guests. They were an uncouth group, and not for the first time he wondered where Selby had recruited them. For the second time he'd failed in his primary purpose in visiting the library, but a stroll around the house would probably be better for him than a book by the fire, and he remembered Belton had said something the previous evening about a Long Gallery. It might be worth a visit.

He sauntered down a corridor running to the right of the galleried landing and came upon the gallery behind open double doors at the end. Long windows along one wall overlooked the parkland, the remaining walls bore ancestral portraits of the usual kind. A few sofas were scattered around on the parquet floor.

Ned took a step into the room and then stopped, moving back into the doorway again.

"I tell you, woman, you'll learn to keep a still tongue in your head . . . what business did you have telling that arrogant son of a bitch about Great Ryle?" Godfrey Belton's voice rose on each syllable.

"It's no secret, Godfrey," Georgiana protested.

Ned stepped back into the room. The voices were coming from a curtained embrasure at the far end of the room. The curtains were open and he could see Georgiana's back, which was turned to him as she faced Belton. He trod softly towards them, keeping himself against the windows so that he was out of their line of sight.

"It's *my* business. And I won't have you blabbing my business to anyone. You're too friendly by half with Allenton, I've seen the way you make eyes at him, don't think that I haven't. And by God, girl, you'll learn that I don't tolerate my woman looking at anyone else."

His voice was a furious bellow and Ned heard Georgiana's swift intake of breath and a bitten-back cry. He moved quickly toward them as she said, "Let go of me, Godfrey. You're hurting my arm."

"Oh, I'll do more than that," her betrothed declared, "if I ever catch you looking at another man—" Whatever else he'd been about to say or do was lost in a howl of pain.

Ned, no longer interested in trying to hide his approach, had a full view of the scene. Georgiana moved with the speed and decision of a striking cobra. Her knee went up into Godfrey's groin and her right hand chopped into the back of his neck as he bent over in agony, gasping and spluttering.

"Don't you *ever* hurt me again, Godfrey," she stated. "Because you'd better believe that I will hurt you more."

She turned in disgust from the collapsed and groaning figure of her fiancé and saw Ned, standing several feet away, out of Godfrey's line of sight.

Ned moved swiftly back to the door and Georgiana followed him.

"What are *you* doing here?" The question was abrupt and angry, the residue of the last few minutes still showing on her face and in her eyes.

"I happened to be passing, and overheard your argument. I thought you might need some assistance. But I see I was wrong."

He stood looking at her, wondering how on earth he could have missed it. No more *déjà vu*. Georgiana Carey was the thief and the pickpocket ambushing unwary travelers in the snow. There was no mistaking the way she moved, no mistaking the similarity in build, no mistaking the businesslike ferocity with which she'd handled her problems. He had felt again the blow to his own neck that had felled him in the snow when he watched her deal the same to Godfrey Belton. No wonder he'd thought there was something familiar about the pony in the stable.

She stood for a moment, her eyes now uncertain, her hands steepled at her mouth, thumbs hinged beneath her chin. "What is it? Why are you looking at me like that?"

He smiled easily. "No reason, except admiration at your ability to look after yourself." He looked beyond her at the still-gurgling Godfrey. "What do you want to do about him now?"

"Leave him," she said coldly.

"Won't he want his revenge?"

"Maybe."

"You could enlist your guardian's support," he suggested. "He surely wouldn't countenance that kind of brutality."

"My guardian is at home in rough company," she said as coldly as before. "Surely you can tell that from the guests he invites. What you may consider brutality he would consider perfectly acceptable."

Georgiana could feel the bruises on her arms beginning to throb and she stood absently rubbing them as she contemplated the consequences of what had just occurred. Godfrey would certainly want his revenge. And she probably should not be here to receive it. But where else could she go in this blizzard?

Ned saw her increased pallor, and the vulnerability growing in her eyes as she stared at something only she could see. "Come," he said. "You need your own chamber. Tell your maid you're unwell and you intend to pass the evening upstairs." He took her hand and drew her away. "Lock the door if you'll feel safer."

"I'm not frightened of that jackass," she denied fiercely, but allowed Ned to lead her away. And then she stopped and looked at him. "Of course, I only had the advantage while he didn't know what I was capable of. Now he knows, and he's a great deal stronger than I am."

"Not as fast though," Ned pointed out, urging her on with a hand in the small of her back. "And by no means as quick-witted. Which way are we going?"

"Left-hand passage, but there's no need for you to come any farther." She moved away from his hand, suddenly afraid that she would start to rely on the strong warmth it was imparting. The temptation was great, as great as was the urge to confide in him. But Georgiana knew she was on her own. She had only herself to rely upon.

"I'm taking you to your door," Ned said. "I actually owe you some thanks, Georgie."

"Oh?" As he'd hoped, the observation distracted her and she looked sideways at him as he eased her down the corridor, his hand still firmly planted in the small of her back. "What for?"

"Warning me about your guardian. Selby is most definitely not an honest broker."

"What did he want?" She lifted the latch on her door, pushed it open, and then gave in to temptation. She didn't want him to leave her and to the devil with the consequences. "Come in and tell me."

He followed her into a spacious and comfortable apartment. The fire blazed, and the lamps were lit. "Well, it seems Selby trapped my never-very-alert brother into some kind of ridiculous property deal, but Rob died while it was still in dispute. Selby seems to think I can be persuaded to settle the debt myself."

Ned shook his head with amusement as he kicked a fallen log back into the fire. "He seems to think I was born yesterday."

"Oh, he'll try anything for a few guineas," Georgiana said, settling into the corner of the daybed, kicking off her slippers. "He's so grasping he can easily mistake his mark." She leaned back, resting her head against a cushion, looking up at him as he stood by the fire, an arrested look in her sharpened gaze.

Ned found himself transfixed by the green gaze. He looked at her, his eyes locked with hers, and he was suddenly overwhelmed by the feeling that this moment, in this room, with this woman, had been lying in wait for him all his life. There was a sense of the absolute rightness of it, of being here with her. Without conscious volition he moved away from the fire, came over to her, leaned down, bracing a hand on the back of the sofa and kissed her mouth.

She didn't move, she didn't resist, but she didn't return the kiss, either. When he straightened slowly, still looking down at her, he saw that her eyes were now full of questions. She touched her mouth with her fingertips, then nodded as if in confirmation.

"What is it?" he asked softly.

She smiled and said, "I always wondered what a proper kiss would be like. I was beginning to think I would never find out. Thank you for showing me."

Somehow that was not the reaction Ned had hoped for. He'd kissed her, not given her a bunch of flowers. He contented himself with a somewhat ironic bow, a murmured "At your service, ma'am," and left her, closing the door firmly behind him. He heard the key turn in the lock almost immediately.

He stood outside her door for a moment, frowning in thought. It was inconceivable to him that she hadn't felt the connection that he had felt. It had been so powerful, an almost palpable magnet drawing him across the room to her, it was not possible that he alone had felt it. Maybe he was being foolish, the strictly pragmatic man of business giving way to a flush of romanticism, but it didn't feel like that.

And the one thing he knew without a shadow of doubt was that he could not in good conscience marry Sarah Hartley. He had accepted the idea of a suitable and convenient marriage between old friends. But he had had no feelings for another woman then. Now—now he wanted

Georgiana Carey, and all the old clichés seemed fresh and bright.

He had lost his heart; fallen head over heels in love; met the love of his life; couldn't live without her.

He laughed to himself in mingled self-mockery and wonder at the whole extraordinary business. He *would* have her. But before he could do that, he had to untangle the mesh that snared her. *Or was she doing that for herself?*

Well, he would find the answer to that a little later. He strode away down the corridor and headed for the Long Gallery again.

Godfrey Belton was standing in the doorway to the gallery as Ned approached. Or rather, he was not so much standing as leaning against the doorjamb breathing rather heavily. His normally high color was rather gray and his skin looked clammy.

He glared at Ned as he approached. "What are you doing here, Allenton?"

Ned gave him a look of innocent inquiry. "I was intending to walk through the gallery," he responded. "A little gentle exercise seemed in order after lunch." He raised an eyebrow. "Is something the matter, Belton? You don't look too well."

Belton grunted. "I'm perfectly well." He pushed himself upright and leaned forward suddenly, one finger jabbing at Ned's chest. "Just keep your eyes off Georgiana, Allenton. She's mine, and she'll learn that soon enough. If you want to do her any favors, then you'll keep well away from her. Understand?"

Ned, with an air of fastidious distaste, caught the jabbing finger and returned it to its owner. "What an uncivilized brute you are, Belton," he said amiably. "I'll thank you to keep your fingers to yourself." Then he stepped around the man and into the gallery.

Godfrey turned to watch him. "You'll regret that, Allenton," he declared. "You don't know your way around these parts anymore, and if you think the Allenton name means anything now, you're in for a rude shock. Your kind have no power now. In a few months Selby and I will own everything from the coast to the Pennines, and we'll drive the Allentons and everyone of your ilk out."

Ned made no response, merely stood looking out of one of the long windows, waiting for Godfrey to leave. And finally he did, limping a little as he walked away.

And what exactly had he meant by that? Everything from the coast to the Pennines?

With his fingertip Ned traced a design in the condensation on the window. He was beginning to see a pattern form.

Georgiana sat by the fire after Ned had left, stretching her shoeless feet to the warmth, wriggling her toes. She hadn't meant to sound so dismissive, but she had spoken out of the surprised recognition that something amazing had happened to her. And foolishly she had expected Ned to understand that. How could he not understand it when it was clear that the same thing had happened to him?

It had come upon her so quickly, that recognition. She had been looking at him, talking naturally enough about Selby, and then she had felt the most powerful need. The need to touch him, to be touched by him, to lean into him, to yield to his strength. How she longed for someone to share her terrors, to make them insignificant. But most of all, she wanted to be loved as much as she wanted to love. Her life was such a desert, a bleak and loveless landscape where the only people around her were intent on getting something from her, on using her. And for the first time, someone had walked into that landscape and filled it with light and warmth, and infinite possibility.

Georgiana hugged herself—an involuntary movement that, while it was no substitute for Ned Vasey's arms, gave her an inkling of what those arms would feel like. She basked again in the glow from those gold-brown eyes, and again her lips felt the pliant warmth of his mouth on hers.

She had disappointed him with her seemingly prosaic response to his kiss, but she hadn't been able to help it. It was all so new and fresh and so full of promise that she hadn't been able to find the right words. But he would come back, she was sure of it, and when he did, she would make certain he was not disappointed again.

Her arms fell into her lap as cold reality reasserted itself. If she was to make a future out of this promise, it was imperative she make her escape before Godfrey could get his hands on her again. She cursed her own foolishness for dropping her carefully preserved pretense of compliance. She had known she had to maintain the play until she could safely make her escape. Instead, in a fit of lunacy, she had shown her true colors at a time when she could not possibly get herself to safety.

And Godfrey would tell Selby what had happened. Or would he? It was always possible he would be too embarrassed to tell anyone of his defeat at the hands of a mere woman. But whether he did or not, the die was now cast.

Chapter Six

Ned dressed slowly and with some reluctance for dinner that night. Christmas night or not, he had no desire to spend another evening under the quixotic sovereignty of the Lord of Misrule, and he suspected that Roger Selby would be less than amiable after their meeting that afternoon. It had certainly not come to Selby's desired conclusion. And then there was Godfrey Belton, of whom Ned had also made an enemy. And he'd find no friends among the other guests. There was no real civility there, and if their host turned against one of the guests, he suspected, they too would turn like an obedient pack of hounds on their master's quarry.

And what of Georgiana? Would she show herself or stay behind a locked door? He rather hoped she would do the latter—it would be one less thing for him to worry about—but he was by no means sanguine that she would choose discretion over valor. Not from what he'd seen of her thus far.

Just what was she doing playing highwayman in the Cheviot foothills? He intended to find out before the night was done. Apart from anything else, he wanted to reclaim his stolen property. He didn't begrudge her the guineas, but his fob watch had belonged to his grandfather, a man with whom he had had much more in common than his own father. It was a valuable piece, but it was worth much more than face value to Ned. She'd had no opportunity to sell or pawn it in the last two days, so he would claim it later, and at the same time get an explanation from Lady Georgiana Carey.

"There, sir. Very smart, my lord." Davis smoothed the coat over Ned's shoulders, patting the soft gray wool with satisfaction. "Is there anything else I can do for you now?"

"No, thank you, Davis," Ned said. "Go and get your supper. And there's no need to wait up for me. I may sit late."

Davis bowed. "Very well, sir. If you're sure, m'lord."

"Quite sure. It is Christmas night, after all. Enjoy your evening." Ned smiled and waved a hand toward the door in dismissal. He waited until Davis had departed, the door firmly closed, and then he fetched his portmanteau from the armoire. Davis had emptied it of everything he could see, but he didn't know of the hidden compartment. Ned lifted the lining at the bottom of the bag and then the stiffened leather base. Beneath he kept a pistol and a lockbox. It was the pistol that interested him tonight. It was small, ivory handled, and in Lord Allenton's hands quite deadly.

He took it out, cleaned and primed it, and tucked it into an inner pocket of his coat, where it lay snugly beneath his arm. Ned checked his image in the glass and nodded his satisfaction. There was not a bulge visible in the beautifully cut garment. Why he thought he might need a pistol tonight was something of a mystery. It was unusual, to say the least, to go armed to a host's dinner table, but better safe than sorry. He'd learned that lesson many times over. No man with half a brain moved around India without his own arms and, more often than not, an armed retinue. Threats came from both the human animal and any number of others.

He felt much more comfortable with the familiar weight under his arm. Although if he had to shoot his way out of the house into the blizzard, he'd be jumping from the frying pan into the fire, he reflected wryly as he went downstairs to the salon.

The guests were all assembled, drinking deep, a group of men throwing dice at a baize-covered table in the window. The atmosphere was more like a tavern or a brothel than a gentleman's salon before dinner, Ned thought, taking a glass of wine from a circulating footman's tray. There was no sign of Georgiana.

He strolled across the room to where Selby stood in conversation with Belton. "Gentlemen, good evening." Ned bowed.

Godfrey walked away but Selby offered a curt nod in response. "I'd like that bill of sale back, Allenton. It's my proof."

"Of course." Ned's smile was soothing. "As soon as I've had my own lawyer look it over, and discussed the matter with my agent, I shall, of course, return it to you."

"We honor our word in these parts, Allenton," Selby stated. "As I've already said, you'll find yourself persona non grata if you don't."

Ned inclined his head in acknowledgment. "I'm sure

that's so, Selby. But if you recall, it was not my word that was pledged." He sipped his wine, watching his host's reaction.

Selby drained his glass in one deep draft and called to the footman to bring him another. "On your own head be it, then, Allenton," he said, and turned his shoulder, ignoring Ned.

Ned shrugged and walked away. He was aware of a slight buzz in the room, of curious glances, low-voiced conversations that died as he approached. Then the door opened and Georgiana walked in.

She was wearing an emerald green gown, caught beneath the bosom with a bronze silk belt. The long sleeves were tight and buttoned at the wrists with tiny emerald studs. Her red hair was caught up on her neck with a bronze velvet ribbon, and two emerald studs gleamed in her ears. Her eyes were filled with fire as she stood in the doorway and looked around the room.

She looked magnificent, Ned thought, his breath catching in his throat. Magnificent and defiant, determined to outface her guardian, her fiancé and the whole drunken tribe of guests.

Georgiana met his eye and smiled slightly. She felt strong, astoundingly relieved now that she'd decided once and for all to drop the pretense. She had nothing to lose now.

"My dear ward, I'm so glad you decided to join us," Selby said, coming toward her. "After your little difficulty this afternoon, I felt sure you would keep to your room."

What exactly had Godfrey told Selby of what had transpired in the Long Gallery? Not the truth, surely. It would be too mortifying for him. Georgiana's smile would have frozen a basilisk. She sketched a curtsy. "I recall no difficulty, my lord. You must be mistaken."

Selby regarded her with narrowed eyes. "I doubt that, my dear. I very much doubt that."

"Excuse me, sir." She moved away from him, crossing the room to where Ned stood, pausing to greet other guests as she made her way to him. She felt rather than saw Godfrey take a step toward her and she forced herself to keep smiling, to continue smiling, nodding, every step drawing her closer to Ned. Surely if she ignored Godfrey he wouldn't force a confrontation here, in front of everyone.

But she was by no means sure of that, and she felt a surge of relief when she reached Ned.

"Good evening, Lady Georgiana." Ned bowed. "May I procure you a glass of wine?" He beckoned to the footman.

Georgiana took a glass from the tray, glancing covertly toward Godfrey, who was staring malevolently at her from a few feet away.

"Don't worry," Ned murmured. "If he makes trouble I have my pistol."

She looked at him, startled. "You *haven't*!"

"Certainly I have," he responded with a bland smile. "I'm a regular knight errant. Always ready to defend a damsel in distress."

Her eyes danced with amusement for a second, and then became grave again. She started to say something but Godfrey interrupted her.

"I take it ill in you, madam, that you ignore your fiancé," he said with distinct menace. "Your duty is to me, and no one else." He turned to Ned, his eyes small and bloodshot and full of hate. "You have no business here. Leave us, sir."

Ned hesitated. But he didn't want to make matters worse at present and nothing would be gained by open warfare. He smiled reassuringly at Georgiana. "Give me leave to leave you for the moment, ma'am." He walked a little way away from them, then took up a position by the fire, resting one arm along the mantel, a foot on the fender, openly watching Georgie and Belton as he sipped his wine.

Georgiana smiled, her confidence once more intact. She could deal with Godfrey with Ned at her back. "What did you wish to talk to me about, Godfrey?" she asked, sipping her wine.

"Talk to you?" he queried. "Why would I want to talk to you about anything? I just won't have you talking to Allenton. I told you that already. And I won't be defied."

"You grow tedious, Godfrey," she said, turning away from him. He grabbed her arm and she stopped, looking over her shoulder at him. "Let go. You don't want a repetition of this afternoon in front of everyone." It was reckless and stupid to provoke him so, but after the many months of enduring his bullying, of smiling and nodding and offering only compliant obedience, it was a wonderfully heady feeling. Tonight she would dare anything. And she knew why.

It didn't stop her taking an involuntary step back as she saw Godfrey's face. He looked capable of anything, his reddened eyes murderous in his flushed face. A purple vein pulsed in his temple and his hand on her arm tightened on the bruises he had already made that afternoon, so that she felt tears of pain spring to her eyes.

"You will be sorry for that, Georgiana," he promised, spittle gathering on his fleshy lips. "Later. I shall make sure of it." Then he released her arm, almost throwing it from him, before weaving away toward the dice players.

A cold shudder crept up her spine. She took a step toward Ned but he shook his head, an almost imperceptible movement that nevertheless stopped her in her tracks. Of course, nothing would be gained by further provocation tonight. She turned away from him and went over to a sofa where two women sat chattering.

"Good evening, Mrs. Eddington, Mrs. Maryfield." She sat down in a chair beside the sofa. "I trust you spent a pleasant day."

"Indeed, Lady Georgiana, most pleasant," Mrs. Eddington declared with a conspiratorial wink at Mrs. Maryfield. "Indoor pursuits can certainly compensate for the lack of the outdoor variety." She winked with vulgar significance.

"Oh, come now, dear Mrs. Eddington," Mrs. Maryfield said from behind her fan. "For shame, ma'am. Lady Georgiana's sensibilities are too delicate for such talk."

Her companion merely laughed. "Only for a few more months, my dear friend. Once she's wedded and bedded, she'll be fit to join the company, you mark my words."

"Oh, yes." Mrs. Maryfield nodded with a significant glance toward Godfrey Belton. "Such a man he is. You are to be congratulated, my dear Georgiana, on such a good catch. He'll make you a fine husband. And that house he's building for you . . . everyone says it will be one of the finest in the county."

"I wouldn't know, ma'am," Georgiana said, hiding her distaste. "I haven't been consulted."

"And how should you be, my dear?" Mrs. Eddington exclaimed. " 'Tis hardly a woman's place to have an opinion on such matters. Leave it to your husband, child. He will know best."

"I'm sure," Georgiana said, tapping the ivory sticks of her closed fan against her knee. "Godfrey must always know best."

Dinner was announced and the party trooped across the hall to the dining room, where servants stood lined up along the walls. The dinner guests stood behind their chairs at the long table and the strains of "The Boar's Head Carol" sounded from the hall. All eyes turned to the door. The cook entered bearing a massive golden salver with the glistening boar's head surrounded by bay leaves and rosemary, an apple in its mouth. He was followed by servants bearing other dishes, garlanded with holly and juniper, their voices raised tunefully or otherwise in the traditional medieval carol.

The guests joined in the final refrain as the magnificent offering was placed upon the table among the brightly burning candles, and Lord Selby took up the carving knife and fork. He looked down the table and smiled.

"Georgiana, my dear, you shall be awarded the apple," he declared amid a small burst of applause. "It should satisfy your somewhat timid appetite." He forked the apple from the boar's mouth and placed it on a plate presented by the cook. The plate was placed in front of Georgiana, who smiled faintly at the jest.

The guests took their seats while the boar's head and a suckling pig were carved and distributed. The smell of meat was rich and heavy in the overheated room, the candles too numerous and too bright for comfort. Georgiana glanced across the table at Ned, who was not looking as if he was enjoying himself at all. He looked up, as if aware of her glance, and very slightly lowered one eyelid. Instantly she felt stronger.

Ned kept to himself as far as it was possible throughout the eternal evening. The Lord of Misrule declared a game of blindman's buff after dinner, with a kiss instead of the customary buff on the shoulder to be given by the blindfolded person when he or she caught one of the players, who would then be blindfolded in turn. The game quickly degenerated into a drunken free for all, furniture knocked to the floor, glasses smashed, kisses becoming lusty embraces.

Georgiana hung on the sidelines of the game, dodging the blindfolded pursuer gracefully as if she was playing in earnest, but making absolutely certain that she was never close enough to be caught. She noticed that Ned was doing much the same. Obviously he was as aware as she was of the potential for malicious mayhem if they found themselves the blindfolded, blundering victims of this dangerously rowdy group.

Godfrey was the blindman as the clock struck midnight. Selby tied the scarf around his eyes amid much merriment, turned him around three times, and then stepped back, raising his glass to his lips, watching with hooded eyes.

Godfrey moved with amazing stealth for such a large man so full of drink, pausing to listen frequently, turning his head this way and that as if to smell someone close by. Georgiana had retreated to the far corner of the salon. Ned was by the door, watching closely. Godfrey turned suddenly toward Georgiana. He began to move through the furniture and Ned inhaled sharply. There was a purposefulness to the man's movements, to his direction, and Ned guessed that he could see. Selby had tied the blindfold leaving enough space for Godfrey to see beneath.

Had they arranged it beforehand between themselves? Georgiana was to be punished for her defiance. Ned held himself still with the greatest difficulty as he saw Georgiana's eyes widen with sudden acknowledgment as she realized that Godfrey was making straight for her. She moved sideways. He followed her. The room was a roaring cacophony of laughter and cheers. It seemed as if everyone was in on the joke except Georgiana and Ned.

Georgiana moved behind a chair and someone jerked it aside just as Godfrey lunged forward. He caught her, trapping her in the corner, tearing off his blindfold as the room exploded in a crescendo of applause. He caught her face between both hands, pressing his mouth to hers.

Georgiana struggled for air, suffocated by the hot vinous reek of his breath, the wet fleshiness of his lips that seemed to be devouring her mouth, the weight of his body pressing her own slight frame against the wall behind her. And her ears were filled with the hateful, cheering applause of the audience.

Ned slipped his hand inside his jacket, his fingers closing over the ivory handle of the pistol. Every instinct told him to hold his nerve. If he fired, even just into the air, it would tip the entire situation over the edge into full-fledged disaster. He'd seen riots, and he knew what could happen, even to such a small group, in the right conditions. And these conditions were ripe for mayhem. They were all drunk; the edge of violence was sharp and would be easily incited by a leader. And Selby or Belton was more than ready to push the boulder over.

But he could barely endure to see Belton slobbering and pawing Georgie, and slowly he began to slide the pistol from his pocket.

And then suddenly it was over. Belton stepped back, breathing hard, a hand on his side. Georgiana slipped out of the corner into the freedom of the center of the room. She appeared composed, but her face was ashen, her eyes glittering.

"If you'll excuse me, Lord Selby, I find myself fatigued," she said, in a voice as steady as the Rock of Gibraltar. "I shall seek my bed. Good night, Godfrey. Ladies and gentlemen." She offered a nod in lieu of a more formal curtsy and turned to the door.

Ned opened it for her, and she threw him a glance as she passed him. He closed the door behind her, wondering what she had done to Godfrey to cause him to sink into a chair, one hand still pressed to his side, his other carrying a glass of wine to his lips. Whatever it was, it had been inconspicuous to all but the victim. He wasn't at all sure Georgie needed any help from him at all.

The atmosphere in the room was deflated, the guests milling aimlessly. Selby declared a game of charades, but there seemed little enthusiasm and the group began to break up, guests drifting toward the stairs to collect their carrying candles. Some stumbled, some weaved uncertainly, clinging to the banister on their way upstairs.

Ned was about to follow the procession upstairs when Selby spoke at his back. "A word with you, Allenton."

Ned turned slowly and found himself facing Selby and Belton, standing shoulder to shoulder. "Certainly," he said with a pleasant smile. "What can I do for you, gentlemen?"

"Not here," Selby said. "In there." He jerked his head back toward the salon.

Ned weighed his options. He didn't trust either of them, but he did have his pistol. And he had a certain curiosity about what they wanted of him—apart, of course, from two thousand guineas for a useless piece of land.

He shrugged. "If you wish." He stepped away from the stairs.

Selby and Belton exchanged a glance and came around him one on each side. "Good man," declared Selby. "I've a particularly fine cognac I should like you to try." And between them they ushered Ned through the salon and into the library.

Belton closed the door firmly behind them and turned the key. He gave Ned a most unpleasant smile. "It would have been so much better for you if you had chosen some other refuge, Allenton," he declared, cracking his knuckles.

"Really?" Ned raised an eyebrow. "How so?"

"You have insulted my hospitality, Allenton," declared Selby. "You've dishonored my ward, Belton's fiancée—"

"And just how have I done that?" Ned interrupted. "Don't be absurd, man. Your imagination is running away with you."

"I've seen the way you look at her . . . and I've seen the way she looks at you," Belton declared, stepping closer. "And I tell you, by the time I've finished with you, you won't be fit to be seen." Without warning he drove his fist into Ned's belly.

Ned inhaled. It hurt, but Belton was drunk and had the

physique of a dissolute. He was vicious, but nowhere near as strong as he thought he was. Ned, on the other hand, was hardened by years of dirty work. He hadn't spent all his time in India behind a desk juggling figures—he'd visited his holdings, his plantations, ridden for days at a time administering his property. He'd hunted game with maharajahs, fenced and shot with officers of the East India Company, and a weak blow, however underhanded, from a Godfrey Belton was more than a flea bite but far from a hornet's sting.

He raised his fist and brought it up under Belton's jaw. The man slumped back into a convenient chair and Ned turned to Selby. "I'm not sure how I've insulted your hospitality, Selby, but I'm certainly sure how you've broken the rules of hospitality. Do you usually set your tame thugs on your guests if they refuse to pay you a guest fee?"

He massaged his knuckles thoughtfully. "I can only imagine that your demand for two thousand guineas is a fee for room and board. It seems a trifle excessive to me. Now, if you'll excuse me, I shall decline the offer of cognac. Good evening, sir." He bowed and walked to the door. He turned the key and opened the door, expecting any minute to hear some response from Selby. But nothing came.

Selby only glanced at the door as it closed behind Ned, and then he looked at the crumpled Belton. "You do appear to be having a hard time of it, Godfrey," he said. "I'm always telling you not to lead with your fist. And particularly with Georgiana. She has more wit in her little finger, dear fellow, than you have in your entire body."

He poured cognac into two glasses and gave one to

Godfrey, who had hauled himself upright in the chair. Selby took a reflective sip from his glass. "I'm beginning to wonder if you're exactly the man I'm looking for," he mused.

Godfrey stared at him. "We had an agreement, Selby. I can control Georgiana. Don't you worry."

"I hope so, Godfrey. I certainly hope so." Selby set down his glass. "I bid you good night . . . and better luck with her tomorrow. I should avoid getting too close to her if I were you. I couldn't see what she did to you just now, but it must have been nasty." He gave a short derisive laugh and left the library, saying over his shoulder, "Snuff the candles before you leave."

Godfrey swore a vile oath. He drained his glass and hurled it into the fireplace, where it shattered into shards of crystal. His side hurt like the blazes but he didn't know what she'd done to make that happen. One minute he was in the ascendancy and the next he'd experienced a stab of the worst pain he could remember.

But she could be subdued. She was so small, so fragile. It was ridiculous to imagine he couldn't control her. He was prepared now. Forewarned, forearmed.

Chapter Seven

Ned sat by the fire in his chamber, sipping cognac and waiting. He'd had some strange Christmases in his life, he reflected. No one could say eating boar's head and brandy-rich Christmas pudding, and singing carols in the midday heat of Madras in December was normal. But the British preserved their traditions religiously however peculiar the circumstances. However, the last twenty-four hours really transcended anything in his experience. And he had the absolute conviction that they were going to change the course of his life forever. The thought brought a smile to his lips.

He let the clock strike one and then he rose and went to the door. He opened it and stepped into the corridor, listening intently. He could hear no sounds and the only light came from a single sconce on the wall close to the galleried landing at the end of the passage.

He walked softly to the landing, listening. Still no sound. On the landing he stopped. The hall below was in semidarkness, also lit only by a single sconce. There was no sound, apart from the general creaking of old boards in an old house. He trod softly down the stairs, across the hall, and opened the door to the salon. The room was in darkness, and when he moved toward the library door he saw that it was closed and there was no telltale line of light beneath.

He made his way back, up the stairs, but instead of going to his own chamber he took the passage he had taken with Georgie earlier. He stopped outside her door. Light glowed from beneath. He knocked softly.

"Georgie, let me in."

There was only silence. He was about to knock again when he heard the key in the lock. It turned and the door opened halfway. He stepped through, and she shut it swiftly, turning the key again.

"I didn't wake you?"

She shook her head, said simply, "No." She turned aside to the fire, where a small pan was heating on a hob. "I was warming some milk for myself. Would you like some?"

"No," he exclaimed. It was so domestic and soothing, and he didn't feel either of those things. "What else have you?"

Georgiana, bending over her saucepan, straightened, laughing. "Cognac on the dresser. I like to put a little in the milk."

"It sounds revolting," he declared, finding the decanter and filling a glass. "What did you to Belton?"

"A jab in the kidney," she said easily. "Undetectable but most effective." She lifted the saucepan, ready to pour its contents into a cup she had ready, and then set it aside. "No, perhaps you're right. This isn't a moment for hot milk." She stood up, turning to face him.

"Where did you learn those tricks?" Ned asked, his eyes fixed upon her. She wore a light peignoir over her nightgown and her hair was an unruly copper mass around her pale face and clustering on her narrow shoulders.

"What tricks?" Georgiana looked at him warily.

"You know perfectly well," he declared. "Would you like cognac?"

"Please . . . and if you're referring to my ability to protect myself from Godfrey, then Jacobs's son taught me. He's a prizefighter."

Ned laughed as he handed her a glass. "I thought there was something unusual between you and Jacobs."

"He stands my friend," she said, taking a sip, still looking at him with some degree of wariness. "He knew my father. They were children together."

"So your family's from Northumberland? Carey . . . ? I don't recognize the name."

Georgiana curled into a corner of the daybed. It seemed pointless to keep her family history a secret. And the urge to confide in Ned Vasey was well nigh irresistible. Ever since she'd found herself in this place, torn from her London roots with such lack of ceremony, she had kept her own counsel, given as little of herself as she could. Confided in no one, trusted no one. All her energy had gone into finding a way out of this calamitous situation that had been forced upon her. But something existed between herself and this man, something unlooked-for. And every instinct told her to rely on it.

"My father was a younger son of the Dunston family. There were six children and by the laws of primogeniture he would have been left nothing." She waved a dismissive hand at the immutable fact of the property laws.

"When a distant cousin, a Jeremiah Carey, offered to adopt him because he and his wife were childless, Lord Dunston jumped at the opportunity. It meant one of the younger sons would be well provided for. So at the tender age of ten, my father was sent to live with the Careys in London, took their name and inherited Jeremiah's property on his death. He married well, I was born, and then both my parents died of typhus within two months of each other."

She sipped her cognac, gave him a rather bleak look across the lip of the glass. "There it is, plain, unvarnished. It's a not uncommon tale."

"And your mother's sister took you in then?" Ned watched her face. He could sense her vulnerability beneath the seemingly calm and matter-of-fact exterior, and he began to have an inkling of the loneliness of her life.

"Aunt Margaret," Georgiana said. "She was good to me, educated me, sent me to a ladies' academy in Bath to finish me off . . . it nearly did too," she added with a rueful chuckle. "So prim and prissy, I thought I would suffocate. But then I had my first Season and was supposed to find myself a husband. Unfortunately," she added mournfully, "I didn't seem to take."

"You had no offers?" He wanted to laugh at the absurdity of such an idea. A young and lovely debutante with what he guessed would be a decent inheritance couldn't possibly have passed her coming-out season without several eligible suitors.

Goergiana's laugh was sardonic. "Oh, plenty of them," she said with a scornful gesture. "Fortune hunters, weak-chinned royalty, even, but no one I would consider going to the altar with." She frowned again. "Of course, if I'd known Godfrey Belton was in my future, I might have compromised my principles somewhat."

Ned began to see how Georgiana's particular way of looking at the world might have put off the more cautious members of London society. There was something wild, untamed about her, a certain carelessness of convention, which would not go down well with the sticklers who made the rules.

"So your aunt died and you somehow found yourself up here?" he prompted when she seemed disinclined to continue.

She shrugged again. "By some quirk of fate it turned out that I was the only member of the Dunston family left when the last earl died. The title has now died out, but the property came to me. My next of kin turns out to be a distant cousin on my mother's side, Roger Selby, and according to the will, I own, or will own when I gain my majority, large swaths of land from the—"

"Coast to the Pennines," Ned interrupted, nodding slowly. *So that was what Godfrey had meant.* He had suspected something of the like, but hadn't been certain.

"Precisely." Georgiana looked at him curiously. "How did you know?"

"Just something Belton said." Ned turned to the dresser to refill his glass. "Was it the will you were looking for last night?"

"If I can't get my hands on it, I might as well give up," she said bitterly. "There's no point getting out of this place without it."

Ned inclined his head in acknowledgment. "No indeed. And you, of course, are very busy acquiring the means of escape." He looked at her with a half smile. "So tell me, Georgie, does Jacobs's son accompany you on your reiver's business?" He perched on the window seat, watching her closely over the rim of his goblet.

"What do you mean?" She watched him in turn, sipping her own cognac.

"Oh, come now, Georgie, you know exactly what I mean. And I would like my fob watch back. It has some significance for me above and beyond its financial value."

For some reason she found that she was neither shocked nor surprised at his knowledge. Ned Vasey wasn't the kind of man to be easily deceived. "How did you find out?"

"The pony in the stable . . . Jacobs said you had been out in the snow yesterday . . . I saw you deal with Belton in the Long Gallery and my own neck remembered that blow." He shook his head ruefully. "My fault for not expecting an ambush, I suppose. But the weather was so dangerously foul, it didn't occur to me to be wary."

"It was our last chance before the blizzard shut us in," she said, as if it was the most logical explanation for a perfectly ordinary activity. "I don't have much time, so I can't waste opportunities."

He nodded. "Well, we shall talk more about those opportunities in a minute. But first . . ." He held out his hand. "My fob watch, if you please."

Georgie exhaled on a resigned breath and kicked aside the rug. She knelt, pushed aside the floorboards and took out the pouch. "Do you want your guineas too?"

"No . . . no," he said with an airy wave. "I'm happy to donate those to the cause. Just the fob watch will do." He watched as she emptied the contents of the pouch on the bed.

"There are several here," she said doubtfully. "I don't know which is yours."

"Oh, what an unregenerate thief you are," Ned declared, getting to his feet. "Let me retrieve my own property." He came over to the bed and looked down at the hoard, a glinting, gleaming pile.

"This is mine." He took his own watch and dropped it into his pocket. "Thank you." He cupped her face between his palms and kissed her, and as he did so he realized that he had come to her tonight for this, not for his fob watch, not for the story of her life. Just this.

Her mouth was at first soft and pliant against his, and then fierce and hungry as her arms came around his neck.

Georgiana was lost in a strange crimson world of urgency. Her body seemed to be one pulse of desire, a sensation so new and yet somehow so familiar that she could only think it was bred in the bone. This was the way a body was supposed to react to the sheer physical wonder of another. Her hands ran down his back, kneaded his buttocks, her loins pressed against his growing hardness. She felt his breath hot on her cheek as his lips whispered a kiss tracing the contours of her face, moving down to the pulse in her throat. Her head fell back in submission as he moved his mouth to her ear, his tongue moist and insistent, his teeth nibbling her earlobe. He pushed the peignoir off her shoulders and her nipples peaked hard and dark against the flimsy white silk of her nightgown.

He stood back for a second, looking at her, her flushed cheeks, her glowing eyes, the soft swell of her breasts showing above the lace-edged neckline of her gown. He looked at her, touched her eyelids with a fingertip, asking a question, even though he knew the answer. And she answered him by swiftly unfastening the little pearl buttons at the neck of her nightgown, opening it to reveal her breasts.

He bent his head and kissed them, lifting them free of their silk containment, running his tongue in a moist caress over their firm roundness before kissing the erect nipples, grazing them lightly in turn with his teeth, and his hands slid over her shoulders beneath the silk, smoothing down her narrow back, reaching her bottom, pulling her urgently against him.

She leaned back against his hands, her upper back curving as she looked up at him, her eyes filled with passion, her lips slightly parted, the pulse in her throat beating wildly. "I want this," she said softly. "Please, Ned. I need this."

He nodded slowly. "I need it too." His fingers moved deftly over the last of the buttons, sliding the nightgown away from her so that she stood naked before him. He knelt and kissed her breasts, her belly, slid a hand between her thighs, waiting for her resistance, but her legs parted slightly for him and he moved a finger in a light caress, touching her core, feeling her center grow moist, opening to his gentle exploration.

She had her hands on his shoulders, her head thrown back, as the exquisite sensation built. It was like nothing Georgie had ever experienced, and yet it felt as if it was the most natural sensation in the world, as if she had been waiting for it her whole life long. And when the warmth flooded her, she leaned over, resting her weight on his shoulders, her lips parted with breathless delight.

Ned lifted her and carried her to the bed. He was filled now with his own need. He laid her down on the coverlet, and swiftly pulled off his own clothes, conscious of her eyes on him as his body was revealed piece by piece. Naked, he straddled her, and immediately she reached for his engorged penis, stroking it with a curious wonder in her eyes as her fingers explored its contours, the corded pulsing veins, the absolute proof of his need for her.

He reached for a cushion, pushing it beneath her hips, elevating her slightly. He touched her again, feeling her open and ready for him, and with a swift movement of his hips drove into her. She bit back a cry of pain at the first tearing sensation and he slowed, his eyes anxious, but immediately she smiled up at him, touched his mouth with her fingertips. "Don't stop."

He bent and kissed her mouth as he moved more slowly within her, feeling her tightness ease around him. He had expected her to be a virgin and she was, but she was no frightened maiden. Georgiana was ready for this moment and prepared to give herself up to it. She felt the pleasure building within her with a kind of wonder, savoring every sensation, relishing the tight spiral that grew ever tighter until she thought she couldn't bear it any longer. Tears stood out in her eyes as she gazed up at him and his own eyes were filled with their own wonder. He leaned back as he continued to move inside her and with a light brush of his fingers touched her core. The coil burst apart, her body convulsed, and she heard herself cry out before he silenced her with his mouth, withdrawing from her body as his own climax pulsed.

He fell on the bed beside her, sliding a hand beneath her to roll her into his embrace, and they lay in silence as their breathing slowed, and the glorious languor of fulfillment slowly faded.

"I wish it could have lasted forever," Georgiana murmured after a long time.

Ned laughed softly. "The tragedy of the human condition, my dear girl. Exquisite delight that lasts but a moment."

Georgiana rolled sideways and propped herself on an elbow, running a hand over his chest. "However, there is one advantage," she murmured with a smile. "There's no limit to the number of times one can enjoy such ephemeral pleasure."

"Up to a point," Ned said, taking her hand and kissing her fingertips, tasting the salt of her skin. "A certain amount of recuperation is necessary, however."

Georgiana chuckled, and sprang from the bed with enviable energy. "I'll stoke the fire and reheat the milk," she declared. "I'm in the mood for it now."

Ned said nothing, for the moment too distracted by the entrancing view presented as she bent to set the saucepan on the hob. After a minute he shook his head as if to bring himself back to reality. "I must leave you now, before the house begins to stir."

"But we have to make plans," she said, looking over her shoulder at him as she knelt before the fire to tend the pan. "We have to get out of this house. Or at least I do, sooner rather than later."

Ned gestured to the window. "Nature seems intent on making that rather difficult for you."

"Not if one uses one's imagination," she declared. "Escaping from the house doesn't necessarily mean going out into the blizzard." She sat back on her heels, still looking over her shoulder at him with a quizzical expression.

Ned raised an eyebrow. "Go on."

"Well, you could always come with me, but it seems to me that if we disappear together certain conclusions will be drawn," she said slowly, dipping a fingertip in the contents of the saucepan to see if it was warm enough.

"Certainly," he agreed. "And they won't be pleasant ones."

She shrugged. "That's of little matter. Nothing could be worse than now, but I have a better idea anyway. I shall disappear. I'm sure Selby will set up some kind of hue and cry, but they won't be able to go far in this. And while they're running around in circles, I shall be snug and warm, watching them."

"Ah." Ned nodded his comprehension as he rose from the bed. He crossed the room naked, aware of her intent scrutiny as he poured cognac into his glass. His body began to stir again under the devouring green gaze. He forced himself to concentrate on the matter in hand. "So, where are you going to hide?"

"In the attics," Georgie said, reluctantly returning her attention to the saucepan. She poured milk into a cup, then swiveled around on her knees to face him. She sounded rather smug as she cupped her hands around the cup. "Right under their noses. I've been planning it for a while. Jacobs will take care of me until I can actually get away. . . . Could you put some cognac in this?" She held out her cup.

Ned brought the decanter over and added a measure of cognac to the milk. He stood looking down at her thoughtfully. "And where do I come in?"

"Ah, well, you see, that's the beauty of it. I haven't been able to count on a partner in crime, if you see what I mean, but now that you're here, that makes everything much simpler."

She maneuvered herself into a sitting position on the rug, her back to the fire's warmth. "I'm guessing that one of the first things Selby will do when he knows I've disappeared will be to check the will. And it seems to me that you could perhaps manage to be around when he does—see where he keeps it. He and Godfrey are bound to panic when I'm gone, and they won't think you have anything to do with it. You're just someone Selby's trying to rob anyway, and he's not going to give up too easily while you're under his roof." She took a deep gulp of her fortified milk.

"So you find the will while I'm hidden away and they're all running around like chickens without heads, and then as soon as the roads are clear enough, we make our escape, take the will to a solicitor in Alnwick, get it proved and safely deposited, and all I have to do is stay out of the way until after my birthday." She beamed up at him with an air of complete satisfaction.

To say Ned was bemused by this sweeping description of his part in Georgiana's plot would be an understatement. "I'm to *steal* the will?" he queried.

"It wouldn't be stealing since it belongs to me and you're acting on my behalf," she declared. "Anyway, I didn't think you'd be squeamish about it, not after what Selby's trying to do to you."

"Well, you see, I haven't had the advantage of your previous experiences," he said apologetically. "I've never actually stolen anything before . . . or, for that matter, spied on anyone."

"Well, it's easy enough," Georgie declared with an airy wave. "And it won't be anywhere near as difficult as ambushing travelers. You'll find yourself quite capable once you put your mind to it."

"You reassure me," he said dryly. He glanced around for his clothes. This didn't seem to be a conversation to be conducted in a state of nature. He pulled on his britches and shirt, and felt instantly more in control. "And once you've made your escape and deposited the will safely, where do you intend hiding until you attain your majority?"

"That's why I have my ill-gotten gains, of course," she said. "They'll pay for some kind of transport and lodging as far away from here as I can manage. And once the business is over, then I shall return to London my own woman, as it were." *And free to love whom I choose.* But this last she kept to herself. It still seemed too soon to be making declarations of that sort, even as she longed to do so.

Ned nodded. It seemed to him highly likely that this unlikely young woman would succeed in doing exactly as she planned. He would suggest his own alterations to the plan at a more appropriate moment.

"So, will you do it?" she asked with sudden urgency, and the confidence in her eyes was diminished slightly by a hint of her earlier vulnerability.

"Yes, my dear girl, I will do it," he stated. "Assuming that I can, and that that thug Belton doesn't do away with me in a dark corridor."

"I don't think Godfrey would resort to murder," Georgie said doubtfully.

"He's not averse to thuggery," Ned pointed out. "I wouldn't put anything past him once he's lost you as his prize."

"No, perhaps not." She frowned into her cup. "You'll just have to be extra vigilant. I'm sure you're a match for him. . . . I could ask Jacobs's son, Colin, to give you a few lessons in unarmed combat, if you'd like. Although, of course," she added with a little frown, "you have killed a man already once."

Ned burst into laughter, forgetting for a moment his compromising position at dead of night in the sleeping house. He stifled his amusement hastily. "Thank you for the vote of confidence," he said somewhat unsteadily. "I think I can handle Belton."

"Yes, I'm sure you can," Georgie said. She uncurled herself from the floor and came over to him. "And you will visit me in my attic hideaway whenever you can." She stood on tiptoe to kiss him.

Her mouth was sweet with a lingering residue of milk and brandy, and her fire-warmed skin had the scent of woodsmoke mingling with rosewater and lavender. He held the slight frame against him, running his hands over the shape of her, committing it to memory. Then reluctantly he raised his head and stepped away from her. "Are you going now?"

She shook her head. "I must talk to Jacobs first. But come with me now and I'll show it to you so you'll know where to come." She dropped her discarded nightgown over her head and shrugged into the peignoir, looking around the floor for the satin slippers she had been wearing. She found one in a corner, the other halfway under the bed.

"How did they get all the way over there, I wonder," she murmured with a mischievous grin as she slipped them on her feet. "Bring the candle." She reached for his hand. "Come." She put a finger to her lips and led him from the room.

She took him up a dark and unpainted stairway hidden behind a door at the end of the passage. Ned held the candle aloft, casting their shadows long on the grimy walls and the steep and curving flight of stairs. At the head she opened a door that should have creaked but opened instead on well-oiled hinges.

Inside was a cavernous space filled with the bulky shapes of old furniture shrouded in dust sheets.

"Through here." Georgiana led the way with confident steps through the obstacle course toward the back of the space. She pushed aside a chest with her hip, and a narrow door was revealed. This too opened on oiled hinges to reveal a small round chamber with a dormer window opaque with snow. A narrow cot piled high with quilts, a charcoal brazier unlit but clearly in working order, a table and chair, two oil lamps and a deep armchair completed its simple furnishings.

"See," she said, flinging her arms wide. "Isn't it cozy?"

"Yes, but you won't want to be immured in here for very long," Ned said flatly. "You have far too much energy, dear girl. You'll go out of your mind with boredom in two days."

She looked at him with a half smile. "I'm assuming you'll be relieving my boredom occasionally, sir. And providing me with the opportunity for exercise several times a day."

"What a wanton you are," he said, gathering her into his arms, pushing up her chin with his palm. "No one would believe you were a maid but an hour since."

"Oh, I have always been a quick learner," she said, nibbling his bottom lip, then teasing the corner of his mouth with the tip of her tongue. "Shall we test the bed?"

"For God's sake, Georgie, it's nearly morning. You

are far too reckless for your own or anyone's good," he chided, half laughing but meaning it. "The servants will be up and who knows who else."

"Not Selby and his guests," she said with a moue of disappointment. "They won't show themselves until close to noon." She sighed. "But I suppose you're right."

"I am," he said firmly, turning her back to the door. "Let's go." He eased her forward with a hand in the small of her back, enjoying the curve of her spine, the warmth of her skin, and trying very hard not to yield to the resurgent wave of desire.

At the foot of the stairs, he gave her the candle. "Go now. I'll follow in a few minutes."

She turned her mouth for a farewell kiss. "I won't appear for breakfast. Come to me this afternoon."

"I might be too busy spying," he teased, kissing the tip of her nose. "Hurry now."

Georgiana slipped through the door, turned to blow him a kiss, and then was gone in a waft of silk and muslin.

Ned waited for close to five minutes, then he stepped into the passage, closed the door quietly behind him, and sauntered casually back to his own chamber. The candles in the sconces were guttering now and he could hear sounds from downstairs as he crossed the galleried landing. Servants would be raking out fireplaces and relighting the fires. He moved quickly back to his own room, closing the door behind him with a definitive click. He had a few hours of peace to think how to go about his part in Georgie's plan, so blithely allocated to him.

Maybe, he thought, as he threw off his clothes and climbed into his cold bed, he should start to be a little more accommodating to his host's demands. String Selby along a little, offering the possibility of capitulation, so that Selby sought out Ned's company. He couldn't be a successful spy if Selby didn't trust him or welcome his company.

Ned smiled with resignation in the dark. If necessary he would pay the man his two thousand guineas. Georgiana Carey was cheap at the price.

Chapter Eight

Georgiana was too keyed up to sleep once she'd attained the safety of her bedchamber. She got into bed and lay propped against her pillows, watching the firelight flickering on the ceiling. Slowly she explored her body, wondering if it would feel any different after those ecstatic moments under Ned's hands, and she smiled to herself, luxuriating in the slight soreness between her thighs. She recognized that a certain desperation had fueled that flood of urgent desire. The knowledge that she might never again have the opportunity to experience the fulfillment of passion—that she might never again feel the need to do so. She certainly couldn't contemplate passion-filled experiences with Godfrey, and until Ned Vasey had entered her life, she had had no reason to imagine anyone else would provide the opportunity. But her life was opening up, offering possibilities once again.

She touched her nipples, and they grew hard under her fingers at the remembered feel of his lips. She felt again the sheer excitement that had coursed through her at the feel of his lips suckling, his teeth lightly grazing the tips of her breasts. Her loins pulsed in memory and her body shifted on the mattress, her legs parting in involuntary invitation.

Until this evening she had thought only of escape. The future after her escape was too murky to untangle until she faced it. But now she could see a path. And she could see who would walk that path beside her.

Impatiently she swung herself out of bed. There was too much to do this morning, and very little time in which to do it. Once she was safely up in her attic hideaway, she could indulge in fantasies of the future to her heart's content.

Ned was still asleep when Davis entered the chamber a few hours later. The valet set down the jug of hot water on the washstand and drew back the curtains at the windows. The rattle they made awoke Ned. He pulled himself up on the pillows and ran a distracted hand through his rumpled hair.

"Davis, bring me up a bath, if you please."

"Oh, you're awake then, m'lord." Davis pulled back the bedcurtains. "Snow's easin' a bit, it looks."

"About time too." Ned turned to look at the window. It was as white as before. "A bath?" he repeated.

"Yes, m'lord. Right away, sir. Should I bring breakfast too?"

"If you please." Ned leaned back against his pillows, staring at the window. If the snow was easing, then it wouldn't be more than a day or two before some of the main roads would be passable. Or at least for a horse if not a carriage. He and Georgie would need horses. She had that pretty mare, Athena, but he had no riding horse with him.

Well, Roger Selby would lend him one. He wouldn't know how generous he was being, of course. Ned chuckled. In the cool white light of morning he was beginning to enjoy the prospect of deception and thievery. Not that it would be thievery to take the will. It belonged to Georgie, after all. He was merely restoring property to its rightful owner—and righting a grievous wrong in the process.

No wonder he felt so full of energy and enthusiasm this morning. Of course, he reflected, getting out of bed, stretching luxuriously, a night of satisfied lust might have something to do with it. That and the prospect of its continued satisfaction.

He sipped coffee while Davis and two manservants labored with jugs of steaming water, filling the copper tub before the fire. He bathed quickly, ate some bread and ham, and dressed. Then he went in search of Jacobs.

He found the butler in the hall, examining the tarnish on a pewter bowl on an oak side table.

"Good morning, Jacobs."

Jacobs turned and bowed. "Good morning, Lord Allenton."

There was something in the man's eye that told Ned all he needed to know. "I imagine that Lady Georgiana is unavailable at the moment," he said casually.

"Yes, my lord, that is so." Jacobs rubbed at the tarnish with a soft cloth. "She asked me to tell you that she will be *apparently* unavailable for the foreseeable future." He chose his words with care, the slightest emphasis making his meaning clear.

"I see. Are her guardian and her fiancé aware of this as yet?"

"No, sir. Not as yet. I expect they will realize it later this morning when they come down for breakfast, sir."

"I see." Ned smiled. "Thank you, Jacobs. You will keep me apprised as necessary."

"Of course, sir." Jacobs held the bowl to the lamplight with a critical frown. "Should you wish to go out, my lord, I will send for your greatcoat."

"I have it in mind to stroll around to the stables," Ned said. "I understand the snow is easing off a little."

"Yes, sir. It looks like it. Would you like my son to accompany you?" Jacobs set the bowl back on the table and looked directly at Ned.

"I think that would be most helpful, thank you, Jacobs."

"One minute, sir, and I will fetch him." Jacobs disappeared, and reappeared in a very few minutes with a stocky young man who carried Ned's greatcoat. "My son, Colin, my lord. You can be sure he will be of whatever help you need."

Ned nodded amiably at the young man, wondering if he recognized him from the ambush, but the visibility had been so bad, he had only really noticed shapes. Colin had a fighter's shoulders, but he was no heavyweight, more a featherweight, Ned decided. However, he had an air of confidence, a comfort with himself, which was a quality Ned had long appreciated, particularly in those who served him.

They went out into the snow, taking the same kitchen route Ned had taken with Georgie the previous day. *Was it only the previous day?*

"I'm going to need a horse, Colin," he said without preamble as they traversed the kitchen garden toward the gate leading into the stable yard.

"Aye, sir," Colin responded phlegmatically. "Thought as much, sir. You'll need a mount with a sure step. Paths'll be slippery and the snowdrifts'll make for slow going for quite some time."

"And Lord Selby has such a mount in his stables?" They entered the yard and Ned glanced up at the leaden sky. The snow was definitely easing and he could swear he caught the faintest hint of blue shifting behind the cloud cover.

"Several, sir." Colin paused to look at his companion, running a knowing eye over the tall, lean frame. "Most of 'em more than up to your weight, m'lord. They're used to carrying his lordship. I'll show you the one I have in mind." He plowed across the snowy yard to the stable block.

Ned followed him into the warmth of the building, fusty with the smell of horseflesh and leather, sweet-scented hay and manure. He checked first on his own carriage horses, which seemed dozy and contented, and then followed Colin along the line of stalls to one at the rear.

A bay gelding, raw-boned with strong shoulders, was cropping hay from the manger. "This here's Magus, sir." Colin leaned on the half door and clicked his tongue at the horse, who indolently turned his head to regard his visitors from long-lashed brown eyes. "Fine strong animal, he is."

"He certainly looks it," Ned agreed, reaching out an inviting hand to the horse, which after a moment decided to acknowledge the greeting and turned in his stall to put his head over the half door.

Ned stroked his neck and murmured to him, and the animal pricked his ears and whickered softly.

"Oh, you and him'll get on like a house on fire," Colin predicted. "When Lady Georgie gives me the word, I'll have him saddled and ready. Him and Athena."

"Good." Ned smiled his appreciation. "I'll just go and find my coachman and postillions, make sure everything's still all right with them."

He looked for the pony as he walked back up the line of stalls, but there was no sign of the animal. He paused on his way outside Athena's stall and the mare came up to him readily, as if recognizing him from the previous day's visit. He stroked her neck, murmured a few words in her ear, and then went on, well satisfied that as far as mounts were concerned he and Georgie would be well equipped.

He returned to the house just after eleven and went into the dining room, where his host and fellow guests were already at breakfast.

"Ah, Allenton, thought you'd decided not to join us," Godfrey said, piling kidneys onto his plate from a chafing dish on the sideboard. "Thought maybe you found the company a little too hot for you." He sat down, glowering at Ned.

"Not in the least," Ned said affably. "Good morning, Selby, ladies . . . gentlemen." He helped himself to eggs and sat down opposite Godfrey. There was, of course, no sign of Georgie, and he waited with some curiosity to see what would happen when she failed to appear.

It took close to half an hour before Selby, who had been consulting his watch at regular intervals, said, "Where the devil has that girl got to this morning? She knows I like to breakfast punctually at eleven." With impatient vigor he rang the silver bell that sat by his plate, and Jacobs appeared immediately.

"You rang, my lord."

"Yes, where's Lady Georgiana? Have you seen her this morning?"

Jacobs looked puzzled, as if trying to remember. Then he shook his head. "I don't believe I have, my lord. I don't believe she's come down yet."

"Well, has her maid seen her?"

"I don't rightly know, sir."

"Well, go and find out, man." Selby shooed at him with an irascible hand and Jacobs bowed and departed.

He returned in five minutes with a maidservant. "Lorna tells me that Lady Georgiana hasn't rung for her this morning," Jacobs declared. "Tell his lordship, girl."

The maid looked terrified, as well she might, Ned reflected, given Lord Selby's heightened color and the wrath growing in his pale eyes. She curtsied. "I've been waitin' on madam to ring, m'lord. But she 'asn't yet."

"Well, go upstairs and see why not." Selby buried his head in his ale tankard. Everyone around the table had ceased eating, eyes bright with curiosity at this mystery. Godfrey Belton, however, continued to chew his way through his mound of kidneys, interspersed with frequent forays into his ale tankard.

The maid came back in a few minutes, her eyes wide and frightened. She curtsied several times, wringing her hands, before blurting, "Lady Georgiana's not in 'er room, m'lord. And 'alf 'er clothes 'ave gone from the armoire."

"*What?*" Selby pushed back his chair, his color ebbing and then rushing back into his florid cheeks. Godfrey dropped his fork with a clatter onto his plate.

Selby strode from the room, Godfrey on his heels, and the guests at the table burst into excited conversation. Ned ate his eggs, buttered toast, drank coffee, and waited. Within minutes he heard Selby giving orders in the hall.

"She can't have gone far in this snow, the roads are deep in drifts," he was bellowing. "Jacobs, send out men from the stables to cover all the roads and paths out of here. See if there are any tracks."

There were no tracks, but that was explained by the constant snowfall throughout the night. However, a pony was missing from the stables.

That explained that, then, Ned reflected. Presumably Colin or one of his compatriots had taken the pony. No one would believe that Georgiana had left the house on foot in this weather, and the pony was a logical choice for a runaway. A sturdy creature, less valuable and certainly less highly bred than the horses.

The uproar surged around him. Selby and Belton did not return to the table and Ned waited for a few minutes before casually rising and making his way to the salon. The library door stood open and he could hear Selby's furious undertone interspersed with a periodic rumble from Belton.

Ned was alone for the moment and he trod softly to the half-open door, listening.

"She won't last half a day out there," Selby was declaring.

"But where the hell does she think she can go?" Belton demanded. "There's no one here about to take her in. They all know who she is; they'll send her right back."

"Yes, but as I've told you before, Belton, Georgiana is no fool. She'll have a plan, so it might take a bit longer to find her. But as long as she can't get her hands on the will, we have nothing to worry about. When we find her—and we will find her—you'll be married at once. Her property will pass into your hands and our agreement stands."

Ned pressed his eye to the crack between the door and the jamb. He could just see Selby, bending over something on the desk. It looked like a lockbox. He waited, ears pricked for the sound of anyone entering the salon behind him. Selby took a sheet of parchment out of the box.

Ned moved sideways, and calmly opened the door wide. "Forgive the intrusion, Selby, but the door was open. I've had some second thoughts about your proposal," he said casually as he strolled into the library.

The two men stared at him. Selby had the paper in his hand, the lockbox open on the desk. "I don't have time for that now, Allenton," Selby declared. "You heard that Georgiana has disappeared."

"Oh, yes, of course," Ned said as casually as before. "But I can't imagine she can have gone far in this weather. I'm sure you'll catch up with her soon enough." He regarded his companions with raised eyebrows. "Strange that she should take such an idea into her head though, don't you think?"

"Just between you and me, Allenton, the girl's not quite right in the head," Selby said, carefully replacing the parchment in the lockbox without looking at it. He turned the key in the lock and pocketed the key. "Gets it from her mother. Strange woman. Had some very fanciful notions."

He moved away from the desk, forcing a smile. "You're right, we can safely leave finding her to my men. So, what are these second thoughts." He took a seat by the fire and gestured to a chair opposite.

Ned sat down, aware of the glowering Godfrey, whom Selby appeared to be ignoring. "Well, I was thinking perhaps you're right. Perhaps I am honor bound to honor my brother's debt. I wouldn't care to start off on the wrong foot among the folk here."

Selby nodded solemnly. "Ah, sensible man," he said. "I knew you couldn't lack for sense the minute I laid eyes on you. You give me a draft on your bank for the two thousand guineas, you keep the bill of sale, and we'll say no more about it." His eyes gleamed.

"I need to settle affairs at the local bank before I am in a position to access such funds," Ned said, crossing his legs, swinging an ankle idly. His smile was pleasant. "But I will give you an undertaking in writing."

Selby looked displeased. "I already have one of those," he stated. "And much good it's done me."

"Ah, but that one is signed by my brother," Ned pointed out. "By my *late* brother. It is basically null and void now, as I'm sure you're aware. However, in the interest of neighborly relations, I am prepared to give you *my* undertaking." His smile was suddenly a little less pleasant. "I am sure you will see your way to accepting a gentleman's word, Lord Selby."

Selby's face was a picture as he struggled with the idea of deferred gratification. But he could not refuse to accept Ned's word. "Well . . . well, I daresay that will have to do," he said finally, grudgingly. "I daresay you'll be able to continue your journey by tomorrow. The snow has stopped altogether now, and my men will be clearing the local road at least as far as the next village."

"I can assure you, Selby, I will not trespass on your hospitality a moment longer than necessary," Ned said, rising gracefully to his feet. He turned to Belton. "Are you intending to join the search for your fiancée, Belton? I have a mind to join them myself."

"There's no call for that," Godfrey said. "It's none of your business, Allenton."

Ned shrugged. *That was a matter of opinion.* "If you'll excuse me, gentlemen." He offered a nod of a bow and left, leaving the door open. The salon was still deserted, quiet and peaceful, but the sounds from the rest of the house, shouts and slammed doors and running feet, were far from tranquil.

So he knew what he was looking for. A lockbox, and quite a large one at that. And it was a reasonable assumption that Selby kept it somewhere in the library. It would be a lot easier to locate than a single sheet of parchment, that was for sure. And he had little doubt that even without the key Georgiana would be able to open it. It seemed entirely feasible that lock picking would be one of her more unconventional talents.

He hovered by the half-open door, hoping for a clue as to where Selby hid the box. Through the narrow aperture he could just make out Selby bending low by the bookcase on the far wall, but he couldn't see what he was doing; his bulk blocked the view. However, he knew a lot more now than he had done earlier. Georgie had been right in her assessment of Selby's first action.

Ned strolled out of the salon to join the frenzied throng in the hall. The other guests were gathered in a chattering knot by the open front door, peering out at the white landscape as if they could conjure the missing woman out of the snow. Dark figures dotted the parkland, searching for some clue. Ned smiled to himself and went upstairs, confident that his own disappearance wouldn't be noticed for some time.

The corridor outside Georgie's bedroom was quiet, although her door stood open, the room in disarray as if ransacked. He moved quickly past and, after a covert glance around, opened the door to the attic staircase and slid inside. He made his way up the narrow stairs, opened the door at the top and stepped into the gloomy space.

He whistled softly as he made his way to the chest that blocked the door to Georgie's eyrie. Jacobs had presumably escorted Georgiana to her hiding place when she made her final move. He shoved the chest aside and tapped once at the door, whispering, "Georgie" against the keyhole.

The door opened and her face appeared, eyes glowing, lips parted. "Come in." She grabbed his arm and hauled him inside, closing and locking the door. "I can hear the kerfuffle even up here," she said. "What's happening?" She was laughing with a curious mixture of excitement and anxiety. "I didn't realize how hard it would be not to be able to see what was going on."

Ned leaned against the closed door. He could feel her tension, like a spring ready to snap, and he controlled his own impulse to sweep her onto the bed, instead saying in measured tones, "Everything is going exactly as you planned, Georgie. I've seen the will in Selby's hand and—"

"Where does he keep it?" she broke in, clasping her hands against her skirt as if it was the only way to keep them still.

"In a lockbox somewhere in the library. I have an idea of where, but I'm not certain. I will find it tonight," he said calmly. "I don't count lockpicking among my talents, but I'm hoping you do."

"Oh, yes, with the right tool," she said almost impatiently. "It seems to have stopped snowing."

"Yes, it has, and by the time Selby's army of searchers has combed the surrounding land they'll have cleared a fair path for us," he said. "We'll get the will tonight, and we'll be on our way at dawn. We can't go in the dark, however tempting it might be."

"No, I suppose not." She sounded doubtful. "It would be better though to have most of the night behind us by the time they discover you've gone too."

"But foolhardy nevertheless," he insisted quietly. "I understand your impatience, love, but sometimes it's best to err on the side of discretion."

Georgiana nodded. She had been gripped by this almost febrile excitement since she'd heard the first sounds of the discovery of her absence. It was partly a terrible dread that she would be discovered and it would all be over, and partly the heady thrill at the whole daring escapade.

Ned smiled. "I have a foolproof way to ease your impatience," he said, reaching for her, drawing her toward the cot. "I hope this doesn't creak too much." He fell back on the bed, pulling her down on top of him. "Would you be interested in trying this very pleasant activity from a new angle, ma'am?"

"Oh, most definitely," she said, lying long against him, bracing herself on her palms as her mouth hovered over his. "I am always open to furthering my education, my lord."

An hour later Georgiana woke from a doze wondering where she was. Her clothing was in disarray, she appeared to have lost her stockings and garters, her underclothes existed in memory only, and she appeared to be alone.

She struggled up on the narrow cot and saw Ned standing at the dormer window, struggling to open it. Relief washed through her and she lay back again, covering her eyes with her forearm as she waited for reality to reassert itself. A blast of frigid air completed the process and she gave a muted yowl of protest, sitting up again, pushing her skirts down over her exposed limbs.

"What are you doing?" she asked.

"Checking the weather," he said, closing the window again before turning to look at her. He smiled. "How deliciously abandoned you look. Can you organize your thoughts sufficiently to talk about our destination when we leave here tonight?"

"Alnwick," she said. "I have to get the will to a solicitor before anything else. It must be secured."

"And then?"

"I don't know." She pushed her tumbled hair away from her eyes. "Where were you going?"

"Ah, well, that's it," Ned said, coming over to the bed. He sat down on the edge and reached for her hand. "I have some business I have to attend to. A mite awkward, I suspect."

"Oh?"

"I was going to Hartley House to spend Christmas,"

Ned explained. "Before I was first ambushed by an enterprising reiver, and then benighted by a blizzard."

Georgiana nodded. "You would know the Hartleys, of course. They're your closest neighbors."

"Yes." He hesitated. "I've known Sarah Hartley since we were children."

Georgie looked at him sharply. She heard something in his voice. "And?" she prompted.

"And I was on my way to spend Christmas at Hartley House and renew a long-ago proposal of marriage to Sarah," he said, a fingertip tracing a pattern in her palm.

Georgiana grinned. "I wish you luck with that," she said. "But I do hope you haven't set your heart on it. I'd hate to see you disappointed."

He enclosed her hand tightly in his, said sharply, "What do you mean?"

"Only that Sarah has been affianced to a lieutenant in the Black Watch these last five years and the marriage is to take place in the summer. He's been in the Peninsula with Wellington and they have had so many put-offs, but at last it looks as if she'll be wedded and bedded by the middle of June."

Ned shook his head in astonishment. "Why on earth didn't Hartley tell me?"

"Did you tell him the main purpose of your visit?" Georgie asked, regarding him with her head to one side, the smile still on her lips.

"Well, not in so many words." Ned shook his head again. "I understood from Rob that Sarah was still unmarried, and I thought . . . oh, what a coxcomb." He laughed in self-mockery. "I thought she had been pining for her long lost love, and I felt in honor bound to renew my proposal. And," he added ruefully, "I thought she would make a perfectly fine wife, and we would rub along quite comfortably together."

"And you were prepared to settle for that?" Georgiana sounded incredulous.

He lifted her hand to his lips and kissed her knuckles. "Until I met you, yes."

"And now?" Her eyes gleamed.

"And now I see no reason why we shouldn't between us own everything between the coast and the Pennines," he declared with a chuckle. He was laughing, but his eyes were not as they held hers. "I love you," he said simply. "I've never felt anything like this before. I want to spend the rest of my life with you. I can't imagine my life without you."

Her green gaze was curiously soft and tender as she looked at him. He still held her hand and her fingers moved against his palm. "Is that a proposal, Lord Allenton?"

"It would appear to be," he replied with a half smile. "I'm not in the habit of making them, so it may lack a certain *je ne sais quoi.*"

"Oh, I think it will do very well," Georgie said, kissing the corner of his mouth. "I love *you*, Ned Vasey."

He gathered her into his arms. "Then this, ma'am, is a contract we should seal with a kiss."

Chapter Nine

Ned spent the remainder of the day with his fellow guests, none of whom seemed to know what to do with themselves. The Lord of Misrule was absent for the main part, appearing briefly at luncheon, and vanishing soon after. Parties of men continued to comb the surrounding area and returned with nothing. Godfrey Belton hovered, casting a malevolent eye over everything in sight and Ned in particular, and as the afternoon drew in, consternation among the guests grew.

"It's such a worry, Roger," Mrs. Eddington said when she could catch her host. "Georgiana is such a little thing. She couldn't possibly survive a night outside. What are we to do?"

"I'm doing everything I can, Bella," Selby said, trying to mask his irritation with an anxious headshake. "My men can't continue to search in the dark. We have to hope she's found shelter in a cottage somewhere. The people around here wouldn't turn her away."

"It's all we can pray for," the lady said with a heavy

sigh. "But I'll not sleep easy tonight, thinking of her out there in the cold."

"It was her own decision," Godfrey growled from the sideboard where he was refilling his glass of port. "If she was fool enough to risk her life, then on her own head be it."

"Good God, Belton, you can't mean that," exclaimed one of the gentlemen, sounding genuinely shocked at this callous statement. "She's to be your wife."

"Aye. The poor girl must have been out of her mind to do such a thing," put in another of the guests. "She'll need some careful attention when she comes back."

"Oh, she'll get that all right," Godfrey muttered with a baleful stare at Ned, who ignored him, concentrating instead on an out-of-date copy of the *Gazette*.

Dinner was a wan affair and the party broke up early. Selby and Belton went to the billiard room and Ned remained in the salon with the pile of ancient periodicals until Jacobs came in to see to the fire and the candles.

"We will be needing the horses just before dawn, Jacobs," Ned said in a conversational tone without raising his eyes from the print.

"Right y'are, sir." Jacobs continued to stoke the fire as if nothing had been said. He left soon after and Ned stayed a while longer before going into the hall, as if on his way to bed. He could hear the click of the billiard cue as he paused outside the room, and the low rumble of voices. There was nothing he could do until Selby and Belton had gone to bed. His only fear was that Selby would take the lockbox to bed with him. But there was no reason for him to do that.

Ned hesitated on the landing, tempted to go to Georgiana in her attic, but he resisted the temptation. It was too risky while Selby and Godfrey were still up. Selby might take it into his head to visit his guest with a renewed demand for the undertaking to pay for a useless piece of land, and would certainly find it strange if Ned was absent from his chamber at this time of night.

He rang for Davis and chatted with him as the valet helped him prepare for bed. Davis was full of the servants' speculation as to Lady Georgiana's whereabouts. "Just between you, me an' the gatepost, m'lord, none of us is really surprised that Lady Georgie's up and gone. Too good by half she is for those what she's intended for. Beggin' your pardon for speaking out of turn, sir."

"I know nothing about it, Davis," Ned said carelessly, settling down in an armchair by the fire with a glass of cognac and a periodical. "That will be all, thank you. I'll see you in the morning."

"Yes, sir." Davis bowed himself out and Ned settled down to wait, confident that when questioned in the morning about Lord Allenton's absence, Davis would have nothing pertinent to say.

After a while, he rose and went to the armoire for his portmanteau. He couldn't be burdened with too much luggage, but there were some things he had to take. A change of clothes, money, a few precious personal belongings, and, of course, his pistol.

When the clock struck three, he left his bedchamber and went soundlessly downstairs to the library. He locked the door behind him. At least there would be some warning of a potential intruder. The room was in darkness except for the ashy glow of the fire's embers and he lit the candle on the mantel before going to the bookcase on the far wall where he had seen Selby that morning. At first it looked to be a perfectly ordinary bookcase. Somewhat dusty volumes lining the shelves, the spaces between the shelves all a uniform size, the books neatly arrayed in alphabetical order.

Ned stood and looked at the bookcase. He cleared his mind and let his eye roam along the shelves. He didn't know what he was looking for, but it had to be there. And then he saw it. In the middle of the bottom shelf the spines of the books seemed very close together, with no space even to push a piece of paper between them. He couldn't see how anyone could have fitted them in so tightly together.

He knelt on the floor and reached to remove one of the books, only to realize that they were not books. It was a solid slab of wood on which a line of book spines had been stuck, covering every millimeter of the slab. It would certainly fool a casual glance, and how many people, anyway, got down on their knees to examine the contents of the bottom shelf of a tall bookcase?

Ned ran his hand over the block that was the width of half a dozen books. About the size of the lockbox, he reckoned. He removed the books on either side of it and felt around. He slipped his flattened palm below the shelf, which lay only a half inch above the floor. And then he felt the catch, embedded in the wood. He pressed it to no avail. He tried sliding it with equal futility. He only had touch to guide him; there was no way he could see what he was doing. Impatience was giving way to desperation as he fumbled around, trying to slide it to the left, then to the right. He slid it to the left again and magically the block became a door that sprang open in front of him, revealing a deep space recessed into the wall behind the bookcase.

It contained only the lockbox, pushed to the rear. Ned edged it out. It wasn't particularly heavy but the padlock looked sturdy enough. It was to be hoped it wasn't beyond Georgie's skills. Once she'd opened it and extracted the will, he would return it to its hiding place, assuming, of course, that he could manage the right trick to close up the shelf again. The longer it took before Selby realized the will was missing, the better start they would have.

Georgiana paced the small attic chamber as she had been doing all evening. She was in an agony of impatience, hating the fact that she could do nothing further to help herself in this business now. She had to leave it in someone else's hands, and she was not accustomed to sitting on the sidelines. She had always taken care of things herself, relied only on herself, and now she was helpless, dependent entirely on Ned.

She knew he couldn't do anything until he was certain everyone was in bed and asleep, but he seemed to be taking an eternity. She had everything ready for the journey. Her treasure trove, a change of clothes, her own jewelry. All she could do was wait, and it was the hardest thing she could ever remember doing.

At last she heard a low whistle and flew to open the door. "Oh, you have it," she exclaimed in a whisper. "Oh, you're so clever. . . . Where was it?" Even as she spoke she was tugging the lockbox out of his arms.

Ned let her take it, following her back into the small chamber, locking the door behind them. "It was in some kind of safe in the bookcase," he said. "It was easy enough to find but I had the devil's own job getting the safe itself open. Can you manage the padlock?"

"Let's see." Georgiana set the box on the table and examined the padlock, frowning. Then she reached up to her head and withdrew a hairpin from the tight knot of curls on her nape. She pulled the lamp closer and fitted the hairpin into the lock.

Ned leaned against the wall, his arms folded, watching her. The tip of her tongue peeped between her teeth as she worked intently, her finely arched brows drawn in a fierce frown of concentration. When the hairpin broke in the lock, she cursed under her breath and Nick grinned despite the tension. It was a reiver's curse, nothing of the lady about it at all.

She took another hairpin and began again, a light dew of perspiration misting her brow. Once or twice she wiped her palms on her skirt. And then there was a click and she said, "Got you, you bastard." She looked up at Ned with a radiant smile. "Success."

"Well done. Let's get the will and I'll put the box back where it came from." He lifted the lid and took out the topmost sheet of paper, guessing that the will had been the last thing Selby had touched in the box.

"Is that it?" Georgiana demanded impatiently. "Let me see."

"Patience, child," Ned teased lightly, laying the sheet open on the table and smoothing it out with his hand. "Why don't we look at it together."

"I can't help being impatient," Georgiana said, bending over the document.

"No, of course you can't." Ned kissed the top of her head as he leaned over her to read for himself.

The reassuring red seal of the lawyer's certification was stamped deep into the thick vellum. They both read in silence and then Ned straightened and said briskly, "That seems to be in order. Put it away and I'll take the box back."

"Let me see what else is in here," Georgiana said, taking out the remaining papers. She lifted out a box that had been on the bottom beneath the papers. "I knew he hadn't deposited them in the bank," she said, opening the box.

Ned blinked at the brilliance of the stones that lay glinting on the black velvet lining. "They are magnificent," he murmured.

"The Carey diamonds," Georgiana said softly, taking the necklace out and letting the stones ripple into her hand. "Selby let me keep all my mother's other jewels, but he took these. He said I would have no cause to wear them up here, and besides, they were too valuable to have lying around. They were to go to the bank and he would give them to me on my wedding day—but I doubt he intended to honor that," she added with a grim smile.

"Well, the sooner we get them somewhere safe the better," Ned observed. He replaced the papers in the box, closed it and clicked the padlock in place. "Meet me at the stables in fifteen minutes."

It seemed he had decided to take complete charge of this enterprise, Georgiana reflected as she deposited the diamonds in the cunningly contrived inner compartment of her cloak bag, which also contained her ill-gotten treasure. She wondered if she minded and then decided that she didn't. At least not at the moment. Indeed, she wasn't at all sure, now that the reality was upon her, that she could have managed to do this entirely alone.

She slipped the will into an inside pocket of her jacket, where it rested against her heart, picked up the small cloak bag, gathered her thick hooded riding cloak around her, extinguished the lamp and crept out of the attic.

It was dark but her eyes grew accustomed quickly until she entered the back staircase leading down to the kitchen. Here it was pitch-black and she felt her way down, using her free hand on the wall to guide her. The kitchen was lit by the fire in the range and she stepped in more confidently, then started violently as the scullery door opened.

"Lord Allenton's just gone out, my lady," Jacobs said. "The kitchen staff will be down any minute, so you'd best hurry."

Georgiana patted her chest, where her heart was thumping wildly. "You gave me such a fright, Jacobs."

"Sorry about that, Lady Georgie," he said. "But you didn't think as how I'd not see you off."

"I suppose I did," she confessed, going up and kissing his cheek. "Thank you, my friend."

"Oh, away with you now," he said, his cheeks turning pink. "You'll be safe enough with Lord Allenton, I'm thinking."

"I'm thinking so too," she said, hurrying to the kitchen door. "Colin will take us along the back paths?"

"Aye, they're still pretty thick, but he reckons you'll get through as far as Mother Jacobs. He's driven the ox cart with a plow through them once this afternoon."

"What would I do without you both," she said, blowing him a kiss. "When I'm settled at Allenton Manor, you'll both come to me there, won't you?"

"If that's in your cards, Lady Georgie, you can count on it." He smiled with pleasure. "Right glad I am to hear it. He seems a good man, the viscount."

"I'm certain of it," she said, and stepped out into the frigid predawn.

Ned was standing with Colin in the yard, stamping his feet in an effort to keep warm. The horses had blankets under their saddles and were shifting restlessly on the snow-covered cobbles of the yard.

"Ah, there you are at last," Ned declared as Georgie appeared. "Hurry, we have to get out of here before first light." He took her portmanteau and handed it to Colin, who strapped it to the back of Athena's saddle. "Up with you." He lifted her, swinging her up into the saddle before swiftly checking the girth and stirrup length. "All right?"

"Fine," she responded impatiently. "Mount up yourself."

Ned swung onto Magus, who shifted beneath his weight and tossed his head as if debating whether to complain. Ned soothed him with a hand on his neck and a soft word in a pricked ear. Colin mounted a sturdy pony and led the way through a back gate in the yard into a field piled high with snowdrifts.

A narrow path had been cleared around the perimeter of the field and Ned dropped back, gesturing to Georgie that she should ride between himself and Colin. It was hard going; the paths were only minimally passable and very narrow. The sun came out and the snow blazed and glittered. Colin dismounted and blinkered the horses to protect them from the glare, but there was no such relief for the riders, who rode almost blind, eyes streaming in the freezing air. But they saw no one else for several hours, and finally Colin gestured silently ahead to a small cottage, a plume of smoke curling from the chimney stack.

"We haven't put enough distance between ourselves and Selby to stop," Ned said from behind Georgie.

"It's all right, it's Colin's grandmother's cottage," she told him. "She's expecting us. Or at least she's been expecting me at some point. I don't suppose Selby even knows she exists. We have to rest the horses and we don't want to be seen in daylight. We'll stay here for the rest of the day and part of the night and go on again before dawn tomorrow, before anyone else is out and about."

It made sense, and Ned was far from averse to warming himself up. They were in no particular hurry, after all. Their only imperative was to stay clear of Selby.

Colin's grandmother was a taciturn woman, like many of her fellow Northumbrians. She welcomed Georgie warmly enough, but looked at Ned a trifle askance until her grandson murmured something to her in an undertone, after which she accorded him a nod that he took as acceptance, and beckoned him to the kitchen table and a bowl of thick, honey-sweetened porridge.

Colin left after he'd eaten and his grandmother went out to feed the chickens and collect the eggs. Georgiana yawned. "I feel as if I haven't slept in two days," she said. "In fact, when I think about it, I haven't."

"Well, now might be a good opportunity." Ned pushed his chair away from the table with a sigh of repletion. "We could both do with it. The question is, *where*?" He looked around the kitchen somewhat at a loss. "You could take the rocker by the fire. I'll make myself comfortable on the settle."

"Oh, I'm sure Mother Jacobs can do better than that," Georgie said. She took her cloak off a hook by the fire and went out into the garden, picking her way over to the henhouse. She returned in ten minutes, her eyes alight, cheeks pink with the cold.

"Up there." She pointed to a ladder in the corner of the kitchen. "In the apple loft. Mother Jacobs says there's a cot made up for me, and enough blankets and quilts for you to bed down on the floor, if you're not too hoity-toity that is," she added with a gurgle of amusement. "I assured her you weren't."

"I could probably sleep on a bed of nails at this moment," Ned stated, making his way to the ladder. "Come on, Georgie, you first." He stepped aside and she set her foot on the ladder and went up with an encouraging push to her rear. Ned followed her into a round chamber smelling of winter apples and the straw in which they nested.

Georgiana, shivering, pulled off her riding boots, then her jacket and skirt, and dived onto the cot in her petticoat, huddling beneath a thick quilt. "Hurry," she insisted, lifting a corner of the quilt in invitation. "It's cold."

Ned wasted no time. He undressed to his shirt and drawers and slid in beside her. It was a tight squeeze but she tucked her slight frame against the contours of his, relishing his body warmth, her head in the crook of his neck, her eyes closing involuntarily. Ned held her as she slipped into sleep, her body relaxing against his. He smiled and smoothed a red curl from his chin where it tickled.

It was midafternoon when Ned awoke, his arm numb from Georgie's dead weight. He tried to extricate it without waking her but she stirred as soon as he moved it and gave a soft protesting groan.

"Forgive me, love, but my arm's gone to sleep," he murmured, rolling her sideways off him. "There, that's better." He sighed with relief and shook out his arm. "How do you feel?"

"I'm not sure yet," she said, trying to sit up without exposing an inch of her skin to the air. "My nose has lost all feeling." She rubbed at it with the heel of her hand. "Every other bit of me is warm though."

"Lie sideways," he said, trying to maneuver her where he wanted her without causing the quilt to slip. "There, that's better." He curled himself around her back, his hands finding the soft mound of her breasts. "Much better," he murmured.

After a minute, Georgiana said, "Have you thought about what we should do once we've secured the will with the solicitor in Alnwick?"

"Actually, we're not going to Alnwick," Ned stated, his breath rustling against the nape of her neck.

She stiffened, struggled to turn around. "Of course we are. It's the most important thing we have to do. It has to be done right away."

"No," he contradicted gently. "It is not the most important thing we have to do."

Georgiana fought against him and won, pushing herself up against his chest. She stared down at him, heedless of the cold air on her back, her green eyes fierce. "This is *my* plan, I'll have you know. And we're going to do exactly as I planned."

He shook his head, smiling into her indignant gaze. He reached up and pushed her hair away from her face, holding it back behind her head. "My love, first I am going to marry you over the anvil. Then we will prove and secure the will."

"Gretna Green, you mean?" She looked as startled as she felt.

"Without a moment's delay," he declared. "I'm sorry if you had grand romantic notions of St. George's, Hanover Square and the rest of the whole wedding circus, but this seems our only option if we're not to wait for six months until you come of age and won't need Selby's permission. And I really don't think we can afford to do that."

"No, of course I don't have notions of a grand wedding," she said, the indignation fading from her eyes. "I just hadn't thought of it. Anyway, I think it's the most romantic thing imaginable. Married by a blacksmith over an anvil. And it's not very far from here, either. How clever of you to think of it. 'Viscountess Allenton' has such a nice ring to it." She leaned down and kissed him.

He caught her face between his hands, letting the red cascade of curls fall forward again, and kissed her, his mouth hard on hers, before rolling her beneath him.

"Do you think we can manage to sidestep the clothes without losing the quilt?" he murmured, pushing up her petticoat, feeling for the string of her drawers.

"Oh, I think we can do anything, you and I," declared Georgiana Carey, her own fingers busy in their own right.

When Sparks Fly

Sabrina Jeffries

To Susan Huggett Williams, for all you do.

And to Ursula Vernon, the daughter I never had—
this is as close as I get to exploding carriages.

Chapter One

Yorkshire
December 1823

Dear Charlotte,

The school must be an empty place with your pupils gone for the Christmas season. I hope you have friends nearby to look in on you. A woman alone is never entirely safe.

Your concerned cousin,
Michael

No more marriage mart. That would be Elinor Bancroft's Christmas gift to herself this year.

Ignoring the antics of her bored young cousins and their friend as the Bancroft carriage hurtled toward Sheffield for the holiday, Ellie gave a heartfelt sigh. She'd rather be a spinster at home in Sheffield than endure another humiliating Season in London. Just the thought of being launched into the social whirl *again* in a mere three months made her stomach churn.

Now all she had to do was convince Aunt Alys and

Papa to give up on marrying her off. She frowned. *That* was unlikely.

"The Christmas goose at Uncle Joseph's house is the best," eleven-year-old Percy Metcalf told his quiet school chum, Charlie Dickens, who'd come with them for the holidays. "He buys the biggest one in town."

"Will there be plum pudding?" five-year-old Meg Metcalf mumbled around the thumb she had stuck in her mouth. "I like plum pudding."

"I hope we play snapdragon," eight-year-old Timothy Metcalf said.

"I wish we could," Ellie said, "but I doubt Papa will allow it. He'll say snatching raisins from a burning bowl of brandy is too dangerous."

"But snapdragon is a Christmas tradition!" Percy protested.

"If Mama lets us play it, why should Uncle Joseph refuse?" Tim said with a pout. "Stop the carriage, and we'll tell her to convince him. I want to ride with *her*, anyway. Percy keeps hogging the seat."

"If you hadn't already driven her mad this morning," Ellie countered, "you could be riding with her now. Let her nap—alone—and I'm sure she'll be happy to have you and Meg back in her carriage when we reach the next town."

After arriving in Hull by ship from London, they'd found one of Papa's coaches waiting to take them the day's drive to Sheffield. Business had called him to Lancashire, but he'd promised to be back before Christmas. Sadly the coach hadn't been large enough for them all, despite the children's nurse being delayed in London with a bad fever. They'd had to hire a post chaise just for their trunks.

"Can we sing Christmas carols?" Meg asked.

"If you want," Ellie said. "What about 'On Christmas Day in the Morn'?"

"Let's sing 'A Jolly Wassail Bowl,'" Tim put in. He seemed to have bowls of spirits on the mind today.

"That one's too long," Percy protested. "I want 'The Holly and the Ivy.'"

"You picked the story yesterday—I should get to pick the carol," Tim complained, thrusting his elbow into Percy's side.

Percy reacted by shoving Tim, which sent Tim into Charlie, who said, "Stop that, you nodcocks!" and shoved them both. Within seconds, the rough-and-tumble boys were brawling. Again.

"Enough!" Ellie protested, leaning forward to separate them. "Stop this nonsense!"

The next thing she knew, Percy accidentally jabbed his elbow into her breast.

"Ow!" Ellie cried, and drew back.

Meg, who worshipped her nineteen-year-old cousin with a passion generally only reserved for kittens and lemon drops, threw herself into the fray. "You hurt her! Mustn't hurt my Ellie!"

She then burst promptly into tears, which brought the fight to a screeching halt, since the boys coddled Meg as if she were a fairy princess.

"There now, don't cry." Percy clumsily patted her shoulder to comfort her.

"Go 'way!" Meg protested, shoving at his hand. "You were mean to Ellie!"

Biting back a smile at Meg's fierce defense, Ellie dragged her onto her lap. "It's all right, moppet." She nuzzled the girl's fragrant blond curls. "I'm fine, really.

No one hurt me." She frowned at Percy over Meg's head. "Not much, anyway."

Percy thrust out his dimpled chin. "I didn't mean to poke you in the . . . you know where."

"The bubby?" Tim supplied helpfully.

"Tim!" Ellie chided. "You shouldn't use such vulgar language!"

"'Such vulgar language,'" he repeated in a prissy tone, sticking his nose up in the air to mimic her. He snorted in disgust. "You've sure become prim and proper lately. You were more fun before you went off to that school."

"She's trying to catch a husband, you chawbacons," Percy said. "That's what they teach them at the School for Heiresses."

Ellie glared at Percy. "Don't call it that. Besides, they taught us etiquette and literature and science, too. It wasn't just about catching a husband, you know."

But it really was, and she was destined for failure. She was no beauty, like her friend Lucy Seton or Mrs. Harris, owner of the School for Young Ladies, which Ellie and Lucy had attended until their coming-out. Ellie was plain and slightly plump. Her unfashionably straight black hair defied any attempt at curling, so she had to wear it plaited in a coil atop her head.

Lucy praised her green eyes, but since Ellie's spectacles hid them, they did her little good. She'd tried leaving the spectacles off, only to discover that it made it hard to *do* anything. Beauty might indeed be but "a flower,/Which wrinkles will devour," according to Thomas Nashe, one of her favorite poets, but she would still like to have been given the flower—at least for a while.

And what did a man know about it, anyway? Nashe

had no idea what it was like to lack any of the physical attributes that might attract a husband.

"What do you need a husband for?" Charlie said. He wasn't very talkative, but he could be quite sweet. "You've got us to look after you."

"Yes, Ellie," Tim put in. "*I'll* marry you."

Arching one eyebrow, she cleaned her spectacles. "I thought you said girls were stupid."

"But you're not a girl. You're Ellie." Tim's face brightened. "Think what jolly fun we could have climbing trees and fishing and riding to hounds."

She flashed on an image of her standing at the altar beside the towheaded Tim while he held a fishing pole at attention, and a smile curved her lips.

"Of course, you'd have to wear something sturdier than *that* silly froofy thing." Tim pointed to her redingote.

"*Froofy* isn't a word," she shot back. "And I *like* this gown." It was the only one that made her look halfway pretty.

"You can't clean fish in it, you know," Tim remarked.

"I don't intend to clean fish *ever,* not even for you. Besides, what would we live on while we're busy fishing?"

"You've got a fortune, haven't you?" Tim said with the matter-of-fact practicality of the young. "We'll live on that."

Her smile faltered, and she donned her spectacles to hide her sudden tears. Even Tim knew that her greatest asset lay in her money. At least he was honest about it, which was more than she could say for most gentlemen. Fortunately, she could spot a fortune hunter from ten paces, thanks to her training at the school, not to mention the information proffered through letters from the school's anonymous benefactor, "Cousin Michael." And fortune hunters were all she ever attracted.

As the richest heiress in north England, Ellie was the most eligible female on the marriage mart—and the least desired.

How naïve she'd been before her coming-out, dreaming of marrying a wildly poetic fellow like Lord Byron—but without his vexing character flaws. Instead, there'd been a steady parade of men who not only lacked poetry in their souls, but possessed the one flaw she couldn't abide—greed. They eyed her as if she were a cow brought to market. They made her feel like a cow, too.

She'd had enough. Once at home with Papa, playing his hostess, she meant to stay there. Forever. Her aunt and her cousins would be returning to London alone.

"You're too young for Ellie," Percy told his younger brother with an air of superiority. "Ellie could marry *me*, except that I don't mean to marry. Charlie and I mean to be soldiers, and she would just get in the way."

Aunt Alys would never let him go off to war. Despite her sweet temper and her young age of thirty-two, their mother had a spine of steel, and her children were her life. So was Ellie, as the beloved daughter of Aunt Alys's only sister. It had been Aunt Alys who'd urged Papa to enroll Ellie in Mrs. Harris's school after Mama died, Aunt Alys who'd sponsored Ellie during her coming-out. She was sure Ellie would find the perfect husband in time. She wouldn't approve of Ellie's plan to give up on marriage.

But Ellie had been preparing for that. She'd been practicing with Lucy, learning to speak her mind and stick to her resolve. She'd never had trouble being firm with the children—she just had to learn to do it with . . . much bigger children.

The thought of children made her sigh. That was a disadvantage to her plan—she'd never have a darling Meg or a clever Percy of her own.

She clutched Meg close. Never mind that. She had her cousins and, eventually, *their* children. Better that than being locked in matrimony to a man who took a mistress because his wife's only attraction was her money.

"Have you looked outside, Ellie?" Percy was watching out the window, deep concern on his plump face. "It's sleeting."

"What?" She pulled aside the curtain nearest her, dismayed to find the trees dripping with icicles. They had no hope of reaching Sheffield by nightfall now.

She heard Papa's coachman, Jarvis, shout something to the postboy driving the hired post chaise ahead of them. She strained to see what was going on, but they were rounding a curve near some woods, and she wasn't at the right angle.

Suddenly a scream sounded from somewhere on the road ahead, and their own carriage skidded. Meg was thrown from Ellie's lap, and the boys were tossed about like matchsticks.

"Damnation!" Jarvis brought the coach to a shuddering halt, then jumped down. After securing the horses, he trudged off across the ice-scarred grass, using his cane for balance.

"Stay here," Ellie ordered the children, then left the carriage to follow him.

Outside, she spotted the bridge where he was headed. The sleet swiftly coated her spectacles, forcing her to tuck them into her redingote pocket. Now she could barely see, although Jarvis seemed to have disappeared over the embankment beside the bridge.

A sudden foreboding seized her as she hurried after him to peer over. Jarvis picked his way down the slope, and very near the river's rushing waters lay the post chaise, crammed up against a thick oak.

"Aunt Alys!" Ellie cried.

"Stay back, miss," Jarvis ordered. "I can't be having you land in the river."

What about Jarvis? His bad leg would make it difficult for him to manage, especially now that snow mingled with the ice to form a treacherous crust over the ground. The postboy had his hands full with the struggling horses.

Jarvis hailed her aunt, but there was no answer, and panic swept Ellie.

"What's going on?" Percy called out behind her.

She turned to find the three boys climbing from the carriage as Meg peeped out the window. "Stay right there, boys."

"Where's Mama?" Tim asked plaintively.

Her heart twisted to see them ranged there, all blue-eyed and blond except for the darker Charlie Dickens. They looked so small and helpless—the slender Tim pulling at his wrinkled breeches, the heavier Percy shoving his curls back with impatience, and their sickly friend Charlie, blinking at the sleet.

Should she tell them the truth? No—they mustn't go near the river, and they surely would if they guessed that their mother was in trouble.

She marched to meet them, pasting a reassuring smile

on her face. "Jarvis is relieving himself, that's all. Get back in the carriage."

"I'm *tired* of the carriage," Percy whined. "I want to go with Jarvis."

"You can't!"

He eyed her suspiciously.

Desperate to distract him and the others, she said, "Weren't we going to sing carols? Come on, let's do 'The Holly and the Ivy' *and* 'The Jolly Wassail Bowl.' Meg would like that." Trying to shoo them toward the carriage, she began to sing, "'The holly and the ivy/When they are both full grown . . .'" until the others joined in.

Within moments the children entered into the spirit of things, but she kept glancing back, wondering if Jarvis was all right, or if she should slip away to help.

Then a voice boomed out from the road. "For God's sake, what's all the caterwauling about?"

Their singing died in their throats. Relieved that help had arrived, Ellie whirled around, ready to commission their rescuer's aid.

The murky image before her struck her dumb with fear. A creature over six feet tall sat atop a massive horse, only the red of his eyes breaking the unrelieved black of his lean figure. For a second, she was reminded of Papa's tales about strange beasts roaming the forests near Sheffield.

Then she squinted and realized that the creature was a man. An inky greatcoat enveloped him, and his ice-encased beaver hat sat perched atop incongruous raven curls. His face was black, except for where the sleet had created smears in what looked like soot. And he smelled of cinders.

A miner? It had to be. Who else would travel the roads looking like *that*?

She stepped forward to speak to him, but Percy grabbed her arm. "Careful, Ellie. Any chap who doesn't like Christmas carols is bound to be a scoundrel."

The man trotted his horse closer. "Any chap who inflicts them on passing strangers is clearly a royal pain in the a—"

"Sir!" she cried, covering her cousin's ears against whatever profanities the man might spew in his Yorkshire accent. "There are children here!"

"Aye, and a worse place to let them run I never saw. Best be on your way, madam, before the ice makes travel impossible." With a click of his tongue, he prodded his horse on.

"Wait, sir, please!" she cried.

When he drew up with a foul oath, she briefly considered the wisdom of involving this ill-mannered fellow, who might be a thief or worse. But Jarvis would never get Aunt Alys free without help, and the miner seemed to have brawn enough to manage that. She dared not look a gift rescuer in the mouth.

"There's been an accident," she said in a rush. "My aunt's carriage went off the road—"

"Where?" he barked before she could finish getting the words out.

She pointed at the embankment, struck silent by his surly manner. He dismounted and hurried for the river. "Just keep those brats out of my way."

Though the harsh words took her aback, she sprang into action. "Come, children," she said, ushering them toward the coach.

But Percy blocked her path, his face pale. "Mama is hurt?"

"I'm not sure," she admitted. "Jarvis is still trying to reach the carriage."

"Then I have to go help!" Percy exclaimed, starting past her.

She grabbed his arm. "Let Jarvis and the stranger handle it."

"But we don't even know if we can trust that fellow!"

"It'll be fine, don't worry." If he'd meant them harm, surely he would have already tried to take advantage of them. His gruffness perversely reassured her, especially after months in society, where the men she could least trust were always the most charming.

When Percy still hesitated, she added, "We have to prepare a place for your mother in the coach. She'll need blankets and cushions, in case she *is* hurt."

That sent the boys scurrying to arrange a comfy bed on one of the seats, while Meg shrank into a corner, sucking her thumb and crying softly.

"It's all right, Meg," Percy told her as he plumped up a cushion. "As soon as Mama is here, we'll go to an inn and get chocolate, won't we, Ellie?"

"Certainly." Giving the boys something to do had been the right approach.

"That man called us brats," Tim complained as he spread a blanket. "He doesn't even know us!"

"I'm sure if he did, he wouldn't call you that," Ellie said soothingly as she climbed out to hunt for Jarvis's flask of whisky. Aunt Alys might need it.

Hearing a noise, she squinted at the embankment and spotted the stranger headed toward her, carrying Aunt Alys. The postboy and Jarvis were at his heels, leading the horses from the post chaise.

"Is my aunt all right?" Ellie asked, her heart in her throat.

"She's alive," the man responded, "but unconscious. I think her leg is broken, and she's taken quite a knock to the head. She needs a doctor right away."

Ellie hurried to open the carriage door. "Is there one in the next town?"

The man leaned inside to set Aunt Alys upon the seat with an odd gentleness for a man so gruff. Then he faced her with a scowl. "As I told your coachman, you won't make it to Hensley. It's eight miles off, even if you *could* maneuver up that icy hill beyond the bridge. My house is nearby—you can sit out the weather there. I'll send someone to fetch a doctor."

"Goodness gracious, I don't know," Ellie murmured. How could this fellow fit seven extra people into his cottage, much less provide food and bedding for the children? They might be trapped for days. "Perhaps you should consult your wife first."

"I've got no wife. And you've got little choice."

If they went on to the next town they could buy what they needed, but he seemed certain of the impossibility of that.

"He's right, miss," Jarvis said. "What lies beyond that bridge ain't navigable at present. And the road back to the last town is sure to be as bad."

They looked to her for a decision. It felt strange to be in charge—usually Aunt Alys arranged everything. But Ellie trusted Jarvis, even if she didn't entirely trust the sooty stranger. "I suppose we have no choice."

As the men discussed how best to turn the coach around, she realized that she and the children needed items from the abandoned post chaise. She would just run back to the river for some clothes and other items. She might even drag a—

"Where the devil are you going?" the stranger called as she headed off.

"To fetch some necessities from our trunks."

"Leave them be." He came after her. "We have no time for such nonsense."

"But there are things we need," she protested.

Grabbing her by the arm, he began tugging her back to the carriage. "Nothing worth the risk of drowning in the river, Miss Bancroft."

"Don't be silly." Futilely she struggled against his iron hold. "I'm not about to—Wait, how did you know my name?"

"Your coachman told me you're Joseph Bancroft's daughter." Without ceremony, he threw open the carriage door and hoisted her inside. "Now stay put, blast you. I've got enough to worry about without risking the wrath of your rich father after you break your damned fool neck rescuing your fancy gowns."

"But that is not what I wished to—"

He slammed the door and walked off.

Taken entirely aback, she sat blinking where he'd dumped her on the coach floor. Well! Wasn't he a churlish lout? If he hadn't rescued Aunt Alys, she would give him a piece of her mind!

And how was it that even *strangers* knew she had money?

With an apologetic smile, Jarvis came up to say through the window, "I'm sure his lordship will be glad to send someone for the trunks later, miss."

"His lordship?" Could that dirty, ill-bred fellow possibly be a gentleman?

Jarvis bent nearer the glass. "The Baron Thorncliff, miss. But don't you worry none about the Black Baron—that nonsense folks say about 'im is just talk."

The Black Baron? Ah, because of his peculiar habit of walking around caked in soot. She shuddered to think what his house might look like. And she was vastly curious to know what people were saying about him.

Before she could ask, Jarvis hastened off and Aunt Alys moaned, shifting Ellie's attention to her. Ellie checked her pulse. It seemed strong, and she was breathing steadily.

"Ellie?" her aunt whispered.

Relief flooded her. "Yes, I'm right here."

Aunt Alys tried to sit up, then sank back with a groan. "My . . . head hurts."

"I know, Aunt." She stroked her aunt's light brown hair back from her pale forehead. "You've been in an accident."

Aunt Alys's blue eyes shot open, though they looked unfocused. "The children—"

"They're here and unharmed. We're taking you to a doctor." She didn't want to tax her aunt too sorely with explanations just now. "You should rest."

With a nod, her aunt closed her eyes.

"Is Mama going to be all right?" Meg asked from her perch on Percy's lap.

"Certainly," Ellie said with as much conviction as she could muster.

Wishing she could do more, Ellie settled her aunt more comfortably on the seat, careful not to jar her broken leg where it lay on the cushion that Lord Thorncliff had used to prop it up. After tucking the blanket around her, Ellie didn't know what else to do except pray that Lord Thorncliff really could fetch a doctor to his home quickly. And that they could trust him.

While Jarvis and their rescuer struggled to turn the coach, she fished out her spectacles so she could peer at him out the window. The stranger's mount did appear to be rather fine, and he did carry himself with a semblance of breeding. If not for his sooty exterior, she *might* believe he was a lord.

A teacher had once told them that men were either beasts, gentlemen, or beasts masquerading as gentlemen. Might there be a fourth category—gentlemen masquerading as beasts? After all, Lord Thorncliff *had* rescued them, albeit grudgingly. Surely that meant he was a gentleman somewhere deep inside.

Very deep inside, judging from his surly temper. Still, perhaps he behaved like that because people around him put up with it, too cowed to do otherwise.

Well, she couldn't help that her family had inconvenienced him, but neither could she let him keep ordering them about without paying any mind to her opinions. She had to think of the children and Aunt Alys. Someone had to stand up to him, and that someone would have to be her.

She just had to keep calm, and make it clear he couldn't keep bullying her. And pray that Shakespeare was right about there being "no beast so fierce but knows some touch of pity." Because if there was no true gentleman lurking inside that rough exterior, they might be headed for trouble.

Chapter Two

Dear Cousin,

I don't mind being alone. Our caretaker lives in a cottage on the grounds, and my neighbor is nearby. When the girls are away, he calls on me to make sure I am well. So you need not fret for my safety.

Your friend and relation,
Charlotte

Martin Thorncliff grumbled to himself as he hunched his shoulders against the snow. Leaving Bancroft's coachman to keep up as best as he could, Martin let his horse pick its own way to Thorncliff Hall. He was already having a bad day. The new fuses he'd invented had burned too quickly when he'd tested them at the coal mine. Then, on his way home, the sleet had begun. Now this.

December was difficult enough for him without intruders fetching up near his land. Rich intruders. With children singing Christmas carols, of all the infernal things.

What had Joseph Bancroft been thinking, to let his family travel so scantily protected? The man owned Yorkshire Silver, the largest silver mining company in England. He ought to have more sense than to rely on an aging coachman and some useless postboy. If those women and children had belonged to Martin, he would have protected them better.

A snort escaped him. Right. The way he'd protected Rupert. After what had happened to his older brother, no female with sense would put herself permanently under the protection of the dangerous "Black Baron."

The nasty nickname society had for him made him wince. He didn't need a wife anyway, mucking with his experiments and giving him one more person's safety to worry about. Though occasionally, he did wish . . .

Ridiculous. His life was as good as he deserved. It was his brother who'd been the jovial lord of the manor, who'd conversed equally well with tenant and duke, who'd run the estate with efficiency while attracting every pretty girl this side of London.

Martin could only blow things up.

And now he had guests, God help him. Thorncliff Hall was no place for a wounded woman and her caroling litter of cubs. Terror seized him at the thought of those boys exploring the old stone barn in back where he did his experiments.

At least he wouldn't have to worry about their cousin doing so. It wasn't the sort of place to entice a fashionably dressed heiress. Everything about her screamed "spoiled rich lass," from her expensive kid boots and matching gloves to the way she looked right through him. Then there was her impractical gown, though it did display her lush figure better than a wool cloak would have done. Probably why she wore it—young ladies like that craved attention. They were raised to enjoy it from early on.

Well, she wouldn't get it from him, no matter how pleasing her curves and sparkling green eyes. He'd met plenty of her sort while Rupert was alive and still forcing him to go into society. He'd even fancied a few. But once Rupert had died and the rumors had begun, they'd turned on him. He didn't fit their notions of what a gentleman should be. Miss Bancroft was sure to be the same.

Worse yet, she lacked sense. Fetch a few items from their trunks indeed. Was the lass daft? Had she no idea how treacherous that ice could be? She was probably worried some miscreant would come along and steal her jewels and furs. As if any would venture out in *this* weather. He scowled. Her jewels could wait—he still had things to do at the manor before the snow got too thick.

Once he reached the drive, he was able to ride ahead. His butler, Mr. Huggett, was already spreading gravel on the icy walk that bisected the low stone wall surrounding the manor. Hell and blazes, Martin hadn't even considered how this situation might tax his small staff.

He'd closed up half the rooms after Rupert's death, and these days he spent every waking hour in the barn. That's why he'd pensioned off all but the most essential servants. Fortunately Huggett excelled at making do. He'd know how to handle this disaster.

"I've brought some people home with me," Martin said as he dismounted.

"Guests?" Sheer joy transformed Huggett's face. "We're having guests?"

"More like unwanted visitors," Martin growled. "Their other vehicle had an accident, and I had no choice but to invite them to stay."

Huggett clapped his hands. "Excellent! Just in time for the holiday, too!"

"Huggett—" he began in a warning tone.

"I know how you feel about Christmas, sir, but it's been three years already, and now that we have visitors, we really must obtain some greenery and perhaps a Yule candle or two, not to mention preparing a goose and plum pudding—"

"Huggett!" When he had the butler's full attention, he added, "This is no time for festivities. One of them is wounded."

"Oh, dear," Huggett murmured.

"I'll need you to send for Dr. Pritchard. And make sure that whoever you send fits the horseshoes with frost nails—there's ice beneath that snow." He glanced to where the coach trundled up the drive. "I suppose we'll need more provisions, although no goose and plum pudding, for God's sake. Just make sure we've got sufficient food for the children."

"Children!" Huggett exclaimed, brightening again. "How many?"

"I'm not sure. Seemed like a lot. And there's a young woman, too, their cousin." As a knowing smile lit Huggett's face, Martin scowled, "Don't get any ideas. She's not my sort. Besides, she took an instant dislike to me."

"I can't imagine why," Huggett said dryly. "You always smile so prettily for the ladies."

Martin glared at him.

"Really, sir," Huggett said with a sniff, "you have to expect the fairer sex to recoil from you when you look like you've rolled through the coals."

"Rolled through—" Martin looked down to find himself covered in soot. He'd been rushing to leave the mine and hadn't washed up. "Hell and blazes."

"You may wish to curb your colorful language around the children," his butler chided as the costly traveling coach approached.

Martin was on the verge of curbing his *butler* with a kick to the rump when the coach pulled up in front, the door opened, and children erupted everywhere.

This time he counted them—three whelps who chattered like magpies and a tiny cherub with a halo of golden ringlets. He only hoped there were no squalling babes hiding under the coach cushions.

Miss Bancroft leaped out next, wearing a pair of spectacles too severe for her soft features. Since she hadn't worn them before, he figured they were an affectation, one of those whims that sometimes possessed society ladies.

She paused near him long enough to say, "My aunt has roused, but someone will have to carry her inside, so if you'd be so kind—"

"Certainly. This is my butler, Mr. Huggett. He's sending for the doctor." On cue, Huggett hurried to a waiting groom to give the instruction, but as Martin headed for the coach, he heard Miss Bancroft exclaim, "*This* is where you live?"

The incredulity in her voice rubbed him raw. All right, so Thorncliff Hall, with its blackened gritstone and mullion windows, wasn't the Greek-Palladian-something-or-other villa that high society deemed fashionable these days—but he was proud enough of it. It might need a bit of work, but it had been in the family for over two hundred years. That ought to count for something.

Not that this lot would appreciate it. That was gratitude for you.

"Aye," he shot back, "this is my home. And judging from the weather, it may be yours for the next few days, so you'd best reconcile yourself to doing without your London luxuries for the nonce."

"I didn't mean— Oh, dear, Meg, don't you dare eat that dirty snow! Excuse me, sir, I must see to the children."

As she ran off, he stared after her in surprise. She was corralling her cousins? It didn't seem like something a spoiled heiress would do. Then again, women like her enjoyed ordering people about. God help any man who married her—he might get a fortune, but he'd have a slew of petulant demands to satisfy in the bargain.

Martin found the aunt reclining on the seat inside the coach with her arm draped over her face. "Madam?" he queried.

"Where are we?" she asked in a disembodied voice much like the one his mother had used before her death.

It alarmed him, though at least she was conscious. "At Thorncliff Hall. You'll be fine now." Leaning in to scoop her up, he carried her toward the house.

The children swarmed around them, tendering questions. Just what he didn't need. "Miss Bancroft, keep those brats—"

"Don't call them brats, sir," she shot back. "They're perfectly well-behaved children who've just seen their mother injured. Have some sympathy, if you please."

The admonishment took him aback. Most women quaked in their boots around him. Why didn't she?

Ignoring Huggett's strangled laugh, Martin tramped into the house with the aunt. As Huggett and a footman kept pace with him, he issued orders, heedless of the heiress and cubs who trailed behind. "We'll put Mrs. Metcalf in my bedchamber, and the rest of them in—"

"You can't do that!" Miss Bancroft broke in as he trod through the great hall and up the stairs. "She's a young widow, and you're unmarried!"

Oh, for the love of God—"I didn't mean I'd sleep in there *with* her, you fool." He shifted her aunt's weight in his arms.

"That's not the point," she said, exasperation in her voice. "It's improper for her to sleep in an unmarried man's bedchamber, whether you're in it or not."

"She's right, my lord," Huggett said. "If word got round . . ."

"Word is not getting 'round' anywhere—I'll make sure of that." He halted in the hall that connected the bedchambers. "I have to put her *somewhere.* And it's the most comfortable room, not to mention the only one ready for guests."

"It's fine," said a thready voice. He looked down to find Mrs. Metcalf gazing weakly up at him. "Really, sir, it's most . . . kind of you."

"You see?" he told Huggett and Miss Bancroft. "Here's a lady with sense."

As he stalked into his bedchamber, he heard one of the lads whine, "Ellie, I need a privy!" The others began to clamor for the privy, too.

"I must see to your mother first," she began, "so if you'll just wait—"

"It's all right, miss," said the footman. "I'll take the wee ones to the privy."

"Thank you." She hurried into the room as Martin settled her aunt on the bed.

At once Miss Bancroft began to fuss over the woman, plumping up her pillow, pouring her water from a pitcher, making quite the show of playing the caring nurse. She wouldn't keep that up long; her sort got bored quickly.

"Which rooms shall I prepare for the young lady and the children?" Huggett asked him.

"I'm staying right here with my aunt," Miss Bancroft said firmly with a veiled look in his direction.

And suddenly he understood. "*That's* why you're being so missish about the sleeping arrangements." Though he generally ignored such reactions, today it tightened a cold knot in the pit of his belly. "You've figured out who I am."

"Who . . . who is he?" queried Mrs. Metcalf softly from the bed.

"Lord Thorncliff, that's all," Miss Bancroft said. "Mr. Huggett, would you please make sure my aunt drinks some water while I speak to his lordship in the hall?"

"Certainly, miss."

Without waiting for her, Martin strode out, then whirled on her as she joined him and closed the door. "That's it, isn't it?" he growled. "You've heard about the Black Baron, so you're afraid to leave her alone in my house."

"I'm afraid to leave her alone because she's ill," she said, a look of bewilderment on her face. "I only want to be there if she needs something."

He ignored her reasonable explanation, annoyed that she hadn't denied knowing what people called him. "Look here, Miss Bancroft, I'm not going to tiptoe around my own house just because you skittish society ladies have heard absurd stories about the dreadful Black Baron. I won't have my staff running after your little br- . . . cousins while you're quaking in your aunt's room, so you'll stay with the children wherever I have Huggett put you, blast it!"

Her eyes narrowed. "You think so, do you?"

That frosty tone should have given him warning, along with her lack of quaking, but he'd put up with enough today, and he wasn't about to quit while he had a full head of steam. "I know your sort is used to being fawned over and coddled and fed all manner of delicacies—"

"My *sort*?" she interrupted, her eyes turning a stormy, crystalline green.

"—but this is a crisis, and we'll have to make do with what we have, so I'll expect you to keep your petty complaints to yourself and not be taxing my staff with unnecessary requests. Otherwise, whatever nonsense you've heard about my being the Black Baron will be nothing to what you see of my true temper!"

"I shudder to think what *that* might be like," she murmured under her breath.

"What?" he growled, not sure he'd heard her right.

"Nothing. Are you quite done, sir?" Though her chin trembled, she didn't look terribly cowed, and that gave him pause.

"Er . . . well . . . yes."

"Fine. I shall do my best to fulfill your requirements." Her voice dripped sweetness, though he swore he heard sarcasm beneath the sugar. "Now if you'll excuse me, I must see to my aunt while I'm still *allowed* to stay with her."

Throwing her head back, she flounced back to the room. That's when it dawned on him that he'd perhaps been a bit too forceful in his statements. In the heat of his temper, he sometimes said things he regretted later.

But before he could soften his words, she swung open the door and paused dramatically in the doorway. "If you don't want people calling you the 'Black Baron,' sir, you might consider washing your face once in a while. I'm sure it would improve your reputation immeasurably."

He gaped at her as she swept into the room like some Egyptian queen. Washing his face? What the devil? A glance at the hall mirror reminded him of his sooty state. But surely she didn't think *that* was why they called him the Black—

Hell and blazes. She didn't know. Apparently she hadn't heard the vile rumors dogging him since Rupert's death. She thought he'd got his nickname because of the soot. *That's* why she hadn't quaked in her boots like other ladies.

He started for the room to explain himself, then halted as the footmen returned with the children. When they rushed past him with the wary expressions their cousin *ought* to have worn, it occurred to him that he didn't have to tell Miss Bancroft how he got his nickname.

Why should he? She would look at him differently, or worse yet, tell her aunt. Then he'd have two hysterical females on his hands, trying to escape his house for fear of their lives or their virtue.

As he stood there mulling the idea of *not* having to be the dreaded Black Baron for once, he overheard Huggett say, "You really don't have to stay in here with your aunt, miss. There's an adjoining chamber that belonged to his lordship's mother. Surely you and the little girl will be more comfortable there, and you can always come in to check on Mrs. Metcalf whenever you please without disturbing anyone. The lads can sleep in the green room. It's got a truckle bed."

"His lordship seems to think I must accompany the children everywhere," she said stiffly.

"It's all right—we can handle a few lads underfoot, and besides, the green room is right across the hall, and I daresay you'd hear them if they came out."

"Thank you, Mr. Huggett. That sounds like the perfect arrangement."

Her warm tone rubbed Martin raw, since she hadn't yet used it with *him*. And *he* was the one who'd rescued them in the first place.

"Now, I suggest we get these children out of their wet things," Huggett said.

"I'm afraid that's impossible," she retorted. "Their fresh clothes are in our trunks, and his lordship didn't see fit to have those brought from the other carriage." Her tone of resentment tested his temper anew.

He strode to the open door. The children flanked her like an army, and the little girl grabbed her hand as soon as he appeared in the doorway.

He ignored the children to focus on Miss High-and-Mighty Heiress. "Surely you packed separate bags for inns and such—"

"Just the trunks." She faced him, her smile chilly. "If you'll recall, I did tell you there were things we needed in them."

Thinking back to their short encounter, he grimaced. She *had* told him, but he'd been concentrating on getting her away from the blasted ice. And he'd assumed that the trunks were extra luggage. Why, he wasn't sure. Probably for the same reason he'd assumed that she knew of his reputation.

He began to wonder if he'd assumed too much.

When they all looked at him expectantly, even Huggett, he had to stifle an oath. "I'll send the footmen back for your trunks," he bit out. Then he modulated his tone. "Is there anything else you require?"

The cordial question seemed to catch her by surprise. Then a soft smile touched her lips. "Not at the moment, no. But thank you for asking, sir."

That smile thoroughly undid him. Three years had passed since the last time a young woman had smiled at him. It made him warm. Too warm. It made him notice her silky black hair and pleasing figure, and the lilt to her words that reminded him of her clear, high voice singing carols—

Hell and blazes. He couldn't be thinking like this about some heiress who didn't know who he was. Besides, there was more to a woman than a pleasing appearance, and he'd be surprised if anything lay in that head but the usual silliness and fascination with fashion. He didn't want a wife. He didn't *need* a wife.

"I'll go see about the trunks," he muttered.

Then he fled.

Chapter Three

Dear Charlotte,

Is your neighbor a man of good reputation? What is his profession? Is he married? Take care—many men prey on women alone by pandering to their concerns.

Your still-anxious cousin,
Michael

Ellie didn't see his lordship again that afternoon. Not that it mattered; she was much too busy to think about him. Shortly after he left, the doctor arrived, and a long discussion followed his examination of Aunt Alys. Thankfully her aunt's head injury wasn't as bad as it looked, but she had indeed broken a leg. The doctor recommended that she not be moved for at least a week.

That sent the children into hysterics, since it meant they would miss Christmas in Sheffield. Ellie and their mother had to make extravagant assurances of future treats and outings in order to calm them. At least their gifts were in the trunks, which had shown up after the doctor left, just as his lordship had promised.

Mr. Huggett, a man who proved as delightful as his employer was frightening, made sure that a messenger was sent on horseback to let her father know what had happened to them. But given the state of the roads and his being in Lancashire, there wasn't much Papa could do.

Ellie spent the rest of her afternoon settling everyone in, making sure her aunt was comfortable, and consulting with Mr. Huggett about the children's meals. By the time the butler came to fetch them to dinner, she felt quite comfortable with him.

That was the only reason she broached her difficult question. "Mr. Huggett," she said in a low voice so the children wouldn't hear as they scampered ahead of her. "Why is your master called 'the Black Baron'?"

The blend of panic and wariness on his face reminded her of Papa's whenever she asked an indelicate question. "I-I . . . well, you see, miss . . ." he began to stammer.

"It can't possibly be just because of the soot," she prompted helpfully.

"The soot? Ah, yes, the soot." He frowned as he escorted her downstairs. "Actually it's . . . er . . . because of his clothes. You may have noticed that he wears naught but black."

She *had* noticed. Still . . . "That's the only reason they call him that?"

"What else would it be?" he said blithely, though he didn't meet her eyes. "Incidentally the doctor told me that your aunt should take soft foods until we're certain her head injury isn't serious, so I took the liberty of having Cook . . ."

As he blathered on, she realized her question had struck a nerve. But it seemed rude to press him into gossiping about his employer. The man seemed oddly loyal to Lord Thorncliff, evidence that his lordship might not be quite as fearsome as he seemed.

There were other indications, too—the way the baron had accommodated them all despite his grumbling, the fact that he'd sent for a doctor *and* their trunks with great speed, his willingness to give up his own bedchamber. And when they entered the dining room, she had the most profound evidence of all.

Lord Thorncliff had bathed. The man who turned from the mantel to greet them bore no physical resemblance to the man who'd rescued them.

He wore the same sort of black coat, waistcoat, and cravat as before, except that these looked freshly washed and pressed. And his face . . . Goodness gracious, the Black Baron might have a beast's temper, but he had rather striking good looks. Indeed, he had much in common with Byron's pirate hero from *The Corsair,* a work that she persisted in enjoying despite its author's now shameful reputation. Lord Thorncliff was "Robust, but not Herculean" and his "dark eyebrow" did indeed shade "a glance of fire." And like the corsair, "Sun-burnt his cheek, his forehead high and pale,/The sable curls in wild profusion veil."

Except that the baron's hair wasn't actually black. It was a dark chestnut brown, with a bit of red glinting in the firelight. And now that he wasn't covered in soot—and she wasn't distracted by the children—she could see the true color of his eyes, too: a smoky gray, fringed with long dark lashes.

He wasn't classically handsome—his face was too angular and his chin too prominent for the sort of refined features that passed for handsome in London. But he was arresting enough to make her weak in the knees. It threw her entirely off guard. Attractive men intimidated her, and that was the last thing she needed around his lordship.

His improved appearance, however, had the opposite effect on Meg, for she went running up to examine him with great curiosity. "Who are *you*?"

"I'm Thorncliff. And who are you, young lady?"

Recognizing his voice from before, Meg shrank back to stuff her thumb into her mouth.

Ellie stepped forward to smooth over the awkwardness. "Forgive me, sir, I forgot that you don't yet know their names." She introduced the children, pleased to see that the boys behaved themselves like gentlemen for once.

When the footmen brought platters of food into the dining room to set on the sideboard, though, the boys went running to see what their fare would be.

"Oh, good, there's beef," Tim said as he gazed at a plump joint. "I'm famished near to death!"

"Look, Charlie, there's ham, too!" cried Percy from the other end. "And pudding."

"Perhaps we should sit," Lord Thorncliff muttered to her, "before the lads devour our dinner where they stand."

And so began their first evening in Thorncliff Hall. Hungrier than she'd realized, she was content to let the boys carry the conversation. They asked impertinent questions about the age of the house, if he had any toys, what streams he fished. His lordship fielded them with good grace, if not great enthusiasm.

Even Meg grew comfortable enough to venture a question. "Why were you so dirty today, sir?"

"Meg!" Ellie chided. "It's impolite to ask a person such a thing."

"Yes, indeed," their host said acidly. "You can gawk at people, make assumptions about them, and gossip about them to your friends, but don't ever ask someone a direct question. Not if you want to maintain the social order."

Was he chiding *her*, the surly devil? "You should listen to his lordship," she put in. "He's a master at the direct question." When his gaze shot to her, she added, "No, wait, it's the direct *order* that Lord Thorncliff has mastered. That's an entirely different skill, but apparently a well-developed one."

Mr. Huggett made a choking sound from where he stood near the sideboard, but Lord Thorncliff actually laughed. "Yes, it has taken me years to perfect it. Thank you for giving me the opportunity to try it out on someone other than the servants and the occasional coal miner."

"*That's* why you were covered in soot!" Percy exclaimed. "You work at a coal mine."

"I own a coal mine, actually. It belonged to my father, and then to my older brother when Father died. But I took over the ownership after—" Pain flashed over his face. "After Rupert died three years ago."

"I'm so sorry," Ellie murmured.

He nodded to acknowledge her condolences, then jerked his head toward Percy's plate and promptly changed the subject. "So, Master Percy, I see you're enjoying the beef."

That sent Percy into raptures about his dinner, but it made Ellie eye his lordship in a new light. Poor man, to lose his whole family so early in life. No wonder he was surly.

When silence fell on the table once more, Meg piped up with another question. "Where's your smelly greens, sir?"

The baron arched one eyebrow. "Smelly greens?"

"She means branches and that, for Christmas," Percy said. "You know, to hang on the banisters and mantels. Mama uses cedar. Meg doesn't like the smell."

"Ah."

When that was his only answer, Tim asked, "Well? Where are they?"

"Don't be rude," Ellie said. "I'm sure his lordship's servants will put up the greenery when the time is right." She couldn't imagine the man doing it himself.

"But Christmas will be here soon!" Tim shot his lordship a pleading glance. "Will you have them do it tomorrow?"

Lord Thorncliff tensed, but said in a perfectly measured voice, "I can't spare my staff for such things. There's few enough to do the work as it is." When a snort sounded, he glared at his butler. "Especially with the house full of guests. Isn't that right, Mr. Huggett?"

"Indeed, sir," Mr. Huggett said in a noncommittal voice.

Now that his lordship mentioned it, he did seem to lack an adequate staff. She'd seen no female servants, and only a few footmen and grooms, a cook, and Mr. Huggett. That might explain the poor condition of the manor.

Or the manor's sad state might be caused by the same thing that caused the small staff. A lack of money.

That must be it! It explained so much—his snide comments about her fortune, his simple black attire . . . his intense involvement with the mine he owned. Her father owned a silver mine, but *he* never came home covered in dirt. Only the men who worked close to the mine did that, and apparently his lordship felt some need to do so. Was his mine failing, perhaps?

And now they were taxing his stores by invading his home. That was surely another cause for his short temper. Like Byron's corsair, he was "Too firm to yield, and far too proud to stoop," unwilling to admit his poverty to the world.

She would have to explain that he needn't go into debt providing for them. They didn't require roast beef and ham—game hens would do them perfectly well. Or she could find some delicate way of offering payment for their lodgings and food. It wasn't right to take his hospitality and not do something in exchange.

"Do you have horses, sir?" Percy asked. "You must, for I saw your groom. Could we go riding tomorrow?"

"Not in this weather," Ellie interjected, not wanting to put his lordship in the awkward position of having to admit he couldn't afford a stable full of horses. "I doubt your mother will want you riding when there's ice on the ground."

His lordship sat back in his chair and wiped his mouth with a napkin. "But when the ice has melted, I have no objection to your making use of my stable. I don't have enough mounts to go around, but you could take turns."

"What's in that stone barn Percy and I spotted out the back window—" Tim asked.

"Stay away from that barn!" Lord Thorncliff snapped, his countenance abruptly darkening. When he caught her raising an eyebrow at him, he added, "This is one direct order I expect to be obeyed, Miss Bancroft."

"As you wish, sir," she said in a caustic voice, but the boys weren't so compliant, especially after his unexpected vehemence.

"Why?" Percy asked. "What do you keep in there?"

"Nothing that concerns *you,*" his lordship growled.

"Is it where you keep your hunting rifles?" Tim said excitedly.

"No, blast it all!" His chair scraped the floor as he rose to his full height. "Don't go anywhere near it! Because if you do, I swear I'll take a switch to the lot of you! Is that understood?"

No one had ever threatened to lift a hand to her aunt's coddled boys. They gaped at him, utterly incapable of answering.

"For goodness' sake, Lord Thorncliff—" she began.

"Is that *understood*?" he repeated, pounding his fists on the table.

The boys visibly jumped. Then their heads bobbed furiously.

Meg burst into tears.

That seemed to jerk Lord Thorncliff out of his fit of temper. He stared at her as if seeing her for the first time, an almost comical expression of horror passing over his features. Then he let out a low curse and stormed from the room.

"Ellieee!" Meg cried, holding up her arms.

Ellie immediately went to sweep her up, her heart thundering in her ears after that violent display from the man she'd been feeling sorry for. He'd banished *that* impulse. How dared he threaten the children?

"I don't like the mean man!" Meg sobbed. "I-I want to g-go home!"

"We'll go soon," Ellie assured her as Mr. Huggett hurried over. "I promise."

"You must forgive my master, madam," Mr. Huggett said in a low voice. "I am sure he did not intend to alarm you, but he is very . . . particular about the barn."

"Yes, he made that quite clear," she snapped. "Though I don't see why he had to be so forceful about it."

"No, madam, you are right. I shall speak to him."

The butler then launched into soothing them all, offering the children desserts, accompanying them upstairs to sit with their mother for a while, helping Ellie prepare them for bed even though that wasn't something butlers generally did.

But although Mr. Huggett offered plenty of suggestions for what the children could do to occupy themselves the next day and answered the boys' questions about the coal mine, when it came to his employer, he was as mysterious as a sphinx. She'd never seen a servant less inclined to gossip. Any question about the baron or his barn was met with "You must ask his lordship," and any sharp comment about his lordship's temper gained the response, "He is under a strain, but I am sure he will be better tomorrow."

She wasn't so sure. Nor was she entirely certain that Mr. Huggett would speak to the baron as promised—or that if he did, it would do any good. But after watching Meg cry herself to sleep and the boys lie whispering together in their beds, probably plotting a secret mission to uncover the magical mysteries of the stone barn, she decided she'd better not leave the matter to the butler.

She wasn't about to let their bullying host take a switch to her cousins. Even if she had to beard the lion in his den.

Martin paced the floor in his study, shedding clothes as he went. First he tossed his constrictive coat over the chair by the fire, then dropped his choking cravat on his desk. It had been years since he'd had to dress formally for dinner, but after making such a spectacle of himself that afternoon, he'd wanted to show that he *could* behave with some semblance of propriety.

And it had seemed worth it at first, when Miss Bancroft had looked at him with a clear feminine interest. After that, even the children's endless questions hadn't plagued him overmuch, not while Miss Bancroft had been offering him her pert comments and occasional soft smile.

Though he'd reminded himself that she was only being nice to him because she didn't know the gossip, he couldn't help enjoying it. Or her endearing habit of pushing up her spectacles every few moments. Or the sweet way she chewed on her plump lower lip whenever something startled her.

Like his outburst at the end. He winced. *That* had made her eye him with horror. You'd have thought he'd threatened to murder her cousins, not merely take them in hand.

He hadn't meant to lose his temper, but the idea of those children gamboling in the barn where he did his experiments chilled his soul.

Not that his threats had helped. The lads were still curious—he'd seen it in their eyes. Tomorrow he'd have to pack everything up before they decided to start exploring. He couldn't be here to keep an eye on them—this close to Christmas and Boxing Day, he had several duties to perform involving his estate. And the lads wouldn't take his stricture seriously. Boys their age never did. *He* hadn't.

But girls were another matter.

He groaned, remembering the cherub's tears. He hadn't meant to startle her, poor lass. Nor Miss Bancroft, either.

Another groan escaped him. Hell and blazes, he'd ruined everything. Miss Bancroft would have no more soft smiles for *him*.

It was probably just as well. Eventually she would learn about the gossip and have the same reaction as everyone else. Even if she didn't, he couldn't allow a woman in his life. So he was better off *not* growing to like her too much. Thinking about her too much.

"My lord, might I have a word with you?"

He nearly jumped out of his skin at the sound of that lilting voice. Did the woman read minds, too? And what did she mean by sneaking up on him in his own study—he'd retreated to this wing of the house for a reason, blast it!

"What is it, Miss Bancroft?" he said through gritted teeth, hoping his tone would put her off from what was sure to be a lecture.

It only seemed to embolden her. She actually entered the room and closed the door. "I need to speak to you about the children."

"So do I." Might as well have it out before someone got hurt.

He faced her, then caught his breath.

She looked entirely different without her spectacles, more approachable and less like a schoolmistress. Though not a raving beauty, she had wonderful eyes, and her skin held a youthful glow that made him think of peaches in spring—soft, tender peaches a man could sink his teeth into. And her lush figure—

"Where are your spectacles?" he bit out, to take his mind off what he wanted to *do* to that figure of hers.

"Where is your coat?" she countered, reminding him that he was dressed inappropriately for a gentleman alone with a lady.

He resisted the urge to make himself more presentable. After all, he hadn't asked her to invade his study. "It's where I always keep it when I'm not expecting company. Tell me, do you even *need* the spectacles?"

She gazed at him, perplexed. "I wouldn't wear them if I didn't."

"You're not wearing them now."

"True." A sigh escaped her. "The fact is . . . well . . . I thought it might be easier to talk to you if I couldn't see you."

That was *not* the answer he'd expected. She'd seemed so sure of herself this afternoon. And how could leaving off her spectacles make it easier to talk to him? "Do you do that with every man or just me?"

"Only men who make me nervous."

He made her nervous? Of course he did. He made most women nervous.

"But that isn't what I came to discuss," she went on.

"I didn't think it was," he said dryly.

"First of all, I realize that we've inconvenienced you greatly."

"You have no idea," he muttered under his breath.

A fetching pink color tinged her cheeks. "I assure you that my father will be happy to repay you for any expenditures on our behalf—the food and the doctor and whatever other expenses you may incur."

"I don't need your father's money." The idea of her trying to *pay* for his hospitality sparked his temper.

"Of course not, but it's only fair that you be compensated for—"

"I don't want your money, blast it! This isn't an inn, Miss Bancroft, where you place your orders and get what you pay for. You'll have to make do with what I can offer. And if you can't, feel free to leave whenever you wish."

A stiff smile tightened her lips. "You know perfectly well we can't do that."

"Then you'll have to put up with my inadequate hospitality."

"I didn't say it was inadequate!" Her expression showed sheer exasperation. "Goodness, you are so prickly. 'You would rouse to anger a heart of stone,' as Sophocles says."

He blinked. "You're quoting *Sophocles*? What sort of heiress are you?"

"I happen to read a lot," she said defensively. "Poetry mostly. Which you would have found out for yourself if you'd conversed with us at dinner instead of blustering and shouting." She crossed her arms over her chest. "That is exactly why people gossip about you. Has it occurred to you that they might call you the Black Baron because of your black temper?"

If she only knew. "Thank you for the commentary on my character, Miss Bancroft. Now, if you'll excuse me—"

"I'm not finished," she said blithely. "As I was saying, we're very grateful for your taking us in under difficult circumstances." She paused meaningfully.

"But?"

"But it does not give you permission to alarm the children."

He hated it when she was right. "I wasn't trying to alarm them," he said testily. "I was trying to make sure they don't go near my barn, something *you* might consider helping me with."

"For goodness' sake, what's so important about your precious barn?"

"It's full of explosives."

"Explosives!" Her eyes widened. "Why on earth would you keep explosives in your barn?"

"I've been developing a fuse to make them safer for the mine. It requires experimentation with black powder and sulfur and the like, all of which are highly dangerous."

"But why *here*? Why not do it there?"

"Because too many people have access to things at the mine. There's too much chance for a visitor or a stranger to get hurt." As Rupert had. "I can keep a better eye on things here. My servants know they risk their positions if they go anywhere near that barn or let anyone else near it." He scowled at her. "But your cousins may be a problem, given how unpredictable boys are."

That seemed to dampen her fire a bit. "If you would just explain to them about the explosives—"

He snorted. "Right. Tell a lot of curious lads that there's a barn full of exciting chemicals next door. That would be like setting a match to the powder. Didn't you see how your cousin's eyes lit up when he asked if I kept rifles in there? Don't you know *anything* about boys that age?"

"No, I don't!" Her tone held desperation. "I'm not used to taking care of them!"

She had a point. According to Huggett, their nurse had been clever enough to escape corralling the rambunctious cubs during the holiday. He could hardly expect their rich cousin to step into her shoes with any degree of competency.

"Then here's a little lesson for you," he said. "Boys of that age enjoy blowing things up. *I* certainly did. It's how I got interested in explosives in the first place. And if your rascal cousins find out I've got something as fascinating as black powder in my barn, it'll be impossible to keep them out."

She sniffed. "Well, now that you've roused their curiosity, they're sure to attempt it anyway. Keeping them in the dark is as bad as telling them the truth."

"Then give them a lie, blast it! Tell them whatever you like—I don't care. Just keep them away from that barn!"

"I'll do my best," she said with a weary shake of her head, "but I can't make any promises. They have minds of their own sometimes."

"Fine. But if they follow their minds into my barn, I will tan their hides."

"You will not!" she protested. "You have no right!"

"That won't stop me."

She planted her fists on her shapely hips. "If you lay one hand on those boys, I swear I'll make you regret it."

"Really?" he said, choking down a laugh. With her

green eyes snapping at him and her bosom shaking beneath her low-cut gown, she looked like an avenging angel. Or at least an avenging dairymaid. "And what exactly will you do?"

Clearly she hadn't thought that far. "I'll . . . I'll . . . tell my father," she said stoutly.

"Go ahead." He stalked toward her. "Tell him that I disciplined his reckless nephews to keep them from killing themselves. I'll wager he takes *my* side in the matter. He knows what explosives can do."

She paled as he neared her. "He still won't approve."

"Let him disapprove—that won't change how I behave. He can thrash me senseless, for all I care."

"Don't be ridiculous. Papa is nearly fifty—he can't possibly thrash you."

"Then what do you hope to achieve by tattling on me to him?" He came right up to where she stood before the closed door and loomed over her in a deliberate attempt to intimidate her. In this one matter, he meant to have his way.

Straightening her spine, she stared him down. "Step back, sir."

He leaned one arm against the door. "Or what? You'll tell your papa?"

"I'll do this." She promptly kicked him in the shin.

"Ow!" he cried as he pushed back from the door and bent to rub the sore spot. The chit had quite a kick, blast it.

"*That* is for acting like a beast," she said primly. "And if you continue to do so, to me *or* the children, I shall kick the other shin. Just see if I don't."

Turning away, she reached for the door handle, but he

caught her by the arm before she could leave. He swung her around, ignoring her expression of outrage, then swiftly bracketed her body between his two arms to trap her against the door.

"So I'm behaving like a beast, am I?" he bit out. "Very well, since you refuse to be sensible about your cousins, you might as well kick my other shin. Consider it an advance payment for when I am forced to tan those boys' hides because they've ventured where they shouldn't!"

He hadn't meant to lose his temper again, but he'd never liked being threatened, and certainly not by some society chit.

"If you don't move back, sir, I *will* kick you again," she retorted, though her cheeks grew flushed and her voice had lost some of its fervor.

Suddenly he realized just how close she was. Suddenly he was painfully aware of how full were the breasts that rose and fell between them, how close were the hips pressed to his. In that moment he didn't care about the boys or the barn or her father. Especially when she chewed nervously on her lower lip, her plump lower lip that tempted him to taste and touch and sample its sweetness.

His gaze fixed there, and his breath quickened . . . along with his blood and pulse and everything else in his body that responded to her soft, warm flesh.

"Go ahead and kick me," he said in a guttural voice. "You're probably going to anyway after I do this."

Then he lowered his head to kiss her full on the lips.

Chapter Four

Dear Cousin,

My neighbor is a respectable married attorney with three children. But if you find those credentials insufficient, you're always welcome to look in on me yourself.

Curious about your identity as always,

Charlotte

Ellie was shocked into immobility. An attractive, virile man was sealing his mouth to hers. And he wasn't after her fortune.

That had never happened. For that matter, only two men had *ever* kissed her, and neither kiss had been like this. Warm. Searching. Thorough.

Very, very thorough. His lips played over hers with the heady assurance of a man who knew exactly what he was doing. And to whom. What an intoxicating thought! A man was kissing her because he wanted to.

No, that couldn't possibly be the reason.

She drew back to search his face for an explanation. "Why are you—"

"I don't know," he said, clearly flustered, though his eyes had turned a molten silver that made her heart race. "You just looked like you needed kissing. And I wanted to be the one to do it."

His gaze trailed down to her mouth, and he swallowed. Then he cupped her chin in his hand, running his thumb along her lower lip. "I'm afraid you'll have to delay kicking me in the shin a little longer."

"What?" That was all she managed before he was kissing her again.

Only this time he did it differently, his thumb pressing her lips apart so he could dart his tongue inside, first warily, then more boldly. It was the most thrilling thing a man had ever done to her.

Her bones wobbled, then liquefied. If he hadn't been holding her against the door, she would have slid right down it. Which left her only one choice—throw her arms about his neck so she didn't fall.

No wonder Robert Burns spoke of being "by passion driven." She seemed to be vaulting into the unknown without a rope.

When her hands locked about his neck, he uttered a sound low in his throat, then dragged her closer, pressing his weight into her, engulfing her with his heat. She could feel the rich warmth even through his lawn shirt. His tongue did heady, wicked things to her mouth, delving and plunging and making her giddy with the pleasure of it—

"My lord?" came a voice so close it sounded as if it were right at her head. That was followed by a knock that made them both jump. "Are you in there?"

Mr. Huggett! Oh, dear.

Lord Thorncliff muttered an oath under his breath, but didn't move away. She didn't mind. She rather liked the feel of his body plastered to hers. It was cozy. And very intimate, especially when his hot gaze pinned her while his hand trailed to her ribs, then her hips, in a caress that left small fires blazing wherever it passed.

"What is it, Huggett?" he asked in a throaty voice.

"I told Miss Bancroft I would speak to you—" the butler began.

"It's all right." A faint smile touched his lips. "She already did herself."

"But I promised her—"

"Good *night,* Huggett," Lord Thorncliff said firmly. "I'm sure whatever you have to say can wait until morning."

"Very well, sir," came the butler's reply, followed by footsteps retreating.

Silence reigned. Painfully conscious of how close they'd come to being discovered in a compromising position, Ellie slid from between the door and Lord Thorncliff.

The reckless kiss had astonished her. Flattered her. *Confused* her, especially having come from the churlish baron. She couldn't look at him or catch her breath, and her belly churned alarmingly, making her feel jumbled up inside.

What was a proper lady to say after a man kissed her senseless?

Actually she wasn't supposed to let him kiss her senseless in the first place.

"Forgive me, Miss Bancroft," he said. "I should not have . . . that is, I know it was impertinent of me to . . ." He trailed off awkwardly.

"It's all right." At least he felt as strange about it as she did. "I didn't mind."

"There's that, at least."

The odd statement made her glance at him. He suddenly looked very young to her. "How old are you?"

The question seemed to startle him. "Twenty-seven. Why?"

"I thought you were . . . older," she said inanely. "But . . . well . . . you're not terribly much older than I am."

A shutter darkened his features. "I'm not looking for a wife," he said bluntly.

After what they'd just shared, the words were a slap in the face.

She must have recoiled, for he cursed, then added, "That didn't come out right."

"Still, I understood it." Dragging the remnants of her dignity about her, she forced a smile. "Fortunately I'm not looking for a husband." She had to escape before he realized how he'd upset her. "With that being the case, I'd better go."

"Miss Bancroft, I didn't mean to imply that you aren't—"

"I'll see you at breakfast, sir," she said before he could make it any worse than it already was. Ignoring his muttered curse, she hurried out.

She managed to restrain her tears until she reached her room, but had to pause outside the door once they started leaking out. Meg generally slept through anything, but she mustn't awaken to find Ellie crying her eyes out. It would mean excuses and secrets no five-year-old could keep. And Ellie would die before she allowed Lord Unpredictable to learn how his cold statement had wounded her.

Curling her hands into fists, she fought for control over her wildly surging emotions. *I'm not looking for a wife.*

Of course he wasn't. Not a plain wife like her, anyway. She leaned against the door. A titled gentleman could have his pick of the ladies, foul temper or no.

Why bother to kiss her, anyway? She thought back to their conversation. Oh, of course. He'd probably figured it would distract her from his threat to punish the boys. It had, too.

Given his probable financial difficulties, she should be glad he hadn't schemed beyond that. If he'd allowed Huggett to discover them in an embrace, he'd have accomplished what no fortune hunter had managed. And that would be disastrous. Truly.

Tears stung her eyes again. It was a pity that she didn't *feel* as if she'd made a narrow escape. But who could blame her? He was the first man to rouse her desire.

A disturbing thought wafted through her mind—was it possible that desire could compensate for the disadvantage of having a man marry her for her money?

Don't be absurd. Nothing compensates for that, and you know it.

Then why did it hurt so much that he'd rejected her? She ought to be glad.

A sound from the stairwell startled her. She couldn't stand out here all night, nursing her wounded feelings. Goodness knew they'd been battered before; she would survive this time, too.

Slipping inside, she undressed, donned her night rail, and joined Meg in bed. The dear girl cuddled up to her when she lay down, and Ellie clung to her for comfort.

But even Meg's sweet smell couldn't make Ellie forget what had happened. If not for his mortifying comment, Lord Thorncliff would fit her fantasy image of a husband. He was certainly dangerous and wild. Though she wasn't sure about the poetry in his soul, there was plenty of poetry in his kisses. She lay awake for hours, replaying every moment.

Even after she fell into a fitful sleep, she dreamed she was a ragweed growing among lilacs. When Lord Thorncliff came to pluck flowers, he trod upon her without noticing, and all she could do was lie there crushed.

After a night of such misery, she was awakened far too early, when the boys rushed in shortly after dawn. "Meg! Ellie! You have to look outside!" they cried as they danced about the bed. "The snow is everywhere!"

Tim tugged on her arm. "Come on, get up! We want to make snowmen!"

"Go away," she groused, burying her head in the pillow. She was *not* in the mood for her cousins.

They didn't care. They bounced on the bed until Meg kicked them crossly. The ensuing scuffle meant there would be no more possibility of sleep.

The children wanted to go right out, but she insisted upon their washing up and stopping in to say good morning to their mother before she made them dress warmly. After that, only Mr. Huggett, with his promises of hot muffins and treacle, could tempt them to stay inside any longer.

As the boys gulped their breakfast, Mr. Huggett bent to say in a low voice, "I understand that you spoke to his lordship about the stone barn last night."

Fighting a blush, she rose and led him out of the children's earshot. "I did indeed. He explained to me about his . . . er . . . experiments. Unfortunately I fear that his reaction at dinner merely heightened the boys' curiosity."

"Perhaps the footmen and I should aid you in keeping them entertained."

"No, Lord Thorncliff made it very clear he can't spare any of you," she said. "Besides, we're already taxing his meager resources to their utmost, and I wouldn't wish to make that any worse."

"His meager resources?" Mr. Huggett said with surprise.

"It's all right." She patted his arm. "I assure you none of the servants have been gossiping, and I understand why you can't discuss such things with strangers. But I drew my own conclusions. The lack of staff, the condition of the manor . . . clearly your employer is having financial difficulties."

Mr. Huggett closed his gaping mouth, then gave her a considering glance. "As you say, it would be wrong of me to discuss the matter."

"I understand. That's why I spent last night considering how to manage the children by myself." During those periods when she was trying *not* to remember Lord Thorncliff's thickly muscled arms and poetic kisses. "Since you and the staff can't be spared to gather the usual Yuletide greenery, I thought the children and I could do it. It would be a way to repay his lordship for his kindness while also keeping the boys out of trouble."

"Gathering greenery!" Mr. Huggett exclaimed, a strange gleam in his eye. "What an excellent idea, the perfect pastime for the young gentlemen."

She nodded. "We've done it for the last few years, so we know what to gather and how. The boys climb trees like little monkeys. I've already spoken to my aunt about it, and she heartily approved. I had some concerns about their handling an axe, but she says Percy has done it before, and his friend Charlie seems sturdy enough. I will need some items from you, however."

"Certainly! We have the axes, of course, and you'll require a cart if you're to gather a great many branches." He lifted one eyebrow. "You *were* planning to bring enough for the entire manor, weren't you?"

"Oh yes, as much greenery as we can find."

"Be sure to strew it everywhere," he said, with an odd glee in his voice. "We could use a touch of the season around here."

"We'll make it very nice. A grand house as lovely as this deserves no less."

He eyed her closely. "So you like the place? You don't find it gloomy?"

"Gloomy! Certainly not." She cast a quick glance around the great hall, with its oak-paneled walls, its aging tapestry hanging at one end, and its weathered floors. "It reminds me of a drawing I once saw of the Royal Palace of Hatfield, where Queen Elizabeth loved to stay. It's the sort of ancient English house that makes me think of glorious days of yore."

Then she colored. "Forgive me, I read a great deal of poetry. Sometimes it seeps into my conversation."

"Nothing wrong with that—it gives you a certain sparkle."

She laughed. "I don't know about that."

"Trust me, Miss Bancroft." With a genial smile, he led her back to the table. "You mustn't let the master's grumbling dim your spirits. You are the brightest thing to have landed on our doorstep in a long time, and you should enjoy yourself. You *and* the children."

"Very well," she said, feeling less melancholy. "I shall certainly try."

* * *

It had taken Martin half the day to pack away the chemicals, black powder, and flints he used in his experiments. It had taken him far longer to stop thinking of Miss Bancroft and her wonder of a mouth. Even riding to the mine to make sure the weather hadn't created problems for the men hadn't driven her from his thoughts.

With a groan, he washed up at the basin in the mine manager's office. But though he splashed icy water on his face, it didn't wash the taste of her from his lips or freeze the warmth that rose in his loins whenever he thought of how yielding she had been, an irresistible blend of fire and innocence. And if he could actually court her—

Court her! He must be mad. He couldn't court anyone, certainly not now, when he was so close to hitting upon the right formula for what he called his "safe fuses." Even after he developed the right mix of powder and the mechanism for conveying it to the explosive, it could take months to test it under different conditions. No woman should be around during such experimentation. It was too dangerous, too distracting.

Besides, Miss Bancroft still didn't know that marriage to him could brand her for life in society. Marrying her would only lend fuel to the fire, too—they would say he married her for her fortune, just as they said he killed his brother for the title and property.

Never mind that he didn't want the title or need her fortune. He didn't follow society's rules for gentlemen, so that gave them excuse enough to gossip about him. God only knew why *she* wasn't put off by his lack of courtly manners.

Or perhaps she was. Certainly his idiot comments after kissing her last night hadn't endeared her to him, judging from how the color had leached from her face. Perhaps he *should* tell her about the gossip to push her over the edge. She would retreat to a safe distance, removing temptation from his reach and ending any chance of unwise intimacies.

That didn't appeal to him, either.

Cursing himself for caring, he donned his clean waistcoat and coat, then headed for home. Darkness had fallen hours ago. He was late for dinner. Not that he minded—he'd rather avoid sharing another meal with Miss Bancroft. She was too potent a temptation, blast her.

He rode up in front and handed his horse to the groom. The smell of fresh-cut cedar assailed him as he neared the entrance. He blinked. There were branches hung over his door. When and how had *those* got there?

Huggett. Of course. His infernal butler had ignored his orders! Just wait until he got his hands on the miscreant. Having strangers in the house had emboldened the man to greater heights of impertinence than usual, and he wouldn't stand for it!

Throwing the door open, Martin tramped inside. "Huggett! Get out here, you wretch! You know damned well what I think of this Christmas humbuggery!"

A voice piped up from the window. "Why do you call it humbuggery, sir?"

He whirled to find a dark-haired lad standing there alone, staring at him with wide eyes. It wasn't a Metcalf; it was the friend. Charlie Dicks or Dickers or some such.

He could hardly tell the boy the truth—that anything to do with Christmas reminded him how he'd failed Rupert.

Then he glimpsed a burst of red color over the lad's head. God help him, the branches over the front door weren't the only ones. Greenery adorned every archway and window and mantel in the great hall. Whorled knots of it dotted the dining table, surrounding thick yellow Yule candles that, according to tradition, weren't to be lit until Christmas Eve. He walked about in a daze, noting how the branches were braided together, entwined with bright red ribbons that erupted at the ends into flamboyant bows.

This wasn't the work of Huggett. Only a woman could do this. One woman in particular, to be exact.

"What do you think?" came the hesitant voice of his tormentor, who'd apparently entered the room while he was looking it over.

Praying that she hadn't heard what he'd said to young Charlie, he faced her. Then he caught his breath, his blood jumping into a frenzy.

She stood surrounded by the other children, ablaze in a gown of fashionable red satin that displayed her lush breasts more temptingly than any Christmas treat.

She didn't seem to notice him gaping at her delicious bosom, for she babbled on. "Mr. Huggett was kind enough to let us into your attic where the Christmas ribbons and such are stored. Fortunately there were even some unused Yule candles. I suppose you stored them from a previous Christmas."

He forced his gaze back to her face. "My mother probably did. My brother always got new ones from town, and I . . . er . . . haven't used any since . . . well . . ."

"His lordship says Christmas is all a humbug," Charlie tattled.

As a stricken look crossed her face, he corrected hastily, "I didn't say that. Well, not *exactly* that. And I was referring to Mr. Huggett's habit of letting his other duties lapse so he can make the manor more festive. I didn't realize that Miss Bancroft—"

"We didn't use the footmen or Mr. Huggett, I swear," she assured him, her hurt expression fading. She pushed up the spectacles that had slipped charmingly down her nose. "The boys and I did it all—went into the woods to cut the greens, found the ribbons and candles, and hung the branches. The only thing Mr. Huggett did was direct us where to look. And provide us with a cart."

"And let you into the attic," he said dryly. He'd wager Huggett had been behind it all.

But his anger was already waning. Oddly enough, the greenery reminded him less of that horrible Christmas when Rupert had been killed than it did his childhood holidays, when Mother and Father had still been present at their Christmas feasts. The bright memory of it burst through his senses, and he had to turn away to hide the quick pain of loss that followed.

"Well, you did an excellent job," he choked out. "It's spectacular."

"So you do like it," she said, the whole tenor of her voice changing.

He nodded, unable to speak. That freed the children to swarm about him, pointing out what parts they'd done, how Percy had chopped the branches with an axe, and how Tim and Charlie had braided them under "Ellie's" instruction.

Although he'd heard them call her Ellie before, he hadn't realized how well it suited her. "Miss Bancroft" or even "Elinor" sounded very elegant and high society. "Ellie" sounded like a fresh-faced country lass that a man could tumble in the hay.

By God, he mustn't think of her like that!

"Is everyone ready for dinner?" asked Huggett from the doorway.

Martin shot Miss Bancroft a surprised glance.

"We didn't want to eat without *you,*" she explained. "That would be rude."

Rude or not, no one had ever held dinner back for him. He didn't count the trays Huggett made sure were waiting in his study once he got around to ending his work for the day. That wasn't dinner—that was filling his belly.

Dinner was what his mother had presided over every night until her death ten years ago. And even she had said that if he wasn't at the table when it was served, he wouldn't get any. That had happened often enough, since he'd been the sort of contrary child to absorb himself so fully in his scientific experiments that he lost track of the time.

"Sir? Shall I have the footmen serve?" Huggett asked.

Martin looked at his butler, this time noticing how nervously he stood watching for his employer's reaction to the greenery. Huggett's question went beyond the matter of dinner. The man was asking for approval. He knew perfectly well he'd overstepped his bounds by encouraging Miss Bancroft and the children. Now he wanted absolution. The question was, would Martin give it to him?

He had to. Because chiding Huggett would mean chastising Miss Bancroft, and Martin couldn't bear to wound her again.

Forcing a smile to his face, he walked to the head of the festive table. "Yes, Huggett, have the footmen serve. We're ready to dine."

Chapter Five

Dear Charlotte,

Be careful, my dear. One day when you least expect it, I may indeed show up on your doorstep and reveal myself to be nothing at all as you imagine.

Your cousin,
Michael

Over the next two days, Ellie noticed that she and Lord Thorncliff had muddled their way through to a sort of truce. He seemed less prickly. She couldn't attribute it to their decorating, because Charlie insisted that his lordship had called *that* "Christmas humbuggery." The man had said something similar about the caroling when he'd rescued them. Clearly he had a peculiar dislike of the season.

Yet he'd not only tolerated their efforts, but was trying to be friendly in his own fashion. Although he spent his days elsewhere while she and the children explored his extensive grounds, he joined them for dinner at night.

He even sat with them afterward in the parlor with the walls painted to resemble walnut paneling. He would go through the newspapers, or watch the children play charades, or listen to her read aloud from Byron's *The Siege of Corinth.* Sometimes he actually read to the children himself.

But the camaraderie ended after she brought the children up to bed. Then he disappeared, and they reverted to being strangers again. Even if she returned to the parlor, he didn't. Sometimes, as she read alone or sat with Aunt Alys in her room, she wondered if she'd imagined their amazing kiss.

On their fourth night at Thorncliff Hall, with Christmas Eve coming in two days, the children suggested that they play snapdragon.

"Are you mad?" his lordship said. "It's out of the question. There will be no burning bowls of brandy in *my* house."

"It's not that bad, you know," she put in, though his response didn't surprise her. "If you take the proper precautions—"

"The best precaution is not to play it at all. Such humbuggery gets people killed."

"Snapdragon?" Percy said skeptically. "It's but a parlor game, sir. Our mother lets us play it every year."

"Then your mother is a fool." When the children bristled at that, he scowled and rose to his feet. "Forgive me, I'm not fit company this evening."

And with that abrupt pronouncement, he left.

What on earth? She would have thought that a man who experimented with explosives would find snapdragon harmless, if not boring. It certainly didn't get people killed. That was ridiculous!

As she stared after him, Percy turned to her. "Can we play it *now*?"

"No, indeed. It would be rude to go behind his lordship's back in his own house."

That ended the discussion. But later, after the children were tucked in and Ellie sat on her aunt's bed relating the day's events, that last encounter stuck in her mind. She wanted to understand why he was so prickly and unpredictable.

So she asked her aunt a question she'd been reluctant to voice until now, having not wanted to alarm Aunt Alys unnecessarily. "Have you ever heard of a gentleman called 'the Black Baron'?"

Her aunt let out a heavy sigh. "I wondered how long it would take for you to hear of our host's reputation."

"You *knew*?"

"Of course. One of the children mentioned the nickname, and I remembered the rumors. At first I was concerned, but he's behaved nothing but kindly to us. In my opinion that speaks louder than any gossip."

"Exactly," Ellie said. "Just because he's the most cantankerous fellow in Yorkshire is no reason for people to despise him. He may sometimes be rude and leap to conclusions about people with absolutely no reason, but—"

"You like him."

"Yes." She caught her aunt's knowing expression. "No! I-I mean, not how you think. I'm merely grateful to him for giving us aid, that's all." As her aunt's eyebrows arched higher, she protested, "He's not my sort, much too uneven in temper. Besides, any man who thinks Christmas is humbuggery isn't suitable marriage material." Even if he *were* interested in marriage. Which he wasn't. But she wasn't about to reveal that embarrassing truth to her aunt.

"You can't blame him for not liking Christmas, given that his brother died during the season."

"What? How did you know *that*?"

"Everyone knows. The man was killed in a mine explosion."

"Oh, dear." *That* was the reason Lord Thorncliff disliked Christmas—because it reminded him of a painful time. Her stomach roiled—how awful of her to have pursued her plans without a care for his opinion! What he must have thought, have felt . . .

But wait, surely Mr. Huggett had known. Why hadn't he stopped them?

"That's why they call our host the Black Baron," her aunt went on. "Some people hold him responsible for the accident."

"Why?" Ellie asked. "What happened?"

"No one's really sure, which is why people invented nasty stories to explain it. It seems his lordship's late brother hosted a house party here at Christmas, and the guests witnessed the two men arguing. Then the present Lord Thorncliff stormed out and went to the mine, followed by his older brother. Some time later, an explosion occurred. And that was the last of Rupert Thorncliff."

"That doesn't mean our host is responsible." She couldn't have mistaken the abject grief on Lord Thorncliff's face at the mention of his brother's death.

"No, of course not, and an inquiry exonerated him of any blame. But he did inherit everything as a result, which is why some said that the younger brother took the opportunity to gain the title and the property."

"I don't believe it," Ellie said stoutly.

"Neither do I."

Ellie's righteous indignation grew the more she thought about it. "Why, he doesn't even seem to care about the title. He's certainly shown no interest in lording it over people. He speaks of society with disgust."

"I think that's part of the problem. His brother was a sociable fellow, loved and admired for his gregarious manner and generosity to his friends. Whereas from what I understand, Lord Thorncliff was much as he is now. People tend to side with the people they like, even if it flies in the face of logic."

"But they shouldn't spread gossip without knowing the circumstances."

"I agree."

"The Black Baron, indeed. That's just *cruel*."

"Absolutely."

"They ought to be ashamed of themselves!"

"Certainly." Her aunt's lips tightened as if she fought a smile. "But I don't know why you care if you're 'merely grateful to him for giving us aid.'"

Ellie dropped her gaze. Her aunt saw far too much. "I just don't like to think of anyone being branded a villain wrongly." Giving an exaggerated yawn, she rose, too full of emotion to endure more probing. "I think I'll retire now. The children want to hunt for a Yule log tomorrow, and that will be exhausting."

"Sleep well, my dear," her aunt said softly.

Ellie pressed a kiss to her cheek, then headed into the next room. But as she settled into bed beside Meg, the mystery of the previous baron's death continued to absorb her.

The very idea of Lord Thorncliff arranging his brother's death was so unfair! She couldn't believe it. She wouldn't believe it. Nonetheless, she spent a restless night in lurid imaginings that only ended when she fell into a dreamless sleep in the wee hours of the morn.

When she awakened, she realized two things at once. She'd slept later than usual. And the house was quiet. Too quiet, given that the boys generally woke at dawn. Even Meg was missing, although a peek into Aunt Alys's room revealed her curled up with her mother, having a story read to her.

"Where are the boys?" Ellie asked.

Aunt Alys looked up. "Outside, I imagine. Percy said that's where they were going while they waited for breakfast. I told them to let you sleep."

Had the boys headed into the woods alone? Surely not. It wasn't like them to go so far without breakfast. But a niggling sense that something was wrong made her rush to the window in her room that overlooked the woods in back. As she threw open the casement, she heard a roar that was unmistakably his lordship's.

Oh, no, the stone barn. A quick glance showed the boys frozen in their tracks at the door as his lordship stalked toward them. Bother it all, that wasn't good.

After throwing her cloak over her night rail and buttoning it up swiftly, she shoved her feet into her half boots. Then she fairly flew down the stairs and out along the path to where the barn squatted a short distance away. As she neared the group, she spotted the barn door's padlock, with what looked like a wire hanging out of it. They'd tried to pick the lock? He was going to kill them!

Lord Thorncliff hoisted Percy and Charlie in the air

by the backs of their coats. As Tim stayed well out of his reach, he raged at them all. "Do you never listen to anyone, you fools? I said not to go near it, and I meant it! By God, I'll cane every one of you for this—"

"My lord, please!" she cried, hurrying forward.

As he turned a wild-eyed gaze on her, she stopped short, remembering the terror on his face when he'd ranted about why they must stay away from the barn. What had he said? That he kept things in there because *too many people have access to things at the mine. There's too much chance for a visitor or a stranger to get hurt.*

Like his brother?

Oh, Lord, *that's* why the idea of anyone going near his explosives enraged him. And probably why he was experimenting to find safer ways to use them, ways that she and the children were jeopardizing by their mere presence here, since he seemed reluctant to work on his experiments while they were his guests.

How could she blame him for being angry at the children? He was trying to keep them safe.

"I have to punish them," he said in a hollow voice, his eyes fixed on her.

She swallowed. "Yes, you're right."

He blinked.

"What?" Percy cried as he squirmed in the baron's grasp. "Ellie, you can't let him cane us!"

Glaring at Percy, she crossed her arms over her chest. Aunt Alys wouldn't be happy about this, but neither would she want to see her boys blown to bits. "He warned you not to go near it. He couldn't have made it more clear. You were the ones who didn't heed his warnings."

"I *told* you we should have waited!" Tim cried at the two older boys. "I told you he hadn't left the manor yet!"

Lord Thorncliff's face flushed a mottled red. "You thought to avoid me, did you?" He shook Percy. "Young fools—thank God I had to fetch something out here. One day you'll be glad of it, even with the caning I mean to—"

"Please, sir, don't!" Charlie cried as he wriggled in the air. He had enough sense to realize that bargaining was their best chance now that Ellie wasn't taking their side. "We swear this is the last time we'll ever go near your barn!"

"Damned right it is!" the baron growled and shook them both again.

"Please don't cane us, sir!" Percy chimed in. "We won't do it again, we swear!"

"You expect me to believe that?" he said gruffly.

She couldn't help noticing that he still hadn't done more than growl at them.

"Upon our souls, we swear it!" Percy said. "Tell him, Ellie!"

It was good to see someone put the fear of God into the boys. "Tell him what? I'm not sure you can be trusted, either."

"Ellie!" Tim's clear sense of betrayal vented itself in violent tears. "We only . . . d-did it because you . . . w-wouldn't let us p-play snapdragon."

"So you're saying it's *my* fault?" she retorted.

"Shut up, Tim!" Percy cried. "You're not helping!"

But Tim was wound up now. "I-it's s-so boring here . . ." he said between sobs. "Our toys a-are at home a-and Mama is . . . always tired, and you—"

"For the love of God," Lord Thorncliff grumbled, lowering the boys to the ground. "Don't blame this on your cousin. She's been running herself ragged trying to keep up with you lot."

She shot him a surprised look. "How did you know?"

"I've got eyes, haven't I? Besides, when I get home, Huggett tells me everything that you . . ." Coloring a little, he muttered an oath under his breath, then turned a scowl on the boys. "All right—I won't thrash you, but you'll spend the rest of the morning scrubbing pots for Cook. Is that clear?"

The boys bobbed their heads vigorously.

"After that, you must promise to stay with Ellie at all times. Otherwise—"

"We promise, we promise!" Percy cried.

Her breath caught in her throat. Not only had the baron softened his stance toward the boys, but he'd defended *her*. He'd even used her given name. Did he realize that? Did it mean anything?

With a glance at the still-sniffling Tim, he sighed. "And if you uphold your promise and behave yourselves today . . ." He cast them a considering glance. "Then we'll play snapdragon tonight."

The boys stared at him, stunned, then let out a whoop of joy. "Snapdragon!" they cried, dancing about him. "Snapdragon tonight!"

"*Only* if you behave!" he shouted over the din. When that sobered them, he lowered his tone. "Because if I catch you near this barn again, I'll thrash you within an inch of your lives. Understood?"

"Yes, sir!" they cried in unison.

"Now go eat breakfast. I'll be along shortly to inform Cook of your duties."

They needed no more excuse to head for safety inside. But Ellie didn't follow them. Instead she watched as Lord Thorncliff unlocked the padlock to make sure it still worked, then went inside the barn. She trailed in after him.

Pushing up her spectacles, she took a quick glance around at the mysterious place that had caused so much trouble. Barrels were stacked at one end, and a long worktable sat at the other, beneath a large glass window set into the roof. Apparently it had been designed to funnel sunlight down on that half of the barn, since the stone walls had no windows. Assorted boxes and cabinets littered the rest of the space, which smelled of fire and sulfur and coal.

"What do you want?" he asked sharply, jarring her from her examination. "You shouldn't be in here. You could get hurt."

The gruff concern in his voice touched her. "Unlike my cousins, I have no interest in rummaging about in your explosives." When he said nothing, she added, "Besides, I wanted to thank you. The boys didn't deserve your lenience, but I appreciate your giving it anyway, my lord."

"Martin," he muttered, pausing in rifling a cabinet drawer.

She edged closer. "What?"

"My given name is Martin. You might as well use it." Withdrawing a penknife, he shoved it in his pocket. "I hate that 'my lord' humbuggery. In my mind, Rupert is still Lord Thorncliff. It suited him better than it does me, anyway."

Her heart caught in her throat. How could society ever

think he would kill his brother for the title? "All right. Then thank you . . . Martin."

A shuddering breath escaped him. "I *will* cane your cousins if they don't behave, you know," he said, a bit defensively.

"I know."

"If you hadn't come along, I would have taken them over my knee."

"I'm sure you would have."

"Because they have no business coming in here—"

Ellie began to laugh.

He whirled to face her. "What the blazes is so amusing?"

"You don't have to keep growling about it now that they're gone. Unlike the boys, I am fully convinced of your capacity to play the dastardly Black Baron as often and fiercely as you must to protect them."

As if noticing for the first time her loose hair and the cloak she'd buttoned over her inappropriate dress, he gave her a long, slow perusal that sent wanton shivers dancing along her spine. "Do you accuse me of pretending, Ellie?"

His intimate use of her nickname sent a little thrill through her. "I accuse you of acting more bad-tempered than is your true nature."

A sudden veil shadowed his face. "You know nothing of my true nature."

"Actually I do." It was time he learned that not everyone was against him. "And despite what people say, I don't believe you killed your brother."

Chapter Six

Dear Cousin,

My, my, you certainly have my interest piqued. Perhaps I should guess at your identity, and you can tell me how far I am off the mark. Might you be a Hessian with a fondness for lemon tarts? An aging spy for the Home Office? A woman, even? No, I know you're not a woman. A woman couldn't possibly be as arrogant as you.

Your "relation,"
Charlotte

Martin stared at Ellie. Had she really said what he thought?

Yes, that's why she was watching him so closely. She'd heard the rumors, and now she meant to find out if they were true.

A groan escaped him. He'd spent the last few days in agony, basking in her warmly innocent smiles, entertaining mad ideas of what it might be like to have her as his wife, looking after *his* children. He'd spent three nights imagining her in his bed, cradling his body between her honeyed thighs, caressing him as only a woman could. He couldn't stand to see her expression when it dawned on her that he really was responsible for Rupert's death.

He headed for the door. "Since you've apparently learned the real reason they call me the Black Baron, there's nothing more to say, is there?"

She caught his arm as he tried to pass her. "I should like to hear *your* account, since all I learned from my aunt were rumors."

He froze, not looking at her, afraid to see what lay in her eyes. "I'm surprised she didn't order you to take her away from here. I'm surprised you didn't demand it yourself."

"Don't be absurd. We know better than to heed some silly gossip. As Shakespeare said, 'Rumor is a pipe/Blown by surmises, jealousies, conjectures.'"

A choked laugh escaped him at her blithely quoting Shakespeare while he stood here expecting her to bolt. "You have no idea how true that is."

"I'm sure I don't. That's why you should explain it to me."

His gaze shot to her. Did he dare? Her face was open, waiting. He saw no reproach in the eyes half veiled by her spectacles, but that meant little. Once he told her, she would despise him. God knew he despised himself.

Pulling away, he headed for the worktable. "You should go. I must hide a few chemicals in case your cousins try again. I packed up the worst ones a few days ago, but yesterday I had to take out some vials—"

"Martin," she said sharply, halting his frenzied flow of

words. "You might feel better if you talk to someone. Tell me what really happened. I promise not to judge you."

Devil take her for saying that. To have someone listen and not judge. . . . No, not just someone—*her*. His men didn't judge him, and neither did the local townspeople. It was only her sort who found him guilty.

That thought spurred him to face her. "It's not a great secret," he bit out. "The miners witnessed it. Huggett knows it. If people really cared to know, they could find out. Yet you're the first in society ever to ask me directly. Most people would rather invent their own tale than search for anything so dull as the truth."

"You don't exactly make it easy to ask," she pointed out.

That stopped him cold. "I suppose I don't." Leaning back against the table, he crossed his arms over his chest.

"But since I've braved your temper to do so, the least you could do is answer the question," she prodded, walking toward him.

For a moment, the silken dance of her hair about her hips distracted him. He couldn't believe she wore it down. Had she come here straight from bed? The very thought made him harden, imagining her lush body spread out on her curtain of shimmering, coal black locks, her mouth smiling, beckoning him to take her—

Idiot—you're letting your mind run away with you again. She couldn't have come straight from bed—society females didn't do that. Besides, her cloak was buttoned up with perfect propriety, and she wore boots and spectacles. Not the attire of a lady fresh from bed. Probably she'd been dressing when she'd heard him with the boys, and hadn't waited to put up her hair.

"At least tell me how a gentleman like you came to do experiments on explosives," she prodded. "Was it because of your brother's death?"

He shook himself out of his distraction. "No. It began long before then." She wouldn't let it go, would she? And perhaps he'd be better off if she knew. Once she recoiled from him, he would no longer be tempted to keep her in his life. His dangerous, demanding life, where no woman belonged.

With a sigh, he began. "I was always interested in chemistry, so when I was a boy Father would let me go with him whenever he consulted the mine manager. One day we arrived right after a bad explosion. I was ten. I saw things my worst nightmares couldn't have conjured up: a miner whose arm hung by a tendon, another without—"

He caught himself, realizing she had gone quite pale. "Anyway, I never forgot it. It galvanized me. So when Father gave me the usual choices for a second son—join the army or navy or clergy—I told him I wanted to study science. I'd read everything I could about mining operations. Explosives might be a necessary evil in mining, but I *knew* they could be safer. I just needed more knowledge to know how. To my surprise, Father agreed to let me pursue my interest."

"Didn't he think it inappropriate for a gentleman?"

"Yes, but he understood it. He'd witnessed plenty of accidents himself. So while he taught Rupert to run the estate, he allowed me to attend the University of Edinburgh. Once I came home, I worked on improvements to the mine. Ours was the first to use the Davy safety lamp."

"Your father must have been very proud of you," she murmured.

He had been—but only because he hadn't lived to see what became of his sons. "After Father died, Rupert and I remained in our circumscribed roles. Though he was the mine's owner by virtue of being the heir, he gave me full freedom to experiment with improvements. Everything was fine between us."

His voice tightened. "Until the Christmas he died." How well he remembered the smell of evergreens and roast goose, the bursts of laughter and carol singing, the crush of people filling every corner of the house. "Rupert invited several guests here for the season. When his guests found out I was testing a new, less volatile explosive at the mine, they clamored to be allowed to watch. Rupert agreed, but I refused to take them. I told him it would be too dangerous."

Fixing his gaze beyond her, Martin saw again the mortification that had crossed Rupert's face. "So we argued about it, and I left, telling him that if he brought anyone there, I'd throw them out. Which, of course, I had no right to do."

"Is that why he went there, to assert his rights?"

"In a fashion. He felt I'd shamed him before his guests. He showed up at the mine drunk, though thankfully alone, and tried to take charge of the blasting. He kept saying he was the owner and knew just as much about it as I did."

Shoving away from the table, he began to pace. "He sorely roused my temper, so I told him to do as he pleased, then stormed off. The men didn't know how to react. He *was* the owner, after all. When he ordered them to set the blast, they did so. But the black powder fizzled before reaching the explosives, which sometimes happens. He went to light it again, even though they cried that he should wait until they were sure the powder really had fizzled."

A shudder wracked him. "It hadn't." If only Rupert had listened. If only Martin hadn't stalked off. *If only . . . if only . . . if only. . . .* The words tortured his nights. "It exploded just as he reached it. He was killed instantly."

The silence that fell between them sent a cold chill down his spine. He was afraid to look at her, sure that she was appalled. And why shouldn't she be? He'd failed his own brother. He'd abandoned him in a rage, with horrible results.

But Ellie was thinking something else entirely—that his story told a tragedy so wide and deep, she didn't know how to begin easing his pain. "I'm so sorry," she whispered. He stopped pacing but didn't speak, so she muddled on. "It must have been awful for you."

"Not awful enough, some would say, considering what I gained from his death." His terse words were guilt-laden.

"Anyone who says that has no heart," she hissed, her own heart breaking for him.

He sucked in a ragged breath. "You don't blame me for what happened?" he said, a note of surprise in his voice, though he still wouldn't look at her.

"Certainly not. Why would I?"

"Because I was responsible, damn it!" He whirled to face her. "I didn't set out to kill him, but I did it as surely as if I'd put a pistol to his head."

"Nonsense!" She hastened to where he stood as rigid and erect as one of the boys' lead soldiers, carrying a weight much heavier than lead. "Forgive me for speaking ill of the dead, but your brother brought his death upon himself."

Martin gave a violent shake of his head. "You don't understand. I shouldn't have let him goad me. I should have stood firm. I should have—"

"It wasn't your fault!" She laid her hand on his arm in comfort. "Brothers argue, even under the best of circumstances."

He turned an anguished face to her. "But I shouldn't have walked away. I should have tossed him off the property as I'd threatened to do to his guests."

"That would have incensed him even more. And the miners would have been put in the intolerable position of going against their owner."

"At least he'd be alive," Martin said.

"Perhaps. Perhaps not. Sometimes people do foolish things no matter how much we try to stop them." She stroked his arm, fumbling for words to help assuage his grief-born guilt. "And the inquiry absolved you of blame."

"Yes, but society didn't. My brother's guests were only too eager to run off and tell the world their version of events. That's why everyone thinks I killed my brother for his inheritance."

"Hang society! Who cares what they think? I certainly don't."

His expression incredulous, he searched her face. "You really mean that."

"Of course." Tears stung the back of her throat to see him still so uncertain of her. "Just because your brother's friends spread gossip about you doesn't mean everyone in society listens. Or believes it." She dropped her gaze from his. "Some of us are good people, you know."

Her wounded feelings must have been evident, for he said, "Oh, Ellie, I'm sorry. I didn't mean to hurt you again." Reaching up, he brushed back her hair, then tangled his fingers in it. "It's just that I'm not used to having a woman think anything but ill of me. Especially one who tempts me so."

"I tempt you?" she said, hardly daring to believe him. He was too near, and his words were too sweet. It made her want everything he wouldn't give her.

His hand slid to cup her cheek. "I've spent the past three years hiding from the world you live in," he went on in a rough voice, "sure that I didn't want or need to be part of it. Now you come along, making me realize what I do want."

She lifted her gaze to his, which proved a mistake. Because he was looking at her as if he'd just found a treat he couldn't wait to gobble up.

Eyes darkening to pewter, he removed her spectacles with deliberate intent and set them on the table. Then his mouth covered hers. This time there was no hesitation, no agonizing uncertainty. He kissed her with the kind of hunger every woman lies awake at night dreaming about, the kind no man had ever shown her.

His hands swept down to unbutton the cloak that encased her from neck to hem, and she was so rattled by his kiss that she scarcely even cared. How could such a gruff man kiss with such feeling, give such delicious pleasure?

And why must he do it to *her*? He said he didn't want a wife, and for all she knew that hadn't changed.

A line from Michael Drayton's sad sonnet drifted through her mind—"Since there's no help, come let us kiss and part." She didn't *want* to kiss and part. That was why she shouldn't let him kiss her at all, shouldn't let him teach her to crave him. He would break her heart, and for what? To soothe his wounded pride? To give him a moment's comfort?

Why did he do it? Why did she let him?

In a desperate act of self-preservation, she tore her mouth from his, but he slid his arm inside her open cloak, dragging her flush against him as he trailed hot, openmouthed kisses down her cheek to her neck.

"Please . . . Martin . . ." she begged.

"Let me just hold you awhile." His hand swept along her ribs before he asked with surprise, "Where are the rest of your clothes, love?"

He spoke the word *love* with the rough intonation of a Yorkshire miner, but she didn't care. No one had ever called her *love.*

"I had no time. . . . I was in a hurry. . . ." That was all she could get out, for his hands were roaming farther now, along the undersides of her breasts, his thumbs brushing the bottom swells, making her heart race.

"God help me," he drew back to whisper, "you're nearly naked." His eyes locked with hers, so beautifully needy that it made her chest hurt. Then they flashed like quicksilver before he took her mouth again.

This time his kiss was so hard and consuming that it left her no room to think of anything but how to wring every moment of enjoyment from his increasingly bold caresses. His thumbs now rose to tease her nipples through the thin cambric, rousing them erect, making them ache and throb.

She knew it was wrong, but she didn't care. He was turning her inside out, making her feel things she'd never felt.

With a little burst of will, she broke their kiss. "We shouldn't be doing this."

"No," he agreed, but instead of releasing her, he drew open her cloak to stare at her. "But I want to touch you, just a little. Will you let me?"

"Someone might see," she protested weakly, glancing toward the open door.

"Not without coming inside. The boys won't, your aunt can't, and the servants know better than to go anywhere near this barn, much less enter it."

"Even Mr. Huggett?" she asked.

His feverish gaze burned into her, making her blood run hot. "Even Huggett," he rasped. Taking her by surprise, he lifted her onto the worktable, then reached inside her cloak to cup one breast.

It felt *soooo* good, nothing like she would have expected. He fondled her breast shamelessly, and when she arched just as shamelessly into his hand, he pressed forward between her legs and began spreading ravenous kisses along her neck.

She grabbed at his shoulders, and her cloak fell off. He took that as leave to unbutton her night rail so he could unveil one breast and seize it in his mouth.

Lord in heaven . . . that was amazing. He sucked and teased, his tongue playing over her nipple, driving her insane with the pleasure of it. She ought to stop him before she was doomed forever, but instead she clasped his head in both hands, urging him to suck the other breast, too. Emitting a low growl from deep in his throat, he obliged her eagerly.

This was madness. Anyone might find them.

Would that be so bad? Then he'd *have* to marry her.

No, she didn't want that, either. But neither did she want to miss her chance to have a man touch her like this of his own free will without a care for her fortune. And not just any man, but Martin, who not only made her body sing, but treated her like a real person. He might not want her as his wife, but he did desire her as a woman, and that was more than she'd ever hoped for.

Then his hand started moving up her thighs, as if lighting a trail of black powder that headed ever closer to the place that awaited the spark, that threatened to erupt any moment in the depths of her belly.

"I should stop this," he rasped against her ear. "Make me stop, love."

She heard him dimly through the haze of pleasure swirling about her. "Why?"

A groan escaped him before he lifted his head to take her mouth again. While his free hand took over caressing her breast, his other hand swept higher between her legs until he was cupping her in her special place, the one she never touched except when washing.

Goodness. Gracious. He was fondling her down *there*! Worse yet, she was letting him. What a wicked creature she was!

But his passion consumed her. She never dreamed men could convey such passion, like a poem full of words so strong and rich she could scarcely keep from bursting into song. He rubbed her as a servant rubs kindling to start a fire, and heat engulfed her, flaming, flaring up, making her ache and quiver and squirm beneath his hand.

"That's it," he murmured, his mouth dropping to take more wild liberties with her breast. "Let me show you. . . .

You're so . . . incredibly sweet. . . . I want to . . . God help me. . . ."

His finger delved inside her, and she nearly leaped off the table. "Martin!"

"Shh, shh," he gentled her, nuzzling her breast and her neck, breathing soothing sounds in her ear. "I want to make amends for hurting your feelings."

"You'll ruin me," she whispered, half hoping that he would.

"No, I swear. I'll give you only a taste. But I have to touch you or go mad."

And all the while, his fingers were working her, tormenting her with the promise of a conflagration she'd never known. "Martin . . . you . . . oh, heavens . . ."

"You're so wet, love, like ripe fruit. . . . I want to pluck you and devour you. . . ." Each word came more dimly to her ears, for she was nearly to the point of exploding, the heat so fiery that she could only moan and thrash beneath his hand.

Suddenly an eruption hit her with the fierceness of wildfire, tearing a cry from her throat that he silenced with his mouth.

As her body quaked and trembled, then finally settled back down to earth in his arms, she realized that *this* was what she wanted—this thrilling intimacy with a man who cared for her.

Now if only she could figure out how to keep him. For after tasting passion with Martin, she could never be satisfied with anyone else.

Chapter Seven

Dear Charlotte,

I suppose you think it amusing to taunt me about my arrogance, but you and I are more alike than you admit. You have a tendency to be rather haughty yourself.

Your cousin,
Michael

As Martin felt her honeypot convulse about his fingers, he wanted to crow—then weep. He'd never desired a woman so much in his life. And he'd never been less free to indulge that desire to its fullest. Instead he had to stand here aching for her, knowing he would never have the chance to fill her flesh with his and claim her for his own.

He must have made some frustrated sound, for she drew back from him, her face pleasingly flushed, and whispered, "Are you all right?"

Hell and blazes, he doubted he'd ever be all right again.

Wiping his fingers on her night rail, he managed a smile. "I should ask *you* that."

Her hands still clutching his arms, she kissed his chin. "I don't think 'all right' begins to describe it. I . . . I feel drunk, but my mind is clear."

A rueful chuckle sounded deep in his throat. "How strange. *My* mind is shattered." Pulling back from her, he drew down her night rail regretfully. "But I didn't mean to go so far."

She was staring at him with alarm. "We didn't . . . you didn't . . ."

"No. You're still chaste."

Laughter bubbled out of her. "Chaste? It felt too good for chastity."

The sparkle in her eyes made him want to go right back to what they'd been doing. The heavy cock in his trousers intensified the urge.

He fought the impulse, drawing her cloak up over her shoulders. He'd never had such shaky control over his desires, especially with a virgin. Ellie was as dangerous to him as blasting powder.

But she wasn't his for the taking, except in the marriage bed—and that was impossible. "That's precisely why it was wrong of me—"

"Don't say that." She touched her finger to his lips. "It was wonderful."

His heart swelled. The adoring look on her face was so sweet that he blurted out without thinking, "Oh, God, how will I ever let you go?"

The minute he spoke the words, he wished them back, because clearly she welcomed them.

Her words confirmed it. "You don't have to let me go," she said softly.

What fresh torture was this? It had been much easier to resist her before. He'd been sure she would lose interest once she heard how Rupert had died. But with her still wanting him . . .

When he didn't answer right away, she dropped her gaze and added, "Of course, that's assuming you would want to marry me, which clearly you don't."

As a flush of humiliation spread over her cheeks, she tried to leave the table, but he wouldn't let her. He couldn't bear to have her think him such a cad. "You're the only woman I'd ever consider marrying," he murmured, bending his forehead to hers. "But I can't." He couldn't risk having her here. It was too dangerous.

"Why not?" she asked in a small voice.

Isn't it obvious? he wanted to shout as he pushed away from the table. *Look around you, look at what I spend my time doing!*

She wouldn't care. Women always tried to deny the risks. Or worse, eliminate the problem by putting conditions on things. And he refused to end his experiments. He was tired of watching people die or be maimed in the mines.

What if she understands that, too? What if she's willing to accept what you feel compelled to do?

He snorted. She could never fully understand the dangers. All it would take was her coming into the barn one night to call him to dinner, bearing a candle in her hand . . .

No, he wouldn't risk it. He wouldn't risk *her.*

She would call his fears irrational. And perhaps they were, but that didn't change the terror that gripped him whenever he pictured her laid out on the ground like Rupert.

Still, he had to tell her something, give her a compelling reason to make her think twice about marrying him. "Your father would never agree to a match between us. I'm sure he's heard the rumors about me, too."

A strange unease crossed her face. "Does his approval matter to you?"

"No, but I imagine it matters to *you.*"

His answer brought a smile to her face. "You have no idea how little it matters. Besides, he's a reasonable man. When I tell him the truth of what happened, he'll see that you weren't at fault."

He tried to swallow past the lump in his throat. "Not everyone has your forgiving heart, Ellie."

"Father will listen to me, I swear." She thrust out her chin as she slid off the table and straightened her night rail. "If I make it clear that I *want* to marry you, he won't object. He wants only my happiness, after all."

She knew so little about men. "I'm sure he does. And he'll know that marrying me won't add to it. For one thing, you won't be accepted in polite society. If you marry me, you'll be the Black Baron's wife. Have you considered that? They'll gossip about you, too—they'll say I married you for your fortune or some such rot, and they'll think you a monster for marrying the man whom everyone believes murdered his brother."

Her eyes flashed sparks. "I don't care."

"You will, in time. You don't know how to handle being cut off from people, being whispered about and avoided—"

"You seem to handle it well enough."

"That's because I don't *like* people. Except for you." When she smiled at that, he sharpened his tone. "I don't care about society but you were bred for it. You're a society female. I won't have time for shopping jaunts to London and Sheffield and York, and you won't want to make them after you see how people react to me there." That was doing it up a bit brown, but how else was he to nip this attraction before it tempted him beyond his sanity?

She glared at him. "Have you noticed *nothing* about me in the past few days? As it happens, I'm perfectly comfortable in the country. I like to read and sew and go for long walks. I'm not remotely a 'society female.'"

"Did you or did you not go to an expensive ladies' school?" he asked.

"Yes, but—"

"And were you presented to the queen? Did you dance at Almack's? Did all your friends do the same?"

"What has that got to do with anything?" she demanded.

"You said you weren't a society female. I'm reminding you that you are." When she opened her mouth to protest, he added hastily, "It's the right kind of life for the daughter of Joseph Bancroft."

"And what about for the wife of a lord of the realm?" she snapped.

"In society's eyes, I am only a lord because I killed my brother. The rules for other men of rank don't apply to me. Trust me, the Black Baron can't give you the kind of life you deserve."

"Perhaps I don't *want* that kind of life!"

He shook his head. "You don't know what you want.

How can you, after only a few days moldering here at Thorncliff? Give it another week, and you'll be bored senseless."

"And you won't even allow me the chance to find out, will you?" she snapped as she buttoned up her cloak. "You're throwing me aside out of some dubious attempt to protect me from . . . from nonsense." She crossed her arms over her chest. "I told you I don't care about any of that, and if you choose not to believe me—"

"I choose to do what I think is right for you. You deserve better."

"Absolutely," she said hotly. "I deserve a man who wants me."

"I *do* want you!"

A blush darkened her fine skin. "If you wanted me, you'd find a way to have me instead of making a lot of excuses."

"They're not excuses!"

At that moment, they heard noises outside. Hell and blazes, he'd forgotten that he'd asked a groom to saddle his horse half an hour ago. That's when he'd seen the boys trying to get in.

Huggett's voice drifted to where they stood. "I couldn't find him in the house, so he's got to be out here."

"P'raps," the groom said. "It ain't like him to keep me waiting so long."

"My lord?" called the butler from a healthy distance, since he knew better than to approach the entrance.

"Blast it all," Martin hissed under his breath. "I have to go."

"Well then, go," she said with a sniff as she turned for the table. She hunted until she found her spectacles, then put them on.

When she made no move toward the door, he growled, "I'm not leaving you in here alone."

"Oh, for goodness' sake." Ignoring his proffered arm, she hurried ahead of him, her sweet hips swaying in a motion that made him wish he could take back everything he'd said.

He moved swiftly up beside her, grabbing her arm just in time for them to walk out together. "I'm here, Huggett. I was just showing Miss Bancroft the barn."

As the two of them emerged into the painfully bright morning sunlight, Huggett and the groom gaped at her. Too late, Martin remembered that her hair was down, though the rest of her looked presentable enough.

"You allowed Miss Bancroft into the *barn*?" Huggett said meaningfully.

Martin was just about to give his presumptuous butler a piece of his mind when Ellie answered. "Actually I followed him in there, which is why he's kicking me out." She shot Martin a cold glance. "Thank you for the tour, my lord." Breaking free of his grip, she gave him a cool nod, then headed toward the house.

As he watched her flounce off wearing the cloak that barely shielded her charms, something twisted inside him. Perhaps he *was* only making excuses. Perhaps a marriage *was* possible. He could still run after her and beg her to forgive him, to stay with him and share his life. . . .

His dangerous, solitary life.

He shook off the impulse. "Huggett, I told the boys they have to scrub pots for Cook as punishment for trying to enter the barn. See that they do it, will you?"

"Yes, sir," he said. As the groom hurried off to where the horse waited in front, Huggett fell into step beside

Martin. "Miss Bancroft has lovely hair, does she not? It compensates for her rather plain appearance."

"Plain appearance!" he snapped. "Are you mad?" When Huggett arched one eyebrow, he groaned. "Give it up, man. I've told you I can't have a woman about the place."

"Why? Because she might make it warm and cozy? Enliven your days?" Huggett's voice grew pitying. "Free you from your blind obsession?"

Anger swelled in him. "Watch it, Huggett!"

"Forgive me, sir," the butler murmured. "I didn't mean to presume."

Martin increased his pace. Of course the blasted man had meant to presume. He *always* presumed.

But that didn't mean he was wrong.

As Martin mounted his horse, he tried to ignore Huggett's apt description of his life. His "blind obsession" had a worthy purpose. If his experiments were successful, he might save hundreds of lives.

While destroying your own.

He snorted as he rode toward town. He'd been fine before the Metcalfs had come to shatter his peace. Before Ellie . . .

A vision of her face rapt with pleasure swam before him. God help him, he wished he'd never seen them on that road. Until then, he'd existed in a blessed numbness that enabled him to do nothing but work.

After knowing her, would he ever be able to do that again?

Ellie spent her morning in a state of fury. Martin and his assumptions! Society female, indeed. He didn't know her at all!

But as the day wore into afternoon, even the task of finding a Yule log with the boys couldn't stop certain thoughts from invading her mind.

Be honest, Ellie. You would miss dancing at balls, and you would want to do some *shopping. And what about visiting the school in London or going to see Lucy? Could you really give that up?*

She wouldn't have to if he would just *tell* people what had happened with his brother. He was merely being stubborn. And proud.

And realistic. Rumors tended to take on a life of their own. Perhaps the nastiness would fade once he married, but it could also increase. The gossips might simply work her into the tale, as he'd said.

She didn't care! As long as she and Martin were together, it didn't matter. With a scowl, she tromped over a rotting stump. It wasn't right. He was a good man. He deserved to have friends around him, and good society, and a wife who loved him.

Loved him?

As the truth hit her like a branch falling from the sky, tears sprang to her eyes, making it hard for her to see where she was going. Look what he'd gone and done—the fellow had made her fall in love with him! It was so unfair.

Still, she couldn't help it. Who could *not* love a man who spent his waking hours trying to better conditions in his mine? A man who didn't care what people thought of him, as long as he could do his experiments? A man who went to any lengths to keep those around him safe. He'd even made *her* leave the barn at the end, because he thought it was too dangerous. . . .

Ohhhh. Could *that* be the real reason behind his refusal to marry her? Out of fear? Or worry that what happened to his brother might happen to her?

She clung to that possibility for one heady moment, since it soothed her aching heart. But much as she wanted to believe it, it made no sense. Why should he worry about her safety? It wasn't as if she'd be going near the mine. And she was perfectly capable of staying out of his way if asked. It was ludicrous to think he might forego happiness for *that.*

What made *more* sense was that he just didn't want her badly enough to make the necessary adjustments in his life.

She swallowed hard. Because she was plain. He might say he desired her, but plenty of men desired women without wanting them as wives. There'd been no females here in a long time, so Martin might just be randy. That didn't mean he wanted to spend his life with her.

Dashing away angry tears, she hurried after the boys and the footmen as they headed down another path through the woods. They'd been in search of the perfect Yule log for two hours now, discarding every stupid piece of wood she suggested. Why was the male sex always so fractious and determined to make a woman's life miserable?

Well, she'd had enough of them all. She wasn't good enough for his lordship? Fine. She would be cordial and aloof with him from now on.

But that night, as they finished dinner, she wasn't so sure she could. Martin kept looking at her with an odd yearning that confused her even further. Did he want her or not? What other secrets lay behind that strange and enigmatic gaze to explain the real reason for his not wanting to marry?

Was she just being fanciful? Or was he simply not interested in her because she wasn't pretty enough to keep his interest?

"So when do we play snapdragon?" Percy asked once dessert was served.

Martin muttered an oath. "I was hoping it had slipped your mind."

"No chance of that," she said dryly. Her cousins never forgot a promise, even one made under duress.

"Very well," Martin said. "I'll go see to the arrangements."

"And I'll take Meg up to bed. She's too young for this." She glanced over to where the girl was nodding off. "Besides, it's late."

Picking her darling cousin up, she headed for the stairs.

"You'll come back, though, won't you, Ellie?" Tim asked.

"Yes," Martin's low voice joined in. "Do come back."

A little thrill darted through her at his words.

But when she shot him a surprised glance, he added, "You can't possibly expect me to handle these lads without help."

She stiffened, tempted to tell him he was on his own, but the silvery heat in his eyes kept her from saying it. "Give me a few minutes."

When she returned, everything had already been arranged. The shallow bowl of brandy held pride of place in the center of the dining table, laden with so many raisins that plucking them out wouldn't prove much of a challenge, fire or no fire.

Nonetheless, Martin was setting down rules as she approached. "No flinging raisins at other people. Huggett will keep count of how many each of you snatches, and you must abide by his count. Take off your coats, and roll up your sleeves. I don't want anyone catching their cuffs on fire."

"What about me?" she asked. "My sleeves are too tight to roll up."

Alarm suffused his face. "You mean to play?"

"Ellie always plays," Tim said matter-of-factly. "She almost beat everyone last time. It's because she has little fingers. She can get in and out quicker."

"God help us." Martin cast her a resigned glance. "I don't suppose I can talk you out of it."

"Not on your life," she said, though his palpable concern softened her.

"Very well." He gestured to her sleeves. "Slide them up as far as you can." He turned to the boys. "If you happen to ignite anything, put it out in one of the pails I placed at each corner of the table. But whatever you do, don't throw water on the brandy. It merely scatters the fire."

"Listen well to him, boys," she put in. "His lordship knows everything there is to know about fire."

"What I know is that it's dangerous," Martin growled.

Everyone roundly ignored him.

Charlie peered into the bowl. "Where's the lucky raisin?"

"What's that?" Martin asked.

Ellie produced the gold button she'd brought along just for this purpose. "In London, we add what we call the 'lucky raisin' to the bowl. Whoever plucks it out is allowed to ask a boon of someone else among the party."

Dropping it into the brandy, she cast Martin a teasing glance. "And whoever is asked must grant the boon or risk a dire fate."

Martin arched one eyebrow. "A dire fate, eh? Then I'll have to make sure *I* am the one to get it."

The husky timbre of his voice thrummed along her every nerve. If he thought she'd let him win this, he was in for a surprise. The Black Baron had already won more from her than she could afford to lose. It was *her* turn to win.

Huggett lit the bowl, then extinguished the candles, leaving only the eerie blue flame playing over the surface. At once the boys began to chant:

> *"Here he comes with flaming bowl,*
> *Don't he mean to take his toll,*
> *Snip! Snap! Dragon!*
>
> *Take care you don't take too much,*
> *Be not greedy in your clutch,*
> *Snip! Snap! Dragon!*
>
> *With his blue and lapping tongue*
> *Many of you will be stung,*
> *Snip! Snap! Dragon!"*

They'd scarcely finished the final verse when Tim plunged his fingers into the luminous glow to snatch the first raisin, and the game was on.

Bracing herself for the quick heat, Ellie darted forward to grab her own prize. She popped it into her mouth, dancing it about on her tongue to extinguish the fire, then chewing up the hot raisin as she reached toward the bowl for another.

For a moment, Martin only watched and shook his head as they complained about their sore fingers even while they thrust them right back in. But then he began grabbing raisins himself with a deftness even she couldn't match.

"Tell me again why we're doing this?" he muttered as he tossed a blue-tinged raisin into his mouth and winced.

"Because it's fun!" she cried, laughing at the chagrin on his face.

When Charlie crowed after snatching up two raisins at once, she noticed that Martin's lips bore a ghost of a smile.

She bent closer, trying to spot the gold button, no small feat with only the blue flame for light. Just as she caught sight of it Percy did, too, and lunged forward. His arm caught the side of her head, snagging her braid loose of its pins to fall right into the brandy. She still managed to seize the lucky raisin, but not before the end of her braid had caught fire.

As the acrid smell of burned hair rose around them, Martin grabbed her braid and tugged her to the nearest pail. "I knew this was insane," he grumbled as he dunked it repeatedly. "Snapdragon indeed. You people have no sense!"

"Ow!" she cried, torn between pain and laughter. "My head is attached to that, you know. Stop pulling so hard! The fire is out, for goodness' sake!"

Releasing her braid, he scowled at her, ignoring the boys, who'd returned to the game as soon as they'd seen she was safe. "What in God's name were you trying to do by leaning so close to the flames?"

"I was trying to get *this*." She held up the lucky raisin with a grin. "And I succeeded, didn't I?"

"You nearly succeeded in igniting your whole head!" he countered, the panic in his voice mirrored by his expression of dark concern.

"I was fine, really." She swept her braid up to examine the end. "It's hardly even burned."

"That's only because you have it so tightly plaited. That slows down the rate of—" He broke off, his eyes going wide. "That's it. Oh my God, that's *it*!"

"What's it?" she asked. "The rate of what?"

But his mind seemed to be elsewhere. Swiftly, he relit a couple of candles, then set a plate over the bowl to extinguish the blue flames.

"Wait!" Percy cried. "We're not done!"

"Yes you are," he shot back. "I have to go, and I'm not leaving you lot here alone with a burning bowl of brandy."

"Where are you going?" Tim asked. "Can we come?"

"Certainly not," Martin growled as he donned his coat.

"It's nearly ten o'clock, sir," Huggett pointed out. "Surely it's much too dangerous to be riding out on icy roads—"

"I'm not riding anywhere." Martin stalked for the door. "Make sure they don't light up the brandy again, Huggett." He was halfway out the door when he halted, whirled around, and returned to where she stood gaping at him.

Before she knew his intent, he caught her hand and

pressed a hard kiss into the palm. "Thank you," he said fervently, his eyes regarding her with such hot intensity that a blush rose to her cheeks. "You don't know what you've done."

"I certainly don't," she shot back, but by the time the words were out of her mouth, he was already heading for the door again.

After he'd gone, Percy shook his head. "He's an odd fellow, isn't he, Ellie?"

Odd wasn't the word she would have used. *Impassioned* was more like it.

Her hand still burned, and not from the hot raisins. She stared down to where he'd kissed it, then curled her fingers into the palm, wishing kisses could somehow be saved. Because just that touch of his lips on her bare skin had brought all her wanton feelings from that morning rushing back.

So much for being cordial and aloof.

"What are you going to do with the lucky raisin?" Charlie asked her.

She opened her other hand to stare at the gold button. "I don't know."

"You could ask Tim to stop being such a nodcock," Percy said, elbowing his younger brother.

"Or ask Percy to grow a brain," Tim countered, elbowing back.

"Stop that, both of you," she said without looking up. "I'm going to save it until I decide."

But what was there to decide? Only one person could grant her what she wanted, and it wasn't her cousins. Because what she wanted was a night of passion with Martin.

Her heart leaped in her chest. It wasn't too horribly outrageous an idea, was it? If she meant never to marry anyway, did it matter if she lost her innocence? What she contemplated might go against every principle Mrs. Harris had taught her, but such principles hadn't suited her very well of late.

She much preferred Nicolas Chamfort's principle, that "when a man and a woman have an overwhelming passion for each other . . . in spite of such obstacles dividing them . . . they belong to each other in the name of Nature, and are lovers by Divine right, in spite of human convention or the laws."

Of course, Chamfort was French. Still, how could she live out her life without experiencing passion for herself with the only man she'd ever loved? She might not have Martin's love in return, but she could have his passion.

She *would* have his passion, at least for one night. He owed her a boon. And she was going to make sure he granted it, no matter what the consequences.

Chapter Eight

Dear Cousin,

I am not haughty, but cautious. I can understand how a man might mistake caution for arrogance, but I assure you no woman would. On the whole, women are far more aware of the world's dangers than men will allow.

Your terribly <u>cautious</u> relation,
Charlotte

Christmas Eve dawned cold and clear, but Martin scarcely noticed. He had passed the night in his barn, working in a frenzy of excitement on his new idea for a fuse consisting of rope impregnated with black powder, and now he was on his third rendition. Each one had worked successively better in his limited tests. He figured that by midday he'd have a version worth testing more reliably at the mine.

Why hadn't he thought of using rope before?

Because he hadn't had Ellie around before. Ellie, with her penchant for braiding things . . . Ellie, with her encouraging glances . . . Ellie, who apparently approved of any Christmas tradition that involved setting fires.

Reckless little fool. He'd nearly lost ten years of his life when her hair had caught fire. And she hadn't even flinched! She'd blithely teased him about finding that idiotic button, as if she hadn't just risked going up in flames.

The wench was a bit mad, as were her cousins. The sooner the lot of them went on to Sheffield, the better. Then his life would return to how it had been before. Predictable. Safe. . . . Lonely.

With a scowl, he bent over the table, cutting strands of jute to wind around the core of gunpowder he'd developed. How had he adapted so quickly to the pleasure of having a cozy group around the dinner table? To evenings filled with books and music? Granted, the boys were rascals, but little Meg had an endearing way of thrusting her thumb in her mouth whenever she was upset, and Ellie . . .

Oh, God, Ellie. Once she returned to London, she'd surely find a husband who wasn't liable to blow her up by accident. He'd be a respectable gentleman with a good name, who would dance with her at balls and dine with her at home and retire with her at night to their intimate marriage bed—

The penknife cut into his forefinger. "Hell and blazes," he muttered to himself, "that damned woman will be the death of me yet."

He couldn't stand to think of her in another man's bed. He hated the idea of some other man kissing that plump little mouth, entwining himself in that curtain of hair, fondling every inch of her lush, warm flesh.

You just have to give it time. You'll forget her when she

leaves. The memory will fade, and your life will go back to normal.

Then why did the image of her not fade from his mind as his experiments continued throughout the morning? Why was it that when Huggett called to him from outside to come eat *something*, he was disappointed to find, when he went in briefly for food, that Ellie and the boys were upstairs with Mrs. Metcalf? He had to restrain himself from going up for just a glimpse of her smile.

That afternoon he went to the mine, bearing his three experimental fuses. They performed spectacularly. Though he could see that improvements would be needed, the men were impressed with the possibilities, and he knew without a doubt that he'd finally stumbled upon the solution he'd been striving for.

Yet despite the congratulations, despite the drinking in celebration of Christmas Eve at the mine, he chafed to be back at the manor. He told himself it was only because he wanted to tell Ellie about his "safe fuse," that he wanted to give credit where credit was due since she'd sparked the idea in his mind. It wasn't because he yearned to see her face bloom in a smile, to hear her praise his accomplishment, to steal a kiss. No, indeed.

Yet instead of drinking into the wee hours of the morning with his miners as on past Christmas Eves, he begged off early. After a quick washup, he rode back to the manor around nine o'clock, praying that Ellie hadn't yet retired.

She hadn't. He found her sitting alone in the great hall, near the hearth that held a monstrously large piece of timber. "I suppose I missed the lighting of the Yule log," he murmured as he came up to where she sat reading before the fire.

She looked up, a smile of welcome flashing over her lips. "Yes. And dinner, too, though I believe Mr. Huggett put a tray of something in your study. He said that was where you generally eat."

"It is, indeed." He suddenly realized he'd had nothing but ale since midday, and not much of that, either. He held out his hand to her. "Will you come sit with me while I eat? I have much to tell you."

"Certainly." Taking his hand, she rose, leaving her book on the chair. As they headed off together, with her hand nestled in the crook of his arm, she added, "You look tired."

"I am. Tired and famished. I only slept in snatches last night, and it's beginning to catch up with me."

"The children were disappointed that you weren't here for the Christmas Eve festivities," she said in a tone of forced nonchalance.

"Only the children?" he said, unable to stop himself.

"Certainly not." Her gaze shot to his, an arch smile playing over her lips. "Mr. Huggett was positively *devastated* by your absence."

He laughed. "The rascal probably had the time of his life with those boys running around setting fire to Yule candles while I wasn't here to put a damper on things." He covered her hand with his. "But I wasn't trying to avoid any of you. I was working out my new invention."

They'd reached the study, where a tray of cold ham, bread, and cheese awaited him. She sat down across the desk from him as he began to eat, describing the safety fuse between bites of his meal. Some of the excitement still beating in his chest must have conveyed itself to her, for her expression soon grew as animated as he felt, even though she probably didn't understand half of what he babbled about blends of chemicals and the proper winding of the jute.

Until now, he'd never realized how much he craved having someone share his successes. She even seemed to understand his enthusiasm. Not even his father had ever done that, and it touched him deeply.

Shoving his tray aside, he leaned forward on the desk. "It's all because of you, you know. Your braid gave me the idea."

"You mean, setting *fire* to my braid gave you the idea," she teased. "Seems to me that since I risked my life for your cause, I ought to receive at least half the proceeds of your safe fuse."

He chuckled. "I do owe you," he said, matching her light tone. "I owe you double, as a matter of fact—unless you've already demanded that one of the others give you your lucky raisin 'boon.'"

Mention of the "boon" inexplicably banished the smile from her lips. She smoothed her skirts and fidgeted a moment, then abruptly rose and went to where the door stood open. "Actually I . . . um . . . kept the fulfillment of the boon for *you.* In fact, I was hoping you'd do it tonight."

She glanced out, then closed the door, and he frowned. Whatever she wanted of him must be very secret indeed. Something for her aunt, perhaps?

But then she stowed her spectacles in her pocket, and he knew this was no ordinary favor. She returned to the desk, looking decidedly nervous. "I . . . um . . . well . . . I've been thinking, and I was hoping . . . that is . . ."

"For God's sake, Ellie, tell me what you want. I'll be happy to give you—"

"I want a night of passion," she blurted out.

The coals that had been smoldering inside him ever since yesterday in the barn leaped instantly into flame. It took all his will to tamp them down. "What in blazes do you mean?" he said, praying he'd misunderstood her.

She set her shoulders as her gaze met his. "I mean I want you to make love to me. Tonight, i-if you're not too tired."

Too tired? He could leap over mountains right now if it meant a chance of bedding her. But that didn't mean it was wise. He rose from the desk so abruptly, his chair fell over. "Are you daft?"

"No!" Her chin began to tremble. "I-I just thought perhaps you wouldn't mind giving me what I want since you . . . seemed to desire me, at least a little."

"Of course I desire you, and more than a little," he bit out, not sure how to handle this. "But that's not the point. You're an untried maiden. Someday you'll marry, and your husband will expect—"

"I shall never marry," she said stoutly. "So given the choice between a spinsterhood without ever knowing passion and a single night with you, I'd just as soon have the night with *you*. If you don't mind."

His blood pounded in his veins. *Mind?* He minded quite a lot. His control was already stretched to the breaking point, and he didn't know how much farther it would hold, now that she'd roused images of her and him together in his head.

"Ellie," he said, attempting a soothing tone as he approached her, "of course you'll be marrying. Why wouldn't you?"

Anger flared in her eyes. "If you're going to be condescending about it, forget what I said."

What did she mean—he was just stating facts!

She turned for the door, but he caught her arm to stay her. "I didn't mean to be condescending. All I was trying to say—badly, it appears—is that some respectable man is sure to offer for you." God rot the lucky bastard.

"Some respectable fortune hunter, you mean."

"No, that's not what I mean at all!"

"Because that's the only type who will ever offer for me," she went on in a tortured voice, her arm trembling in his grasp. "I can't take another season of their insincere smiles and their polite conversation while they follow my friend Lucy with their eyes. I'd rather die than marry a man who doesn't care for me."

Pulling free of his grip, she faced him. Her eyes held so much pain that it shocked him. "I understand why you don't want to marry me, either. Sadly enough for me, you're a man of character, and like most men of character, you can't be tempted by a mere fortune. I can even"— her voice caught on a sob before she steadied herself—"accept that. But I don't see why that should prevent you from showing me what passion is."

He was still trying to follow her skewed reasoning when she added in a heart-wrenching voice, "I . . . I know I'm not pretty enough to marry . . ." She was crying now. "But surely you find me . . . desirable enough . . . to share your bed . . . for just one . . . night."

"Ellie, my God," he whispered as it finally dawned on him what notion she'd taken into her head. Catching her face in his hands, he forced her to look at him. "Pretty enough to marry! Are you mad? I've spent the past few days in a torment trying to keep my hands off you. I can't sleep for dreaming of what it would be like to have you in my bed."

"Then why won't you make love to me?" she choked out. "I promise no one will ever know. It will be only the one night—"

"One night would never be enough," he said fiercely. "Hell and blazes, don't you understand? You're everything I dream of in a wife. You have a heart as big as the world. You're honest, and clever, and you make my blood run hot whenever I see you." He brushed the tears from her cheeks with his thumbs. "And yes, you *are* pretty. To me, you're as pretty as a woman can be. I don't know what those idiots in London have been telling you, but they're wrong."

She dropped her gaze. "You're just s-saying that to be kind."

"When have I ever been kind before?" he said, desperate to relieve her pain. "I'm saying it because it's true, love. I swear I would marry you in an instant if not for—"

"If not for what?" She lifted her lovely, innocent gaze to meet his. "And don't say it has anything to do with the gossip, because you know I don't care about that. Besides, none of it could hurt me nearly as much as marrying a man who doesn't love me. Or remaining a spinster. Because if you don't want me, that's what will happen. I'll live with Papa and never know the passion of the marriage bed—"

"At least you'd be alive!" he cried, the words torn from him. But he couldn't let her think that he didn't want her; that would be cruel.

Her face was incredulous. "*That's* what this is about? You won't marry me because you're worried about my safety?"

"Don't you see? I couldn't bear it if anything ever happened to you." He *had* to make her understand. "I won't marry you at the risk to your life. I can't."

Chapter Nine

Dear Charlotte,

Men don't believe that women are cautious because we witness their recklessness time and again. Even you must admit you let your emotions lead you into trouble.

Your cool-headed cousin,
Michael

Ellie laughed, giddy at the thought that he really *did* want her, incredulous at his willingness to let fear for her safety come between them. Here she'd spent the entire day feeling sure that he didn't care for her, and *that* was what worried him?

"I mean it, blast you!" Martin said angrily, stepping back from her. "It's too dangerous here at Thorncliff." From the look on his face, he really believed what he was saying. "What I do has risks."

Ellie sobered as he began to pace his study in quick, jerky steps. "I realize that. And I'm not asking you to give up what's important to you. But your servants live here safely while you perform your experiments."

"Notice that none of them are women. That's done on purpose."

"Because women catch fire more easily than men?" she quipped, incredulous that this was his reasoning.

A scowl knit his brow. "Mock me if you want, but my male servants accept the risks. No female can be expected to do so. It's bad enough that I require *some* staff, but the idea of a poor maid dying because she passed the barn at the wrong moment—" He rubbed the back of his neck. "I could never bear the thought."

"Yet you could bear the thought of a male servant dying in an accident?"

"No!" He swore under his breath. "You don't understand. I keep my staff small to lower the risks. But a wife needs more servants—maids and footmen and a nanny for the children . . ." He cast her a horrified look. "*Children*. God help me! Can you imagine? You've already seen how hard it is to control *them*."

"If you don't tantalize them with warnings about the mysterious barn, and if you teach them from the beginning to be cautious, they can be controlled as well as anybody. So can servants." She thrust out her chin. "*And* a wife. There's no reason people can't follow reasonable precautions if they know the purpose."

"The way you followed reasonable precautions last night?"

"Oh, for goodness' sake, that could have happened to any of us! Besides, you put out the fire before it half began, and I would have done so if you hadn't."

"The point is—"

"The point is," she cut in, "you act as if the rest of the world is generally safe, but it's not. Fire is a constant threat in the best of homes, what with candles and coals and sparks from the hearth." She ticked things off on her fingers. "People take falls down stairs—will you block off your stairs, too? And it was purely by God's mercy that my aunt didn't die in that carriage. Or that we weren't sent flying into the trees when we skidded on the ice. Shall you banish carriages from your life, too?"

"If that's what it takes to keep the people I love from dying, then yes!"

And just like that, she understood his fears. It had naught to do with anything rational—it sprang from a deeper source. Instantly her heart went out to him. "Oh, Martin, I'm so sorry."

He cast her a wary glance. "For what?"

She walked up to cup his cheek in her hand. "For everything—for what happened to your brother. For what that has done to you."

His eyes were a stark, steely gray as they locked with hers. "I don't know what you mean," he said hoarsely.

"Yes you do." She caressed his beard-stubbled jaw, wishing she could soothe his wounded soul just as easily. "This is about punishing yourself for Rupert's death."

He closed his eyes, his throat working convulsively. "It has nothing to do with punishment," he ground out.

"Doesn't it? You could have put an end to the gossip by telling your story and brazening out the rumors. Instead you trumped up these ridiculous reasons for staying here alone, cut off from anyone who might care about you. Because you're doing a self-imposed penance for Rupert's death."

"No . . ." he whispered, and tried to move away.

But she looped her hands around his neck and wouldn't let him go. "Yes. It hurts less to condemn yourself to a life alone than to face the hard truth that life is not safe. That you can't control what happens to those you love. That some things must be left to fate." Her voice dropped to a whisper. "Your guilt gives you an excuse not to get too close to anyone, so you don't risk it happening again."

"You don't understand." His eyes blazed at her, dark in their torment. "I would die if you were hurt. Or our children or—"

"So would I." She pressed a finger to his lips. "But the answer is not to deny yourself family or friends or love. That only poisons the soul. Samuel Johnson said that 'Solitude is dangerous to reason, without being favourable to virtue.' By condemning yourself to this lonely life, you save no one, not even yourself."

"But by bringing you into my life, I risk putting you into danger."

"No more than the danger you put yourself into every day. As long as we face it together, I can handle any such dangers."

A muscle flicked in his jaw as he stared at her. "And what if *I* cannot?"

"Then you condemn me to a life of loneliness as well—to serve your penance with you against my will."

"I don't believe that. Surely others will see what a jewel you are, men who can give you everything that I . . ." He choked on the words.

She took advantage of his jealousy. "And that's what you want?" She stretched up to brush her lips across his throat, desperate to make him understand what he'd be giving up. "For me to find some other fellow?"

His pulse beat hard beneath her lips. "I want you to be safe and happy."

"In another man's bed?"

He uttered a low curse.

"Letting him do all the wonderful things you did yesterday when you put your hands on me?" she went on ruthlessly. "Letting him kiss and caress me—"

"No, blast you, no!" he growled, covering her mouth with his hand. "You know that's not what I want."

When she kissed his palm, he seized her chin and stared at her a long, painful moment. Then another oath exploded out of him, and he took her mouth with his.

As he kissed her with a savage passion he'd never shown before, she exulted. Here was the fervent lover she'd imagined in her dreams, who couldn't live without her. He couldn't seem to get enough, plundering her mouth as his hands roamed her body to take wanton liberties with a reckless urgency that thrilled her.

"Ellie," he rasped as he branded her cheeks and jaw and brow with burning kisses. "Ellie . . . why must you persist in bedeviling me?"

"Because that's what it takes to have you," she answered truthfully. "And I am willing to fight for what I want."

A rough laugh escaped him. Then he scooped her up in his arms and stalked toward a door at the back of the study.

"Where are we going?" she breathed.

"You win, love." His raw gaze pierced hers. "You wanted a night of passion, so I'm taking you next door to where I've been sleeping this past week." His voice grew husky. "I'm taking you to my bed."

Her heart leaped. Having him make love to her was more than she'd hoped for. But as they entered the room, she knew it would never be enough. Even his temporary lodgings bore traces of him—a monogrammed shaving set left askew on a table, a black waistcoat dangling from a chair post, the scent of saltpeter he could never erase from his clothing . . .

She buried her face in his chest. She didn't want to think about tomorrow.

Apparently neither did he, for he set her down beside the bed and began to claw off his clothes, a wild creature wanting freedom from the trappings of civilization. "You think you can handle the dangers, do you?" His eyes darkened to slate as she took down her hair and undid her gown. "You think you can live with my unpredictable hours, my unsociable moods, my risky experiments."

The unspoken promise of a future that lay in those questions made her heart leap. "Yes." She shimmied out of her gown. "I'm not afraid of danger or risk." As he ravished her with his gaze, she reached back to untie her corset. "And I'm not afraid of *you.*"

"Such a brave little soul," he growled. Now wearing only his drawers and shirt, he slipped behind her, clearly too impatient to wait for her fumbling attempts to remove her corset. As his fingers worked the laces loose, his mouth burned a path of kisses up from her shoulder to her ear.

"But I wonder," he went on, "how brave you'll be once you see what's to come." He dropped her corset to the floor, then filled his hands with her breasts, kneading them through her chemise. "I wonder how you'll react once you realize the many wicked, lascivious things I want to do to you—"

"Do them all!" she cried, turning into his arms. "Every single one!" She tore open his shirt in a frenzy of desire, and when he yanked it off she reveled in the sight of his bare chest, swathed in muscle, ornamented with black curls, and all hers for the taking. "Do everything, I beg you."

"God help me," he muttered as she explored him with her hands, his breath growing more ragged by the moment.

When she paused shyly at the waistband of his drawers, he caught her hand and urged it inside to caress him *there.* "You said you weren't afraid. . . ." he taunted her.

"I'm not," she said shakily, though she wasn't sure what to make of the hard, thick length of him. Seeing the modest privates on statues had given her a rather different expectation of what a real man's might be like. "I must say this is quite a substantial . . . collection of parts."

With a ragged laugh, he moved her hand to his buttons. "Then take off my drawers. Let's see just how brave you really are, love."

She did as he bade, feeling a bit nervous. But that was nothing to what she felt when she unveiled his rigid flesh, saw it thrusting forward boldly, eager for her perusal. "Heavens," she whispered, half in excitement, half in alarm.

"Still want your 'night of passion'?" he asked hoarsely.

Her answer was to slip off her chemise, then climb onto the bed and lie back with a tremulous smile. His eyes went wide, then scoured her with excruciating leisure, taking in her heavy breasts, her rounded belly, her wide hips.

"I was wrong," he uttered in an aching whisper as he followed her onto the bed. "You're not merely pretty, love. You're beautiful. More beautiful than any man could ask for."

Her tears started anew, not only because of his words, but because of his worshipful expression. She'd never hoped for such from any man, and now . . .

Now he lavished his reverence on every part of her that she'd maligned for being unattractive. He molded her breasts, licked at her belly, fondled her between the legs until she ached so badly for him that she began to beg for release. By the time he rose up to press his flesh against her tender parts, it was almost a relief.

His gaze played hotly over her body as he prepared her with his fingers. "So warm, so lovely," he murmured, easing himself inside her. "And all mine."

"Yes, yours." She clung to his shoulders, more than a little anxious at the unfamiliar sensation of having him there, so palpable and hard and insistent.

"Be brave a little longer, love," he whispered, his brow taut with the effort of taking his time with her. "If you can hold on, I promise not to make it too awful."

Awful?

Then he drove himself to the hilt inside her. The surprise of having him seated so deeply startled her more than it pained her. Then he began to kiss her above, and move inside her below, and even *that* fleeting pain was swiftly forgotten.

Because she was riding with the corsair, undulating over seas, hastening before the wind, toward adventure and discoveries and, yes, danger. The more he moved, the more she craved it, arching to meet his plunges, digging her fingernails into his back.

"Ellie . . . love . . . I want . . . I need . . . God help me . . . I need *you*," he rasped as he brought her closer and closer to the pleasure he promised with every shattering thrust.

"I need you, too," she whispered, afraid to tell him that her feelings were far more reckless than mere need. "Take me, Martin." *Forever.*

Then they were climbing higher, farther, faster, until they crested a wave to crash in a glory of wild, impetuous danger.

She cried out. Or perhaps he did. All she knew, as he shook and strained against her, was that she would rather die than leave him after this.

Did he feel the same? The question plagued her even as he slumped upon her, his mouth dragging languid kisses along her cheek and neck and hair. While he slid off to lie beside her, she tried to ignore the pesky question, preferring to savor the simple joy of having him pull her close, nuzzle her ear, and twine his fingers idly in her hair.

But as he settled himself against her with a sigh of pleasure, she knew she had to ask what their lovemaking meant for the future. Perhaps *he* thought it was settled, but he'd said nothing about love *or* marriage amidst all the sweet words he'd murmured. If this was to be only the night of passion she'd asked for, she had to know, so she could begin learning to hide the broken pieces of her heart.

"Martin," she whispered after a moment.

Silence. She drew back to stare at him. His eyes were closed, and his breathing steady and even. Why, the unfeeling wretch was asleep!

"Martin!" she said sharply.

He roused only enough to settle more comfortably beside her, then slipped right back into his doze. She threw herself upon the pillow with a frown. Then she remembered that he'd barely had any sleep in the past two days.

She sighed. There would likely be no rousing him for hours. Unfortunately she couldn't stay in his bed until he awoke. Meg might stir in the night and wonder where she was. She had to be in the room when the children and her aunt rose for Christmas morn anyway, and if she lay here much longer, they might *both* end up sleeping until noon. That was too risky even for the new, bold Ellie.

Besides, it would be better to have this discussion in the morning, when he was fully in command of his faculties. She still had no desire to force him into marriage: he was a grown man who knew his own mind, and she had made her arguments. If he was still fool enough to prefer his solitary life, she wouldn't beg for his love. Even spinsterhood was preferable to that.

Leaving the bed, she dressed as best she could without help. Then she returned to him just long enough to brush the chestnut curls from his forehead and press a kiss to his smooth brow. "Good night, my love," she whispered.

He didn't even stir as she slipped out the door.

Chapter Ten

Dear Cousin,

You mean that I let my heart lead me into trouble. I admit to that freely. But unlike you, sir, I believe that one's heart will never steer one wrong.

Your emotional friend,
Charlotte

After a night spent in fitful, erotic dreams, Ellie was wakened shortly after dawn by sounds of loud confusion. She hurried into the adjoining room, where her aunt hobbled about on the crutches she'd just begun using the day before. She was trying to soothe the boys and Meg, who were clustered atop her bed, each fighting to tell her their own version of some dire news.

"Oh, thank heaven you're up," Aunt Alys said as she spotted Ellie. "Your father has arrived. And apparently he's bent on taking us all off at once, as soon as we pack. Or so the children tell me."

"At once?" she exclaimed, her heart dropping into her stomach.

Tim rushed to her. "Yes, it's too horrible. Uncle Joseph said to rouse you and Mama because we're going right away! We're not to open our gifts yet or anything! And we're going to miss the goose and plum pudding and Yorkshire pudding and—"

"What does Lord Thorncliff say to this?"

The children exchanged glances. "Don't know. He wasn't downstairs," Percy said.

He was probably still asleep. "Stay here, children. I'll go talk to Papa."

"Yes, talk some sense into him," her aunt said. "Whisking us all away on Christmas? I don't know what he can be thinking. . . ."

She dressed as her aunt clomped about voicing loud complaints from the other room. Then Ellie hurried downstairs to find her father making demands of a very flustered Mr. Huggett. Martin was nowhere in sight, though how he could sleep through such commotion was beyond her.

"I don't care what elaborate dinner you've had prepared, sir," her father boomed, his barrel chest shaking with outrage. "My daughter and the others shan't remain one moment longer under this roof. Where are your footmen with those trunks, man—"

"Papa!" Ellie cried, torn between delight at seeing him and dismay about what he was attempting.

"Ellie, my girl!" Hurrying to meet her at the foot of the stairs, he gathered her up in his arms as if she'd been lost to him for years rather than a week. "I'm sorry I couldn't come before this. I didn't even receive word of it until two days ago, and the roads are still slick. That's why it took me so long to get here."

"It's all right," she reassured him. "We've been perfectly well. Lord Thorncliff has been very kind."

"Thorncliff is the devil himself," he hissed. Casting Mr. Huggett a foul glance, he pulled her out of the man's hearing. "I know you haven't heard about the fellow's reputation, but it's believed that he *murdered* his brother to gain this property. Why the local folk didn't arrest him is anyone's guess, but he certainly has no business allowing two respectable females to tarnish their reputations by residing under his roof without a chaperone."

"Nonsense, he had no choice," she bit out, annoyed that he should swallow the gossip about Martin so thoroughly. "We're very grateful to his lordship for taking us in. Otherwise we would have been in dire straits indeed. And I do know the rumors, but they're wrong. Lord Thorncliff has been nothing but courteous to us. If you won't trust me in this, ask Aunt Alys."

He snorted. "Your aunt was injured and hardly in her right mind to form an opinion. Otherwise I doubt she would have allowed the Black Baron to take advantage of you all."

"Don't call him that!" She groaned when her father's eyes narrowed dangerously. "He didn't take advantage of us. Nothing untoward happened."

"All the same, we're leaving as soon as those blasted footmen get the trunks packed."

"But, Papa, it would be rude to leave without even thanking his lordship!"

"I would gladly have a word with the man if he were

here, but he is not." Her father jutted his chin toward Mr. Huggett. "Or so his servant claims."

"What?" She went over to take Mr. Huggett aside as her father went to the door to look for the coach's approach. "Where is Lord Thorncliff?" she asked, fighting to keep her voice even.

"He came down shortly before dawn, miss, and asked if any of you were up. When I said no, he said he was going out and would be back in a few hours." Mr. Huggett leaned close with a knowing air. "He said to make sure that I told *you* most specifically, in case you should happen to come down early."

What was she supposed to make of that? "He didn't say where he was going?"

"I'm sorry, miss, no. But someone has already checked the barn, and it's locked. He might have gone to the mine, but it's closed today so I don't think he went there, either."

"Find him, please!" Trying not to panic, she strode back to her father. "Papa, we must at least stay until his lordship returns."

"No, indeed. I shan't wait on that scoundrel's leisure. If he wishes to speak to us, he can find us easily enough at the inn in Hensley."

"Hensley?" Her alarm eased a little. Hensley was nearby.

"I stopped there to reserve us rooms before I came here. I want to consult the doctor about your aunt before we go on, and since it's Christmas, I thought we could stay the night there and return to Sheffield on the morrow."

"An excellent idea," she said in a rush, struggling to hide her relief.

Her father hailed a footman coming down the stairs. "You there, are the trunks being packed?"

"I believe so, sir."

"Ellie, go help your aunt." He cast a dark glance about the sparsely furnished hall. "I am impatient to be away from this gloomy place."

"It's *not* gloomy!" Ellie protested. "I find it rather . . . poetic."

He shook his head, as he always did at what he called her "fanciful notions." "Poetic or not, the sooner we are away, the better."

For the next half hour Ellie did her best to stall him, though once he came up to hurry the packing along, she could stall no more. She consoled herself that Martin would surely follow them to Hensley if they left the manor before he returned. He had to, if only to say good-bye.

Unless he sees this as his chance to be rid of me without any fuss.

No, she couldn't believe that. She wouldn't.

When everything was packed, and Papa had carried her aunt down to settle her comfortably in the carriage, she took Mr. Huggett aside. "Tell his lordship that he is invited to join us for Christmas dinner at the Rose and Crown in Hensley today."

"Yes, miss." But he wouldn't look her in the eye.

"You *will* tell him, won't you?" she pressed.

"I will, I swear." Mr. Huggett sighed. "But I cannot promise he will go. You know how he is."

"He must," she said, determined to listen to her heart and not her fear. She dug into her pocket for the gold button. "Give him this. Tell him he owes me a boon."

He might come after her just to dispute that lie. Either way, she had to see him again before they left the area for good.

"Aye." Mr. Huggett cast her a wistful smile. "Whatever happens, you should know that it's been an honor to serve you. I think I can safely speak for the servants in saying that we would be happy to have you return anytime."

"Thank you, Mr. Huggett," she whispered past the lump lodged in her throat. "I hope to see you again soon."

As they rode off in her father's two carriages, she clung fervently to her hope of a return. Because it would be no Christmas for her if she didn't.

When Martin had awakened near dawn to find that Ellie had returned to her bed, he'd gone downstairs to find Huggett and the footmen bustling about in preparations for Christmas morning. Though he'd given up on stopping any of that days ago, it had been too much for him to handle with his thoughts in such a turmoil. He'd had a sudden violent urge to escape it before the children awakened and added their own brand of chaos to it. He had to think, to plan.

After walking aimlessly, he'd somehow found himself at his brother's grave, which lay in a far spot on the estate that had always been Rupert's favorite, overlooking the lake where he'd enjoyed rowing.

Martin had visited it every week since his brother's death. He'd told himself he did it as a reminder of what he owed to his brother and the miners, but after last night he knew differently. Ellie had been right. It had been a penance. All of it—his isolation, his rigid rules for the staff, even his neglect of the manor. He *had* been punishing himself—not just for his part in Rupert's death, but for being allowed to work and eat and breathe while his brother languished forever in the grave. It wasn't right. It wasn't fair. But then, life wasn't generally right or fair.

Or safe, as Ellie had pointed out. He'd used Rupert's death as an excuse to protect himself from life, and instead he'd condemned his heart to a vast wasteland where his guilt had become a kind of solace. A deadly and ruinous solace.

Then she'd burst upon him with her bright smiles and her ridiculous quotations. And her wonderful, forgiving, open heart. Now he had to make a choice. Embrace the happiness she offered or sink further into the guilt that had become his prison. It couldn't be mere coincidence that her coming had given him the solution to the problem of his fuse that had plagued him for three years. It was hard to think straight when one's mind was mired in misery.

He couldn't banish the guilt that still lay heavy upon his soul, and doubted he could ever rid himself of it entirely. But perhaps he could put it into its proper place and turn to living his life. With Ellie. With the woman he loved.

A moment of panic seized him. Loved? Oh, God—the very idea struck fear into his soul. Loving was the greatest danger of all. If he loved her, and something happened to her . . .

The answer is not to deny yourself family or friends or love. That only poisons the soul. Samuel Johnson said that 'Solitude is dangerous to reason, without being favourable to virtue.' By condemning yourself to this lonely life, you save no one, not even yourself.

A faint smile touched his lips. Leave it to his Ellie to quote some stuffy old writer to make her point.

His Ellie?

Yes—his. He couldn't live without her, come what may.

He stared down at the grave another moment, then clapped his hat back on his head. "Forgive me, Rupert, but I must go. It's Christmas morn. And I think it's time I stop mourning a death on Christmas, and start celebrating a birth instead."

With lighter steps he turned for home, eager to embrace his future. But the moment he entered the manor to a stillness too like the grave he'd just left, he knew something was wrong.

Where were the children clamoring for their presents, the footmen setting the table? *Where was Ellie?*

"They're gone," came a weary voice. He whirled to find a disconsolate Huggett slumped in a chair by the hearth where the Yule log still smoldered. "Mr. Bancroft came and took them all to the Rose and Crown in Hensley. They're leaving for Sheffield tomorrow."

Ellie was *gone*? Without waiting to speak to him, to settle what lay between them? No doubt that was her father's doing. But for the merest moment, Martin was tempted to accept it as a sign that he wasn't meant for happiness, that he must have been mad to think otherwise.

Then he remembered her sweet face and the chatter of the children and the hope she'd brought thundering in the moment she'd arrived. *I am willing to fight for what I want,* she'd said.

And now, so was he.

"The young miss said I was to invite you to join them for Christmas dinner at the Rose and Crown." Huggett rose morosely and came toward him. "And I was to give you this." He handed Martin a gold button.

What the devil? Ah yes, the "lucky raisin."

"I told the young miss that like as not you wouldn't wish to go, but she said to remind you that you owe her a boon."

With a laugh that startled Huggett, he stuffed the button into his pocket, his heart lighter than it had felt in years. He should have known his Ellie would never let him go so easily.

"Tell me, Huggett, do you think the Rose and Crown will be able to get a goose today? Or any of the other trappings for a decent Christmas dinner?"

Huggett's face reflected a faint hope. "I would be quite surprised if they could, my lord, especially at this late date."

"And do *you* happen to have such necessities lying about the house somewhere, enough to feed a large family?"

"I do indeed, sir," Huggett said, his voice thrumming with excitement.

"Well, then, man, pack it all up—every pie and pan and loaf of bread. We're going to town."

Chapter Eleven

Dear Charlotte,

Follow your heart if you must, madam. I suppose that is the way of all women, especially at this time of year.

With best wishes for a Merry Christmas,

Michael

If not for the worry in her heart, Ellie might have been amused by the heated conversation taking place between her father and the innkeeper. The Rose and Crown hadn't expected seven people for dinner. The innkeeper's wife had only planned a modest repast, since the other staff were celebrating with their families, a fact the innkeeper, a grizzled Yorkshireman, kept trying patiently to explain.

"We should have stayed at Thorncliff Hall," Aunt Alys murmured beside her. "Your father can be so impetuous."

Ellie sighed. The boys had done naught but complain since they'd left, and Meg kept asking when they were going to see Lord Thorncliff again—a question Ellie wanted answered as well.

Suddenly Charlie called out from the window, "Come see, everyone! There's a parade!"

A parade? On Christmas Day in a provincial town like Hensley? That was hardly likely. But when the others rushed to look out the window, she did, too. And what she saw struck the breath from her lungs.

Martin led a procession of servants in carts, his great black mare stamping majestically, ribbons streaming from his saddle. The greenery she and the children had used to deck the manor now adorned a cart pulled by a horse Huggett rode as he held a Yule candle high. And in the cart were . . .

"Look!" Percy cried. "His lordship has brought us Christmas dinner!"

As tears stung Ellie's eyes, she held her hand to her mouth to contain a sob of joy. He had indeed. More important, he had come for her. He had come!

At that moment, Martin looked up and spotted her in the window. Doffing his hat, he cast her a smile so brilliant that it warmed every inch of her heart.

"Now that's a sight for sore eyes," the innkeeper said as he stared out. "Ain't seen his lordship smile like that since the terrible day his brother were killed. Some said he would never recover, he was that overwrought."

Her father glanced to the innkeeper and then to her. "Is that so? I'd heard otherwise."

Papa probed the man for more details and the innkeeper began supplying what he knew, but Ellie paid them no mind. She lifted her skirts and ran out.

In moments she was downstairs, reaching the door just

as Martin opened it. Heedless of who might see them, he caught her up in his arms and kissed her soundly, his servants behind him letting out a cheer.

When he drew back, his eyes were shining and she had every answer she'd wanted. But before he could give her the words, too, her father appeared at the top of the stairs.

"See here, sir, unhand my daughter!"

"Papa—" she began.

"Let me handle this, love," Martin murmured as he drew her to his side, keeping his arm anchored about her waist. "Good morning, sir. I see that you arrived safely."

"Don't 'good morning' me, you scoundrel," her father said as he descended. "I want to know what you think you're doing with my daughter."

The boys and Meg scrambled down behind him, eyes alight with curiosity, and the innkeeper helped her aunt move down enough to see what was happening.

As Ellie glanced at Martin, her heart in her throat, a twinkle appeared in his eyes. He pulled something from his pocket. "It's very simple. Your family and I played snapdragon the other night, and in the process I acquired this." He held up the gold button. "I'm told it's the 'lucky raisin,' allowing me to demand a boon of someone in the party. So I've come to demand it of your daughter."

Percy snorted. "But *Ellie* was the one who—"

"Be quiet, Percy!" Aunt Alys hissed, making him jump.

Papa's eyes narrowed as he marched toward them. "And what boon might that be?"

Martin squeezed her side. "Her hand in marriage, sir." He turned to her, his gaze as bright as the gold button. "I love you, Ellie, and I can't live another day without you. I will give up my penance for you. Will you take me, dangers and all?"

"Yes, Martin, yes," she whispered. "I love you, too."

"Now see here," Papa broke in. "You're not the first man to be tempted by my daughter's fortune, but that doesn't mean—"

"I don't care about her fortune, sir," Martin said evenly, turning to meet her father's stern gaze. "Though we would prefer to have your blessing."

"What if my blessing comes at a stiff price?" her father asked in a hard voice. "Will you give up her fortune to have my blessing?"

"Papa! I *want* to marry him, and he deserves—"

"It's all right, Ellie," Martin murmured. "I told you from the beginning, I don't need your money."

"He don't, 'tis true," the innkeeper put in. "Everyone knows that his lordship's estate brings in over five thousand a year. And the mine is earning more now than it ever did when his brother owned it."

"What?" She twisted round to look over at the servants. "But Mr. Huggett said—"

"Forgive me, miss," the butler replied with a blush. "You were so convinced that his lordship had fallen on hard times that it seemed rude to tell you otherwise."

She let out a laugh, remembering how neatly Huggett had manipulated her into decking the manor in greenery despite his master's wishes.

She glanced up at Martin, who was eyeing her and Huggett with a perplexed expression, and flashed him a giddy smile. "Very well, sir, I shall grant your boon—though I do have one condition of my own."

"Oh?" he asked, arching an eyebrow.

"You must promise never to get rid of Mr. Huggett."

Martin began to laugh, and so did she. Then the boys joined them, dancing about while her father stood there stunned and her aunt beamed.

"Come now," Martin cried, pulling Ellie out of the doorway. "The food is getting cold, and we have a dinner to eat."

As the servants hauled in the roast goose and Christmas pie and plum pudding, the boys were beside themselves with joy, exclaiming over each new treat in wonder.

"His lordship knows how to keep Christmas well, if I do say so myself," the innkeeper pronounced.

Little Charlie Dickens stared round at all the feast, and in a burst of pleasure cried, "God bless us, every one!"

And so He did.

Author's Note

Yes, I took the ultimate dramatic license—I put Charles Dickens himself in my book and gave him some of his own lines from *A Christmas Carol.* Fortunately the timing of my book was perfect for it, occurring exactly between when his family moved to a suburb of London and his father entered debtor's prison. How could I resist?

I also appropriated the invention of the safety fuse for my hero. The real inventor was a man named William Bickford, who lived in a mining town and decided to do something about all the needless deaths from explosion. His invention came about when he saw a man weaving rope and had a "Eureka!" moment. His design is the same one used today for fuses for explosives.

And yes, snapdragon was not only a real game, but it became quite popular in the Victorian era. It's not as bad as it sounds (I experimented to be sure). The song (contained in Robert Chambers's *The Book of Days*) is also real, although longer. The "lucky raisin" is a variant I was delighted to be able to use!

Snowy Night with a Highlander

Julia London

Prologue

London
1806

Lady Gilbert, a self-proclaimed great admirer of dogs, was compelled to bring her talented terrier to an afternoon tea party in Mayfair one cold afternoon, where she commenced to command the little dog to perform many canine feats. Up on his hind legs he went to beg eagerly for a treat, over he rolled at the lilting suggestion of his owner. And the *pièce de résistance*: he leapt vertically two feet into the air and latched on to a piece of leather Lady Gilbert dangled before him, then hung there, twisting and turning in his determination to have it. When Lady Gilbert at last relented, the little dog strutted proudly with the leather in his mouth, pausing only to lift his leg and mark Lady Osbourne's hem.

In the ensuing mêlée, the Earl of Lambourne's London butler appeared in the salon and informed the tea's hostess, the earl's sister, Lady Fiona Haines, that two official-looking gentlemen had called and insisted on having a word.

Fiona received them in the drawing room. She was a bit flushed, having tried to help Lady Gilbert corral the culprit, which led only to the toppling of a chair and crystal vase. She explained that her brother, the earl, was away just now, as she tucked a strand of rich brown hair behind her ear. Away indefinitely, she added.

Forever, as far as she knew, given the scandal brewing in London.

Fiona loved her brother, Jack, fiercely, but she was aware that he was an inveterate rake, both in their native Scotland and in London—and perhaps as far away as Ireland. She was also aware that Jack had been accused—falsely and unjustly, according to him—of having committed adultery with the Princess of Wales. The Prince of Wales intended to exploit that accusation, if he could manage it, in a very public trial of divorce. That could be devastating for Jack, for as everyone knew, adultery with any woman was morally reprehensible, but adultery with the Princess of Wales was a highly treasonable offense.

As Jack wrote in his hastily penned letter to Fiona from Eastchurch Abbey, he'd rather be hanged than spend his life in Newgate, and that he'd be in Scotland until "this bloody bad business was done."

Fiona glossed over these small details when she said to the gentlemen Woodburn and Hallaby, "I canna say when he might return, but I should be delighted to give him your card the moment he does."

The two gentlemen, who did indeed look rather official, exchanged a look with one another. "Forgive me, madam, but Lord Lambourne is in a spot of trouble."

Fiona's heart fluttered a bit. "Oh?"

"If I may speak indelicately?" Woodburn asked.

Fiona swallowed and nodded.

"The Prince of Wales has been egregiously offended by the rumors that your brother, his friend, may have lain with the Princess of Wales. He is determined to bring swift justice to *anyone* who might have compromised the rightful succession of his daughter to the throne."

She must not have appeared to be suitably alarmed, because Sir Woodburn stepped forward. "It is a very serious offense, my lady. If the earl is found to be guilty, he could very well be sentenced to hang for his crime."

A small swell of panic filled Fiona's breast, but she managed to remain calmly inscrutable. "That is very distressing news, sir, although I am confident my brother would be found innocent of these ridiculous accusations were it to come to that. Nevertheless, I canna imagine what you'd have me do. My innocent, virtuous brother is away presently." She mustered what she hoped was the sincerest of smiles.

"Perhaps there is something you might do, my lady," Lord Hallaby interjected regally. "The king does not necessarily believe *all* the ugly rumors that swirl around London. In fact, he, too, considers Lambourne to be his friend and remarks with great fondness the memories he has of a royal hunt a few years ago at Balmoral."

"How very kind of his majesty."

"The king would not like to see the earl involved in what has all the markings of being a very public and ugly scandal," Hallaby continued. "The king would like to think of his friend tucked safely away until this wretched ordeal is at an end."

If she understood them correctly, the prince would have Jack hauled to London and tried for adultery, while his father, the king, hoped Jack would remain tucked away to avoid it?

"The king is hopeful," Hallaby said very low, "that you might impress on your brother the serious nature of the offense of which he has been accused and suggest that perhaps he might move deeper into Scotland. You know—into the hills there."

"The Highlands," Fiona said, and wished she could sit down to think a moment. How did they suppose she would warn him? "I appreciate his majesty's concern," she continued uncertainly, "but I canna say anything to my brother at present as he is away."

Woodburn looked at Hallaby, then at Fiona. "The Christmas season is almost upon us, is it not? The king hopes that when you travel to join your family, you might find your brother and bear him this message—before the prince's men find him."

To Edinburgh? The wanted her to go all the way to *Edinburgh*?

"I do not wish to alarm you, madam, but the prince's men are looking for your brother as we speak," Woodburn said softly. "It is the king's genuine hope that you find him first and warn him properly. His highness should very much like to see this delicate investigation put to rest as quickly as possible. Perhaps you might want to depart at dawn's first light."

"Dawn's first light?" she echoed weakly, her mind reeling.

"A traveling chaise will be made available to you and your maid." Woodburn smiled thinly. "Good journey, Lady Fiona." He bowed his head and turned on his heel. With a quick smile for her, Hallaby was right behind him, leaving a dazed Fiona behind them.

Wasn't it peculiar how one's life could change in a mere few moments?

Chapter One

Edinburgh

The Buchanans' Edinburgh butler presented a folded letter to Duncan Buchanan on a silver tray. Duncan snatched the letter with his good hand and turned quickly—he didn't like the way the butler looked at him, as if he were a ghastly apparition. He stalked to the end of the salon to stand before the fire.

The letter made Duncan curious. He was rarely in Edinburgh since the accident had occurred, and even more rarely did he receive invitations or callers. He was something of a pariah to polite society.

He studied the writing on the letter. It was from a Mr. Theodore Seaver, a name that stirred a buried memory. He tucked the letter under his useless left arm and broke the seal with his good hand, then quickly read its contents. Mr. Theodore Seaver hoped that the Laird of Blackwood—Duncan—might receive him and his late sister's daughter, Lady Fiona Haines, at five o'clock. It was a matter of some urgency, Mr. Seaver wrote.

Fiona Haines. Duncan remembered her—a rather plain girl, save a pair of big, catlike amber eyes. But that was all he remembered about her. However, her brother, Jack, now the Earl of Lambourne, was quite another story. Duncan remembered him very clearly: a black-haired, gray-eyed roué with a liking for redheaded women. Many years ago, before either of them were really men, Jack Haines and Duncan had vied for the same redheaded woman from Aberfeldy, and Duncan had lost to him.

Duncan could not imagine what any of them would want with him now, but as he was a solitary man these days, his curiosity was piqued.

He turned partially toward the butler, glancing at him from the corner of his good eye. "Send for Mr. Cameron if you would, then. We are expecting guests at five o'clock."

As the butler went out to fetch his secretary, Duncan turned his gaze to the fire and wondered what, after all these years, could possibly bring a Haines to his doorstep.

"I canna believe what I am about to do," Fiona muttered beneath her breath as her uncle's carriage clattered down Charlotte Street en route to the estate known simply as The Gables—or, as her uncle had called it, Buchanan Palace.

"Eh? What's that you said, lass?" her uncle asked, peering at her over the rims of his spectacles, which were perennially perched on the tip of his nose.

"Naugh' that bears repeating, Uncle," she said, and sighed as she looked out at the gloomy façade of the buildings they were passing. It had done nothing but rain since she'd arrived in Edinburgh, coming down in hard, icy pellets. Christmas was still several days away, yet it was as if the worst of winter was setting in.

"You must no' fret, *leannan*," her uncle said. "I shall speak for you. No need to say a thing if you'd rather no'."

Fiona couldn't help but smile. Her aging Uncle Theodore and Aunt Lucy had always been very protective of her. "Thank you, Uncle," she said. "I've no fear of speaking for myself, and you mustna think so. But I'll be honest, sir—I do no' care for Duncan Buchanan, and I never have, and the less I must say to him, the better."

"Eh? What's that?" her uncle said, cupping a hand behind his ear.

Fiona smiled and said loudly, "I said thank you!"

He smiled, obviously pleased with his role as defender, and leaned across the carriage and patted her knee.

It was dark by the time the carriage rolled to a stop in front of the very large and cheerless estate. Only two windows showed any light from within, and a pair of crows was battling over something near the entrance. Just looking up at the cold gray monolith made Fiona shiver; she pulled her hood up over her head.

The Gables was just like Blackwood, the enormous Buchanan estate situated in the Highlands. Blackwood had always seemed rather oppressive to her, even when it was the site for celebrations. Her cousin had married in the chapel there when Fiona was a girl, and Fiona recalled thinking how strange it was to see all the flowers and cheerful music and smiling faces with thick stone walls and foreboding parapets in the background.

Jack, blast him! It was just like the rapscallion to have gone there, off for a bit of sport while he waited for the scandal to die in London and for Fiona to sweep up after him! Aunt Lucy said he'd gone to see Angus Buchanan, a distant cousin of the awful laird there, but one who enjoyed duck hunting this time of year. Now *she* would be forced to darken the threshold of the one place in all of Scotland she swore she'd never visit again.

The door suddenly swung open, and a swath of light spilled out onto the drive. A butler stepped out and held his lantern high. "Mr. Seaver, I presume?"

"What's that?" her uncle called back to him.

"Yes sir," Fiona said.

"Seaver!" her uncle shouted, having ascertained the question. "Theodore Seaver at your service, sir!"

"This way if you please," the butler said, and stepped back, gesturing for them to enter the narrow passageway that led to the house.

Uncle Theodore did not hear well, but he understood the gesture, and with his hand firmly cupping her elbow, he propelled Fiona forward.

As it turned out, the house was not nearly as imposing as it looked from the outside. In the main foyer, a woolen rug warmed the stone floor, and in addition to the usual sets of armor and swords that families like the Buchanans felt obliged to display on their walls, there was a vase of fresh hothouse flowers and a portrait of a beautiful woman gracing the small hearth.

They weren't all ogres, then.

"Shall I have your cloaks?" the butler asked, extending his hands.

Uncle Theodore was quick to help Fiona out of hers, and as he methodically removed his hat and gloves, his greatcoat, his scarf, and yet a second scarf and handed then to the butler, Fiona shook out her skirts and smoothed her lap.

She was wearing one of her best gowns—it was brocade, claret in color and intricately embroidered. It had been fashioned for her by one of the finest modistes in London, and her friend Lady Gilbert had remarked that it showed her figure to its fullest advantage. Not that Fiona cared a wit what Duncan Buchanan might think of her figure, no sir, no indeed. She had ceased to care about anything to do with that arse several years ago.

Having divested himself of what seemed a mound of clothing, Uncle Theodore grabbed the ends of his waistcoat and gave it a good tug before looking expectantly at the butler.

The butler handed off the mound of clothing to a waiting footman, then bowed his head. "Welcome to The Gables," he said. "If you please." He stepped into a dark corridor, indicating they should follow.

Fiona looked at her uncle. Her uncle winked and held out his arm. Fiona sighed again, put her hand on his arm, and lifted her chin. In a matter of moments, Buchanan would discover that she was not the shy, uncertain young girl she'd been when she'd last seen him, if he remembered her at all. It had been more than a few years; she really wasn't certain how many years it had been. She would have to give it some thought. But one thing was certain—he was undoubtedly still the most tiresomely supercilious man in all of Scotland.

They were shown into a rather large drawing room that had been divided into two rooms by a pair of heavy drapes. A man who was most decidedly not Buchanan rose from a chair as they entered and bowed respectfully to them.

Fiona curtsied as she quickly glanced around the room, searching for the magic door through which Buchanan would strut and pause to look at her with disdain. There was no door. There was only the gentleman—Mr. Cameron, he said his name was—who was saying something about being the laird's secretary and how he was authorized to hear their petition.

Petition! As if they were serfs come on a rickety cart pulled by their aged mule to ask the laird for a bit of leniency! She was hardly aware that her uncle was speaking. She was scarcely aware of anything, as it seemed that all her thoughts had been obliterated by her fury.

Behind the drapery, Duncan stood with one hand behind his back, the other hanging listlessly at his side, and his head down. He was not expecting the woman who swept impatiently into the room. And frankly, he was more than a bit taken aback. Had he not known it was Fiona Haines who would be calling, he would not have recognized her. Granted, he scarcely remembered her at all, but this woman was resplendent in the claret gown, and seemed much more sophisticated than the girl he remembered.

If she had looked like this years ago, he would have remembered her . . . he would have *bedded* her.

"Please, do sit," Mr. Cameron said, directing them both to a settee.

It was clear that Lady Fiona Haines did not want to sit, judging by the way she hung back, but her uncle gave her a stern look and put a hand to her back, steering her to the settee.

"Now then," Mr. Cameron said as he took a seat across from them, "What might the laird do for you?"

The lady made a strange choking sound and politely put her hand to her mouth and cleared her throat as Mr. Seaver bellowed, *"Pardon?"*

Cameron inched forward in his seat and said loudly, "What might the laird do for you, sir?"

"Oh, 'tis naugh' but a favor, really," Seaver said congenially. "My niece has an urgent matter she must discuss with her brother, the Earl of Lambourne. You know of him, eh?"

"I am acquainted with the name, but I've no' had the pleasure, no," Cameron said.

"Eh, what?"

"I've heard of him!" Cameron said loudly.

"Right, right. Well then, the earl, he's gone off to have a bit of a hunt, then, for he didna know Fiona would be joining us in Edinburra—indeed, none of us knew, else I would have sent a man to fetch her, but there she came, in the king's chaise no less, which, I said to me wife, Lucy, was quite a step up for our girl, it was—"

"*Uncle,*" Fiona said stiffly.

"Pardon?" he said to her. But with one rather stern look from her, he nodded. "Aye." He glanced at Cameron again. "Here she is, then, our lass, Fiona, returned to us, but desperate to speak to her brother, the earl, and there he is, all the way to Blackwood. She's determined to go to him and the wife and I, we canna stop her, for Fiona can be a bit headstrong when she's of a mind," he blithely continued as Fiona sighed heavenward.

"Nevertheless, the wife and I thought perhaps the laird or some of the Buchanan people would be returning to Blackwood for Hogmanay, eh? And would it no' be lovely, sir, if Fiona could just"—he made a gesture with his fingers that looked like someone running—"tag along? Mrs. Seaver and I could rest comfortably knowing she'd gone on with the Buchanans and no' on her own with naugh' more to protect her than the wisp of a girl she calls a lady's maid."

"I beg your pardon, sir, but the lady wishes to travel to Blackwood at this time of year?" Cameron repeated carefully.

"What's that you say?" Seaver said.

"Yes sir, to Blackwood," Fiona said politely.

Cameron fidgeted nervously with the cuff of his shirt. "My lady, you are surely aware that the roads are hard to travel this time of year, aye?"

"I am indeed aware of that. But they *are* traveled, sir."

"Aye, they are," Cameron said. "Would you be traveling alone?"

"With a lady's maid, as my uncle said. If she can be accommodated, of course."

"What'd he say?" Seaver demanded, leaning into Fiona.

"He inquired if I would have a proper chaperone!"

"Oh aye, of course," Seaver said, nodding. "You donna think we'd send her off willy-nilly, then, do you, sir? Aye, of course she'll have her lady's maid. Good solid lass, that one. Sheridan is her name, but we call her Sherri. Been with the family for nigh on ten years now, and she'll brook no tomfoolery. She's no' always been with Fiona, no, but she had a hankering to see London, and there was Fiona, off to London to be with her brother. We were sorry to lose her—"

"Uncle," Fiona said, laying a delicate hand on his arm. "I am certain Mr. Cameron does no' have time to hear our entire family history."

Seaver looked at Cameron. "All I mean to say is that Sherri's done quite right by my niece and is a proper chaperone."

"That's . . . fortunate," Cameron said uncertainly. "Lady Fiona, I must warn you that what with the snow and rain we've had, no' to mention the bitterly cold weather, the roads to Blackwood are treacherous. And there is the constant threat of highwaymen once you reach the Highlands."

From where he sat, Duncan could see Fiona folding her hands primly in her lap. "While I appreciate your concern, sir, I must speak with my brother as soon as possible. It is a matter of great urgency."

"A letter willna do, then?" Cameron gamely tried.

She shook her head. "I wouldna risk putting it to paper."

That was curious. Duncan knew Lambourne was a risk taker with a penchant for trouble, just as Duncan had been once. He guessed there was a debt of some sort, and probably a sizable one to prompt this foolish venture on his sister's part.

"And what if the laird declines?" Mr. Cameron asked.

"Then I shall take a public coach," the lady said.

"The public coach only goes as far as Aberfeldy," Cameron reminded her.

She straightened her back and raised her chin stubbornly. "I shall make do from there."

Make do from there? She was mad! Duncan certainly did not recall Fiona Haines as being mad as an old hen.

"Well then," Cameron sighed. "I shall present your request to the laird. You should have word at week's end."

"Week's *end*?" she cried.

"What comes at week's end?" Seaver demanded, cupping his hand to his ear.

"A response, Uncle," she said, and looked at Cameron. "As long as that, sir? Shall no one be leaving ere week's end?"

"I will do my best," Cameron assured her.

"His best what?" Seaver demanded.

Fiona looped her arm through her uncle's. "His best effort, Uncle!" she said loudly. "He shall call at week's end!"

"Ah," Seaver said, and smiled at Cameron. "We canna ask for better than that, eh? Thank you kindly, my good man. Our regards to the laird, then. Come along, Fiona—we've taken enough of the man's time."

Duncan waited behind the drapes until Cameron returned from seeing Fiona Haines and her uncle to the door, then slowly stepped out. Cameron was one of the few people he allowed to see him when he wasn't wearing a patch over his eye. The fire had done the most damage to his neck and left arm, which hung awkwardly and often uselessly at his side. But there was also a swath of burned, puckered skin that ran from his eye to his jaw, tugging his left eye down slightly in a manner that seemed ugly to Duncan.

If Cameron had ever been repulsed by his visage, Duncan had never seen it.

"You heard it all, milord?" Cameron asked simply.

"Every last foolish word," Duncan said gruffly, and ran a hand over the top of his head. It *was* foolish—a woman had no business traveling alone save for a lady's maid into the Highlands. But Fiona Haines seemed inordinately determined, and Seaver had guessed correctly—at the very least, Duncan would be returning to Blackwood for the Christmas feast and Hogmanay, an important Highland tradition and celebration that ushered in the new year. As the laird of Blackwood, Duncan was expected to be on hand to deliver the annual blessing of the estate's houses and livestock.

He could see from Cameron's expression that he was thinking the same thing—that he would be making the journey, and it would not do to let a young woman travel alone. He sighed. "It's bloody foolish of her. But I suppose I must, eh?"

Cameron merely nodded.

Chapter Two

Still vexed from having been summarily uprooted from London to Edinburgh, Fiona's lady's maid, Sherri, was in high dudgeon when Fiona informed her they would be traveling on to Blackwood.

"To *Blackwood*?" she echoed, her voice clearly conveying her displeasure. "Where's that, then? No' the Highlands, milady! Say it is *no'* the *Highlands*!"

"What could you possibly dislike about the Highlands?" Fiona demanded irritably. "You've never been north of Edinburra."

"And with good reason! There be naugh' but heathens up there—I've heard it said all me life."

"Heathens!" Fiona scoffed. "That's absurd! *I* hail from the Highlands, Sheridan—do you think me a heathen?"

"No, mu'um. But you've left those hills and the murderers and thieves who live in those nooks and crannies."

"Oh, for God's sake, Sherri," Fiona groaned. There was no point in arguing—she'd not convince Sherri, who was superstitious to the point of distraction, that there were good and decent people throughout the Highlands until she saw it for herself. Murderers and thieves indeed! "Pack our things," she said archly. "We've had word from the Buchanan throne that we will be departing Saturday morning."

"The laird is to take us, then?" Sherri asked as she picked up a dressing gown.

"Ha!" Fiona scoffed. "*That* would require a jewel-studded litter and a host of escorts. No' to mention a herald."

"Pardon?" Sherri asked, confused.

Fiona waved her hand at Sherri. "Nothing so lofty as the laird, I'm afraid. I understand we are to travel with the supply coach, no' in a laird's conveyance."

There was more grumbling from Sherri as she folded the gown. "Ye must know the laird, then," she said. "What's he like? An unkempt beard, I'd wager, and hands as big as chickens."

Fiona snorted. "He's clean-shaven as I recall, and I canna say the size of his hands. What I recall is that he is pompous and vulgar."

She didn't want to tell Sherri that Duncan Buchanan was the most sought-after bachelor in all the Highlands, or that he was wealthy and handsome and physically gifted in sport. Or that he had a reputation for hunting and bedding beautiful women, a skill that was rivaled only by Fiona's dear brother, Jack, the bloody rogue. Duncan Buchanan lived recklessly, enjoying the life privilege and good looks had given him. He was vain and proud and arrogant . . . and *virile*. Completely and exceedingly virile.

On her life, she'd yet to meet a man as virile as he.

And just like every other female in Scotland who could draw a breath, Fiona had been very taken with him when she'd come of age. She'd been all of seventeen and violently infatuated with the dashing young laird. She'd even suggested to Molly Elgin, whom she thought she could count among her friends, that she thought she believed she was a good match for him.

Molly had seemed surprised, but of *course* Fiona believed it was true, and why shouldn't she? She was of age, she was generally agreeable, she was the daughter of an earl, and she was a Highlander, just like him. What more could a man possibly want in a marital match?

But on the night of Fiona's coming-out, Molly Elgin—who, in hindsight, had perhaps the same lofty marriage goals as Fiona—intentionally suggested to Buchanan within earshot of her that Lady Fiona Haines might be the perfect match for him. She said it coyly, as if she meant to impart some astounding news that he would certainly find agreeable.

The moment Fiona realized what Molly was about, her heart had begun to pound so hard she could scarcely hear what he said—but she'd heard it. Every last cruel word.

"Fiona Haines?" he'd repeated, his brow wrinkling as he obviously tried to conjure her up from the scores of women in his memory. Fiona had felt her life ticking by in long, interminable seconds. She stole a glimpse of him just in time to see the light dawn in his green eyes (or were they brown? Memory had dulled his image), and for a single, glorious moment, a young and naïve Fiona had teetered on the brink of the utmost happiness.

She imagined him gazing at Molly with an expression of sheer gratitude for enlightening him on this most wonderful opportunity. An opportunity, no doubt, he had missed because Fiona had not yet come out . . . until that very night. And tonight, he would look past the other four debutantes and see her for the first time. *Really* see her.

"Lambourne's younger sister?" he said, and Fiona knew instinctively by the incredulous tone of his voice that her hopes had been dashed. "Brown hair? About so tall? Slightly reminiscent of a woodchuck?"

His friends howled.

Fiona had died a thousand deaths.

"Thank you, Miss Elgin," he said to a dumbstruck Molly, "but I'd sooner *marry* a woodchuck." And with that, he turned away, accepting the congratulatory claps on his shoulders from his friends who apparently thought his ability to liken a girl to a woodchuck was brilliance in wit.

Fiona had fled into the crowd before Molly could gauge her reaction. She had pretended not to have heard it, and for weeks after, as his remark about her made its way through the glen, Fiona laughed and pretended that it didn't bother her in the least.

Yet privately, his remark had been devastating, and when Jack left for London the following year, Fiona was close behind.

She had not returned to Scotland until now. And while she'd not had much luck on the marriage mart in the intervening years—Lady Gilbert said her fortune wasn't great enough and really, she was a *Scot*—no one in London had ever likened her to a woodchuck.

At least not to her knowledge.

Therefore, she would simply call at Blackwood, ask to see her brother, deliver the urgent message, then ask—no, *demand*—that Jack take her from Blackwood straightaway.

It was all really rather simple.

"Donna forget to pack the fur-lined cloaks and muffs, Sherri," Fiona said. "It can be quite cold in the Highlands."

"Lovely," Sherri muttered irritably on her way to the dressing room.

The Seaver townhouse was on Charlotte Square, a famously fashionable block that sat in the shadow of Edinburgh Castle. Their neighbors included some of the most prominent Scottish citizens.

That was precisely the reason Duncan preferred The Gables, which was located on the edge of the city. There were no prying eyes, no children staring, and no one to recognize him from an earlier time. Nevertheless, he arrived promptly at eleven o'clock Saturday morning as promised. He was on horseback, accompanied by Ridley, a longtime servant who drove a team of four and pulled a wagon. A wire frame, over which a tarpaulin had been erected for the ladies' convenience, created a cave over the bed of the wagon with an opening at the rear. Duncan had seen to it that a bench of sorts had been installed within the cave's walls on which the ladies would sit, but most of the space in the wagon was taken up with supplies.

The original plan had been for two Buchanan men to drive the wagon to Blackwood while Duncan led a pair of stallions he'd bought from a horse trader in Stirling. The unusual request from the Seavers, however, had prompted Duncan to make a small change—he would be accompanying the wagon now, and had sent one of the men on with the horses.

The day was bracingly cold but bright. Duncan wore his greatcoat, hat, and gloves, and in addition, he'd wrapped two scarves around his neck and face so that only his eyes—and his eye patch—were visible.

He sent Ridley, the driver, to the door to fetch the ladies. His staff was used to his idiosyncratic behavior regarding his burns—Ridley, in particular.

When summoned, the Seavers and their ward spilled out onto the walk, halting uncertainly at the sight of the wagon. Not one of them spared Duncan a glance, and Fiona Haines, in particular, looked at the wagon, then at her uncle, and then looked at Ridley with a gaze that would melt snowcaps. "I beg your pardon, sir, but you canna mean that we are to travel in *that*."

Ridley, a small, nervous man, looked anxiously at the wagon. "There's a bench within, mu'um," he said. "Put in special, for you and the lass," he said, nodding toward a petite woman standing a bit behind the family.

"A *bench*," she repeated, and marched to the end of the wagon, her fur-lined wool cloak flapping around her ankles. She leaned forward, squinting to look into the interior.

"And a brazier, mu'um," Ridley quickly added. "To keep your feet warm."

Her uncle hurried as fast as his stout legs would carry him to Fiona's side and he, too, leaned forward to peer inside. "Well then!" he said, puffing out his cheeks. "It's right cozy! Look here, then, Fiona—they've put in a bench!"

On the walk, the young woman tossed her head back and groaned audibly.

"*Lord*," Fiona said, and straightened up, clapped her gloved hands together as if she'd built the bench and was knocking the sawdust from her palms. She pressed a pair of remarkably full lips together and gave Ridley a curt nod. "It will have to do."

"Are you certain, dear?" Mrs. Seaver asked, peering into the wagon. "I donna understand why you canna wait for Jack to come back to Edinburra."

"The journey is no more than two days, Aunt Lucy. I *must* go. I should no' have waited as long as I have."

"I canna imagine what message is as urgent as that. If you'd but tell us, dear, we might be able to help you," her aunt pleaded.

For a moment, Fiona looked as if she wanted to do just that. She looked longingly at her aunt and the Charlotte Square townhouse. But then she bit her bottom lip and shook her head. "I dare no'," she said, and looked directly at Ridley, giving him a bright smile. "We've a few bags, Mr. . . . ?"

"Ridley, mu'um. Ridley."

"Mr. Ridley. As I was saying, a few bags," she said, and pointed to the footman who had emerged, laden with bags.

"Aye, mu'um," Ridley said.

Duncan dismounted and moved to the walk to help with what seemed like far too many bags for a quick trip to the Highlands, passing close to Fiona on his way. She glanced at him, but he saw no hint of recognition, nothing but a pretty frown furrowing her brow as she studied the wagon.

She'd been gone from Scotland too long, then, if she feared a ride in a wagon. But he supposed that being conveyed to Scotland in the king's chaise might color one's perspective on such things.

With the bags loaded, the women safely tucked inside, Ridley bid Mr. and Mrs. Seaver a good day. Not one of them had glanced at Duncan, apparently believing he was a servant. That suited Duncan—he really had no need to speak to them. In a matter of two days, he likely would never see any of them again. So when Ridley looked at him, he gave him a nod, and Ridley sent the team trotting forward through the streets of Edinburgh.

* * *

They'd been underway a little more than an hour, but Fiona feared she would strangle Sherri if she could but feel her fingers. Sherri complained incessantly—it was as cold as a Norseman's breath, her bones ached from all the pitching about, and in spite of the grill that covered the brazier, she did not feel like stomping out every bit of ash that was sent flying for Fiona's apparently baseless fear that it might set one of the thick woolen lap rugs afire.

It wasn't that Sherri wasn't perfectly justified with her complaints—it was terribly cold, and the little brazier scarcely warmed their feet. And without benefit of the sort of springs that equipped a proper carriage, each dip in the road was, admittedly, bone-jarring. Nevertheless, there was naught they could do about their less-than-comfortable accommodations now, and Fiona could not endure endless hours of carping. Her usually cheerful mien had been terribly compromised. "By all that is holy, Sherri, please cease complaining!" Fiona begged the maid. "I canna bear another moment of it!"

"And I canna bear another moment in this blasted wagon!" Sherri shot back.

Fiona looked at her with surprise, but Sherri returned her gaze defiantly. "We were in a king's chaise no' a fortnight past, but look at us now, will you, in the back of a wagon like a pair of swine."

Fiona gasped.

"I didna want to leave London," Sherri angrily continued. "And I donna want to go up into the Highlands where thieves and murderers lie in wait to cut our throats!"

"Oh, dear *God*," Fiona said irritably. "Your imagination has taken hold of your common sense!"

"I should no' have come," Sherri said, ignoring her, folding her arms tightly across her body.

"And where might you have gone, then?" Fiona demanded.

"You're no' the only lady in Edinburra, mu'um," Sherri sniffed. "No' at all. Or in London, for that matter. Lady Gilbert said to me more than once that if I was ever in need of a position, I should come to her."

"*What?*" Fiona cried. "Lady Gilbert *said* that?"

Sherri shrugged and looked straight ahead, to the patch of road they could see out the back of the wagon.

Before Fiona could speak, the wagon shuddered to a rude halt.

Both women leaned forward, trying to see out the back opening. They could see nothing but the torsos of many horses that appeared to be tethered. A moment later, Ridley's head popped up in the small opening. "Beg your pardon, mu'um," he said. "We're on the outer reaches of Edinburra. We'll take on some grain before we start up. There's a public house if you're of a need."

He disappeared again.

"Beg your pardon," Sherri said, and moved off the bench.

Fiona watched her go, picking her way through the supplies, and then sliding off the end of the wagon. "I'm quite all right!" she snapped after Sherri. "No need for your assistance!"

But Sherri had already disappeared from sight, and with a sigh of exasperation, Fiona pushed aside the lap rugs.

Her legs were stiff, making it hard to step around the supplies. When she reached the end of the wagon, she lifted the hem of her cloak and attempted to disembark gracefully. Unfortunately, she half leaped, half fell out the back opening with a cry of surprise, and was caught—quite literally—in the strong hands of the man who rode with them. He gripped her arm tightly and put a steadying hand to her waist, righting her.

Fiona glanced up at him. Because most of his face was covered by a scarf and one eye was covered by a black patch, she could see nothing but a fine brown eye. It was remarkable in its clarity and was, she noticed a little uneasily, quite intent on her.

She smiled thinly. "I beg your pardon—thank you."

His hands drifted away from her body, and with a bow of his head, he stepped back, giving her berth. Fiona looked at him again. "What is your name?" she asked him.

He hesitated a moment. "Duncan."

"Duncan," she repeated. There were scores of Duncans in this part of Scotland, but this man did not seem like a Duncan to her—at least not the sort with whom she was acquainted. "Duncan," she repeated, her eyes narrowing. She glanced at his hands. They were as big as chickens. "Thank you, Mr. Duncan." She walked briskly toward the public house, trying to ignore the feeling his hand had left on her waist, which lingered a bit longer than it ought to have done.

The public house was teeming with patrons, mostly men. There were a few women in addition to a handful of children who were playing some sort of game that had them running through the throng. The inn was a way station, Fiona gathered, and struggled through the crowd to the retiring rooms.

The accommodations for ladies were lacking, to say the least, but Fiona made do.

She emerged and labored again through the crowd to the door, pausing only when one young lad collided with her in his haste to get away from the pair of girls who pursued him. After skirting two men who were shouting at one another about a dog, of all things, Fiona stepped outside, took a moment to straighten her cloak and draw a deep breath of fresh air.

She glanced around. Sherri was nowhere to be seen.

"If you please, mu'um, we'd best be on our way."

She started at the sound of Ridley's voice and twirled around. He was standing in front of Mr. Duncan, a full head shorter. Fiona looked at Mr. Duncan's remarkable brown eye and hastily looked away. His expression caused a curious little shiver to course through her.

"Of course," she said, and walked to the wagon. Duncan followed her, and moved to help her up—which, Fiona realized, she was anticipating perhaps a wee bit too much—but she suddenly realized Sherri was not in the wagon and stepped back, out of his reach. "Sherri . . . my maid. She's no' here as she should be."

"What's that, mu'um?" Mr. Ridley asked, popping around the end of the wagon as he stuffed his hands into gloves.

"My maid, Sheridan Barton. She's no' here."

Mr. Ridley looked at Duncan, then at the public house. "Perhaps she's within?" he asked gingerly.

"No . . . I was just inside and there was no sign of her. Ah, but she must be around, then. I'll just have a quick look about," she said, and hurried back to the public house.

But Sherri was nowhere to be found. She was not standing out in the cold, she was not in the public house, and another examination of the wagon revealed that Sherri's portmanteau was missing.

When Fiona realized Sherri's bag was gone, too, she leaned against the wagon and sighed up at the blustery blue sky. The wench was trying to make her way back to Edinburgh—there was no other explanation.

"Mu'um?" Mr. Ridley asked anxiously.

Fiona glanced at him from the corner of her eye. "I believe, Mr. Ridley, that Sherri has decided to return to Edinburra."

He looked confused by that.

"She was fearful of traveling into the Highlands because of all the murderers and thieves waiting to nab her," she said with a roll of her eyes. "She mentioned something about finding another position—but I didna think she meant *immediately*."

Mr. Ridley's eyes widened. He glanced at the public house, then at Fiona.

"Are you . . ."

"Certain? Quite," she said, folding her arms. "Silly, foolish girl!"

Mr. Ridley looked so uncomfortable that Fiona feared he would jump out of his skin. "Then . . . then what will you have us do, mu'um?" he asked a little frantically, squinting at her.

"An excellent question," Fiona said irritably. *Damn* Sherri! Now what was she to do? And how could she go off and leave Sherri to walk back into Edinburgh?

Fiona put a hand to her forehead and shielded her eyes from Ridley. She just needed a moment to think.

Chapter Three

The good and noble reasons for which Duncan had, reluctantly, agreed to take a very foolhardy woman to Blackwood completely escaped him as Ridley explained that the foolhardy woman's even more foolhardy lady's maid had decided to return to Edinburgh.

"How?" he grunted.

"By foot?" Ridley guessed.

Oh, how bloody splendid. A woman with no more sense than the cows standing across the road was attempting to *walk* to Edinburgh?

A quick search for her on horseback turned up nothing. When Duncan heard that a public coach bound for Stirling had come through the way station, he could only assume that the chit was clever enough to at least find her way onto that coach.

Ridley looked frantic when Duncan told him that there was only one thing left to do: Ridley would take the horse and ride for Stirling, hopefully intercepting the public coach and the maid before she got herself into worse trouble. If he could not find her, he was to return to Edinburgh and deliver the news to Seaver.

In the meantime, Duncan would take the wagon and the other incorrigible female and continue on to Blackwood. He had reasoned with Ridley that he had little choice. The sun was already beginning to slide to the west and they had three, perhaps four, hours of good daylight left. He might make it as far as Clackmannan if he was lucky, and that was being optimistic. If Duncan was going to reach Blackwood for Christmas in two day's time, and begin the necessary preparations for Hogmanay, he could not turn back and lose a day.

Ridley nervously explained this to Lady Fiona, who took the news with her hands clasped demurely before her. The only indication that she understood a bloody word Ridley said was her elegantly winged brows, which slowly rose up until they seemed to disappear under the rim of her bonnet.

"Do you mean to suggest that I should go on to Blackwood with . . . *him?*" she said, nodding at Duncan, clearly not recognizing him in the least.

"You'll come to no harm," Ridley said quickly. "But we canna allow the lass to wander off by herself, aye? We canna say how much longer we might be detained, and the supplies must reach Blackwood."

The lady seemed to consider that for a moment; she looked at the wagon, then at Duncan, who glanced away from her intently curious gaze.

"You realize, Mr. Ridley, that my reputation will be called into question under your scheme, do you no'?"

Ridley's face turned very red. "I . . . I—

"Let us carry on," Duncan said brusquely. They were wasting time.

His interruption drew a startled gaze from Fiona Haines.

"We canna leave Miss Barton to the dangers of the road," Ridley suggested.

She gave him a sharp look, but shook her head no, they could not leave her.

"If you'd prefer, milady, we could arrange a seat on the public coach to Edinburra? It comes round four o'clock," Ridley suggested.

"What? No! No, no, I canna go back to Edinburra! No' now, Mr. Ridley—I've tarried too long as it is. I *must* find my brother before it is too late."

"Aye," Ridley said, and eyed the wagon. "Well then . . ."

"Oh, for God's sake!" Lady Fiona snapped, and whirled around, marching for the back of the wagon. Ridley scarcely reached her in time to help her before she launched herself into the back.

Duncan watched the wagon bounce and move from side to side as she made her way to the bench and the brazier that had surely gone cold by now. He imagined her stomping through the supplies and sitting hard on the even harder bench. It had been a long time since he'd been in the company of a woman, but he'd not forgotten the strength of a woman's ire.

When Ridley had put the gate of the wagon up and locked it in place, he gave Duncan a look of pure misery. Duncan sighed. "It remains to be seen which of us has drawn the worst hand, Ridley."

"Aye, milord," Ridley said weakly, and took the reins of Duncan's horse. Duncan waited until he'd mounted and was on his way before he climbed up onto the wagon's outside bench. He wrapped the reins around his bad hand, picked up the driving whip, and touched the neck of the lead horse with it. "Walk on," he said to the team, and flicked the reins against them.

As the coach lurched forward, he heard a tiny squeal of alarm just behind him and glanced heavenward in a silent appeal for strength.

Fortunately, his passenger remained quiet for most of the afternoon, save a cry of alarm every so often when the wagon hit a rut. He was lost in thought when he realized the sound he was hearing was not a squeak of the axle, but Lady Fiona, who, at that very moment, shouted, "*Pardon!*"

He did not stop the team from trotting along but leaned to one side and said, "Aye?"

"Will you *please* stop?" she cried. "I really *must* have you stop!"

Duncan reluctantly pulled the team to a halt. The horses had been in a rhythm of their own and stomped and snorted their displeasure.

"Aye?" he said again.

"I need . . . I should like . . . *Lord,*" she said, and the wagon began to bounce a bit. She was climbing out.

Duncan quickly unwound the reins from his hand and leaped from the bench, striding to the back of the wagon, reaching it just in time to see a lovely derrière sliding over the back gate. He reached up with the thought to help her, thought the better of it, and dropped his hand as she took the last step—misjudging it, of course—and stumbled to her feet, knocking against the wagon in a desperate bid to keep herself upright. When she was certain she was on the ground, she adjusted her bonnet, turned, and looked up at him with a pair of golden eyes with a coppery tint.

He wondered fleetingly how he'd missed such remarkable eyes all those years ago.

"I didna wish to disturb you, sir, but the truth is, what with all the jostling and banging about, I really must . . . I *need* . . ."

She was too much of a lady to bring herself to admit it, so Duncan bowed and gestured grandly to the forest that lined either side of the road. She squinted in the direction he pointed and then bit her lower lip before glancing at him sidelong. "I donna suppose there is another alternative, then?"

Under his scarf, he allowed himself a ghost of a smile.

"What if there are creatures? Or worse, highwaymen?"

He moved slightly, just enough to open the vent of his greatcoat, and showed her the pistol he wore at his side.

"Ah," she said, nodding. "That should come in quite handy . . . for *you*. Likely I will be dead, either from shame or shock, by the time you reach me. If indeed you intend to reach me." She glanced at him again. "Well then, Mr. Duncan, if you will excuse me?" And with that, she marched off the road, stepping gingerly into the trees. She paused and glanced back at him. "You may wait on the other side of the wagon, if you please!"

Duncan touched the brim of his hat and walked around to the other side of the wagon. But he peeked around the back, watching her enter the forest with her arms held wide, as if she were surrendering to someone, and slowly, carefully, made her way into the forest.

Fiona Haines, Duncan was discovering, was a curious and surprisingly lively young woman.

* * *

When Fiona emerged from the woods, the Buchanan man was standing at the back of the wagon, one arm folded across his chest, the hand resting beneath his other arm, which seemed to hang at an odd angle from his body, and one leg casually crossed over the other. His head was down and the brim of his hat was pulled low, over his face. He was tall, well over six feet, a big man with very broad shoulders.

He was intriguing, this big, silent man with the damaged arm and the patched eye, and she was curious to know what he looked like beneath the scarves and the wool coat and gloves and the eye patch. If he hadn't spoken a word or two at the way station, she would have thought him mute.

He straightened when he saw her and opened the wagon's gate. He leaned over, cupping one hand to help her up. Fiona followed him and stood a moment, looking at his hand. "Come on, then," he said low, the irritation evident in his voice.

But his voice! It was quiet and low, like a dark whisper. It sparked something in her, a rush of blood and a distant memory or a dream so fleeting she could not catch it. "I am coming," she said. "No need for a fit of apoplexy." She slipped her booted foot into his hand, felt his fingers close tightly around her foot, then vault her up, as if she were light as a feather. She put one knee down, a breath catching in her throat when he put a hand to her hip to keep her from falling backward.

Fiona quickly moved inside and glanced over her shoulder, looking at him. The Buchanan man put his good hand on the gate, and swung it shut, locking it into place, and returned her look. Their gazes held a long moment. A long, crackling moment.

"Ready?" he asked.

"Yes. Thank you," she said, and reluctantly turned away from him to pick her way through the crates and bundles to her little spot in the wagon.

When his weight dipped the wagon to one side, and he started the team to trotting again, Fiona could not help but think of that broad expanse of his back, just inches from her, and the delicious feeling of his hand on her hip.

The thought of it lulled her into a shallow sleep; she lay down on the bench, pillowing her hands beneath her face. She thought she dozed only briefly, but when the wagon came to a halt—almost flinging her to the floor—Fiona noticed it was dusk.

She pushed herself up and winced at the pain in her neck, the result of napping on the bench. The sounds of people and animals reached her—a village, she supposed—as did the growl of her stomach. Fiona made her way to the end of the wagon and climbed down, forcing a devil-may-care smile to a pair of men in dirty buckskins who—how lucky for her—were on hand to watch her emerge from the wagon. "Good evening," she said, and turned away from them, almost colliding with Mr. Duncan.

"Oh. Pardon," she said. In the waning light of day, he looked even more darkly mysterious. "Please tell me we have stopped to dine. I am famished."

"We've stopped for the night."

"For the night," she repeated, and glanced around her. The village was rather small—a few buildings on the high street and one inn. "Where are we?"

"Airth." He leaned over her and removed a saddlebag

from the back of the wagon and manuevered it over one shoulder.

She was not familiar with Airth, and wanted to ask him more, but he was moving. So Fiona moved with him.

Mr. Duncan stopped and nodded at the wagon as if she were a child. "You stay."

"Pardon, but I donna believe you are at liberty to command me about."

A look came over Mr. Duncan that suggested he did indeed have liberty, and as if to prove it, he suddenly swept her up in his arm, took three steps back, and deposited her at the wagon. "*Stay*," he ordered her, and walked on.

"What? Who do you think you are?" Fiona called after him. "My brother will hear of this!"

But Mr. Duncan was striding along, ignoring her.

"Inquire as to supper!" she added hastily.

She thought about following him, but thought the better of it, and stood next to the wagon, wincing a little against the hunger pangs she was suffering. Dusk was turning into a clear night; it would be quite cold. She hoped the inn was properly heated.

Several minutes later, Mr. Duncan appeared again, striding toward her.

"Ah! There you are! Did you order a supper?"

"They've no lodging," he said.

Fiona blinked. Then looked at the wagon. "Oh no. Oh *no*, you canna expect me to stay in that all night, sir! I'll catch my death, I will! I could perish! I could very well perish in that wagon!"

He stepped around her, slid the saddlebag off his shoulder, and tossed it into the dark interior.

"You may be quite accustomed to sleeping in the elements, but I am no'! I require a bed! And a bit of food!" she exclaimed, pressing her palms to her belly. "I grant you that your laird is something of a beast, but he would naugh' stand for this, I am really fairly certain!"

That seemed to give the man pause. He stilled and looked down at her so fiercely that Fiona recoiled a bit. "What?"

"Wait here," he said, and turned on his heel.

"Wait here?" she exclaimed, hugging herself tightly as he strode up the road. "Where are you going?"

He did not respond, naturally, and left Fiona to stand at the back of the wagon as a curious couple walked by her, eyeing her suspiciously.

"For the love of Scotland," she muttered, and peered up the road.

The Buchanan man had disappeared from sight.

Chapter Four

The innkeeper had pointed Duncan to Mrs. Dillingham, a widow who lived down the road in a whitewashed cottage. The innkeeper said she would take the occasional family or young couple in need of lodging when the inn was full.

Mrs. Dillingham looked rather alarmed to see Duncan at the door, but he hastily pardoned the intrusion and explained he was a Buchanan man, ferrying Lady Fiona Haines, the Earl of Lambourne's sister, to Blackwood.

The moment the word *lady* left his lips, Mrs. Dillingham's doughy face lit with pleasure. "A *lady*!" she exclaimed happily in a thick Scots accent. "I've naugh' had the pleasure of keeping a lady!" Her eyes were shining as Duncan imagined they would shine on a child or a favored pet.

"If you would be so kind, I will compensate you well for it."

"I'd be *delighted*! Oh, but me abode is too humble for the likes of a lady, is it no'?"

"She would be honored." He hoped to high heaven she would be honored. She certainly wasn't honored by wagons. "Might you have a bit of supper for her?" he asked, reaching for his coin purse.

"Supper! Oh, good sir, I've no doubt a lady is accustomed to finer fare—"

"She would be grateful for whatever you might have. She's no' eaten this day."

"No' eaten! Poor thing! I've a stew in the kettle, if that will suit."

"Perfectly," he said, and holding the coin purse in the claw of his left hand, he fished three coins from the bag and handed them to Mrs. Dillingham.

"*Three* pounds?" she exclaimed, looking wide-eyed at the money. "Oh, she must be a *fine* lady *indeed*!"

"Mind that you take good care of her," he said. "Look after her properly, for she's had a rough go today. I'll fetch her."

He left Mrs. Dillingham scurrying about to tidy her cottage.

Lady Fiona was precisely where he'd left her, at the back of the wagon, stomping her feet for warmth. When she saw him, she threw her arms wide and looked up at an increasingly dark sky, making a sound of relief. "You scared the wits out of me, you did!" she blustered as he approached. "For all I knew, you'd walked back to Edinburra as well, leaving me to stand here all night until the wolves came to feast upon my flesh!"

Beneath his scarf, Duncan smiled. "You've quite an imagination, lass."

"And just where have you been, then?" she demanded as he reached around her into the wagon for the smallest of her portmanteaus. "There's hardly a village here at all—I canna imagine where you've been off to, but I hope it was in the pursuit of food. On my word, I've never been so famished. Have you brought us anything to eat?"

He glanced at her as he hooked the handles of the portmanteau on his bad hand. "No."

"*Aaah,*" she exclaimed, bending backward a bit and closing her eyes. "I would eat your glove were it presented on a proper plate. Honestly, I would eat it were it presented on a *stick*."

Duncan smiled in spite of himself. "Have you what you need in here?" he asked, lifting up the portmanteau.

"What I *need*? What I need for what, pray tell? I can tell you this—there's no' as much as a morsel in there."

"Come," he said, and began walking.

"Where?" she demanded, but fell quickly in with him, glancing over her shoulder at the wagon. "Where are you taking me? If any harm comes to me, sir, I can assure you my brother, the earl, will find you and exact the proper revenge! He's rather fierce when provoked."

He gave her a withering look. "So you've said."

"What, then?" she asked with a shrug of her slight shoulders as she marched alongside him. "I've quite a lot of cause for concern, really, if you consider it from *my* shoes. My maid has deserted me, I've been left in the hands of a man I donna know, and really, you have no' said where we are going. Into the woods? It looks as if this road curves into the woods. I will grant you, it is dark, and I suppose it is possible there is more of the village around that bend, but . . . Oh my, do you smell that, Mr. Duncan?" she asked, pausing midstride and putting a hand on his useless arm to stop him. "*Do* you?" she asked, smiling up at him. "That is the most heavenly smell!" she exclaimed, clapping her gloved hands together at her breast. "*That* is the smell of roasted venison."

Duncan began to walk again, turning into the little gate of Mrs. Dillingham's cottage.

"One might find that sort of venison only in Scotland," Fiona continued to prattle, following closely behind him. "The venison in London is rather stringy—even at the queen's table, if you can believe it. She's awfully frugal, the queen, and will settle for stringy venison."

Duncan gave the door a quick rap with his knuckles.

"I would *never,* were I queen. When I was a girl, Cook used to make the most *delicious* venison stew. She used potatoes and—"

The door swung open and the smell of venison stew wafted across the tiny courtyard. "Oh!" Mrs. Dillingham said, nervously patting her hair with her hand. She suddenly remembered herself and curtsied a bit lopsidedly. "How do you do, milady?"

"Very well," Fiona said, reaching to help her up. "I beg your pardon, Mrs. . . . ?"

"Dillingham, your ladyship. Mrs. Dillingham at your service."

Fiona looked past her into the small cottage. "Something smells simply divine, Mrs. Dillingham."

"Oh, that's just a wee bit of stew I've got on the fire," she said, stepping back to give Fiona entry. "Come in, come in! My home is right humble, but I think it rather cozy."

Fiona looked uncertainly at Duncan.

"Your lodgings," he said. "I'll come for you in the morning."

"*My* lodgings?" she said as Duncan deposited the portmanteau on the stoop. "But what about you?"

He tipped his hat to Mrs. Dillingham and turned around, walking through the small yard and little gate. He paused to latch it and glanced back—Mrs. Dillingham had her firmly by the elbow, but Fiona was looking at him. Looking, he thought, a little worried for him. It was a strange thing to see—no one worried about him. Quite the opposite.

He continued walking up the hill, resisting the urge to look back. He had the horses to rest and water, and a space in the stables to sleep for which he'd paid a small fortune. If there was one thing he agreed upon with Fiona, it was that the stew smelled divine. It made his cold scones rather disappointing fare, but they would reach Blackwood tomorrow evening, God willing, and he would feast then.

Duncan went about the business of unharnessing the horses and bedding them down with a sack of oats, then made a bed for himself in straw near a small fire that another driver had made. With his greatcoat and a pair of furs taken from the wagon, he was warm. He stretched long on his makeshift bed, his head propped up on a saddlebag, and chewed cold bread while he thought of a pair of beautiful golden eyes.

It had been a long time since he'd beheld a woman's eyes and the sparkle of happiness in them. Since the fire, his associations with women were confined to inns like the one here, with women he did not know and would never know, and in darkness so that they did not see the burns that had marred his left shoulder and arm.

How ironic that there had been a time when women like Fiona Haines had flocked to him, their parents desperate for a match. He'd once been the most sought-after bachelor in all the Highlands, vain and proud and arrogant. He might have had his pick of any number of them, but he'd been more intent on sampling their wares than wedding himself to one of them for all eternity.

And then, three years ago, on the eve of his twenty-seventh birthday, a fire had swept through Blackwood.

Duncan rarely thought of that horrendous night—it was too painful to recall the event that had precipitated so much loss in his life—but he'd been at Blackwood with his usual coterie of friends: Devon MacCauley, Brian Grant, and Richard Macafee. There had been a pair of women from the village with them, as well as two of his cousins. His mother was in Paris, where she spent most of her time, and his cousins had retired early to another wing of the house, having lost their enthusiasm for the antics of four drunken men and two loose women.

Aye, the four of them, notoriously fond of drink and women, had fallen well into their cups that night as they were wont to do, drinking from what seemed an endless vat of Scottish whisky.

Duncan could remember very little of the events before the fire other than crying off when another bawdy parlor game was proposed. He remembered seeing Brian and Richard with the girls they'd brought up from the village, and supposed Devon must have been somewhere within the room, but for the life of him, he could never recall seeing him.

Fortunately—or unfortunately, depending on one's perspective—Duncan never made it to his suite of rooms in the east wing. He'd been obliged by the amount of whisky he'd consumed to take refuge on a divan in the study just down the corridor from where they'd been engaged in adult games. Given his state of inebriation, it was nothing short of a miracle that he was awakened by an awful crash and the smell of smoke. After a moment of gaining his bearings, he'd rushed into the corridor—and into a wall of smoke. It was billowing out of the salon, where he'd left the lads.

Brian and one of the lasses stumbled out of the room,

coughing. Duncan had rushed to help them, but Brian had waved him off, urging him to save himself, they were all out.

But they weren't all out. As servants rushed past them toward the fire, and Duncan and his guests gathered in the front lawn, he realized Devon was missing. Brian and Richard could not say where he was. Duncan had felt a surge of sickening panic unlike anything he'd ever felt in his life, and had run back into the burning wing.

Cold, hard fear was a sobering agent; he clearly remembered yanking his shirttail from his trousers and holding the tail over his mouth and nose. He remembered how intense the heat was from the blaze in the salon—the furniture, the draperies, the carpet, all in flames. He pushed past the brave souls who were trying desperately to beat the fire into submission, ignored their cries to come back, and entered the room.

The smoke was so intense that he'd dropped to his knees. But still Duncan had crawled, searching for his friend, desperate to find him.

He never found Devon. A moment after he entered the room, a piece of drapery and its apparatus had come tumbling down in a fiery blaze. His shoulder and arm and a sliver of his face were badly burned. His servants had pulled him out of the fire and rolled him on the carpet to extinguish the fire on his body. Duncan remembered only that; the rest of it, including the rapidity with which the fire spread, destroying the western wing of what had been a grand estate, he did not recall.

The charred remains still stood—Duncan had not yet found the will or energy to repair it. The shell stood as a silent but constant reminder of all that he'd lost.

Devon's remains were found a few days later—or rather, the soles of his boots and a gold ring were found in the salon. He'd fallen so far into his cups he'd passed into oblivion, and his absence had gone unnoticed by his equally inebriated friends.

The cause of the fire was never discovered, but no one needed to suggest it was a drunken mishap that had sparked it. Most around Blackwood blamed Duncan and his libertine ways for it. So did Duncan.

He spent weeks in a painful fog, and it was months before he could manage the physical pain. He suspected it would be years before he could manage the emotional pain of it. To make matters worse, people who had once flocked to him were repulsed by his burns and disgusted by the unnecessary death of his friend. Duncan had gone from king of Highland society to pariah.

Yet he could scarcely complain—after all, his life had been rather shallow before the fire. He'd lived from one moment to the next without regard for anyone but himself.

And while he still dreamed of himself as a whole man, with a functioning arm and an unmarked face, he nonetheless felt himself a profoundly changed man. He kept to himself these days, using Cameron as a front man to do his business so that he did not repulse anyone with his unsightly appearance. He did not enjoy the genteel company of women as he once had, but then again, he had come to regret his cavalier treatment of them and everyone else in his life when he'd had a life to speak of.

He regretted so many things.

Duncan shifted beneath the coats and rugs and closed his eyes, methodically stretching the fingers of his scarred hand as far as he could, then closing them again, over and over as he did every night, hoping that somehow some use would come back to the gnarled fingers.

Chapter Five

Fiona was awakened by the smell of cooked ham. Mrs. Dillingham was at the long table in the kitchen cutting thick slices of bread when Fiona came down from her attic bedroom. At her elbow was a pail.

"Good morrow, milady!" she said cheerfully, "I hope you slept with the angels."

"I did. Thank you."

"'Twas me pleasure, it was. Eat, eat!" she exclaimed, gesturing to the feast that graced the table. "I've made your breakfast."

Grateful, Fiona sat. As she ate, Mrs. Dillingham stood at the table and put the slices of bread, ham, and other items wrapped in paper into a pail. When she'd filled it with what seemed like enough food to feed an army, she picked up a handful of straw and began to stuff that in the pail, too.

"You must hurry on, then, for your man is anxious to be on his way," Mrs. Dillingham said. "He says he feels snow coming, and you've still a way to go to Blackwood." She smiled at Fiona as she stuffed more hay into the pail. "He wouldna even have a bite, if you can believe it, but

I'm no stranger to stubborn men, no I'm no'. I insisted he take some food along."

"How very kind of you."

"A big man like that canna work and see after you on an empty belly, can he, now?"

Apparently, she'd not be traveling on an empty belly, either. The food was delicious; Fiona ate until she was quite stuffed.

Mrs. Dillingham tested the heft of the pail. "There we are," she said, apparently satisfied with her work, and as Fiona stood, she handed the pail to her. "Here you are, milady. A bit of food for your journey."

"For me?" Fiona asked, surprised. "How very kind, Mrs. Dillingham. Thank you. I've some coins in my portmanteau—"

"No, no, your man has paid for it."

"He did?" she said, startled.

"He was right generous when it came to your lodging, milady. Said I was to take proper care of you." She smiled. "Take it, then, and Godspeed."

Fiona took it. And when she walked outside the little cottage into a gray day, her man, as Mrs. Dillingham had put it, was standing at the fence, waiting for her. "Good day, sir!" Mrs. Dillingham called out to him. He nodded in response.

Fiona walked across the yard to him, her portmanteau in one hand, the pail of food in the other. "Good morning," she said.

He hardly spared her a glance as he took the portmanteau from her hand and placed it carefully onto his bad hand. "Morning," he responded as he took the pail from her. "Shall we?"

"Yes." She turned and waved to Mrs. Dillingham, then

followed Mr. Duncan up the road. Mr. Duncan kept his gaze on the road, but Fiona looked curiously at him. "Mrs. Dillingham said you paid for my keep."

"Aye."

"Why?" she asked. "I can pay my way," she said, her eyes narrowing suspiciously.

"We'll settle at the end of the journey."

"Will we indeed? You are quite free with your commands, Mr. Duncan. Funny, I did no' think you looked like a Duncan when first we met, but now I think I am beginning to see it."

That earned her a curious glance. "Pardon?"

"I did no' think a Duncan should be quite as tall as you," she said, eyeing his torso. *Or as broad.* "Or as taciturn," she said. "I thought a Duncan would be a bit of a prattler. A rooster."

"*Rooster?*"

"Mmm," she said, looking at him studiously. "*Rooster.* You have a bit of it in you."

His gaze took her in, from the top of her hood to her hem, before he opened the gate on the wagon. For the first time since they had begun this journey—which seemed many days ago instead of only one—he really looked at her, his gaze lingering a little too long on her figure, and then rising slowly again to her eyes.

The *way* he looked at her was alarmingly arousing. Her heart began to beat a little wildly, the pace picking up as he leaned toward her. For one moment of sheer insanity, Fiona thought he meant to kiss her.

But he handed the pail of food to her. "So that you willna perish," he added unnecessarily.

Surprisingly disappointed, Fiona smiled coyly and took

the pail from him, sliding it onto the back of the wagon. Mr. Duncan leaned down, cupping his good hand, and once again, she put her foot into it and allowed him to push her up as if she were nothing more than the pail of food. He watched her move to the front of the wagon—the brazier was full and warm, she noted—then put her portmanteau just inside the wagon's gate. He closed the gate, then paused to look at her again. She thought he would speak; but without a word, he disappeared. A moment later, the wagon dipped to one side as he climbed up on the bench. A moment or two after that, the wagon lurched forward.

Fiona tried to keep her thoughts from the mysterious Mr. Duncan, but it was an exercise in futility. This was what she deserved from playing so many bawdy parlor games in London and flirting outrageously. But it was different here. Given the difference in their stations, a flirtation would lead him to think her a lady bird.

So Fiona amused herself for a time by counting the various crates and sacks and bundles surrounding her. When she tired of that, she thought of Sherri, hoping that she'd walked miles and miles before Mr. Ridley found her, but then began to fret that Mr. Ridley hadn't found her, and that Sherri was wandering about the countryside, the potential victim of any number of predators.

After a time, she tried to lie on the bench, but every bump in the road required her to catch herself from falling.

Fiona finally sat up. This was really not to be borne. There were only the two of them, separated by a thin sheet of tarpaulin. Why should they pretend not to be in one another's company? Because she was a lady and he was a— Honestly, she wasn't precisely certain what he was, other than a very virile man, but he was a man who was a stranger to her. It wasn't as if the rules of society had to be obeyed on this road or really beyond Edinburgh. They were two people traveling through a landscape so vast and remote that it was possible to believe they were the only two people in all the world.

Fiona twisted on her seat and looked at the tarpaulin, pulled taut over the wire frame. She leaned forward, saw where the tarpaulin was attached to the wagon, and gave it a pull. "Stop," she said, her voice barely audible above the creaking and moaning of the wagon and its wheels. "Stop!" The wagon pitched along. "*Stop!*" she cried, and hit the tarpaulin with the flat of her palm. "*Stop, stop, stop!*"

The wagon lurched to a sudden halt, propelling her into the tarpaulin and back again, then tilting to one side as Mr. Duncan climbed off the bench. Fiona had scarcely turned herself around on her little bench when he appeared at the back of the wagon, looking at her through the opening as if he expected her to be bleeding. When he saw that she wasn't hurt, the expression in his eyes melted into impatience.

"I canna' abide riding in the bed of the wagon all day," she said in response to his question before he could ask it. "I should like a proper airing."

"An *airing?*" he echoed incredulously.

"Aye, an airing! Is it really too much to ask?" she demanded as she made her way forward. She tripped on the corner of a bag of grain and quickly righted herself. "It's dangerous in here!"

"*Mi Diah,*" he cursed softly.

It had been some years since Fiona had heard Gaelic spoken, and it made her pulse leap a bit—there was nothing that brought her back to Scotland and home faster than the language of the Highlands. She'd grown up with Gaelic spoken around her, particularly by her father, who insisted she and Jack learn how to read and write it along with the languages of society and court, English and French, which they spoke every day.

Duncan's speaking a bit of Gaelic now drew her to him like a magnet; she paused, looking down at him. "There are only the two of us, Mr. Duncan, and it seems rather pointless to continue on in complete silence, does it no'? I, for one, would prefer some company." Even if he was the most taciturn man she'd ever met.

He sighed as if he was vexed beyond endurance—but he held up his hand to help her down.

Fiona smiled triumphantly, slipped her hand into his, and felt his thick fingers close tightly around hers. She slid one foot off the end of the wagon, looking for the undercarriage. But her foot missed it and she slipped; Duncan let go of her hand and caught her around the waist. Her fall was stopped by his unmovable body. He held her there, his eyes piercing hers. After a moment, he allowed her to slide, very slowly, down the length of him to her feet.

The contact was brief, but the effect was entirely intoxicating. This man was as hard-bodied and big as a tree, his grip as firm as a vise yet surprisingly gentle.

Fiona's body was tingling all over. She stepped away, drew a quick but steadying breath, and glanced over her shoulder at him. Duncan's startling gaze was filled with the look of a man's hunger, a look of gnawing desire—Fiona knew it, because regrettably, she was feeling it, too.

A warm flush filled her cheeks, yet she pulled her cloak around her and adjusted her hood. "The air will do me good," she said, apropos of nothing but a suddenly pressing need to fill the silence that seemed to crackle around them. She did not look at him, did not give him the chance to argue, and began walking to the front of the wagon.

Fortunately, there was a wooden step to help the driver up, of which Fiona availed herself. She settled on the driver's bench, looking straight ahead, waiting for Duncan to ask her to come down, to go back into the little cave.

She heard nothing. She looked up at the trees towering above them and the stone gray sky, breathing in the heavy scent of pine. When she at last risked a look at him, she discovered he wasn't even there. But he appeared a moment later with a pair of furs tucked up beneath his bad arm. He pulled them out and tossed them up onto the bench. Fiona quickly moved them, spreading them over her lap while Duncan lifted himself gracefully onto the bench.

He did not look at her; he picked up the reins and wrapped them around his bad hand, then reached across himself to release the brake. With a whistle and a hitch of the reins, he sent the horses to trotting once more.

Fiona could not help but smile to herself. She'd put herself in a terribly shocking situation. Look at her, a woman who dined at the queen's table, riding on a wagon's bench with a servant or tenant of some sort! She could imagine herself relating this tale to the royal princesses, who would be all agog as they tried to imagine riding in a wagon in the company of a man they did not know.

Especially a man as enigmatic as Duncan. She stole a glance at him; he kept his gaze to the road. His eye creased in the corner with his squint; his jaw was square and strong. He had the growth of a beard that showed above his scarf that made him look even wilder than she imagined him to be. None of the gentlemen in London looked like this. None of them had so much as a curl out of place. None of them could handle a team of four with one hand, or catch her in one arm and hold her so effortlessly. . . .

Stop. This was insanity.

"Do you think we might reach Blackwood today?" she asked in an effort to make idle conversation that would take her mind from him.

"Aye."

She spread her hands on her lap and looked at her fur-lined gloves, a gift from her aunt. "It seems a wee bit colder here than in London," she remarked. "I didna remember it being quite so cold as this."

He said nothing.

"Are you no' cold, sir?"

"No."

"Then your cloak must be a fine one indeed. Mine is lined with fur, yet still I feel a chill. When I was a girl, I never felt the chill. Then again, I was quite active, always out-of-doors, engaged in games with my brother. My father was of a mind that physical exercise was good for the body's humors." She looked at him for a response.

He kept his gaze on the road.

"What of you? Were you an active lad, then?"

He gave her a look that clearly indicated he found her prattle tiresome.

So did she, truthfully. But she *had* to talk. If she didn't speak, she would dwell on the closeness of his deliciously masculine body, eyes the color of tea leaves, and unspeakable things. "Perhaps you were put to work at an early age," she suggested. "Our housekeeper had three sons who worked alongside her. I shall never forget the sight of Ian standing on his brother's shoulders to light the candles in the chandelier, as steady as you please."

Duncan turned his head and seemed to be looking at the trees as they passed them.

"I was always rather fond of Ian, in truth. He was a very likable lad. I have no' the slightest notion what has become of him, as I've no' been home in some time." She paused. "Eight years it is now."

Duncan gave her a passing glance before turning his attention to the road again.

Fiona shivered. "No doubt you are wondering why I've been in London all this time, but it's all rather complicated. There are times I long for Scotland, but then again, there's little for me here." She laughed. "I'd be living in my brother's home, Lambourne Castle, which, I can assure you, would be a trial. No one likes to be beholden, do they?" She looked at Duncan. "And besides, I should no' admit it, for he's my blood, but my brother is a wee bit of a rogue, he is, and always has been." She smiled and looked forward again. He was a rogue, but she loved him dearly. "I followed him to London," she announced, as if her mouth was suddenly connected to her thoughts. "Our parents were gone, and he's my only family to speak of, really, save my aunt and uncle, but they are getting on in years, aye? I wanted to be close to Jack."

For some reason, Duncan glanced at her when she said this.

"And now he's the reason I've come back to Scotland," she admitted, as if Duncan had asked her why. "I fear he's gotten himself into awful trouble in London," she added with a soft shake of her head. "Shall I tell you what he's done? No, no . . . I should no'. The less you know, the better, I suspect. But if he's no' at Blackwood, I donna know what I shall do."

She realized that Duncan was looking at her curiously and she smiled. "He may be a rogue, but he's always been right good to me. That's why I followed him to London. Oh, aye, I suppose I would have remained here had there been any real prospects for me," she continued, as if Duncan had inquired. "Society is rather small in the Highlands, is it no'?" she asked, thinking of her own coming-out. How many had been in attendance—perhaps one hundred people? That seemed so small in comparison to London gatherings, particularly those hosted by the Prince of Wales, which numbered well into the hundreds.

"It's no' that I had *no* prospects," she added hastily with another shiver. "I had a few." If one could count Mr. Carmag Calder a true prospect. He was a studious young man, interested in the Greek classics, and could name all of the Greek deities, which he had done for Fiona on more than one occasion. She admired him for his scholarly pursuits, but she'd also found conversation with him awfully dull.

Which, for some inexplicable reason, she decided to share with her driver. That, as well as some other startling moments in her life—such as the day she fell from the window at Lambourne Castle and broke her arm. And the night she was introduced to the Prince of Wales for the first time and couldn't help but marvel at how intricately and perfectly his neckcloth had been tied. It was precise in a way that defied human nature, and she'd pictured a bevy of valets working on that neckcloth—until Jack nudged her with his elbow to make her stop gaping at the prince.

A hard dip in the road shook her and made her realize that she was indeed prattling on, and she suddenly felt rather silly sitting next to this man, speaking so openly about her life.

She watched the bare tree limbs that passed along over their heads for a moment, and then asked, "Have you been to London?"

"Once or twice."

She waited for him to say more. *I liked it very much* or *London is very crowded.* But he said nothing. "Really, Mr. Duncan, I beg of you, please do stop nattering on!" she said. "Your endless chatter is beginning to wear on my poor nerves."

She could see the skin around his eye crinkle. He was smiling.

"I've been to London, but that was several years ago," he admitted.

"Aha!" she said brightly. "You are indeed capable of conversation!" He sounded, she thought, as though he belonged to the gentry. He was a tenant, she guessed—not a servant. She folded her arms tightly around her.

"Move closer," he said.

"Pardon?"

"Move closer," he said again. "You are cold. Sit close to me for warmth." When she made no move to do so, but gaped at him, he put his arm around her waist and pulled her closer to him.

Fiona made a sound of surprise; he removed his arm.

But that didn't remove the feeling of him. Their bodies were touching, her shoulder to his arm, her thigh against his large one, her lower leg against the smooth leather of his boot. She was aware of every inch of their bodies that came together. She did indeed feel warmer; in fact, she felt a deep warmth at the very core of her begin to spread, sliding out to her fingers and toes and tingling across her scalp.

It took her a moment to notice her fingers were digging into her palms.

Duncan glanced at her, and Fiona would have sworn he knew precisely the titillation she was feeling, because his eye seemed to glow with it. "Continue, then," he said.

"Beg your pardon?"

"You were telling me of your life. Carry on, if you will."

"Oh!" Her face felt flushed. She must sound perfectly absurd to him. "There's really very little to say, actually. My life has been utterly uneventful." She looked at him. "What of you, sir? How long have you been at Blackwood, if I may ask?"

She felt an almost imperceptible stiffening in his body and rather imagined it was because conditions at Blackwood were as bleak as she imagined, being under the thumb of such a reprehensible laird. He probably treated his tenants with complete disdain, walking over them as if they were objects instead of people and demanding exorbitant rents, whereas *she* had always taken care to treat her servants admirably. If Sherri were here, that bloody stupid girl, she would vouch for Fiona's fair treatment, she was certain.

She looked at Duncan. "It's quite all right—you may speak freely, you know," she said. "I am well acquainted with the character of your laird," she said with a slight roll of her eyes.

Duncan looked as if he wanted to inquire, but being a Buchanan man, he just clenched his jaw and stared straight ahead. Highlanders were notoriously loyal.

"Tell me, Duncan, is Mrs. Nance still in the laird's employ? I—"

Her question was lost when the wagon hit something hard, sending it skidding behind the team and riding very rough.

"Ho, there, *ho, ho*!" Duncan shouted at the horses, reining hard. When he'd pulled the team to a stop, he quickly unwrapped the reins from his left hand and jumped off the bench in one fluid movement. He strode around the back of the wagon and around to Fiona's side. With his hand on his hip, he stared down at the wheel, then muttered a Gaelic oath that, fortunately, Fiona could not make out.

"The wheel is damaged," he said with a hard kick to the offending wheel.

She gasped and leaned over, bracing herself against the wooden armrest as she peered down at the wheel. She could see one of the spokes jutting out, perpendicular to the wheel. "Oh no."

Mr. Duncan squatted down to have a closer look. Fiona could only see the crown of his hat and the wide rim. The hat was dark brown, and when the first fat snowflake fell and landed on the brim, it was so large it made her think of dandelions. But when another followed it, and another, she looked up to see that snow had indeed begun to fall.

"Oh, look!" she said with all the brightness one typically feels at the sight of new snow. "It's begun to snow!"

Duncan lifted his head and looked up at the sky and said something in Gaelic that, if Fiona's memory could be trusted, was loosely translated to mean *Bloody, bloody hell.*

Chapter Six

The sight of the broken spoke was bad enough, but when snow began to fall, a very bad feeling invaded Duncan. It likely would be impossible to reach Blackwood by nightfall now. Frankly, he feared they would not reach *any* place by nightfall.

He sent Fiona into the trees to gather wood before it became too wet from the snow in the event they needed to build a fire. He had her stack it in the back of the wagon, under the tarpaulin awning. He was both amazed and relieved that she did not argue, but only voiced her opinion that she was being sent on a fool's errand so that she'd not be underfoot while he tried to repair the wheel, and went off cheerfully to do as he'd asked.

She wasn't wrong. It was difficult enough to repair a spoke in the wheel cog, particularly when one arm refused to cooperate. It took him much longer than it would an able-bodied man, and as a result, the lady had stuffed the wagon with as much wood as she could find without wandering too deep into the woods, and was now sitting on a rock beneath the bows of a towering Scots pine.

From his position on his back beneath the wagon, where he was working to force a spare spoke into the fittings on the wheel, Duncan could see a pair of ankle-high boots that were attached to a pair of very shapely legs covered in thick woolen stockings. Legs that disappeared beneath the dirtied hem of her gown and cloak.

Her arms were wrapped around her knees, drawn up to the chest, and her chin perched atop her knees. She watched him work, chattering on about something to do with a ball in London. He'd been unable to follow her conversation as his attention was diverted by the task at hand and that pair of shapely legs peeking out at him from beneath her skirts.

He might have gone on all day stealing glimpses of that tantalizing view, but she suddenly dipped her head, catching his attention. "I said, I'd never been to a proper ball before I attended the one at Gloucester."

Duncan had no idea what he should say to that and grunted. He'd positioned himself around the wheel, tucking it in between his body and his bad arm so that he could keep it from moving. With his good arm, he worked to set the spare spoke into the notches of the wheel.

Fiona stood and began to pace just beyond the wheel, kicking what was, fortunately, a light accumulation of snow. "I rather thought London would be different somehow," she said. "I rather thought the whole of society would be different, but it's really rather remarkably similar to society in the Highlands—what wee bit exists here, that is."

He could not imagine that the Highlands were anything like London. Her small boots passed by his face, turned sharply, and passed again. "I truly believed there would be some sort of enlightenment in London," she continued, one hand waving airily. "But I discovered that while there are good souls to be found in London society, there are others who can be as mean-spirited and churlish as the Laird of Blackwood."

There it was again, her complete disdain for the man that he'd been.

Her feet paused in their pacing; she suddenly squatted down beside him. "I donna mean to disparage your laird, if indeed he remains your laird and has no' been shot in a duel or otherwise brought down."

"But you have disparaged him, aye?" Duncan asked curtly.

One lovely dark brow rose high above the other. "I did no' *mean* to. I merely assumed he might have met with trouble, naturally, given his general disposition."

Duncan gave her a look that he hoped would end the conversation, but the lass was bold. Or oblivious. Instead of politely demurring as she ought to have done, she smiled as if she pitied him his laird. "I beg your pardon if I've offended," she said sweetly. "But perhaps you do no' know your laird as *I* have known him."

"Have you *known* him?" he demanded, and hit the spoke with the flat of his palm. He hit it too hard—it shoved the spoke past the notch. Duncan muttered under his breath and started the laborious process over again.

"I have," she said.

"If I a may ask, Lady Fiona, what's he done to you to leave you with such an unflattering impression of his character?" Duncan demanded.

"He likened me to a woodchuck."

Duncan stilled and glanced at her through the spokes.

She colored slightly and shrugged a little. "No' that it matters to me, for it does no' in the least."

"A *woodchuck*?" he echoed disbelievingly. Now he doubted her completely. He never would have said such a thing about a lady.

But Fiona nodded adamantly. "It was such a silly thing, really. It happened at my debut, at Gunston Hall. My friend was having a bit of sport with me, and she suggested to your high and mighty laird that perhaps I might make a good match for him, and he said, '*Fiona Haines*?'" She mimicked him, speaking in a low voice and looking comically studious as she rubbed her chin with her hand. "'*Lambourne's younger sister? Brown hair? About so tall? Slightly reminiscent of a woodchuck*?'"

Duncan blinked.

"Aha!" Fiona cried triumphantly. "You are no' the least bit surprised, then! You know perfectly well that he's wretched!"

Oh, but she was wrong. She was terribly wrong—he was surprised and appalled.

"His friends had quite a laugh at it, which undoubtedly encouraged him even further, for he turned to my friend Molly and said, '*Thank you, Miss Elgin, but I'd sooner* marry *a woodchuck*.'" Fiona laughed, but it sounded forced.

"Perhaps Miss Elgin fabricated the conversation?" he suggested, hoping that was so.

"Why should she do that?"

Any number of reasons. Duncan remembered Molly Elgin—she'd been rather keen to be near him, by any means she could devise.

"Oh, I've no doubt that Molly Elgin was up to no good when she broached the subject with him," Fiona said airily. "Yet I know he said it, for I *heard* him. I was standing not two feet away. I heard him *quite* plainly." Her laugh again sounded stilted, and she abruptly stood and began pacing again. "I hardly cared, mind you. I'd set my sights on London."

A direct contradiction to what she'd said this morning, he noted. He swallowed hard—he was never prepared to be reminded of the man he'd been. Vainglorious and, apparently, cruel. He hit the spoke with the flat of his palm; it popped into the notches on the wheel. He grabbed the spoke and pulled hard to assure himself it was locked into place. Satisfied that it was, he disengaged himself from the wheel and stood up. As he stuffed his hands into his gloves, he said, "Knowing the laird, I rather imagine you are right—he surely said what he did for the amusement of his friends. Yet I am certain he would be ashamed and regretful if he realized the distress his words had caused you." He looked at her from the corner of his eye. "I am certain of it."

Fiona laughed. "Do you realize that is the most words you have spoken to me at one time? And all of them in defense of a profligate. Oh, aye," she said, nodding vigorously, "he is a profligate of the *worst* kind. If ever there was a man who delighted in trampling the feelings of others, it is your laird, sir. I've heard more tales of him, but I will keep them to myself, then. Honestly, I would no' have brought it up at all had you no' asked. I've quite forgotten it! Really, I am surprised I've remembered as much of it as I have. Look here, it's begun to snow again." She leaned her head back and closed her eyes, and stuck out her tongue, trying to catch a snowflake on the tip.

Something about that stirred Duncan deep inside.

He did not want to be intrigued or otherwise aroused—it would only lead to frustration and pain, and he had a long way to go with this one yet. But he could not help but wonder where life might have taken him had he not been so dismissive of Fiona so long ago. If he'd met her, *really* met her. . . . Such were the regrets in his life—he would never know now. Bloody hell, he couldn't even tell her who he was now without making everything she'd said of him seem true.

Nevertheless, he racked his memory for the night in question, and vaguely remembered an encounter with Molly Elgin, but for the life of him, he could not remember saying such a thing.

He did not remember it, but he could not doubt it. She was right—he'd been terribly cavalier with other people's feelings then. Especially women. But where he'd once treated pretty young women as cattle, he would now be on his knees with gratitude if but one of them could see past the scarring of his skin and the scandalous death of his close friend.

A deep sense of regret and loss pervaded him as he checked the wheel once more. That he could have been so cruel to someone as vibrant and lively as Fiona Haines made him feel more inhuman than he normally did, and he'd not thought it possible to feel any lower.

He dusted off his buckskins, walked to the driver's bench, and shoved the broken spoke beneath the bench. One of the horses whinnied nervously; he assumed the horse wanted a warm stable. But another horse snorted and bumped against the harness, and Duncan glanced over his shoulder at Fiona.

What he saw made his heart stop beating.

Now all of the horses were shifting nervously and tossing their heads. Fiona was oblivious to it—she was holding out her gloved hand, watching the snow fall into her palm. Behind her, not more than ten feet away, was a very lean wolf, crouched low on its haunches, stalking the horses.

The number of wolves had been drastically reduced in the Highlands to save sheep, but Duncan had heard tales of the occasional desperate and hungry lone wolf. He could see the ribs on this one; it was hungry, and Fiona stood between him and a meal.

All of the horses were stomping and snorting now, whinnying at Duncan.

Fiona glanced at the horses, then at Duncan. "They must be hungry," she said brightly. "Look at this snow, will you? It's really beautiful, aye?"

Duncan nodded as he carefully reached beneath the driver's bench for his pistol.

"Have you blankets for the poor things?" she asked. "Perhaps they are cold." The wolf was only five feet from her now. If she cried out, if she made any sort of threatening move, Duncan feared what the hungry wolf might do. He had one clear shot, but he couldn't sight the wolf properly with the patch on his eye.

"Lass . . . listen to me now," Duncan said softly as he pushed his hat from his head. "Stand where you are, but donna move a muscle. Do you understand me?"

"Why ever no'?" she asked laughingly. "You sound so ominous, sir. Why should I no' move? Please allow that I might at least stamp my feet, as it is right cold."

He pushed the patch from his eye and wrapped his hand around the pistol, snaking his finger into the trigger. He'd have only seconds to fire.

Fiona's smile faded. "Why are you holding that pistol? You are frightening me," she said, the gaiety gone from her voice.

"Donna move," he said again, shifting his gaze to the wolf, who had begun to inch forward. The horses sensed it; one of them tried to break forward, but the wagon was dead weight, the wheels locked by the hand brake. The horse whinnied again, high and shrill, prompting the others to do the same. The sound of their nervous cries startled Fiona—she moved.

Duncan lunged toward the wolf to draw his attention from Fiona and fired. Fiona screamed, covering her ears with her hands. One of the horses tried to rear, shaking the wagon as the wolf fell to its side with a bark of pain. He began to claw his way up; Duncan pushed Fiona behind him, trained the gun again, and fired, killing the wolf.

The horses were frantic now, bumping against one another and dragging the wagon behind them. "*Fuirich, fuirich*!" Duncan shouted at the horses to steady them as he whirled around and grabbed Fiona up before she could scream, before she could see the blood of the wolf pooling darkly against the thin layer of snow and spreading toward her. He twisted her away from the sight of the dead wolf, clasped her in his arm, and pressed her face into his shoulder. "Steady, lass," he said. "Steady."

"God help me, I never saw it!" she cried, her voice shaking. "I was almost eaten alive!"

Duncan smiled wryly above her head. "I assure you, he preferred horsemeat," he said. "He is dead; you've naugh' to fear. But come now, let us be on our way—the wheel is repaired."

She reared back and looked up at him. "Mr. Duncan!

You saved my *life*!" she cried, her eyes searching his face. "With no regard for your own safety, you saved my life!"

"I had a gun," he reminded her, but Fiona would not accept that and wildly shook her head, her eyes searching his face. Duncan was painfully aware that his bad eye was exposed to her and out of habit, turned his head.

"I owe my life to you! How shall I ever thank you?"

"By getting in the wagon," he said, pulling her toward the enclosure.

"What? Oh, no," she said, firmly shaking her head. "I donna intend to ride back there after *that*," she said, gripping his wrist. "I shall stay close, if you donna mind. We might be set upon by packs of them at any moment. Aye, we should hurry along before they come!" she said, and let go of him.

"He was a lone wolf," Duncan tried, but she was already marching past him, and helping herself up onto the driver's bench.

He'd not win this battle, that was plain. With a sigh, Duncan saw after the skittish team before gathering his hat and his eye patch. If she'd noticed his eye in the ruckus, she gave no indication, but Duncan quickly pulled the patch over his eye nonetheless. He tugged his scarf up over his nose, donned his hat, and pulled the brim low over his eyes before climbing up and sending the horses to a trot.

The snow was coming down heavily now, wet and thick. He figured they had perhaps three hours of light left and worried how far they would be able to travel. His team trotted along, throwing their heads back to sniff the air. Beside him, Lady Fiona felt compelled to relate all the ghoulish tales of wolves she'd heard as a child, but as the snowfall thickened, she delighted in it, and recounted a sledding episode on a hill at an English country estate that had ended with the Prince of Wales tumbling head over heels down an embankment like a drunken snowman.

Fiona really was quite entertaining. She had a talent for telling stories that made even him chuckle, someone who had not laughed in so long he could no longer remember the last time.

But the heavy snow made travel difficult, and he could feel Fiona shivering next to him. As much as he enjoyed her company, it was dangerous to expose her to the elements. So Duncan pulled the team to a halt and climbed down from the driver's bench.

Fiona looked down at him with a smile. The tip of her nose was bright red, and the brim of her bonnet had begun to sag under the weight of the snow. "Come down," he said.

She instantly twisted about, looking back at the road they'd traveled. "Why? Are there more wolves?"

"*No,*" he said. "But you should be under the tarpaulin."

"I'm really quite all right."

"Come *down.*"

Fiona blinked wide eyes, but reluctantly came down off the bench. He helped her down, took her by the hand, and dragged her to the back of the wagon.

She tried to lift the latch of the gate. "This is really unnecessary," she said, her voice straining with her effort to unlatch the wagon's gate. "From the look of it, there are only the two of us in all of Scotland. What harm is there if we enjoy a bit of human companionship? I doubt nations will fall if we sit together."

"I will no' be responsible for any ague that comes on you."

"I am made of the hardiest Highland stock, sir! And what of you?" she demanded as he covered her hand with his and easily lifted the latch. "Are you impervious to ague?"

"I'm fine," he said. "Up with you, then. We should no' tarry."

"At least take another rug with you to the bench," she said, showing no sign of hurrying things along.

Duncan impatiently dipped down, caught her around the waist, and ignored the squeal of surprise as she grabbed his shoulders. He lifted her up and sat her on the wagon's gate—but he did not let go as he'd intended. Something happened to him—he was captivated by her amber eyes. He could not look away.

Nor did she. Her hands remained on his shoulders, her eyes locked on his.

Something passed between them, something intensely magnetic.

Duncan was the first to move, slowly sliding his arm away from her waist. Such attraction as he was experiencing was pointless, useless. She despised him. And even if she could be persuaded that he was indeed a changed man, she had not yet noticed his face. When she saw his face . . .

"You can get yourself under cover, I've no doubt," he said abruptly, and retreated to the driver's bench. But as he climbed up and dusted the snow from the seat and pulled a pair of furs over his lap, he heard her grousing behind him.

Something about being ordered about by a Highlander.

She fell silent as he sent the horses to a trot again, their breath rising in great plumes. Duncan imagined Lady

Fiona Haines on her bench inside the wagon, bouncing along, her hands gripping the edge.

A headwind picked up, pushing the snow into neat piles alongside the road. The limbs of the pines under which they were passing were hanging low under the snow's weight.

After another hour of traveling in wretched conditions, Duncan realized they were far from a village and even farther from Blackwood. The team was tiring, and if the snow kept falling, it wouldn't be long before it would be too deep to pull the wagon. Duncan did not relish a night spent literally on the road.

It was dumb luck that as the horses began to labor up a hill where the trees thinned, he happened to see a cattle enclosure on the sheltered side of a large rock. And he considered it nothing short of a miracle that the enclosure held three sheaves of hay.

"Whoa, whoa," he said, pulling back on the reins, bringing the horses to a stop once more.

When he helped Fiona out of the wagon, she only grumbled a bit when he explained their predicament and pointed to the enclosure. "We shall freeze to death," she said.

"We will no'," he countered.

"It will scarcely matter if we freeze, for wolves will feast on us."

"The wolf is dead," he patiently reminded her. "And if he were alive, he'd no' come near a fire."

She pressed her lips together, studying him, and nodded. "All right, then. What must we do?"

"Help me remove the tarpaulin."

Between the two of them, they removed the tarpaulin from its frame and dragged it up the hill to the enclosure.

She helped him make a shelter of sorts. With hay on the ground and one of the lap furs to cover it, he used the rest of the hay to form a lee around the fur. On the edge of the enclosure, he scuffed a circle and kicked hay and snow away, leaving the earth bare. "Stay here," he said to Fiona. He trooped down to the wagon again, loaded wood onto his damaged arm, then returned to the space he'd made. He made the trip to the wagon thrice more.

As Fiona watched, he built a fire, held his hand over the flame a moment, and when he was certain it would not go out, he touched the brim of his hat. "Here is wood," he said, pointing to the little pile. "Keep the flame burning while I tend the horses."

The snow was beginning to thin, but now the wind was blowing and he was chilled to the bone. He disengaged the horses one by one from the harness frame and led them to a stand of Scots pines, where he hobbled them together. He hung oat bags on each of them—no small feat, given their height and his useless appendage. And with the four of them munching away, he draped them each with horse blankets.

Satisfied that the horses would huddle together and survive the night, Duncan returned to the wagon and fetched the pail of food Mrs. Dillingham had made for them. He also dug out a flask of whisky from beneath a sack of grain and leaned down, tucking it inside his boot.

He had a feeling that being trapped in a small shelter with an attractive, alluring woman might make this the longest night of his life, and he was going to need every bit of help he could get.

Chapter Seven

Fiona was relieved to see Duncan when he emerged from the gray mist that was settling around them, a fur rug draped over his shoulder, the pail of food in hand. He'd been gone long enough that she'd begun to fret something had happened to him.

But then again, she'd noticed today that things were not easy for a man with a wounded arm.

She stepped out from beneath the tarpaulin to relieve him of the pail. He followed her underneath the cover and shrugged out from underneath the rug, letting it fall between them.

Fiona glanced at the fur as she kneeled down and began to remove the straw Mrs. Dillingham had packed into the pail. "Only one?"

"You're sitting on the other," he said as he squatted down and added more wood to the fire.

The import of that statement slowly sank in—there was only one rug for the two of them to use to cover themselves, one rug between the two of them and nature's icy grip.

The idea that they'd have to share a lap rug, while entirely titillating, was also alarming. There had been that moment at the back of the wagon in which Fiona actually feared she might have kissed this Highlander had his face not been wrapped in woolen scarves.

She was courting disaster—she might be in the Highlands with no one about to observe her ruin, but that didn't mean she'd be any less ruined if she gave in to temptation.

"What is it?" he asked.

Startled, Fiona looked at him, then down at her hands. She was holding two rock-hard scones.

"Perhaps if you put them near the fire," he said, as if she were undecided as to what to do with them.

She quickly put them on a rock near the fire and looked into the pail again.

It hardly mattered that there was only one rug between them—the space was so small that she couldn't help but lie or sit beside him in this tiny shelter. Lord God, how did she get herself into such predicaments? It very much reminded her of the time that she and Lady Gilbert had taken it upon themselves to climb up to the old ruins on the Gilbert estate. But the ruins were not where Lady Gilbert had believed them to be, and they'd become lost in a stand of aspens. It had begun to rain, and without a proper umbrella between them, the two of them had been forced to crouch together in a tiny little cave. It was so cramped that they'd become rather cross with one another. It was a fortnight before they'd patched things up.

Fiona had learned a valuable lesson that day—in times of turmoil, people either came together or were torn apart.

"Is something amiss?" he asked, his voice low and gruff.

"Amiss? No, no—I was just having a look at the pail." She pulled out a hunk of cheese wrapped in cloth. There were apples and nuts, too, in addition to the bread and ham. She handed the ham to Duncan, who speared the meat on the end of a stick and stuck it near the fire to warm it.

They ate in silence, both of them staring out at the white landscape, huddled in their cloaks. But the cold was seeping through the hay and the fur on which they sat, making Fiona's bones ache.

Seated on her left, Duncan watched her hold her gloved hands out to the fire. "You are cold."

"I'm no'."

He gave her a look that said he knew better. "I can *see* you shivering, lass."

"*Shivering?*" She tried to laugh. "I am no' *shivering.* I am . . ." Honestly, she couldn't think of an excuse. She was shivering.

Duncan removed his hat. He had sandy brown hair, streaked gold by the sun. With his gaze on the fire, he unwrapped a scarf from his face, leaving a second one wrapped around his lower face and neck. He returned the hat to his head and pulled it down low. "Here," he said, handing the scarf to her. It was dry, protected by his collar and hat from the snow. "Put it around your neck and ears."

"I could no' possibly," she protested.

"Put it on," he commanded her. "You'll catch your death."

She did not want to take his scarf, but she was freezing. She quickly removed her damp bonnet and tossed it aside. She wrapped the scarf around her head and neck. It smelled of him—a spicy, musky scent that stirred her blood. A violent shiver caught her by surprise, and this one had nothing to do with cold.

"Better?" he asked.

She nodded. "Thank you."

He reached for his boot and retrieved a flask. Fiona watched him open it and take a long draft from it. Then he handed it to her. "Drink."

"What is it?"

"Scotch whisky."

"Oh no, I shouldna—"

He turned and looked at her with a gaze warmly limpid in the firelight. "*Drink*, my lady," he insisted low. "It will take the chill from your bones."

That suggestion persuaded her far too easily; she gingerly drank from the flask. The liquor burned so badly it made her eyes water. Fiona blinked to clear her vision. She felt a little strange in the gut, but she did indeed feel warmer.

Duncan smiled a little lopsidedly when she took another, longer drink and handed it back to him. He took a sip, then passed it to her again, as if they were a pair of sailors sharing a bit of gin on a moonlit deck.

"May I ask you a personal question?" she asked after taking another sip and dragging the back of her hand across her mouth.

He did not respond, which she took as tacit agreement. "What happened to your arm?"

He shifted slightly, as if the question made him uncomfortable. "An accident."

It was obviously the result of an accident. Fiona tapped him on the arm with the flask and handed it to him. But before she let go of it, she said, "There are many types of accidents . . . carriage accidents, hunting accidents . . ."

"It was a fire," he said stiffly. "Now may I ask you a personal question?"

Fiona smiled. She was beginning to feel very warm and airy, open to all examination. "Please ask me—but I assure you, I've no' omitted a single detail of my life today."

"Did you no' settle on a matrimonial match in London?"

Except perhaps *that* detail. Of all the things she thought he might ask, that was not among them. Fortunately, the whisky had done quite a lot to soothe any feathers before they could be ruffled, and she laughed at his audacity as she took the flask from his hand and sipped again.

"No," she said with a cock of her head, smiling at him. "It would seem I am a wee bit of a problem in that regard."

One brow rose high. "How so?"

"Well . . . " she said breezily, "I have a fortune . . . but it is no' a great fortune by London standards. And I'm no' what one would call handsome."

Duncan snorted. "You are a very handsome woman."

The compliment, so tersely and adamantly spoken, thrilled her. "You are very kind, but I am well aware of my shortcomings."

"You've no shortcomings," he said gruffly. "If someone has allowed you to believe it, they are a bloody fool."

She grinned. "Lord, dare I believe my own ears? The Buchanan man flatters me!"

"It is no' flattery. I am a man, madam. I know a handsome woman when I've laid eyes on her." He snatched the flask from her hand and tossed his head back, taking a long draft.

Fiona's grin broadened. "Then perhaps it is my cheerful countenance that serves me so poorly," she gaily suggested. "Lady Gilbert swears that I am no' as circumspect in social situations as I ought to be, all for one small mistake I made. One teeny, tiny mistake," she said, holding up her finger and thumb just a breath apart to show him how tiny.

"Aye?" He seemed interested as he handed her the flask. "What mistake, then?"

Fiona snorted. "On my word, when Señor Castellano inquired directly of me if I thought Miss Fitzgerald would be a good match for him, I answered truthfully! I said that Miss Fitzgerald seemed particularly fond of Lord Randolph, and that I rather doubted she'd seriously entertain the advances of a Spaniard. I said it only because I thought it would be kinder to disabuse him of his false hope than to encourage him further. Was I so wrong, then?" she asked rhetorically before taking a drink from the flask. "Unfortunately, I was no' privy to the fact that Lord Randolph had *his* eye on Lady Penelope Washburn, who is a very close friend of Miss Fitzgerald, but Señor Castellano was, and when Señor Castellano informed Miss Fitzgerald—and everyone else in jolly old England, for that matter—Miss Fitzgerald discovered for the first time that her dear friend Lady Washburn had no' turned away Lord Randolph's attentions as she'd promised she had, and . . . and it was a rather big to-do," she said with a dismissive flick of her wrist.

She glanced at Duncan. He was smiling again. "Oh no, no, no," she warned him as she casually settled back against the hay, feeling remarkably warm for the first time that day. "You've no right to laugh. You were no' there, you did no' witness my dilemma."

"Any other mistakes?" he asked, clearly amused.

"*Nooo*," she drawled. "I am no' entirely hopeless. Only one or two." She shrugged. "A bit of horse gambling and what no', that's all. How was I to know proper English ladies donna gamble?" She lifted the flask to her lips, drank liberally. But when she lowered it again, Duncan took it from her hand.

At Fiona's look of surprise, he said, "Another drink, and you may very well float off into the snow." He sipped once more and stuffed the flask in his boot. "I'll just check on the horses. You should try and get some sleep, for the morrow will be a rather long day."

"I'm too cold to sleep," she complained, and tightened the scarf he'd given her around her head.

With a wry smile, Duncan stood and pulled the fur over her before moving to the edge of their shelter. He paused and glanced back at her, taking all of her in—*all* of her—from her head to her toes. When he lifted his gaze to her eyes once more before going out, she found his expression to be entirely provocative.

In fact, his lustful look had made her flesh heat in a most enticing way. Fiona meant to wait for him to return, but he was gone awhile, and the fire was lovely, the thick fur rug even lovelier, and when she laid on her side and pillowed her face on her hands, it was only to be nearer the fire.

She did not recognize the moment she slipped into a whisky-induced sleep.

* * *

Fiona wasn't the only one feeling the effects of whisky and a sexual attraction. Duncan had to walk about in the frigid snow just to get her out from under his skin. When he returned with another armload of wood, Fiona was lying on her side next to the fire, snoring lightly.

He could not help but smile. As she'd talked this evening—her face flushed from the whisky, her eyes sparkling with her many memories—he'd pictured her in the finest salons of London, a young and elegant woman from the Scottish Highlands who knew more about horse gambling than social maneuvering, but whom he rather imagined had a natural talent for it. He guessed she was admired in London.

He admired her for it. When he'd been whole, moving in even limited society had not been easy for him. He never clearly understood what was expected of him; it seemed men wanted him to be bold and aloof, women wanted him to be kind and solicitous. And they all wanted something from him.

It required a lot of courage for Fiona to have gone off to London without knowing what awaited her, and quite a lot of courage to have remained and negotiated her way through court society all these years. Duncan liked her honesty and envied her ability to see her place in the world. She seemed to harbor no illusions about who or what she was, and seemed to take everyone she met at face value, without regard for their social standing.

That she had attempted to befriend him, believing him a driver, made her all the more captivating to him.

Duncan went down on his haunches beside her, and in the light of the fire he watched her sleeping for a moment. She was pretty. Not beautiful, but certainly pretty.

She had the look of a Scot, a freshness he'd seen only in Highland women. More important, Fiona was real—there wasn't the slightest bit of artifice about her. She was refreshingly different from the debutantes he'd once known. They'd all been trained from the cradle to be serene and delicate and demure. Fiona was serene but in a natural way. And she wasn't particularly delicate or demure, a fact that made him chuckle quietly.

He stoked the fire, removed his hat and eye patch, then eased himself down next to her, very gingerly lifting the fur rug and sliding underneath it beside her. There was nothing to be done for it—if they were to survive this night, they'd need to huddle together for warmth, just like the horses.

He propped his good arm behind his head and looked out over the fire. The snow had passed and bright starlight was reflected off the snow. The air was completely still; it would be bitterly cold tonight. But on the morrow—Christmas Day—they'd be able to travel. They *had* to travel—he did not have enough grain to see the horses past another day, nor was there any food left but a pair of scones for the two of them.

It would be a long, hard day, and Duncan closed his eyes, wanting to sleep—and to dream. To dream of himself with his old face and a pair of working arms.

He slept badly, the cold seeping too quickly into his bones and settling there. He was awakened at some point in the night by Fiona's trembling. She was making a strange noise that he realized was the sound of her teeth chattering. He reacted without thought, sitting up to stir the embers and put more wood on the fire, then easing down and moving closer to Fiona, pulling the fur up to her chin. He then slid his arm around her abdomen, drawing her into his chest.

For several peaceful moments they lay there, the warmth of their bodies seeping into his joints. But then Fiona stirred.

Duncan did not move or speak. He did not want to be sent back across the gap of cold earth that had been between them. But Fiona grabbed his hand and pried it from her middle. He began to move away, but she suddenly rolled onto her back and held his hand and removed his glove. She was, he sheepishly realized, awake.

"Have you had your palm read by a seer?" she asked softly.

He shook his head.

A slow smile curved her lips as she idly traced a fingertip down the length of his palm. "*I* have. The Prince of Wales was quite entertained by the art and invited a seer to Carlton House to read the palms of all of his friends."

"You are a friend to the Prince of Wales?"

"Oh no. But Lady Gilbert is. Or rather, Lady Gilbert's husband. *This* line," she said, tracing slowly from his forefinger to the bottom of his palm, "represents the path of your life. I am no expert, sir, but by the look of it, you shall have a long one."

"Shall I indeed?"

"You seem skeptical."

He smiled wryly. "Perhaps a wee bit."

"Mr. Duncan, you must have faith in your hand." She tapped her finger against his palm. "This line speaks to your intelligence," she said, running the tip of her glove across his palm. "I am fairly certain it is this one. But this," she said, wrapping her fingers around his forefinger and drawing another line across his palm, "indicates your heart." She studied it a moment by the firelight. "There is a small break here, do you see? A broken heart, no doubt. Oh, but look! The line is renewed and goes on for quite a length! It means you have survived the heartache and will be strong again."

"Certain of that, are you?" he scoffed.

"No, no' at all," she said. She turned her head and looked up at him, looked directly at his damaged eye. "But I am hopeful, for your sake."

That tiny profession of hope was his undoing. Duncan could not resist her—she was the one person who did not look at him with horror or disdain. Her *joie de vivre* was infectious, her hope uplifting. And her body, curving in all the right places, as soft as butter, smelling of rosewater, was too much for the man in him. He could not endure another moment in her company and not touch her.

He put his fingers to her chin and turned her face completely to him. Her eyes were glimmering; he could feel something rising up in him, something human, something pleasing and agreeable. Her skin, her smile, her eyes beckoned, and he slowly, deliberately touched his lips to hers, unmindful of the consequences, caring for nothing but the feel of a woman in his arms.

She kissed him back.

Her mouth set him aflame, firing his blood from an internal hearth that had been cold for far too long. He slipped his tongue between her lips, and Fiona pressed against him, her body touching the length of his, inch by excruciatingly pleasurable inch.

The sensation was overwhelming to a man starved for affection. He roughly pulled her to him, wrapping her in a tight one-armed embrace. He'd kissed many women in his life, but never in this way, not with such torrid need, and never so dangerously close to losing all capacity for reason. He rolled her onto her back and came over her, slipping his hand to her breast, filling his hand with the soft pliancy of it.

He dipped his head down, working the clasp of her cloak with his teeth, then pressing his lips to the warm skin at her throat. Fiona sighed with pleasure and swallowed; he could feel the contraction under his lips.

It drove him absolutely mad with desire.

He slipped his hand beneath her cloak and undid the buttons of her traveling coat, one by one, pushing fabric aside until his hand touched silken flesh.

A wave of prurient desire engulfed him, and Duncan helplessly buried his face in the curve of her neck where the scarf had fallen away. When his hand found her bare breast beneath layers of wool, she gasped softly and arched into his palm.

He could feel his heart beating. *His heart, his heart!* It wasn't dead, it was very much alive. "*Fiona,*" he whispered, and pressed his lips to the skin of her neck, then to the hollow of her throat, and the mound of her breast.

She did nothing to stop him—her hands were on his shoulders, her fingers scraping down his back, and up to his chest. She was panting lightly, and in something of a lust-filled daze, Duncan cupped her face with his hand and lifted himself in order to seek her mouth with his, filling her once more with his kiss.

Fiona sighed into his mouth and began to move against him in a way only a woman could move, slow and sultry. He sucked and nibbled on her lips and her tongue, feeling pent-up need thrumming through him, swelling into every vein, every muscle, and flooding him with emotions he'd not felt in a very long time. He wanted her with a desperation that left him breathless; he needed—desperately needed—to be inside her, to feel her body hot and wet around him.

As if to answer his silent wish, her leg rose up on one side of him as he teethed a rigid nipple. Duncan caught her ankle and slid his hand up her calf, beneath her cloak and skirt, over thick woolen stockings, to the bare flesh of her inner thigh, to the warm, damp apex of her legs—

Fiona suddenly surged up, cupping his face in her hands, and in doing so, pushing the scarf from his head. She must have felt his puckered skin of his cheek and neck, because she suddenly reared back and looked at him, her eyes widening with shock.

Duncan panicked at the thought of what she was seeing, and everything in him crashed in that moment. He felt a searing twist of his heart.

"Dear God," she whispered as she stared at his face.

He knew what she saw: a left eye tugged down by the burned skin of his cheek, a misshapen ear. There was scarring on his neck and shoulder that she couldn't see, but was just as bad. He expected her complete revulsion and tried to pull away, but Fiona held his head in her hands, and remarkably, she touched her fingers to his putrid skin.

Duncan jerked back so suddenly that she toppled to her side. He quickly returned his scarf to its rightful place, and his suddenly lifeless heart to its lockbox. He felt awkward and exposed, did not know what to say, what to do. He was accustomed to the shock, but this time he was not prepared. He'd been so unguarded and lost in the moment.

He occupied his hands and his sight with tending the fire.

"Duncan . . . I beg your pardon."

He shook his head. It was he who should be begging her forgiveness.

"I was surprised."

Repulsed, she meant.

"It must have been quite painful."

He pushed the stick around the fire, stirring the embers, desperately seeking his voice. He finally managed to speak, but he was unable to look at her. "Do please forgive me. I have overstepped my bounds. Excuse me. I should see to the horses."

He tossed the stick in the fire and stood, walking out of the shelter. He could not bear to see revulsion in her eyes, or far worse, her pity. Moreover, he realized she'd seen his face fully and did not recognize him yet. Was he so changed? Had the fire taken all his recognizable features from him? Perhaps he should admit now who he was, he thought bitterly, and explain that her wish to see him brought down had been fulfilled.

He did not return to the shelter until the bitter cold had left his extremities numb, his thoughts dull.

Thankfully, Fiona was sleeping. Duncan stoked the fire once more, then took a seat next to her, propped himself against the hay, and stared into the fire, unable to sleep.

Chapter Eight

A fire was roaring the next morning when Fiona awoke, and the last two scones were warming on a rock near the fire.

But Duncan was nowhere to be seen.

Fiona ate one scone, then slipped out of the shelter. She was stiff and her bones ached, but the sky above her was a glorious shade for blue. She used the snow to wash her face, gasping at the burning cold of it. When she had finished, she stood up and glanced around.

She spotted Duncan then, tending to the horses. It amazed her how fluidly he moved for a man with a useless arm. He'd learned to compensate for it, and it seemed as if there was nothing he could not do.

The sight of his face had kept her from sleeping much through the night. She'd feigned sleep when he'd returned because she'd sensed his discomfort and because she'd not been able to rid her thoughts of the burns or the pain in his eyes—God, his *eyes*. The pain that shone in them was so powerful that it reverberated in her. She could not imagine how he must have suffered, both physically and emotionally. Her heart had overflowed with sympathy, and then empathy, and now she wanted to assure him that it was not his scars she'd noticed, but *him*. And his eyes. They were expressive and deep, and last night they'd been filled with a passion that had ignited her. He was a man of few words, but with those eyes and hands and mouth, he hadn't needed words.

Fiona realized that in spite of the impropriety and futility of it, she was very taken with this stoic man. She didn't care that he was a tenant and she a lady; she told herself that in Scotland those things mattered less than they did in London.

There was something else, too, something that niggled at her thoughts, something vaguely familiar about this man she'd met only two days ago. In some strange way, she felt as if she'd known him quite a long time.

She watched Duncan trudging up the hill to the shelter he'd made. He stooped down, picked up big handfuls of snow, and dumped them onto the fire as she made her way through the snow to help him. "Merry Christmas!" she said cheerfully.

He barely spared her a glance. "Merry Christmas." He was wearing the patch, had wrapped his head in the woolen scarf again, and his hat was pulled low over his eyes.

"Will we reach Blackwood today?" she asked, for the sake of conversaton.

"God willing, aye."

"Oh, that's marvelous news! I'm frostbitten through and through, I am. And how do you fare this morning, Mr. Duncan?"

He rose, gathering the fur they'd slept under and stuffing it under his arm. "Well." He began to take the tarpaulin down. Fiona immediately moved to help him. "That's no' necessary," he said.

"I beg your pardon, sir, but the sooner we've put these things away, the sooner we will be on our way."

He eyed her warily, his gaze flicking over her. "Aye," he admitted.

Fiona smiled and continued to pull the tarpaulin down. "We shall fold it neatly and tuck it into the wagon, for I refuse to ride beneath it," she blithely informed him. "I, for one, intend to bask in the sun's warm glow."

Duncan clenched his jaw before he turned away.

But Fiona was not the least bit deterred.

When they were at last on their way, Fiona sat beside Duncan, chattering like a magpie, attempting to regale him with more tales of London. Once or twice, she thought she saw a look of amusement on him, but save for the occasional terse remark, Duncan remained quiet.

Fiona's imagination began to run wild, as it was wont to do. Did he regret the passionate kiss they'd shared? Did he regret that she had seen his face? Perhaps he'd been treated very ill in his life and it made him reticent now. It was really too heartbreaking to even contemplate . . . yet she could not help but contemplate it. Perhaps he did not care for her. Could she have misread his passion so completely?

Feeling quite flustered, Fiona did what she typically did—she talked. She talked and talked, filling the air around them and the vast and vivid blue sky with her words.

But a day of chatter wore on her; by midafternoon, there was still no sign of Blackwood. "I imagine it's around every bend," she said, her spirit somewhat daunted.

"It's quite a way yet," he said. "The snow has slowed our progress."

The thought that they might spend another night under the stars made Fiona's skin flush. It wasn't the cold that worried her—quite the contrary. She almost hoped this little adventure would never end, for there was something about Mr. Duncan that had settled into her blood as no one ever had. *Another night.* The very thought rattled her, titillated her, and launched her into yet another tale of London.

She told him about an afternoon she and Lady Gilbert had taken Lord Gilbert's phaeton on a drive through Hyde Park. "He was quite beside himself, his lordship," she said, after explaining how the team had gotten away from her normally firm hand and they had inadvertently terrorized a few elderly women on their walkabout. "He was very clear in his opinion that ladies ought no' to drive a carriage, particularly at such reckless speed, to which Lady Gilbert complained that why should no' women drive, as they are generally very keen on the small details, which would, naturally, make them the better drivers, but Lord Gilbert was very cross with us both, and he said, 'This may be the way of things in bloody Scotland,'" she said, affecting Lord Gilbert's voice, "'but it is no' the way of things in London,' and really, sir, I was rather offended, for while indeed I was the one driving, it was no' my idea, was it, then? I would no' presume to make use of his property—"

Duncan suddenly put his big gloved hand over hers, startling Fiona into a moment of speechlessness. She looked down at his big hand on hers, his silent way of telling her that the nattering on wasn't necessary after all. She understood him completely.

She turned her palm up beneath his, closed her fingers around his, and looked at him.

His eye shone with a hint of his smile, and once again she was struck by something familiar. "We'll no' see Blackwood today, will we?" she said, perhaps a bit too hopefully. "I know last night was right cold, but I . . . I was . . . last night was . . ."

"Fiona," he said, abruptly removing his hand from hers, the warmth in his eye fading a bit. "There is more than you know. More than meets the eye."

He was speaking of his injury, and she nodded fervently that yes, she understood what he meant. "I donna care, Duncan. I donna care in the least."

He seemed startled, confused.

"I mean . . . I understand about . . . about your face," she said.

Duncan instantly recoiled, turning his face away.

"I am sorry!" she cried, seeing how it pained him. "But it is obviously uncomfortable for you. What I mean to say is that it is no' for me! I could no' possibly care any less. I—"

"Fiona," he said, reining the horses to a halt. "Listen to me, lass. There is something you really must know—"

"Merry Christmas! Merry Christmas to you, then!"

Both of them jerked around to the sound of the voice, and watched as five people—two adults and three children—emerged from the woods. They were all carrying baskets.

It suddenly dawned on Fiona—they were carrying

wheat or pies, as was customary, to the poor on Christmas Day.

The man, wearing a patched brown cloak, hurried forward. As he neared, his round face lit with a smile. "My lord! I did no' recognize ye from afar. Old eyes," he said with a laugh, gesturing to his face. "*Fàilte, fàilte,* milord, how good of ye to come this Christmas Day!"

The man had mistaken Duncan for someone else, Fiona thought, and she looked at Duncan expectantly, assuming he would correct the man's impression and identify them. But Duncan wore a pained expression as the man approached.

"We've been visiting your tenants!" the man said. "The snow is too deep for our old cart. Are ye coming to pay a call, milord?" he asked. A light suddenly dawned in the man's eyes, and he looked behind him. "Karen! Karen, *leannan*, the laird has come to pay a call!" He turned back to them, his face beaming. "We'd no' expected ye, laird—but ye are right welcome, ye are."

Laird. The word slowly entered Fiona's consciousness like a whisper, a whisper that grew louder and louder as the truth began to sink in. She suddenly understood why Duncan had seemed so familiar to her. *Laird.* Duncan Buchanan! He'd not even bothered to hide his name, and yet she'd failed to recognize him! He'd stood before her the whole time, listening to her rail about him, and she'd been so absorbed in her little adventure she'd not even recognized him!

She looked at him now, her eyes narrowed on the features of his face. She had failed to take note of his face in her haste to accept his burns. In fact, that was *all* she had seen—the purple, scarred skin, the evidence of a tragedy that had made him even more mysterious than she'd first believed. She had not looked *at* him, *really* looked at him until this very moment!

She felt like a colossal fool. An addlepated, loose-tongued fool. How could she possibly have developed feelings for a man who had once so rudely likened her to a woodchuck? "*Mi Diah*," she said low.

Duncan jerked his gaze to her as Fiona bent over her lap, mortified by the depth of her stupidity.

"Fiona—"

"It is an honor, laird," the man was saying.

An honor! An honor to receive a man who once reviled her and now deceived her!

"I assure you, Mr. Nevin, the honor is mine," Duncan said. He touched Fiona's hand. "Lady Fiona Haines, allow me to present Mr. Nevin. He is my tenant."

She could hardly make herself sit upright. But she did. She stared at Mr. Nevin, her heart and mind in a nauseating whirl of wretched thoughts.

"A pleasure to make yer acquaintance, mu'um," Mr. Nevin said anxiously. "Ours is but a humble home, just round the bend here, but ye are most welcome. *Ceud mile fàilte*," he added in Gaelic, welcoming her.

"*Tapadh leat*," she responded, thanking him.

"May I also present Mrs. Nevin, Master Tavin Nevin, his brother, Collin Nevin, and the lovely Miss Robena Nevin," Duncan stoically continued as the entire family made their way to the wagon.

The lads bowed their heads; Miss Robena curtsied without taking her eyes from Fiona.

Fiona nodded. She could not speak. If she uttered anything, it would be a scream or a curse.

"Climb on," Duncan said. "We'll see you home."

Mrs. Nevin ushered the family into the wagon, while Mr. Nevin gestured to Duncan's hand. "I could ride up top with ye, milord, and handle the reins."

"It's no' necessary."

"Please, milord. It would be my honor," Mr. Nevin insisted.

Duncan nodded, and Fiona numbly watched him unwind the reins from his deformed hand and pass them to Mr. Nevin. With Mr. Nevin up top, the wagon lurched forward.

She could feel Duncan beside her, could feel all of him, pressing against her. But she could not look at him. She was mortified to her very core.

After only a few minutes, they reached a thatch-roofed cottage from which a tail of smoke curled up out of the chimney. With Mrs. Nevin at her side, Fiona was ushered into the cottage. She made the obligatory remarks, but she hardly saw the place, her mind was rushing so. A table was laid with dinnerware and wine. The scent of roasted goose and bannock cakes wafted through the air, and Fiona's stomach responded with a hungry growl. Boughs of evergreens were scattered on the floor before the hearth, a few of which Miss Robena picked up to show Fiona. Candles had been lit and placed in the windows, symbolically lighting the way for the holy family.

"Tavin, set two more places at the table. Robena, mind you have a care with those boughs!" Mrs. Nevin instructed her children, then smiled at Fiona. "We've no' had a lady to dine with us," she said anxiously. "And from England, no less!"

"England?" Fiona said, startled. "I beg your pardon, but I'm no' English."

"No?" Mrs. Nevin said, blinking clear blue eyes at her. "Forgive me—I thought, given your accent . . ."

"Scottish," Fiona said adamantly, and removed her bonnet. She sheepishly put a hand to her hair, certain it looked a fright. "I am as Scottish as you, Mrs. Nevin, reared no' very far from here at all." She smiled at Robena, who was looking at her bonnet as if it were a fine work of art. She handed it to the lass, who took it carefully and held it away from her with awe. "Scotland is home," she added, and realized for the first time since returning how deeply Scotland was imbedded in her blood.

Just when she'd begun to realize it, the shock of seeing Duncan Buchanan after all these years had put her to sea all over again.

Chapter Nine

Mr. Nevin could not have been more accommodating when Duncan explained their predicament and how they'd been caught in the snow. There was not the slightest bit of censure in his tenant's expression. In fact, Mr. Nevin seemed more than pleased to be able to offer lodging for the night.

That had always been Duncan's experience with the Nevins. They were good, honest Christian people, full of charity. The very sort of tenants he'd once ridiculed as too rustic in the company of his friends.

Now he wished for all the world he had an ounce of Mr. Nevin's integrity. If he'd possessed it, he might have told Fiona who he was in Edinburgh instead of hiding behind his bloody vanity.

When he entered the cottage directly behind his host, his gaze fell upon Fiona standing at the hearth, her hands held out over the heat. She looked tired, and her gown was in an awful state of dishevelment, stained by snow and ash and tree sap. Her hair, which had begun the journey bound up nicely, had come undone in several different places. Thick strands of brown hair fell here and there down her back and over her shoulder.

He'd never seen a lovelier sight. To him she was beautiful.

He'd had every intention of telling her who he was when he'd pulled the team to a halt on the road. He would not have waited so long had he not already lost his heart to her. He could not bear to see her censure when she realized he was the one who had so stupidly and rudely dismissed her all those years ago. He'd thought all day how best to broach it—but he'd not counted on the Nevin family's appearing so unexpectedly from the forest path.

"Shall I take your hat, laird?" Mr. Nevin asked as Mrs. Nevin bustled about the table, helping Tavin add two place settings.

"We are delighted you've come, laird!" she called to him. "Please, take off your cloak and warm yourself by the fire."

There was no reason not to do as she asked—the Nevins had seen his face, as had most of his tenants. There was no reason to keep the scarf on besides his foolish vanity. He glanced at Fiona again—she was looking at him now, watching him closely.

He shrugged out of his cloak first, sliding it over his bad arm. And as it hung uselessly at his side, he unwrapped the scarf from his head and handed that, too, to Mr. Nevin, and stood in all his grotesque glory.

"To the fire, milord—I'll pour a whisky for you, shall I?"

"Aye, please," he said, gazing at Fiona. She had every right to hate him. He looked for it in her expression. But whatever she was thinking was carefully hidden behind an inscrutably polite expression.

"The children are tying boughs together to hang on the hearth," Mrs. Nevin said proudly. "It's something we've always done on Christmas Day."

"It's a lovely tradition," Fiona said. "May I help them?"

The Nevin lass looked as is if she might float away; her gaze flew to her mother with a very loud but silent plea.

"They'd be honored," Mrs. Nevin said.

Duncan watched Fiona sink to her knees beside the girl and begin to put the boughs together, helping her tie them with ribbon. Collin, the youngest boy, who Duncan knew had the aim of a grown man when it came to shooting grouse, leaped over a stool to join them. He stood at the fire, watching the three of them binding the boughs together. Fiona's bright smile had returned, and she told the children a tale of Hogmanay from her childhood that included such excitement as spears, beavers, toppled bonfires, and general mayhem.

When they had at last finished tying the boughs, the elder boy, Tavin, dragged his father's stool to the hearth and stood upon it, trying to reach the mantel. His reach was short, however. Mr. Nevin moved to help him, but Duncan waved him off. He took the bough from the boy and said, "Allow me."

"I'll fetch the others, milord!" Tavin exclaimed, and leaped off the stool to gather the others.

With the children gathered round, Duncan proceeded to tack the boughs to the cottage wall above the mantel. He methodically went about it, his heart and mind on Fiona while he mindlessly stuffed the boughs beneath his bad arm, then used his shoulder to hold them in place while he tacked them up. How she must despise him! *Good.* It was no less than he deserved. He did not deserve to think her light had shone through to his marrow. He did not deserve to feel her body, soft and small next to his, resting so perfectly in his arms. He deserved her complete disdain. He should wallow in it, for heaven's sake.

He was rudely brought back to the present when Collin asked what had happened to his face.

Time seemed to stop for a moment—no one moved, no one so much as breathed until the lad's mother cried, "*Collin*!"

Duncan quickly held up a hand. "It is quite all right," he assured her. "My scars are a curiosity, naturally." He smiled at Collin. "I was caught in a fire. I could no' escape before I was injured."

"Was it a very big fire? Was it so big that it burned the ceiling and floor and walls and all the furniture?" Collin asked, gesturing wildly to indicate a flame out of control.

"Enormous," Duncan assured him. "It burned half my house."

Collin gasped and looked at his older brother. "Were ye forced to leap from a window from the very top of the house?" Tavin asked hopefully.

"No. I was pulled out of the fire by my servants."

"What the laird does no' say is that he was attempting to save the life of his friend," Mr. Nevin added as he steered the boys away. "He is a very brave man."

"I was no' brave, Mr. Nevin," Duncan said with a bitter laugh. "I scarcely knew what I was about."

"Did ye save him, then, sir?" Tavin asked.

Duncan shook his head. "Devon MacCauley perished in the fire."

Fiona gasped; Duncan looked at her. She'd put a hand over her mouth to stifle her cry, but was looking at him with horror. Of course, she knew nothing of the fire.

"The good Lord was watching over the laird. Thank God he survived the fire," Mrs. Nevin added stoutly.

"But what of his friend?" Collin asked. "Was the Lord no' looking out for him?"

Mrs. Nevin blinked. "The Lord works in mysterious ways, young man, and we've better things to think of now. We are blessed to share our Christmas meal with our laird. If you would, then, milord—supper is served."

Collin slipped his hand into Duncan's and led him to the table.

He and Collin sat across from Fiona and Robena. Duncan tried to keep his gaze from Fiona, but the smooth skin above her décolletage and her slender neck were impossible to avoid. He was mesmerized by her, entirely smitten, which just added to his pain.

She, on the other hand, was very good in her efforts to avert her gaze from him. If she hated him, reviled him, it was impossible to detect. She was, quite simply, the life of the party. She exclaimed gleefully with the children when they related their plans for Hogmanay. She beamed with delight when Mrs. Nevin spoke shyly of how she and Mr. Nevin had met at a Hogmanay celebration. She then related a rather embellished tale of how she'd ended up in London, as well as her grand return to Scotland in a grander carriage.

After a supper of roasted goose, potatoes, and the traditional bannock cakes—perhaps the best meal Duncan had ever eaten in his bloody life—Mr. Nevin produced a fiddle and began to play some old Scottish tunes. Fiona was instantly on her feet, coaxing Mrs. Nevin to hers.

Mrs. Nevin's shyness quickly evaporated, however, and the two women were soon dancing and laughing with the children, spinning round to Scottish reels, tapping their toes and heels to jigs and strathspeys.

When Mrs. Nevin grabbed Duncan's hand and tried to pull him up, he resisted. But Fiona grabbed hold of his burned arm and smiled at him. He was powerless to decline.

They danced until they lacked the stamina to dance anymore. Mrs. Nevin collapsed on a chair, one arm slung over her middle. "Ye are an excellent dancer, milady," she said approvingly.

"It's a hobby," Fiona answered breathlessly with a flick of her wrist. "My brother and I once competed with one another. I felt rather obliged to best him, so I practiced." She laughed.

"A sword dance!" Mr. Nevin cried.

"Oh no," Fiona started, but Mr. Nevin was already pointing his bow to another room. "Fetch me walking sticks!" he cried merrily to his sons.

The boys scampered out while Mrs. Nevin fretted about where to move chairs.

Duncan stood back and watched them all as suitable "swords" were found and placed on the floor before Fiona. How strangely comforting this all felt to him—he'd always believed he would marry and produce the obligatory family only when it was absolutely necessary. And even then, he'd assumed he would continue to enjoy the favors of other women. He'd viewed a wife as nothing more than a vessel for his heirs and a hostess for Blackwood.

Things were so vastly different now. He was a different man—a lonely man—a man who would welcome the companionship and intimacy of a wife. He'd even come to despise Blackwood for its bleak emptiness, where he'd once cherished his independence there.

He'd like to have children, too, he thought, chuckling to himself when Collin tripped and fell over a thick woolen rug in his haste to move. He'd never given children any thought at all. But since the accident, he'd discovered that young children were the most accepting of the human race. They accepted his face for what it was and went on about their business, much as the Nevin children had tonight.

How ironic it was to finally realize he did want to marry and bring children into this world now that his prospects had burned in the fire. Most of the privileged women he'd once known did not want a man as damaged as he was, both physically and morally.

As he watched Fiona dancing the sword dance, her face full of light, her step quick and accurate and graceful, he fantasized about marrying her. He imagined them at a restored Blackwood, on Christmas day, with their own children.

But in his fantasy, his face was repaired and she had forgiven him.

It was just a fantasy. He harbored no illusions.

Chapter Ten

Dawn arrived too quickly as far as Fiona was concerned—she was loath to leave this idyllic little cottage in the woods. She'd enjoyed one of the best Christmas feasts she'd ever attended, in this cottage, with this family who'd been strangers to her yesterday and were now dear friends. And, surprisingly, with Duncan Buchanan.

She simply must be mad.

Of course, she'd been shocked to discover who he was, that she could not deny. She'd been angry, mortified, and furious. But in the course of the evening, something had happened. She'd seen with her own eyes how different he was from the man she once knew. Pain and disfigurement had humbled him. The man she remembered would never have condescended to speak to these people, much less share their Christmas meal, and it went without saying that he would not have noticed the children in any remarkable way. Or *dance*!

It had given her a sense of just how far the handsome, arrogant laird's pride had fallen. The change in him was extraordinary.

But she was still angry, very angry. He'd known very well she did not recognize him and had allowed her to carry on, saying horrible things about him . . . not to mention her wanton behavior! She was just as angry with herself for being so daft that she'd not recognized him. By all that was holy, he'd said his name was Duncan, and still she'd been too stupid and blind to see him!

There was something else she'd learned that cold Christmas night, when the world had seemed bathed in the white of a pristine snow and a full moon—she missed having a family. Oh, aye, she'd told tale after tale of *her* family, but the truth was that there was only her and Jack now. The atmosphere here—a warm hearth, a warm home, a loving family—seemed a world away from London, figuratively and literally. The Nevins's lives seemed so much simpler than her life in London, yet in some respects, they seemed much fuller than hers could ever hope to be.

She envied them that.

But dawn brought reality streaming in through the window of the room she'd shared with Robena. She dressed early, wanting to reach Blackwood and deliver her message to Jack, then remove herself as quickly as she could with what little dignity she had left. In the family room, however, she found only Mr. and Mrs. Nevin and their children. The laird was nowhere to be seen.

"Good morning, Lady Fiona!" Mr. Nevin said cheerfully. He was wearing a thick cloak and had his hat in hand.

"Good morning, sir."

"Please, break yer fast. When you've done, I am to take you on to Blackwood."

"Beg your pardon?"

"The laird was gone before dawn, mu'um. He asked me to drive you over when you are ready."

He'd *gone*? After all they'd endured—and not forgetting the bloody apology he owed her—he'd *left* her here and gone on? Fury swelled in her; she forced a bright smile to her face and swiped up her hat from the table. "Thank you kindly, sir, but I am without appetite this morning. You fed me too well yesterday, I fear."

"No' a morsel?" Mrs. Nevin asked.

"I could no' possibly," Fiona said, patting her belly. She would choke if she ate a thing, she was so angry.

She said farewell to the Nevins, truly hating to leave their happy home and truly dreading Blackwood.

Unfortunately, the drive to Blackwood went smoothly and quickly. The snow was rapidly melting, but the ground still hard enough that the team clipped along. Mr. Nevin was a pleasant traveling companion, full of interesting information about the area and the estate. Yet he did not prepare her for the sight of Blackwood.

They turned onto the long road to Blackwood that Fiona remembered well. In just a mile or so she would see the massive structure built on a hill with the Highlands behind it and a valley before it. But instead of the imposing towers coming into view as they drew closer, Fiona saw a blackened shell rising above the landscape. "God in heaven!" she cried. "Is there nothing left of it, then?"

"The east wing still stands."

"But . . . but why has he no' rebuilt it?"

"I've wondered that myself," Mr. Nevin admitted. "I rather imagine he canna bring himself to do so yet."

That made no sense to Fiona. The man she knew was too proud to leave his home in such a state. Yet it was a monument to a devastating fire, a reminder of that awful night he'd been disfigured and his friend had died.

They drove around to the entrance, lavishly marked by iron gates that were anchored in the open mouths of a pair of massive stone lions. But the vista was ruined—the fire had devoured one half of a fine mansion, and nothing but stone columns, a hearth here and there, and various stairways remained, blanketed by snow.

The butler—a different man than the one Fiona had known—walked out onto the stone portico that had somehow remained untouched by the fire. "*Fàilte!*" he said, bowing low. "Gaines at your service, milady."

"Thank you," Fiona said, allowing Mr. Nevin to help her down from the wagon. "Is the laird about?"

"Unfortunately, he is occupied with his solicitor, but he asks that you be made comfortable and join him for the evening meal."

"I had no' planned to stay as long as that, sir," she said pertly. But she wasn't leaving before giving Duncan a thought or two. "May I inquire—is my brother, the Earl of Lambourne, in residence?"

"No, milady, there are no other guests in residence. The earl has joined the laird's cousin, Mr. Angus Buchanan, for a hunt at Bonnethill."

Bonnethill! Good Lord, did Jack ever stay in one place? Was nothing easy? "Might you know when he will return?"

"I canna say, my lady, but Mr. Angus Buchanan is expected back for Hogmanay."

"Hogmanay! I canna wait as long as that! Is it possible to have a message delivered to him? It is rather urgent that I speak with him."

Gaines bowed and gestured toward the entrance. "I shall inquire of the laird straightaway. Shall I show you in?"

"You might show me to a hot bath, sir, if you please," she said, and turned to say good-bye to Mr. Nevin.

Before she could do so, however, a footman appeared at the wagon carrying a large bundle, which he presented to Mr. Nevin.

"What's this?" Mr. Nevin asked, surprised.

"The laird sends his gratitude for your hospitality, Mr. Nevin," Gaines explained. "He sends these gifts to you and your family with the hopes you will enjoy them at Hogmanay."

Mr. Nevin looked down at the bundle. "*Diah* . . . what is it, then?"

"Some toys for the children, a bolt of fine silk for Mrs. Nevin, and one of the laird's prized hunting knives for you, sir."

Mr. Nevin gaped at the butler. "No, sir, I canna accept it—"

"The laird is quite insistent, Mr. Nevin. You did him a great service, and he should very much like you to accept these gifts, which are a token of his appreciation."

"You must take it, Mr. Nevin," Fiona urged him.

"It is too much," Mr. Nevin insisted, and looked at Gaines. "You must tell him it is too much, sir. We did only what he would do in our shoes, aye?"

"Take it, Mr. Nevin. You were so very kind to us," Fiona said again.

He shook his head as he looked at the bundle, but could not help his smile. "The children will be right pleased, aye?" he said excitedly, and put the bundle on the bench. He climbed up, took the reins in hand, and waved at Fiona. "Good day, milady, and a very happy Hogmanay to you!"

"Good day, sir, and thank you!" she called after him. As she watched him pull away, Fiona didn't know how happy her Hogmanay would be, but if Mr. Nevin's beaming smile were any indication, his family's Hogmanay would be a very happy one indeed thanks to Duncan's generosity.

Bathed, shaven, and somewhat rested after a night spent lying in front of the hearth in the Nevin home, Duncan was in better spirits. He'd gone about his business, reviewing his accounts and the plans for the Hogmanay celebration. At Fiona's request, he sent a messenger to Bonnethill, requesting that Angus and his guest return to Blackwood at once, as an urgent matter had arisen.

The underbutler, Ogden, who had become a passable valet after the fire, helped Duncan dress for supper that evening. When he had finished tying Duncan's neckcloth, Duncan did something he rarely did—he looked at his face in the mirror. It made him ill, but tonight, of all nights, he felt the need to be completely honest about who and what he was.

As he walked through the hallways of what was left of his house, his boots striking a steady rhythm on the pine floors, Duncan tried to see Blackwood through Fiona's eyes. This part of the house was still rather magnificent—portraits, fine works of porcelain art, and carpets imported from Belgium adorned every room.

In the red drawing room, he allowed Gaines to pour him a tot of whisky, which he quickly tossed back before extending the tot to Gaines once more. He glanced at his hand—he could detect an almost indiscernible tremble.

Bloody hell, but he was as anxious as a goose at Christmas about this meeting with Fiona Haines. It astonished him that he could not recall a time he'd really cared what a woman thought of him, but *this* woman had crawled under his skin and rooted there. He cared very much what she might think.

He cared very much.

Too much—such desire would only lead to crushing disappointment. He had to remind himself of this during his interminable wait for Fiona.

When at last she arrived, she made quite an entrance. The doors of the drawing room swung open and she stood there in the threshold, her arms held wide as she gripped both doors, staring at him with glittering gold eyes, full of a woman's ire. She was wearing an emerald green velvet gown that picked up the flecks of green in her eyes. It was tightly—and magnificently—fitted to her. The flesh of her bosom swelled enticingly above a low décolletage. Fiona looked as if she belonged in a king's court, every lovely inch of her.

Bloody hell, she looked as if she belonged in his arms. *Now.* He could feel his body react, could feel that unconquerable male urge roar inside him. But it was insanity to hope—Fiona Haines would fare far better than him, and besides, the way she was looking at him now was a far cry from the way she had looked at him on the cold, snowy night they'd shared under the stars. She looked as if she could and might strangle him with her bare hands, here and now.

Duncan braced himself for it, clasping his good hand behind his back.

Fiona folded her arms, lifted her chin, and walked imperiously into the drawing room, her eyes narrowing on him as she neared.

Duncan swallowed. Whatever she would say, let her say it—just *say* it. He wanted this over and done so that he might return to his lonely existence and forget her.

Fiona cocked her head to one side. "You *left* me."

"Good evening," he tried.

"You forced poor Mr. Nevin to accompany me to your home as if I were a wayward orphan!"

"I assure you, that was no' my intent. I thought to spare you any question of impropriety."

She snorted and walked in a slow circle around him. "Perhaps you sought to spare yourself any questions from your friends about your traveling companion."

His *friends*? He had no friends, not any longer. "No' at all," he assured her. "I thought only of you."

She came to a halt before him, tilted her head back, and peered up at him. Her eyes were sparkling with her wrath, her lips, plump and red, curved in a devilish smile. "If you thought only of *me*, laird, then why did you no' tell me?"

"You were sleeping."

"No' that!" she cried, punching him in the arm. "You know very well what I mean!"

He rather supposed he did, and no less than one thousand responses sloshed about in his brain. "I did no' want to alarm you."

She arched a brow high above the other. "No' even when I was telling you what a wretched man you were?"

He could not help the tiny smile that curved one corner of his mouth. "Especially then. By that point, I was too mortified to admit it was I for whom you held such contempt."

"You were no' the only one to be mortified, I assure you," she said low, and spun away from him.

"I offer you my sincerest apology. I should have told you."

She glanced over her shoulder at him. "*Aye.* You should have indeed." She smiled thinly. "But I suppose the damage is done. We should no' dwell on it, aye? Let us just . . ."—she made a whirring gesture with her hand—"go on from here, shall we?"

He felt a current run through him, the first wave of crushing disappointment. "Of course." He gestured toward the door. "Shall we dine?"

"I thought you'd never ask," she said, and gave him such a brilliant smile that he felt a bit weak at the knees.

In the dining room, he said very little. He felt incapable of conversation. He felt like a shell of a man, his body shrinking under the glow of her countenance, which brightened considerably over the course of the meal. She was animated, laughing at something Mr. Nevin had told her.

He could sit for the rest of the night and watch her talk, her hands moving expressively, her face lit with her smile. Not once did she look away from his face. It almost seemed as if she did not see the ravages of the fire there. When she spoke, she looked him directly in the eye. Occasionally, while she was talking, she would touch his damaged hand and seem not to notice it at all. She was, he slowly realized, remarkably unfazed by the awful sight of him.

Fiona then unabashedly mentioned her shock at seeing Blackwood, and her walkabout in the ruined wing this afternoon. "You could rebuild it," she suggested.

That brought his head up. It was a difficult subject for him. Part of him wanted to leave that burned shell to remind himself of his folly, of the shallow man he once was. Another part of him feared his ability to make it right.

The two parts had left him paralyzed with indecision.

"There is a home near Bath that I recently had the pleasure of visiting," Fiona said airily. "It was built in the French style, with lots of windows and turrets. The French style with turrets would be quite lovely here, set against the hills, do you no' think so?"

Turrets. Why she thought them particularly French, he could not guess. He cleared his throat, glanced at Gaines, and nodded for him to begin clearing the dishes. "I have no' decided."

"But the fire was quite a long time ago, was it no'?" she asked. "The girl who tended my bath said it was very long ago."

"Aye, but . . ."

"But?"

"Lady Fiona, it is a rather complicated matter," he said, looking at her once more.

She drew a breath, but seemed to think the better of responding, and nodded.

With the meal concluded, Duncan could think of no reason to keep her. He feared any polite parlor games, feared being remotely close to her because then he would want to touch her and he would lose himself to a false hope all over again. As it was, he could not take his eyes from her. He could not *breathe.* "It is late," he said, rising from his chair. "You've had quite a long journey. I will leave you to retire at your leisure," he added as a footman stepped forward to help Fiona out of her chair. "Gaines will see you to your rooms."

He bowed his head and made himself turn. He quit the room without looking back, leaving his beating heart behind with Fiona.

Chapter Eleven

The supper had seened interminable to Fiona. Duncan hardly spoke and had kept looking at her as if he could not understand what she was doing at his gold inlaid dining table.

She'd wondered that a time or two herself. But as she watched him stalk from the dining room—he could scarcely wait to free himself of her, she thought—it occurred to her that it was ridiculous to wait for Jack at Blackwood. She could just as easily wait for him at Lambourne Castle.

"If you would like, mu'um, I could have a tot of whisky sent up to your rooms," Gaines offered.

"Where is the laird going?" she asked the butler, ignoring his offer.

"I canna rightly say, but it is his habit to repair to the morning sitting room after supper."

"The *morning* sitting room?"

"It is where he has situated a library," Gaines explained. "The library was in the west wing before the fire. A wee bit of whisky, then?" he asked, holding up the decanter.

"Actually, Mr. Gaines, I shall have it now," she said, and

held out her hand for the tot. She extended the other for the decanter. "All of it."

He looked surprised by that, but handed it all to her nonetheless, and watched, his brows almost to his hairline, as Fiona poured a tot and tossed it back. "Thank you," she said hoarsely as she handed him the empty tot. She smoothed the lap of her gown and marched from the dining room, gripping the decanter. But instead of turning left toward her suite of rooms, she turned right, toward the morning sitting room.

When she reached the door at the end of the corridor, she rapped lightly, then leaned forward, listening.

"No whisky, Gaines, thank you," he said from within.

"No whisky indeed," she muttered, and opened the door.

"No whis . . ." Duncan's voice trailed off when he turned his head and saw her there. He hastily came to his feet; the newspaper he was holding in his lap fluttered to the floor. "I beg your pardon," he said, and put his good hand behind his back, standing stiffly.

"No, laird, I beg yours," Fiona said smartly, emboldened by the tot of whisky. "I must thank you for seeing me to Blackwood, but as my brother is no' here, I have come to a decision."

"Oh?"

"I see no reason to burden you further with my presence. I see no reason for us to continue this . . . familiarity, aye? Lambourne Castle is but a half day's drive from here, and I shall be perfectly fine there until the earl returns from his hunting or . . . or whatever he is doing at Bonnethill," she said with a dismissive flick of her wrist. "If you would be so kind, I should like to go home for a time."

"Home," he echoed.

Was he daft? "Aye, *home.* The house where I was brought up. The house where I shall now reside. Lambourne Castle."

Duncan swallowed. He glanced at his bad hand, then at her again. "Do you mean . . . do you mean to say you intend to remain in Scotland, then?"

What did he care if she did or did not? She shrugged and set the decanter down with a *thwack.* She hadn't thought it through entirely, but it suddenly seemed the place for her. She could be the little spinster who lived at Lambourne Castle. She would tend her garden and make remarks about society and people would flock to her to hear her tales of spending a few years in the highest reaches of London society. Perhaps Lady Gilbert would call on her here, and she would have a large soirée.

Except that she didn't think Lady Gilbert's husband would be in favor of the journey.

"Perhaps I will!" she said firmly. "Much depends on my brother, of course—he might need me in London—but Lambourne Castle is quite nice, is it no', if one enjoys the moat and parapets?"

Duncan pressed his lips together and nodded. "Quite," he said curtly.

He seemed almost pained to hear it. Well, he could bloody well be pained! Fiona was not a shy young debutante so easily influenced by his remarks as she'd once been. She would not run to London! "I am sorry if that displeases you, but I shall be very busy at Lambourne, I assure you. No one has been about for so long, I imagine there is quite a lot to be done."

"Lady Fiona—"

"And really, I should no' bother you in the least, as

there is quite a lot to be done *here*. How can you leave such a magnificent home in such a state?" she cried, throwing one arm wide. "It is a jewel in the Highlands, yet you let it rot! If I am to remain in Scotland for a time, I could be persuaded to help you, you know."

She could scarcely believe she'd just said it. She hadn't even really thought about it before it came tumbling out of her mouth. But there it was.

He stilled and looked at her closely. "Perhaps I shall accept that offer," he said low.

"*Good*."

He was looking at her in a way that made her feel oddly exposed, and Fiona blushed. He'd always had that effect on her—just a look with his brown eyes could make her feel warm and a little weak in the knees. "You need someone like me, if you must know," she added pertly. "Someone who is no' afraid to say what must be said."

A soft smile curved his lips. "No one would ever accuse Lady Fiona of being afraid to speak, that is true."

Oh Lord. She was beginning to feel very wobbly and put a hand to her nape as she cast her gaze at the carpet. "But now I think there is naugh' more to say," she said. "Other than that I should very much like to thank you for delivering me home. I . . . I could no' have come alone. It would seem my uncle was right again."

"It would seem."

"Aye." She was surprised by the feeling of sadness that suddenly rose up in her. She looked up and smiled sheepishly. "Well then. Thank you, laird. I shall leave you in peace."

That was it, then. The night they had shared notwithstanding, that was it, all that could be said between the two of them. And as she was not one to reveal how distressed she truly felt, Fiona turned to go.

But Duncan suddenly moved, crossing the room, shutting the door and locking it. He turned around, his back to the door, and looked at her again, only this time, his gaze locked with hers, and in that gaze was a world of meaning. "*Fiona* . . ."

The way he said her name was like a caress. It was soft and low, trickling warmly into her consciousness like the bit of whisky she'd drunk.

"I . . ." He paused and stared helplessly at her.

The mighty laird of Blackwood seemed unsettled. Uncertain.

He cleared his throat, looked down as he ran a hand over the top of his head, then looked up once more, catching her gaze and holding it. She could feel the intensity of it, could feel that magnetic pull between them again.

"I . . . I canna express to you how . . . how much I regret what I said all those years ago. I will be honest—I donna remember it, but I've no doubt I said it. What I can no' understand is how I might have possibly dismissed someone as . . ."

He paused and let his gaze drift over her, and Fiona felt herself on the edge of some precipice.

"As beautiful," he said, his voice breaking slightly, "or as *vibrant* as you. Fiona, in a very short time, I have come to simply . . . adore you."

Fiona's mouth gaped. It felt as if time had rewound itself, and he was saying the things she'd wanted him to say eight years ago.

"I was a bloody fool," he said, his face darkening somewhat.

"What?"

"A bloody, ignorant fool," he repeated, only more adamantly, and Fiona's heart swelled in her chest, choking the breath from her.

"And now?" he said, clenching his fist at his side. "Now I would give what is left of Blackwood to make amends to you. But I harbor no illusions, lass—I know I canna repair it."

"What—why?"

He scowled and turned away from her. "Must I say it? The scandal that surrounded Devon's death. My useless arm, of course. My . . ." He gestured impatiently to his face. "My scars."

Fiona took a step closer to him. "What scars?"

Startled, he turned to look at her. "Fiona! I treated you contemptibly—you and others. I was vain and proud and . . ." He made a sound of disgust. "I am a changed man, Fiona. In my heart I have changed. I am ashamed of what I was then and I leave the burned shell of my house to remind me of it every day."

Her heart went out to him. Oh, how he must have suffered! She took another step toward him, and another. "Have you no' punished yourself enough for it, then, Duncan?" she asked him softly. "Can you no' see that it is time to build a house as a testament to the man you are now?"

His eyes filled with helplessness. "I am but a shadow of the man I was."

"Oh, but that is where you are wrong," she said, moving closer. "You saved my life by risking your own, Duncan! You saved my *life*. And . . . and your generosity to the Nevin family was astoundingly kind." He glanced skeptically at her; Fiona nodded adamantly. "I was there when your gift was delivered to Mr. Nevin. You cannot imagine his happiness. Do you see? You are more than the man you were then," she said again. "You are strong and giving and handsome and . . . breathtaking in your sincerity."

As she spoke the words, she realized how true they were. He was a completely different man now, a better man.

"Ah, Fiona," he said sadly. "Can you really see past this deformity? It is no' a pity you are feeling?"

She responded by taking the last few steps to where he stood. She reached up; he recoiled, turning his face, but she caught his chin in her hand and turned his face toward her. With her eyes on his, she pressed her palm against his damaged flesh. "I see no deformity. I see only you, a man greater now than he was before. A man who is kind and thoughtful and sincere. I see only you."

With a groan, Duncan abruptly caught her up in his arm. He kissed her as he twirled her around, putting her back against the wall. "I canna resist you. You've made me feel more alive than I have felt in a very long time."

His kiss was urgent, his embrace fiercely possessive. It filled Fiona's heart—she wanted to be possessed, body and soul. She threw the last vestiges of her pride and virtue to abandon, raking her hands through his hair and returning his kiss with an urgency of her own. She'd never felt so wildly aroused as she did the moment he swept her up, never felt so emotional as this.

She caught his face in her hands as his mouth moved from her lips to her neck, then down her body, to her bodice, nibbling and kissing the flesh of her bosom.

Fiona closed her eyes and pressed her head against the wall, reveling in his attention to her. She was an alluring woman who could entice a man to do this. She felt feverish, on fire, as if they'd denied themselves for a lifetime instead of a day or two. Duncan's mouth and hand caressed every curve of her body, every patch of exposed flesh, so that her body was quivering with anticipation, her skin consumed by his touch.

She slipped her hands inside his coat, running them across the breadth of his hard chest, the flat plane of his abdomen, and up again to his neckcloth, which she quickly untied, loosening it so that she might put her hands into the space between his collar and his shirt and feel his flesh.

But Duncan caught her up again, holding her against him in a one-armed embrace, and strode to a divan. He deposited her there, then stepped back and hastily unwound the neckcloth. His fingers flew down his waistcoat, which he discarded along with his coat. He went down on one knee beside her and tenderly caressed the hair at her brow. "I was a bloody fool all those years ago, lass. You are beautiful, Fiona, a Highland beauty."

He could not have seduced her more completely. Fiona sat up, put her hands to his waist, and pulled his shirttail from his trousers. She moved to lift the shirt over his head. Duncan's immediate reaction was to try and stop her, but Fiona caught his hand and pushed it away. With her eyes on his, she slowly lifted his shirt, her hands sliding up the skin of his chest, her fingers grazing his nipples, his sternum, and up, until she felt the ravaged skin of his shoulder.

Duncan winced; Fiona stilled her hand. "My . . . my body is hideous," he muttered.

"It is beautiful," she assured him, and she meant it. His skin might be horribly scarred, but he was a strong, virile man, and no puckered skin could change that.

She rose up on her knees and pulled the shirt over his head, tossing it aside, and looked unabashedly at his arm and shoulder, running her fingers over the worst of it. It was misshapen; the skin had healed in such a way that it pulled his arm to a strange angle. She leaned forward and kissed his chest. His shoulder, his arm.

"'*Bòidheach,*" she whispered as her fingers fluttered over his shoulders and neck, across the ball of his throat and down, to the hard plane of his chest. *Beautiful.* . . .

Duncan drew a ragged breath as she explored him with her hands. "I thought the journey would never end," he said roughly. "I could no' bear to sit beside you and no' touch you. I could no' lay beside you and no' think of loving you. You are right, Fiona. I need you. I have needed you desperately."

"If you need me, then make me yours," she said audaciously.

He cupped her face, pressed his forehead against hers a moment, then lifted his head and looked at her, his brown eyes probing deep. He watched her eyes as he slipped his arm around her back and expertly sought the fastening of her gown, his fingers moving down the row of buttons. He pushed her gown from her shoulders, along with her chemise, down her body until her breasts were bared to him. His gaze dropped to her breasts; he drew a ragged breath as he caressed them with his fingers before catching her around the waist once more and carefully lowering her to the divan again.

He kissed her madly before moving down her body to her breasts, taking one into his mouth and sucking the hardened peak onto his tongue.

The sensation was spellbinding. Fiona closed her

eyes—a consuming desire began to rise up in her; she could feel it growing with every stroke of his tongue, with every caress of his hand until she felt frenzied with it. She kissed his head, kneaded his shoulders, ran her fingers down his back and up again as he laved her breasts. When he lifted his face to kiss her, she took it in her hands and kissed his eyes, his lips, his chin.

But Duncan faded from her again, moving down her body, his mouth on her abdomen, his hand pushing her gown down to her hips, and over them, baring her body to him. His breath was hot on her sex, his hands cupping her hips.

Fiona's blood felt as if it scored her veins; she was dangerously aroused, desire seeping into her marrow and pooling in a cauldron inside her.

Duncan rose up to kiss her at the same moment he put his hand between her legs, against her hot, slick flesh. Fiona moaned against his mouth; she was lost, completely lost. But when his fingers slipped inside her and he began to stroke her with his thumb, she was mad. She gasped into his mouth and shifted against him, pressing against his hand and body, moving seductively against him, her body begging for more.

"I canna bear it," he said roughly, and withdrew his hand, unfastening his trousers, pushing them from his magnificent hips, and quickly coming over her again, sliding in between her legs. He leaned down and kissed her tenderly, holding himself aloft with one arm, his knee nudging her thighs apart. "I want to make you mine, Fiona," he said. "Completely. Always."

She rose up on her elbows and kissed him. "Always."

He groaned; she held his gaze as the tip of him, hot and hard, nudged her. Duncan shifted on top of her and moved his hand to her thigh. He caressed her with his palm, pushing her legs farther apart, then guided himself inside her.

It was an exquisite sensation—her body working to open to him, the tightness easing a bit to allow him. There was a moment of pain, and Fiona closed her eyes. When it had passed, she opened her eyes and looked at him.

He was watching her closely, his eyes full of longing.

Fiona raked her fingers through his hair. "Always," she whispered.

With a hiss of restraint, Duncan began to move in her—slowly, easily. But Fiona wanted the frenzy of their shared desire again, and kissed him until he let go of his inhibitions and was moving fast and deep inside her.

She ached at the intrusion but longed for more. She moved with him, burying her face in his neck, anchoring her fingers in his flesh. She whimpered with the undiluted pleasure of his body filling hers. When he shifted again, he put his hand between their bodies and began to stroke her as he moved inside her.

The effect was as exhilarating as it was shocking. Her body was responding, and when she found her release, Fiona cried out, tightening hard around him.

He responded with a strangled cry and shuddered deep inside her. She could feel the contractions reverberate throughout his body, and Fiona understood in that astonishing moment that she was precisely where she was meant to be.

Somberly, Duncan gathered Fiona in his arm and rolled to his side. She nuzzled her face into his neck. "I need you, Fiona," he said again. "Lord God, how I need you."

She smiled into his neck.

She was home.

Chapter Twelve

Duncan Buchanan was so rejuvenated by Fiona's love that in the following days he not only began plans to rebuild Blackwood, he also planned a great Hogmanay celebration. As he was something of a pariah in Highland society, it would be attended only by the tenants and the servants and their families, but it would nevertheless be the finest Hogmanay celebration Blackwood had ever seen.

At last there was cause for celebration, and the tenants and residents of the estate all seemed to feel it—they'd gone from the gloom and doom of living in the shadow of a burned mansion to living in the bright rays of hope. Everyone seemed to have a new spring in their step. Everything seemed warmer and sparkling.

The weather cooperated, too, and they were able to build large bonfires on the south lawn, which they would set ablaze on the night of Hogmanay.

The only cloud in that week of blue skies was a message from Fiona's uncle, warning her the prince's men were on their way to Lambourne Castle. Duncan's messenger had been unable to find Jack and Angus, and Fiona fretted that he would return to Lambourne Castle before coming to Blackwood.

But on the evening of Hogmanay, Jack Haines arrived at Blackwood in the company of Angus, just as they had planned. The pair was met at the gates of Blackwood by a grinning Ridley, who, having found the runaway maid, Sherri, and returned her to Mr. Seaver, had waited in Edinburgh until the weather had passed. He'd only arrived two days past, but was instantly caught up in the new atmosphere at Blackwood.

"What's this?" Angus asked as Ridley fell in beside them on his horse. "Ridley, you old dog—has the laird returned, then?"

"Indeed he has," Ridley said. "He's hosting the Hogmanay celebration tonight. There's to be bonfires and fireworks after the official blessings."

"You donna say!" Angus said, apparently as surprised as Jack. Jack understood that since the fire, Duncan Buchanan had become a recluse. It was hard to imagine the king of Highland society having fallen so far.

"What news from Buchanan?" Angus asked casually.

"Quite a lot of it, sir," Ridley said. "But it's to be a surprise, it is."

Angus laughed. "I rather doubt I shall be even a wee bit surprised," he said confidently. "I know the laird far too well."

They arrived on the grassy east lawn of the main house just in time for the *saining,* or the blessing of the household and the livestock. From the back of the crowd of servants and tenants, Jack recognized Duncan as he climbed up on makeshift scaffolding. Jack had heard of

Duncan's burns, but he was taken aback when he saw the scars across Duncan's cheek.

Duncan held up two juniper limbs, then leaned down, extending them to someone in the crowd. When he lifted them again, they were lit. A moment later, he'd extinguished the fire, and used the smoking limbs to conduct the ancient blessing and prayer for prosperity in the new year.

When the *saining* was done, a raucous cheer went up. The footmen began to move through the crowd carrying small barrels of whisky, which they ladled into tots.

Jack readily took one when it was offered, as did Angus.

Just as he was about to drink the whisky, another man hopped onto the dais and shouted for the crowd's attention. When the crowd had quieted, he called out, "Have you all got a tot, then?"

A chorus of *ayes* was raised in addition to the tots.

"Who's he?" Jack asked.

"Cameron," Angus responded. "Duncan's secretary."

"Then lift a toast to your laird, lads, for this happy day he announces his engagement!"

Jack and Angus exchanged a look and Angus, Jack noted, was quite surprised, in spite of his boasting earlier.

"A hearty Highland welcome to the future lady of Blackwood!" the man called out. "Lady Fiona Haines!"

Jack dropped his tot.

Angus clapped him on the back. "Bloody hell, the devil you are!" he laughed. "You've no' said a word!"

Everyone around them was shouting, "*Slàinte, slàinte,*" cheering the happy couple as they stepped up onto the dais. Jack gaped, disbelieving. But it was Fiona, all right, his baby sister, smiling and waving at the crowd.

For a moment, he felt as if he were in a dream. He could not conceive how Fiona had come to be here or engaged to Buchanan, but he intended to find out, and rousing himself from his shock, he began to push his way through the crowd. When he reached the dais, he had to grab the hem of Fiona's cloak and give it a good tug before she noticed him.

She looked down, smiling broadly, and in that moment before she recognized him, Jack thought she looked as happy as he'd ever seen her.

"*Jack!*" she cried, and fairly leaped at him.

He caught her with both arms and set her on her feet, and Fiona instantly twirled around. "Duncan!" she shouted. "He's come, he's come!"

Duncan looked down, saw Jack, and grinned. *Grinned.* Jack could count on one hand the times in his life he'd seen Duncan Buchanan genuinely *grin*.

"Lambourne!" he said. "On my honor, I intended to speak with you, I did—"

He never finished his sentence, as two men climbed up on the dais and distracted him. Jack took the opportunity to glare at his sister. "Fiona Haines, what in bloody hell have you done, then?"

"He would have spoken to you, but you were gone!" Fiona exclaimed, hitting him playfully in the chest. "And no' a word to where you'd gone!"

"Fiona!' he cried, grabbing her arms. "Why are you here? What in God's name are you about? What sort of jest is this, that you are engaged to be *married* to Duncan Buchanan?"

Fiona laughed gaily. "I think because of the snowstorm!" she cried gleesfully. "Had we no' had to sleep under the stars, I donna think—" She suddenly blinked and hit him squarely in the chest. "*Jack!* What am I thinking? You canna stay here!" she cried, and gripping his arm, she began to pull him away from the crowd. "You must go at once!" she said. "The prince's men are coming for you, and by our best guess, they should be here any day now!"

"The *prince*'s men? What are you prattling on about?"

"I'm no' prattling!" she insisted, frantically pulling him along. "Woodburn and Hallaby came to me and said the king wanted you to know that the Prince of Wales had sent men to find you and bring you back to London for questioning with regard to . . . *you* know very well with regard to what," she said, punching him in the shoulder. "How could you be so careless, Jack?"

"There is no truth to it, Fiona!"

"It hardly matters—the king said you were to go deeper into the Highlands until it's all passed."

She was confusing him. Jack shook his head. "I canna begin to guess what you are saying, lass, but before I try and untangle it all, I will know how you have come to be at Blackwood!"

"I told you! The king sent me," she said, and leaned forward, glancing anxiously at the crowd. "For all we know, they could be here now, disguising themselves as tenants—"

"The *king* sent you?"

"Aye, aye, the king!" she cried impatiently.

Jack was dumbstruck for a brief moment. He'd not heard Fiona say *aye* in ages.

"Listen to me, Jack! They are rounding up the men who . . . who *know* the princess," she said, glowering at him, "and I've had word from Uncle that they've already been to Edinburra. They are en route to Lambourne Castle as we speak if they have no' arrived already! There is no time to waste! You must flee!"

"Dear God," he muttered, furious with his old friend George, furious with those who had named him an adulterer. "All right, all right, then. But I will no' go until I understand how you came to be engaged to Duncan Buchanan!"

"There is no time to tell you that now! Do you think it happened so easily? Without the least bit of scandal, then? Of course no'! It will have to wait, Jack. Just know that I love him! I *love* him!"

"Fiona," he said, catching her by the arms. "You've no' done something so monumentally stupid as—"

"It is too late, if that is what you are asking," she said defiantly. "There is naugh' you can say to change it."

"*Mi Diah*!" Jack cried.

"He's no' the same as you remember, Jack!"

"If you are referring to me," a deep voice said just behind them, "I can assure you I have changed, Lambourne."

Jack whirled around, glaring at Duncan Buchanan.

"Do you think you can debauch my sister and live to tell about it, then?" he demanded. "I shall call you out, sir. I shall delight in putting a bullet in your chest!"

Far from having the desired effect, Buchanan laughed. "Come now, Lambourne—have you no' enough trouble as it is?" he asked congenially. "I asked politely, and she consented. I adore her and am quite unwilling to part with her. You must no' fear it, for I will honor her and protect her—even from you."

"From *me*?"

"Aye, from you. As the Prince of Wales has sent his henchmen for you, I will no' allow any dishonor to be brought to Fiona. Go, Lambourne. Go save your own hide."

Jack's head was spinning. He knew how George could be when he was angry. But still— He was rudely interrupted from his thoughts by a hearty shove from Fiona.

"*Go,* you bloody fool! Go deeper into the Highlands while you can! You may question me to your heart's content when the danger has passed!"

Jack groaned. He caught Fiona's chin and kissed her cheek, then wagged his finger at her. "You've quite a lot of explaining to do."

"I shall be delighted to tell you all at the first opportunity." She pushed him again.

Jack looked at Buchanan. "If you so much as—"

"You donna have to say it. There is no one dearer to me than Fiona. I shall keep her safe and well."

"Fine," Jack said crossly, looking at the two of them. It seemed as if he'd entered another world entirely. "I will be back."

"I've no doubt of it," Fiona said. "Now *go,*" she said, gesturing impatiently. "And keep an eye out for wolves!"

So Jack went, with no destination in mind but "deeper in the Highlands," as Fiona had said, just some place far from humanity—and wolves, apparently—for a time.

He paused at the gates of Blackwood at the first celebratory explosion and glanced back to see the fireworks of Hogmanay falling from the sky.

What an astonishing start to the new year, he thought, and with a shake of his head spurred his mount forward, into the dark.